continued . . .

The Wife Test . . .

"[A] witty, rollicking romance . . . Krahn's amusing follow up to *The Husband Test* quickly blossoms into a bright, exciting adventure."   —*Publishers Weekly*

"An absorbing read. Add in Ms. Krahn's unique and witty humor and, once again, she scores a winner with the Convent of the Brides of Virtue series."   —*The Best Reviews*

"A delightful romp of a read that delivers joyous wit and comic action."   —*BookPage*

"Betina Krahn never disappoints her readers. Her plots are always exciting and unusual. Her characters are always fresh and unique. I thought she couldn't improve on the first book of this series but she has. *The Wife Test* is delightful. This is a 'Don't miss it.'"   —*Rendezvous*

. . . AND THE NOVELS OF
BETINA KRAHN

"Packs the romance punch that fans have come to expect from this bestselling novelist . . . smart, romantic . . . sure to delight readers."   —*Milwaukee Journal Sentinel*

The Book of the Seven Delights

Betina Krahn

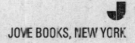

JOVE BOOKS, NEW YORK

THE BERKLEY PUBLISHING GROUP
Published by the Penguin Group
Penguin Group (USA) Inc.
375 Hudson Street, New York, New York 10014, USA
Penguin Group (Canada), 10 Alcorn Avenue, Toronto, Ontario M4V 3B2, Canada
(a division of Pearson Penguin Canada Inc.)
Penguin Books Ltd., 80 Strand, London WC2R 0RL, England
Penguin Group Ireland, 25 St. Stephen's Green, Dublin 2, Ireland (a division of Penguin Books Ltd.)
Penguin Group (Australia), 250 Camberwell Road, Camberwell, Victoria 3124, Australia
(a division of Pearson Australia Group Pty. Ltd.)
Penguin Books India Pvt. Ltd., 11 Community Centre, Panchsheel Park, New Delhi—110 017, India
Penguin Group (NZ), Cnr. Airborne and Rosedale Roads, Albany, Auckland 1310, New Zealand
(a division of Pearson New Zealand Ltd.)
Penguin Books (South Africa) (Pty.) Ltd., 24 Sturdee Avenue, Rosebank, Johannesburg 2196,
South Africa

Penguin Books Ltd., Registered Offices: 80 Strand, London WC2R 0RL, England

This is a work of fiction. Names, characters, places, and incidents either are the product of the author's imagination or are used fictitiously, and any resemblance to actual persons, living or dead, business establishments, events, or locales is entirely coincidental.

THE BOOK OF THE SEVEN DELIGHTS

A Jove Book / published by arrangement with the author.

PRINTING HISTORY
Jove mass-market edition / July 2005

Copyright © 2005 by Betina Krahn.
Cover design by Lesley Worrell.
Cover illustration by Leslie Peck.
Book design by Kristin del Rosario.

ISBN: 0-515-13972-6

JOVE®
Jove Books are published by The Berkley Publishing Group,
a division of Penguin Group (USA) Inc.,
375 Hudson Street, New York, New York 10014.
JOVE is a registered trademark of Penguin Group (USA) Inc.
The "J" design is a trademark belonging to Penguin Group (USA) Inc.

PRINTED IN THE UNITED STATES OF AMERICA

10 9 8 7 6 5 4 3 2 1

For Michael Christian Lord Krahn

May the road rise to meet you.
May the wind be always at your back.

One

"To the *right* are the Grenville Library and the manuscript department," the assistant to the director and principal librarian of the British Museum, Jonas Pratt, declared with a wave before turning emphatically to the *left*.

Abigail Merchant paused for a moment in that juncture of the marble-clad exhibition halls, scowling at the archway they weren't headed for. Gripping her letters of reference more tightly, she quickly caught up with her guide.

"These, of course, are our famous galleries," he continued briskly. "The Roman . . . and through that doorway is the Greco-Roman . . . with the Priene Marbles, including the Venus from Ostia, the Discobolos, Giustiniani Apollo, Clytie, and so forth. And through here are the Assyrian Galleries." He led her quickly into another long hall with soaring ceilings. "Steles from Ninevah . . . the great winged bull from the palace of Sargon II and the great winged lion from the Palace of Ashurnasirpal II at Nimrud. And of course, the Assyrian cuneiform tablets, which are—"

"Unparalleled. A whole library unto themselves," Abigail said, staring into the glass case and feeling her heart begin to pound. All around her, captured in stone, bronze, and clay, were glimpses and whispers of the history of humankind. It was little wonder that there was a reverent hush all through the galleries; entering them was like being admitted to the memories of God Himself.

She shook her head and attempted to steer him back to the topic of her suitability for employment.

"My letters of reference will show that I am, by training and experience, a fully qualified librarian. I spent two years preserving and cataloging the archives of the State of New York. If you would just look at my credentials. . . ."

Pratt looked at her around the side of his wire-rimmed spectacles.

"That won't be necessary. We know your qualification. This way please."

Qualification: singular. There was only one thing he could mean: She was the daughter of renowned classical scholar Sir Henry Merchant. Before leaving Boston she had written to her estranged father, asking for a letter of introduction to the librarian of the British Museum. Apparently he had provided it.

The starchy little assistant led her through the remaining galleries and straight past the priceless Rosetta Stone . . . to the rear of the museum and down a set of narrow metal stairs that descended into Stygian gloom.

"Pardon me, Mr. Pratt, but"—she halted on the second step—"this seems most irregular for an employment interview."

There, at the bottom of the darkened steps, he declared: "You are not being interviewed, Miss Merchant. It is my task to inform you that you have been hired . . . at a salary of one hundred twenty pounds per annum."

Before she could make sense of the fact that he was delivering that longed-for pronouncement while standing in what appeared to be a darkened basement, he flipped the switch of an electrical light to reveal a cavernous underground chamber stacked floor to ceiling with crates, barrels, and cartons.

"This will be your workplace," he said, gesturing to the stacks. "Every publisher in the kingdom is required to submit a copy of each book, journal, pamphlet, and paper they have published to the museum. It will be your task to open, process, and catalog these 'copyright acquisitions.'"

She nearly slid off the step.

"There must be some mistake. My expertise is in authentication and preservation of manuscripts, not acquisitions or cataloging." She hurried down the stairs. "If you will just take a moment to review my references—"

Again he waved off the documents.

"*All* assistants at the museum begin in acquisitions, Miss Merchant." His ferret-dark eyes glinted with condescension. "Of course, some assistants find the work here too demanding and prefer to seek employment elsewhere." His gaze flickered down her sensibly clad frame and back up to her face. "Handling heavy crates and boxes and lifting bundles of books is taxing for even a robust *man*."

That look. That scarcely cloaked disdain. Here was the root cause of his objection to her. It wasn't whatever influence might have been exerted on her behalf that caused his resentment, nor even the fact that she had spent most of her life in Boston . . . though the way he winced when she spoke left no doubt that he found her American accent appalling. What truly galled him was the fact that such influence had been exerted on behalf of a *woman*.

She should have anticipated such an attitude, she thought irritably. Her beloved mother had spoken of it often enough. Women might be the backbone of the burgeoning library movement in America, but in Britain they were still considered inferior scholars who did not belong in libraries . . . much less in the crowning collection of the British Empire, the British Museum.

The Social History of Idiots . . . the 300's . . . Social Sciences.

She gave the peplum of her fitted woolen jacket a determined jerk.

"I am hale and hardy, Mr. Pratt. I am not put off by honest work."

"How gratifying," he said from between clenched teeth. "Then I suggest you make a start." He waved to the endless stacks of crates and turned to go.

"Mr. Pratt." She just managed to contain the anger in her voice. "I shall need access to the museum's catalog, as well as supplies for the work."

"The catalog, as everyone knows, is in the Reading Room." He paused on the bottom step without looking back. "You shall have to make an application to the superintendent for admission."

"Application? I must *apply* to use the Reading Room and catalog?"

He turned enough to give her a condescending look.

"The superintendent is charged with maintaining the *standards* of the Reading Room. It is always his decision whether or not to grant admission."

"Fine." She raised her chin. "If you will just direct me to the female employees' retiring room—"

"We have no such facilities for *female staff*." He stiffened as if the very mention of "women" and "staff' in the same breath was an affront to British manhood. "You will have to use the facilities for female *guests* of the museum." He exited up the stairs and the sound of the door closing wafted down to her.

She stood for a moment staring at the space he had vacated.

Never mind. It didn't matter that the assistant principal librarian was an arrogant, narrow-minded ass. Never mind that she had to apply for permission to enter the sacred precincts of the Reading Room. Never mind that there were no facilities for female staff . . . and very likely no other female staff with whom to commiserate that lack. She was now gainfully employed by the British Museum at a salary of 120 pounds per annum. She was where she had planned and worked for years to be. She was here and she intended to show them the mettle of a graduate of the New York State Library School.

A *woman* graduate.

See if she didn't.

A month later she sat in a dim circle of electrical light in the cavelike basement, staring at a copy of *The Philosophical Lepidopterist's Wanderings in Sussex* and trying to decide whether it belonged in the 100's, Philosophy; the 500's, Natural Science; or the 900's, Geography and History. Stuck in that gloomy hole, day after day, without access to the museum's precious catalog, she had to work in the dark in more than one respect.

Proving her mettle? Striking a blow for womanhood? Right now she would settle for proving just her existence. Every few days she would hear the door at the top of the steps open and when she went to see who was there, she would find a number of muttonchop-clad faces peering down at her in dismay.

"You see?" one of them would say to the clearly horrified others. "I told you . . . there *is* a female down there."

She had come more than three thousand miles to become a blessed ghost in the basement. Hardly the bold and glorious adventure she had expected when setting out from Boston to make a name and a life for herself in the world of British scholarship. She had expected to have to earn a place of responsibility and respect . . .

. . . but not by sorting through moldering copies of *An Aesthete's Guide to the Mosses of Western Cornwall*, *Principles of Ancient Roman Sanitary Engineering*, and *A Spinster's Tour in France*. She glanced at the stack of books at her feet. Who on earth would want to read such stuff?

Someone, she heard her old instructor's voice declare in her head. It was a librarian's calling to organize and preserve and make available to readers all products of human inquiry without passing judgment.

It was a sad truth that one age's ignorance was often remedied by the next using discoveries that lay unheeded in the first's annals. To make absolute judgments might be to disrupt the flow of knowledge and discovery. There were terrible examples in history, like the descent into ignorance called the Dark Ages that came after the destruction of the classical civilizations. So much learning was lost in the destruction of the Great Library of Alexandria, for example, that it had taken humankind a whole millennium to overcome it.

Having wrestled her disappointment to a standstill, she forced herself to looked around her ill-lit workplace with a more hopeful perspective. Somewhere in those crates might be a work that would change lives, even society itself, for the better. She should think of herself as an explorer facing the unknown . . . an archaeologist of the printed word.

A few days later she was bashing the crates of an unexplored row with the carpet beater she had brought from home—giving whatever vermin might reside there time to evacuate—when she was startled by a scratching noise and lurched back into a stack of crates and cartons, sending them toppling.

When she recovered enough to investigate, she realized the container that had just missed cracking her on the head was not the usual pasteboard carton or wooden crate, it was a piece of luggage: long and square with a leather handle on top, a steamer trunk, with a key tied to the top handle.

On the side of the battered chest was a shipping label that read: FROM: THE ESTATE OF PROFESSOR T. THADDEUS CHILTON, PH.D. TO: LIBRARY OF THE BRITISH MUSEUM, GREAT RUSSELL STREET, LONDON.

Professor T. Thaddeus Chilton? He must not have been one of the leading lights of his field, else the museum wouldn't have abandoned his final bequest to the rats in the basement. The shabbiness of the museum's treatment of his gift made her feel a furious kinship with the old boy.

She tipped the trunk up onto its end, untied the key, and inserted it into the lock. An avalanche of books and documents threatened to tumble out and she closed the trunk hastily and wrestled it onto a trolley to take it back to her worktable.

As it happened, there were three containers of T. Thaddeus's things: a trunk of lecture notes, maps, correspondence, and journals; a barrel filled with reference books on classical antiquities; and a pasteboard carton of memorabilia: faded tassels, silk cording, a weathered wineskin, a pair of brocade Persian slippers, and yellowed photographs of tents, camels, and sand dunes.

"What did you study, Professor?" she muttered, removing the leather-bound journals from the trunk and thumbing through the pages of the one on top. She froze. It appeared to be written in Greek. *Classical* Greek. Inside the front cover she found in somewhat faded ink: "The journals of T. Thaddeus Chilton, Ph. D., assistant professor of Classical Studies, Oxford University . . . the search begun in the year A.D. 1849."

A search? Almost fifty years had passed since those journals were begun. Had the old fellow been on a single scholarly quest throughout his entire career?

On the first few pages of the first journal she found her answer and fell a little in love with old T. Thaddeus. He was a man after her own heart. It seemed he had spent his entire working life looking for a *library*.

Two

"*Seasickness,*" world traveler Maude Cummings had said in her best-selling book *A Female Adventurer Abroad*, "*is very much a state of mind.*"

Abigail gripped the edges of her narrow bunk aboard the storm-battered *Star of Persia*—and fought the urge to hurl herself across the cabin to the chamber pot once again. Clearly, Maude Cummings was full of horse manure. Abigail couldn't remember ever being this miserable. Her stomach roiled and heaved—standing, sitting, or lying, it was all the same—she felt like her body was turning itself inside out.

The *Star* was a steel-hulled freighter with double smokestacks and deep cargo holds covered by a quarter acre of weathered decking . . . built for the quick and efficient transport of goods and materials—not passengers. The *Star* did, however, have half a dozen cabins that could be booked by persons in need of conveyance. And since the renowned Maude had stated with such authority that the best value for one's money when it came to sea travel was to be had on a freighter, and since Abigail was paying for her passage from her modest inheritance from her mother, she had felt no qualms about booking an economical cabin on the *Star of Persia.*

Thank you so very much. Maude. May you be seized by a violent case of the scours while riding on the back of a camel somewhere.

But in fairness, Maude Cummings had stated that her advice was based on the fact that freighters sailed to places that ocean liners and cruising ships did not: far-flung ports of call favored by adventurers. And Abigail was not exactly an adventurer.

Her earlier Atlantic crossing—Boston to Bristol—five months ago, had been on an ocean liner filled with staterooms and salons and a surprisingly well-stocked library. It had been a most agreeable crossing; no gales or unsettling incidents. She had decided, on seeing the way other lady travelers spent days in their cabins "indisposed," that she must be something of sailor.

She was rethinking that conclusion.

Torrents of rain beat at the porthole that was her only source of light and the ship gave a shuddering roll and bucked sharply, throwing her against the side of the bunk and smacking her head on one of the metal flanges that ribbed the seaward wall of the cabin. Dazed, she lay for a moment, disoriented, seeing flashes of the last few months swirling like a kaleidoscope in her head.

The ship from Boston . . . *Travel, the 900's, Geography and History* . . . the British Museum . . . *Museums, the 000's, Generalities* . . . her employment interview with the irksome Jonas Pratt . . . *Abnormal Character Development, the 100's, Psychology* . . . weeks spent in the dark basement of the museum, sorting and cataloging things no one would ever read . . . the *Emancipation of Slaves, the 320's, Social Sciences* . . .

The ship pitched violently, tipping her from the bunk, sending her sliding across the tilted floor toward the cabin door. Unfortunately she wasn't the only thing sailing across the cabin; her open trunk was headed her direction and picking up steam.

As she braced for impact, all movement around her—cabin, trunk, and contents—abruptly stopped. The ship hung suspended, motionless for a moment, then seemed to drop a long way and landed with a thunderous splash. The trunk toppled over, and one of the straps on the open front snapped open and books and documents came pouring out. Then the *Star* rolled back toward level and her trunk slid back toward its original position, spewing papers along the way. An overturned pitcher on the nearby table came rolling toward the edge, slinging water in a wild arc.

"Aghhh!" She scrambled across a carpet of strewn documents in time to snatch several of them out of the water's path. Teetering on hands and knees, struggling to swallow her stomach back into place, she lost her balance and fell over into the spreading puddle.

It took a moment for her to realize that the danger to her precious maps and journals was past; she and her nightdress were soaking up most of the water. She issued a miserable sigh just before the metal pitcher cleared the table and hit the floor beside her with a jarring clang.

"What the devil are you doing here, Abigail Merchant?" She pushed herself up and maneuvered so that her back was against the door and she could brace against the movement of the ship. "Charging off on an expedition by yourself . . ." Her mouth was dry; her words were more difficult to form. "Risking life an' limb . . . spending the money you should be using to buy a sensible little house and settle down to a sensible job in a sensible profession. . . ."

Sensible. Her mother rose in her mind, speaking oft-repeated words: "You'll have the rest of your life to be *sensible*, Abigail."

Her gaze went to the large, battered trunk and leatherbound volumes strewn across the cabin floor—the gift fate had dropped into her lap—or, more accurately, almost dropped on her head. Keys to the adventure of a lifetime.

"She's right. The rest of my life to be sensible." Her tongue felt thick and clumsy. "The professor may have started this quest, but it's mine now. Just what Mother would have wanted me to do with her legacy. 'Go and explore, Abigail,' she'd have said. 'Do something bold and breathtaking.'" A roll of the ship made her stomach clench, and she gritted her teeth and fought through the urge to be ill. "After all . . . who b-better to finish the search for the greatest library ever assembled than a classically trained librarian?"

Anybody. Or at least, anybody with sea legs, she thought moments later, sitting on the cabin floor . . . chilling in her soaked nightdress, clutching an armful of journals, and trying desperately to ignore the way the cabin floor seemed to be undulating around her. She was so cold she was shivering, yet she could feel sweat running down the side of her face.

Hubris—she tried to force her thoughts from her physical misery—it was pride in her own intellect and judgment that had propelled her into this disaster. *Repentance . . . the 200's . . . Religion.* That, and just possibly a reckless desire for glory and fame and scholarly vindica—

Oh, God—not again.

She pressed her head back against the door closed her eyes and fought the contraction working its way up through her. Spotting the chamber pot nearby, she flung the journals she was clutching across the cabin, onto the dry part of the floor, and headed for that vessel. After a few moments of pure misery, she sagged and the motion of the ship began to damp in her consciousness.

Everything began to grow blessedly darker and warmer and easier. . . .

Pounding on the louvered wooden door of his cabin jarred Apollo Smith awake, and he burrowed deeper into his bunk and clamped his arms around his head to ward off the racket. After several minutes he realized it was the ship's steward thumping the door and calling his name, and that, despite his lack of response, Haffe showed no sign of going away.

"Damned ship had better be sinking," Apollo muttered as he swung his legs over the side of the bunk and gave the porthole a dark glance. Sunshine, not seawater. His eyes felt like they were filled with sand as he struggled to keep them open and staggered across the tilting floor to the door.

"What the bloody hell—"

The wild-eyed Moroccan rattled off something in a puree of Berber, French, and English as he pulled Apollo out into the narrow passage. The belated sense of what the steward had said and the stench of sickness struck Apollo at the same time.

"Good God." He clamped a hand over his nose and mouth, muttering into his palm, "Who died?"

"*Engleesh* m'am . . . *assistez!*"

"Englishman? It's not like we're all related, you know."

Haffe dragged him frantically to the open door of the adjoining cabin and pointed to a form in a wet cotton nightdress, crumpled on the floor and wedged between an open steamer trunk and a chamber pot. Papers and books littered the cabin floor and female garments dangled out of open baggage.

"*Assistez!* English m'am. *Assistez . . . vite, vite!*"

"Ohhh. Not English*man*, English m'am."

The little Berber pointed at the unconscious woman and thrust Apollo by the arm into the open doorway. Apollo didn't resist at first; he was torn between scrutinizing whatever catastrophe had taken place in the cabin and averting his eyes and nose. Then the steward's demand dawned on him.

"Ohhh, no."

Haffe scuttled around behind him, jammed a shoulder into his back, and braced both feet against the opposite passage wall, pushing with all his might. Apollo caught the sides of the door frame and held on for dear life.

"Sympathies, old man. It's a mess. But it's *your* mess." Then he looked back at the woman on the floor and re-called an even better reason for not getting involved.

"She's the one who kept banging on the wall that first night. I could barely hear the bets. Lost the fattest pot of the night thanks to her."

He pivoted, deflecting Haffe's force and sending him sprawling in the passage. But Haffe quickly recovered and darted around Apollo to make a stand between him and the bunk that was calling his name. Through the throbbing in his head, he made out the words "English," "lady," and "infidel."

It was suddenly all too clear. As a good steward, Haffe felt responsible for the woman's welfare. But as a good Muslim and an even better Berber, he could not bring himself to handle an infidel female, even a sick one.

"*Assistez,* Smeeth." Haffe was gray with desperation. "*Pleeeease.*"

Apollo squeezed his eyes shut and fought a growing urge to retch himself. *Steady on.*

"Where's her husband? Let *him* help you."

More linguistically mixed exclamations and ejaculations, of which only one was understandable to him: "no man."

"Figures. Who'd marry a chit who pounds the walls during poker games?"

He turned back to the woman's cabin and stood for a moment weighing the situation. They were still the better part of a week out of Casablanca and she was clearly in bad straights. Left untended, she could die before they reached port. He might be a lot of less-than-sterling things, but he was not the sort to stand by and let a woman die without raising a finger to help. Muttering a few choice oaths, he sucked a deep breath and ducked into the woman's cabin.

"Get me a couple of blankets," he ordered Haffe, and knelt to pick her up.

"*Merci,* Smeeth!" Haffe began to rip blankets from her bunk. "May all your wives be gloriously fat!"

•　　•　　•

The distant voices of crewmen wafting up from the cargo deck awakened Abigail. She grew steadily more aware of her surroundings; the roar of the storm and the groans and shudders of the sea-battered ship had subsided, and monstrously fierce light was stabbing straight through her eyelids. She squeezed her eyes tighter shut, but something prevented her from turning away.

After preparing herself for the onslaught of light, she pried her eyes open enough to see that she was on the deck of the *Star*, wrapped in a restrictive cocoon of blankets and propped in a chair like the one in her cabin.

She had no idea how she'd gotten wrapped up like a mummy, why she was on deck, or what was wound so tightly around her head and under her jaw.

Opening her eyes wider, she took in the metal railing, the weathered wooden decking, and the rusted metal stairs nearby and realized she was on the narrow upper deck. Looking up she found she was wearing her own straw sun hat, tied firmly around her head with—good Lord—with her own stockings!

With concentrated effort, she was able to slide one of her arms up under the blankets to her face. Rubbing her eyes turned out to be a bad idea; they burned as if she were grinding salt into them. She groaned and a deep male voice from nearby startled her.

"Don't do that. Here. Open up."

Three

She squinted and made out a hazy human outline moving between her and the fierce sun. Coming toward her was a cup of something dark and smelly. The man holding the cup didn't give her a choice about drinking or much of a chance to swallow; he just kept pouring the lukewarm liquid in a steady stream between her parched lips and down her ravaged throat. She gulped and gurgled and finally drew air enough to protest.

"You're drowning me," she croaked out.

"It's good for you," came masculine tones with a pronounced English accent. "You need liquids." He sighed with exasperation when she fended off the cup a second time. "That is, assuming you aren't one of those females who make a career out of hovering on the edge of oblivion."

He lowered his face toward her and she could finally make out that there was a black leather patch over one of his eyes. The sight caused her to gasp, and her parched palate rattled so that she emitted a resounding snort. He winced at the sound and she clapped a hand over her mouth in horror.

"If that's your game, I suggest you turn around and head home on the next boat. You're not particularly fetching as a near-corpse, and you'll get no points for 'delicate languishing' where we're going."

"I am not *languishing*," she declared, despite the pain speaking caused in her throat. "I'm seasick."

"You are that." Her tormentor gave a wicked smile. "A fact that would probably make someone, somewhere extremely happy. Not, however, our overwrought steward. He seems to think he'll be blamed if you kick off in one of his cabins. He's below right now cleaning . . . scrubbing the varnish off everything in your quarters."

"He's *whaaatt?*" She struggled to sit up and free her legs.

"Stay right where you are." He pushed her firmly back into the chair and reached for something on the deck beside him. A spoon. Heaped with grim-looking paste. "Open up. You have to get something into your stomach." When she tightened her mouth and glared, he wagged the spoon back and forth. "It's this or a snout full of whiskey. Which will it be?"

"I'll be s-sick again," she whispered, unable to hide her fear of that prospect. To her surprise, he sighed and lowered the spoon. That was when she noticed his face had strong, cleanly chiseled features that were sun-bronzed and framed by sun-streaked hair. But her eyes kept going back to that eye patch.

"Look, this is the best, the only *real* cure for seasickness," he declared. "You stay on deck, where you can see the sea move and get fresh air, and you keep something in your belly . . . not much . . . just enough to keep things moving the right direction. Oat porridge. Fruit. Light fare. No bloody meat or grease."

At the word "bloody," her stomach rebelled and he watched her fight it.

"Open up."

They hadn't been introduced, but in the next few minutes, Abigail deduced his identity. *The Spawn of Satan.* In the flesh. Sardonic, determined, and utterly merciless with a spoon. He shoveled dose after dose of that plasterlike porridge into her, barely giving her time to swallow each bite. The lukewarm paste would have glued her mouth together if he hadn't paused periodically to force her to sip that vile liquid, which she now recognized as tea adulterated with foul-smelling herbs.

When he deemed her sufficiently stuffed, he ordered her to watch the horizon, picked up his implements of torture, and disappeared into the cabin area of the ship.

Her gaze was drawn to the horizon; not because he ordered her to keep her eyes on it, but because there wasn't anything else to watch. The waves were lulling and, as the sun rose and the glare lessened, watching became soothing. Her stomach was so occupied with the mass it had ingested that it ignored her, and she was so grateful to be ignored that she relaxed enough to doze.

Shadows were lengthening on her side of the ship by the time her tormentor returned with another cup of that wretched tea and a glass of amber liquid that proved to be a heavily sweetened infusion of mint. She extracted one of her arms from the blankets to hold the cup for herself, but he applied a finger to the bottom of the cup to hasten the process. By the time he handed her the glass of mint tea, she sat up straighter in her cocoon and brushed away his assistance.

He stood for a moment watching her drink, then stooped slightly to peer past the jutting edge of her hat, searching her face.

"Better?" Again that eye patch drew her attention.

"Some." She did a quick inventory and realized she spoke the truth. At the moment she didn't have a serious physical complaint, just hideously sore muscles and a fiendish thirst caused by that syrupy mint concoction.

"Well, you have to feel better than you look," he said.

Jolted, she glanced up at her misshapen hat, over at her lank hair, and then down at the soiled sleeves of her nightdress. The skin of her face and throat felt burn-tender, probably blotchy from her being upended over a chamber pot.

"Who *are* you?" she demanded, tightening her grip on the top of the blanket and wishing he would go away.

"Your neighbor. The cabin next door."

So, the Blackbeard lookalike staring at her was the wretch who had conducted a gaming-hell next door and kept her awake for the first four nights of the voyage. Spawn of Satan. And they said there was no such thing as women's intuition.

"Don't you have something better to do than torture me?"

"Not at the moment." He crossed his arms over his broad chest. She couldn't see his stare, but she felt it. "You know, you don't sound very English."

"I'm an American. From Boston."

"And your name? All I could get out of Haffe was something about a 'merchant.'"

"That's my name. Merchant. Abigail Merchant."

"Right." He cut a look at her from the side of his good eye. "And what are you doing on a freighter bound for Morocco, Miss Merchant? You can't be a missionary—you're not packing Bibles and prayer books. All you've got is books and maps."

"How do you know—" The question, together with a memory of him saying the steward was scrubbing her cabin, set off an eruption of anxiety in her. "You were in my cabin?" She fought her way out of her cocoon of blankets.

Dizziness hit as she rose, and she staggered. He stepped forward to steady her but she fended off the assistance and bent over to improve the flow of blood to her brain. When she finally regained her balance, she straightened more slowly, pulled her blanket and dignity tighter around her, and headed for her cabin.

"I told you—you have to stay on deck." He followed at a distance, watching her feel her way down the steps and along the passage to her cabin door.

The water on her floor had dried, her bunk was straightened, and on top of the bedclothes lay two piles, one of garments and another of documents. She rushed to the heap of papers and frantically began to evaluate their condition.

There were water spots on some of the pages, but overall the writing had escaped disaster. As her anxiety subsided, it took with it some of the energy it had provided and she wilted onto the bunk.

"What's so important about these papers?" he said, ducking into the cabin and strolling over to reach for one of her maps. "Does that say 'Timbuktu'?"

She snatched it out of his reach and rolled it up to stack it with the others. "These are historical documents. From my family." She had given some thought to what she would say if asked about where she was going. Miraculously, she managed to recall it. "It's imperative that I get them to my family. In Morocco."

"Where in Morocco?"

"Casa"—dark spots were circling the edges of her vision—"blanca."

"And what do they do there? This 'family' of yours."

She wanted to confront the disbelief in his tone, but her vision was starting to swim and her throat and stomach were tightening in an all-too-familiar way.

"Trade," she said, her voice sounding oddly far away in her own ears. "Dates . . . buying and exporting. Verrry . . . verrry big . . . in dates."

She lurched from the bunk, looking for the chamber pot.

A moment later she'd been seized by the waist and was wilting over Spawn of Satan's rock-hard arm. He half dragged, half carried her back up on deck and propped her unceremoniously against the railing so that her head hung over the side.

"Don't you dare lose that oatmeal," he ordered. "Take deep, slow breaths and think about something else. The burn of good Scotch. Fat, fragrant cigars. Or dancing girls. The ones at Le Maison d'Houri always work for me . . . especially that one with the long legs and the henna on her belly. . . ."

She had never understood the urge to wreak bloody mayhem until now.

She did, however, manage to keep her oatmeal down.

Several hours later, she awakened on the deck in the dark; covered once again with blankets, her feet now propped in a second chair. There was a bracing hint of chill to the breeze, and a surprising peace in her midsection. For the first time in days she wasn't in some sort of agony. She floated in and out of a comfortable trance, until she spotted in the distance a darkened strip beginning to intrude between the shimmering night sea and the dark velvet sky.

Land. With surprisingly clarity of mind, she recalled Emily Woodbine's description of her voyage from England to Africa in her book, *An Englishwoman on Safari*. This hazy blue streak on the eastern horizon meant they had reached the last third of the voyage, where they hugged the coastline of North Africa. That meant, somewhere to the east was the port of Tangiers, with its spice markets and rugs and dates and oil and hammered brass. And women with "henna" on their bellies. Whatever the devil that meant.

"You're awake. Good." Her one-eyed tormentor appeared—at least the lower two-thirds of him did—and placed a bowl of mush in her lap. "Eat."

As he ducked back down into the dimly lit passage, she felt the warmth of whatever was in the bowl spreading through her blanket and nightdress. It surprised her to realize that she did indeed feel hungry. She slid her arms free of the blankets and lifted the bowl to her nose. There was a novel sweetness to the aroma. At the first bite she could tell he had done something to make the oats more palatable.

Honey, she thought, chewing on a lump of some kind and praying it was meant to be there. At least it wasn't moving. Then a burst of flavor surprised her; the lumps in the oatmeal appeared to be dried fruit . . . dates and apricots. *Exports of Morocco . . . the 960's . . . Geography.* She finished the bowl in record time. Now, if she only had something to drink . . .

As if in response to her thoughts, a hand soon appeared with a cup in it. She followed that arm up to the face that for some reason made her own heat.

"What is your name?" she said, taking the drink and filtering the potent sight of him through her eyelashes. "I mean, you've been"—helping? badgering?—"*seeing* me through this illness and I don't even know your name."

There was a pause, in which he seemed to be manufacturing a response.

"Smith," he said.

Not a very inventive product.

"Just 'Smith'?" When he nodded, she rolled her eyes and then sipped her tea. "English, obviously. What are *you* doing on a ship bound for Morocco?"

"Tending to family business . . . regarding . . . important documents."

She nearly choked on the liquid.

"I merely asked a civil question," she said, straightening.

"And I merely gave you a civil answer." He leaning closer to intercept her averted gaze. "I am returning to Morocco on family business related to some important documents."

In spite of her annoyance, her gaze was drawn to his eye. Hazel. Worldly. Full of urges and experiences she didn't want to know anything about His hair was wind-ruffled and the collar of his shirt had blown up against his neck. Bronzed . . . muscular . . . like his face. His full, neatly curved mouth turned up on one side in a wry grin. Reddening, she shifted on the chair and buried her nose in her cup of tea.

"So does this family of yours live in the dusty old *medina*?" he asked.

"Not exactly." She wasn't sure what he meant, but it sounded unpleasant.

"Oh, *outside* the city walls, then," he said, sounding impressed.

"Yes." She melted slightly. "Just outside."

"And they buy and export dates," he said, propping his hands on his waist.

"Yes."

"They must make a killing, then. Morocco is lousy with date palms. Especially those Smyrna dates. Of course, the locals prefer the Kadota. Not me. I'm strictly an Adriatic man, myself. What about you?"

"One kind of date is the same as another to me," she said, shoving her empty cup into his hands, annoyed that he seemed to be testing her and that she had no idea if she'd passed or not. "Now if you don't mind, I'm fatigued."

What she was — Apollo thought as he carried the empty cup below and found himself ducking into her cabin — was *lying*. Nobody lived outside the *medina*, the walled city . . . except a few goat herders in shanties and poor, tent-dwelling nomads who came to trade. And Smyrna, Katoda, and Adriatic were varieties of *figs*, not dates.

He, on the other hand, had told the truth.

He stood for a minute surveying the writings piled on her bed. She had been fiercely protective of her things. He pulled an envelope from his shirt and looked between it and the books and papers tucked together on top of the bedclothes. It might be safer to . . .

He thought of her prickly attitude and penchant for disaster. She could disappear the minute they reached the dock and he might never find her again. More likely, she'd stumble going down the gangplank and drop her bags straight into the damned water.

He stuffed the envelope back into his shirt, exited, and pulled the door shut behind him.

●　　●　　●

It was galling to admit, she realized as the sky brightened the next morning, but her one-eyed nursemaid's prescription for seasickness worked. It meant, however, that she would have to camp on deck for the rest of the voyage; eating, sleeping, washing, and dressing in the open air. The thought of conducting all but the most personal of necessities on deck was intimidating. But, despite the calm seas, there was enough motion to the modest vessel to make her fear a return of illness if she closeted herself in her cabin again.

This would be good practice for the rigors of expedition life, she told herself. Washing with a minimum of water; maintaining modesty while dressing and grooming in the open; and keeping her belongings in useful order under difficult conditions . . . all were practices she might find useful later. After all, Mabel Crawford, in her book *Through Algeria*, insisted that an Englishwoman traveling alone must be all things at all times—careful, alert, mindful of her coin and possessions—prepared for anything a strange land could put in her path.

What the new day put first into her path was the captain of the *Star*, an amicable Greek fellow named Demetrios, who stopped by to check on her. In charmingly flawed English, he informed her that the deck she now inhabited was officially off-limits to everyone but her and the steward, Haffe, who would resume seeing to her needs now that the weather and her stomach had calmed.

She thanked him and realized as he gave her a backward glance and shook his head that he was probably reacting to the sad state of her appearance. She gave her nightdress a cautious sniff and grimaced. It was time for a quick foray into her cabin to wash and retrieve some fresh garments.

Once below in her cabin, her stomach began to knot with warning. She quickly washed her face, snatched up several garments and one of the professor's journals, and darted back out into the passage, where she ran smack into her one-eyed rescuer.

"What are you doing below deck?" he said gruffly, watching her pick up the journal she had dropped and back away under his searching gaze.

"Getting a few of my things." She fought a flush of embarrassment at being caught in her bare nightgown. "If I have to spend the rest of the voyage on deck, then I intend to do so properly dressed."

He cocked his head, looking at the garments she was clutching against her.

"Surely not in those."

"I beg your pardon." She edged backward toward the steps.

"That cincher. You can't wear that," he said, gesturing to a daintily embroidered garment dangling from the stack.

"Really." She stuffed it out of sight, picked up the hem of her nightdress, and climbed the five steps to the deck. He followed and emerged onto the deck just as she dropped her garments onto her chair. "Need I remind you"—she inserted herself between him and the stays visible on top of the clothes—"that the captain has declared this part of the deck off-limits to all but me?"

"You'll suffocate."

"I have been dressing myself quite successfully since I was four years old."

"Not in Morocco, you haven't." He widened his stance and crossed his arms. "You have to wear loose, breatheable clothing. Strap yourself into one of those things and you'll be keeling over on an hourly basis."

"I appreciate the advice," she said irritably, realizing that this was a test of her recent resolve. "Now if you don't mind, I am *trying* to dress."

When he continued to stand and glower, she snatched up her combinations, gave them a shake that produced a snap. Still no movement toward the hatch.

"Fine." She hiked up the bottom of her gown. Modesty asserted itself, and she turned her back to him before raising her nightdress past her knees. Then, with the knickers at her waist, she realized she would have to make a tent of her nightgown in order to insert her arms into the straps of the attached camisole. Grumbling silently, she withdrew her arms from the voluminous sleeves to continue dressing.

Four

Apollo Smith stood with his legs braced apart and his arms crossed over his chest. His gaze was fixed on an expanse of rumpled white muslin and on the silhouette of a naked female outlined against it by the rising sun. He closed his eye to clear his vision, but the brightness had scored her image into the back of his exposed eye: a glowing light-shadow against the dark wall of his mind.

Curved breast, waist, and hip . . . bared leg rising . . . He flipped up his leather patch and narrowed both eyes to filter the sunlight that was penetrating the fabric, skimming her bare flesh, and carrying stolen impressions to him.

His fingers twitched as he watched her draw garments over that outline, blurring it. The sound trapped in his throat was part protest and part relief. Then she wrapped something around her midsection that began to define the curve of her waist in a way that was both foreign and familiar. Pink, he recalled. A boned, embroidered rectangle edged in lace and trimmed with ribbon roses.

Until two months ago, he hadn't been close to a female in European dress for five long years. Corsets, petticoats, lacy knickers, silk stockings—the hallmarks of femininity imprinted in him during his formative years in England were utterly foreign to the rough and rugged world of Berber mountain tribes, desert Arabs, and French Legionnaires. The few women accessible to him and his comrades-at-arms were denizens of brothels or serving girls in taverns who, despite their adoption of European affectations, would never be mistaken for English women or ladies of any kind.

In his long, tumultuous years of service to the Legion, he had all but forgotten the tantalizing swish of petticoats, the temptation of a tautly drawn corset, and the fascination provoked by a deeply cut neckline. Then he arrived in London just more than a month ago, took rooms in a comfortable West End hotel, and found himself plunged into a flood of forgotten titillations. For a month he stalked the streets of London in a continuous, adolescent-like state of arousal. It was a damned relief to learn of a quiet little house in St. James where he could purge that sexual tension for an affordable sum.

Now, it seemed that fleeting indulgence had only roused old memories and focused his interest all the more on accouterments of Western femininity. And the annoying bit of muslin he'd been forced to rescue was determined to upholster herself with a full complement of female garb.

He lowered his eye patch, intending to retreat in silence, when the chit abruptly lifted her nightdress and dragged it off over her head.

She stood fastening the sleeves of a starched white blouse while a gray tweed skirt hung open from her waist on one side and down along her hip on the other. The breeze blew her long hair such that it caught on her blouse and wrapped about her arms and shoulders. Chestnut brown hair. Lapping suggestively around her.

His mouth went dry.

"I'll tell Haffe to check on you in an hour," he managed gruffly. "You'll probably need reviving by then." He headed for the door to the cabin passage, feeling suddenly too damned warm himself. "Oh, and if you know what's good for you, you'll get rid of those silk petticoats, too. Where you're going, you won't want to draw attention to what's under your skirts."

"I'll have you know, the quantity and quality of my petticoats is—" She stalked after him to the top of the stairs he was descending, determined to have the last word. "Proper ladies wear petticoats all over Arabia and Africa. I've read the accounts . . . Lillias Campbell Davidson . . . Mary Kingsley, too, in West Africa . . . Amelia Edwards in *A Thousand Miles Up The Nile* . . . Ella Sykes in *Through Persia on a Side-Saddle* . . . Mabel Crawford in *Through Algeria* . . . they all wore plenty of petticoats!"

His cabin door was slamming behind him before he realized she was citing titles and authors. *Books.* Good God. She was heading off to Morocco armed with the advice of a bunch of lunatic females who had gone gallivanting all over the globe and somehow survived to write about it. In glowing terms, no doubt. Making it sound like a tea party in paradise.

A raving innocent. With a boatload of pride.

Headed straight for disaster.

He groaned and ripped off his eye patch, rubbing the scars around the eye it had covered, purging the lingering silhouette of her cool, naked curves. Stubborn chit . . . sailing into a town like Casablanca with no idea who or what lay in wait for her . . . refusing to listen to the voice of reason and experience . . . just like he had years ago. . . .

Somebody ought to save her from herself. Somebody who actually cared if she "corseted" and "petticoated" herself into oblivion. Somebody who didn't mind simple-minded lies and high-handed manners. Somebody with a lot more patience than common sense.

Somebody *else.*

He had far more pressing matters to contend with . . . like how to win back some of his stake money from the crew, and how to get off the ship when they docked without getting spotted, captured, and very likely killed.

• • •

Life on deck wasn't really so bad, Abigail decided, except for her tendency to awaken at the slightest noise and the ship's penchant for making worrisome noises night and day. Over the next few days, she regained her strength and made increasingly longer visits to her cabin to bathe, wash her hair, and restore order to her belongings. It was a relief to find that none of her journals or maps were missing and that her cache of money remained undisturbed.

Haffe, the rotund little steward with the ever-present turban and horse-toothed grin, was diligent in his efforts to see to her needs. It was from him that she learned that the racket from "Smeeth's" cabin, meant that the gambling had resumed and that the crew were making nightly contributions to his "luck."

It was just like him—she fanned herself with the book she was reading—to spend his time drinking, gambling, and taking advantage of the poor crew. Thank heavens she didn't have to deal with him anymore. Her one regret was that he couldn't see just how well she was faring, corset and all. She fanned harder.

Two mornings later the horizon filled with a coastline of beaches and cliffs that gave way to glimpses of rolling hills and the fertile plains beyond. North Africa. *Morocco*. The place of spice markets, minarets, and men in turbans . . . of sand dunes and oases . . . of caravans of camels stretching off into the Sahara. . . .

Past the vivid blue water and fringe of white surf, the sand of the beaches was a thousand shades of red and gray and tan. Dark rock jutted up through the uneven shoreline, ragged spires pocked with holes that provided roosts for seabirds. Here and there, ruddy stuccoed walls enclosing clusters of flat-topped buildings extended the tops of cliffs overlooking the sea. Below those villages, fleets of wooden fishing boats with patched sails plied the waters or were pulled up around fires on the beaches.

As the *Star* drew nearer to the coast, the sea grew calmer and a land breeze reached the ship, bringing with it a faint but tantalizing scent of sand and spice. A reassuring sense of completion settled over her. She had survived the voyage to Casablanca and had learned a few things in the process. Her confidence in her ability to carry on Professor Chilton's search for the great library was renewed.

As the city walls came into view, Haffe appeared with a cup of tea and a mixed linguistic pot of descriptions of the city. He pointed out the minarets of the great mosque, the *Bab el-Marsa* or "sea gate" in the great city wall, and below that, the area of makeshift warehouses and taverns and enterprises catering to just-paid sailors. Between that area and the ships waiting to unload cargo stretched a number of stone quays and wooden docks that swarmed with activity. Off to the south sat a separate walled complex the little steward called a *sqala* . . . a bastion built a century ago and now occupied by an uneasy alliance of Moroccan forces and a regiment of the French Foreign Legion.

With butterflies in her stomach, she retired to her cabin and began to repack her garments, books, and papers.

Emily Lowe, in *Unprotected Females in Norway*, was emphatic that a single woman traveling alone should never attempt to travel with more luggage than one portable carpetbag, in the event she might have to serve as her own porter. Since she would be traveling with a guide and porters of her own, Abigail favored Mariana Starke's better-equipped approach. She had dutifully acquired the items suggested in *Travellers on the Continent*, but—conceding to Emily that horse and camelback travel might require some flexibility—had secured three capacious carpetbags and had them reinforced with leather and fitted with interior pockets. Her trunk would be stored at her hotel in Casablanca until she returned.

Yes, she was well prepared, she told herself as she transferred the last of her personal items from her trunk to a carpetbag. All that remained was asking the captain to have someone summon a carriage to take her to the British Consulate. The British Foreign Office had assured her the consulate would be more than happy to recommend comfortable lodgings and a trustworthy guide.

The water around the docks was dark with slime, bilge oil, fish offal, and rotting God-knew-what. Apollo Smith fought both to breathe and to keep from breathing as he swam toward the dock, towing his leather valise behind him. It was a foul end to a long journey, but it was either this or risk arrest by the retrieval squad he had seen prowling the dock as the *Star* approached its berth.

He had expected no less. The Legion was fiercely protective of its enlistees . . . especially those whose enlistments were less than voluntary. And his own enlistment five years ago had been about as involuntary as they came. After a night of drinking and carousing, he'd awakened in a metal box in a prison yard . . . arrested for killing a man in a fight. He was given the choice of remaining in that stifling cell until he was roasted to a turn or joining the Legion.

He resisted at first, demanding to see the British Consul, demanding a trial, and demanding to at least send a message to his uncle . . . all of which amused his jailors. After two weeks of searing heat, starvation, and the occasional beating, he finally surrendered and signed an enlistment that placed his life and limb at the disposal of the French Foreign Legion for a stated period of five years.

He might be mad for coming back here, but at least he wasn't mad and *stupid*. He knew what to expect in Morocco this time. He had scanned the dock as the ship approached and spotted Legionnaires prowling the area. They had fight-scarred faces and bellies that hung over their belts from too much time drinking beer in dockside taverns. A retrieval squad if he'd ever seen one.

He had taken off his shirt and boots, stowed them in his valise, and then slipped overboard to swim down the dock to a place where the cargo being unloaded from another ship would provide cover for him to climb ashore. Once on the dock, he shook off as much water as he could, dressed, and climbed to the top of the stacks of crates to watch the Legionnaires.

Raising his patch and squinting away the glare that plagued the vision in his left eye, he recognized one of the men . . . a fellow named Banane . . . a wiry little weasel with a nasty temper and a nose flattened into a half crescent against his face. Apollo snarled silently. Just the sort the Legion would assign to do their dirtiest, most disgusting work. A human dung beetle. With apologies to upstanding insect dung beetles everywhere.

From his vantage point on the cargo, he scanned the dock in both directions and realized that there was no cover for further escape for fifty yards in either direction. With an oath, he flattened against the top of the crates and reconciled himself to waiting there until the retrieval squad moved on or darkness fell.

Then he spotted *her.*

Abigail Merchant was standing at the top of the gangway, arguing with one of the shore officials about an impromptu "tax" required of all persons disembarking from ships in the harbor. It was just like her, he thought, to come all the way to Morocco and then refuse to leave the damned boat because of scruples over a few *dirhams* in shore bribes.

An abrupt movement at the bottom of the gangway caught his eye and he spotted several dirty, half-naked wharf rats snatching up three large carpetbags and hauling them off at a dead run.

Pay attention, woman—they're robbing you blind! It was all he could do to keep from shouting it at her.

"My bags—they're taking my bags!" She finally saw what was happening. "Stop them—somebody stop them!" She rushed down the gangway, shoving her way past the porters returning up it for more cargo, but the thieves had already reached the corner of a nearby street and were disappearing.

"Un voleur—arrêtez-vous!" Haffe shouted, pointing

from the cabin deck. But his call only caused confusion amongst the crew and dockworkers, many of whom had checkered pasts and thought he was accusing rather than alerting them. *"Legionnaires!"* Haffe tried calling to the soldiers loitering at the corner. *"Allez, allez! Un voleur!"*

The Legionnaires seemed startled at first, then indignant at the notion that they were being asked to exert themselves in so mundane a cause. Tightening their grips on their truncheons, they took off in the opposite direction.

Captain Demetrios rushed up from one of the cargo holds to see what the yelling was about and quickly ordered some of his men to drop what they were doing and give chase.

As the *Star*'s crew erupted in arguments about which way to go, where the thieves were likely to be headed, and what they might use as weapons against such brazen criminals, a handful of men came running from further down the quay . . . burly dockworkers bearing spars and lengths of iron pipe . . . followed by a stocky, nattily dressed man in a white three-piece suit. The man came to a stop beside the trouble-prone Miss Merchant and doffed his hat.

Apollo froze, unable to expel the breath he'd just taken.

"Please . . . allow me to be of service, mademoiselle," the man declared in a mellifluous French accent, planting his silver-headed walking stick on the dock and striking a pose beside it. When she nodded permission, he waved his white Panama hat to send his men rushing after the thieves.

"Thank you, sir," she responded, sounding a bit breathless. "But surely I must contact the authorities . . . the police. . . ."

"I fear the authorities here in Casablanca will be of little assistance," he said with a rueful wag of head. "Theft is an all too frequent occurrence on these docks. Fortunately, my employees are knowledgeable in the ways of the streets. If it is at all possible, mademoiselle, they will retrieve your bags." He produced a smile that oozed admiration. "Permit me to introduce myself. I am—"

"Ferdineaux LaCroix," Apollo muttered, watching the

oily Frenchman plant a kiss on her hand and feeling like he needed to spit. Badly.

"Abigail Merchant. I am grateful, sir, for whatever you can do to retrieve my bags. They contain items that are irreplaceable."

Just then, LaCroix caught sight of Captain Demetrios standing in the middle of the gangplank watching them.

"*Capitaine.*" LaCroix acknowledged him with a nod.

"Monsieur LaCroix."

Demetrios paused for a moment, looking as if he wanted to say something, but then nodded brusquely and headed back to his cargo. La Croix smiled and turned his attention once again to Abigail Merchant.

"*Quel dommage*, mademoiselle, that we must meet under such circumstances. If you will give me the name of your host in Casablanca, I shall see that your bags are delivered to you as soon as they are recovered."

"*Don't tell him.*" Apollo ground out through gritted teeth.

"I had planned to go first to the British Consulate," she said with a hint of indecision. "The captain has said he will send for a carriage. And he has suggested a hotel called the Exeter."

"The Exeter. A fine old establish—" LaCroix smacked his forehead with his palm. "The fire. There was a fire recently, mademoiselle. I fear the Exeter is not available. But, there is another hotel . . . the Marrat." He brightened and gestured down the dock to a handsome black carriage with fashionable yellow wheels. "I can take you there and save both you and *le capitaine* much trouble."

"*The Marrat?*" Apollo groaned. "*There isn't a door in the place that doesn't have at least fifty keys.*"

As if on cue, two of LaCroix's beefy employees came rushing back around the nearby corner bearing two carpetbags. Abigail all but melted with relief.

"Oh, thank you, Mister LaCroix!" She squeezed the Frenchman's hands and then fell to her knees to undo the buckles and open the valises. "Thank heaven, they didn't—wait—there is still one bag missing. My books and papers—"

"*Dammit.*" Apollo clenched both fists. "*It would be that one.*"

"We will find it, mademoiselle." LaCroix watched her refasten her bags and then offered her assistance in rising.

"Your kindness overwhelms me," she said, swaying to her feet.

"*Me, too,*" Apollo snarled, shifting on the cargo to get a better view.

"I don't know how I can ever repay you," she continued.

"*He'll think of a way.*"

"The delight in your lovely face is my sole reward, mademoiselle," LaCroix said, staring at her as if she were edible. "And perhaps the honor of your company at dinner this evening in the Marrat's dining room."

"*She'll say yes, of course.*"

"I would be honored, monsieur."

Apollo watched, feeling thwarted and furious, as the Frenchman claimed her arm, escorted her down the dock, and helped her to his carriage. It wasn't that he actually cared about the stubbornly corseted Miss Merchant. But just now he had something of a stake in her well-being; when he saw the retrieval squad, he had visited her cabin and tucked his papers into her bag after all.

He waited to be sure the Legionnaires didn't return before climbing down from his hiding place. Taking no chances, he slid around the cargo in stages, listening and watching. The coast seemed clear and he stepped out onto the main dock—right into Haffe's incredulous stare.

"Your eye, Smeeth—praise be to Allah!" He was about to fall on his knees, when Apollo clamped a hand over his mouth and dragged him behind the cargo.

"Quiet." He released the little steward and flipped his eye-patch down into place, which made Haffe shake his head in bewilderment. "It's a disguise." Haffe still looked baffled. "I'm incognito. Hiding. *Cachant.*" The light finally dawned.

"Did you see Miss Merchant leave?" Apollo said.

"Meez Mer-chant? *Oui.*" He pointed to where the carriage had stood. *"Avec sa pappa."*

"He's not her papa, my friend," Apollo's nose curled. "Not by a long shot."

Five

The Frenchman's carriage sent people scrambling for open doorways as it barreled through the narrow, deeply shaded streets of Casablanca. The air was hot and laden with the scents of dust, dung, and the dyed wool that hung in colorful skeins from lines strung across the streets. When the way broadened, a breeze dipped toward them, bringing scents of drying jute, foods cooking on charcoal braziers, and newly tanned leather.

Exotic sounds floated from the buildings they passed: the rhythmic thud of treadles from rug-weavers' shops and the *pling* of stringed instruments floating out of cafés, the calls of food vendors in the markets. The turbans and sun-bronzed faces of the men; the jingling jewelry and veiled faces of the women . . . stalls packed with fabrics, slippers, and beaten brass . . . pushcarts overflowing with olives, oranges, dates, and melons . . . everything looked so *foreign*. And felt so foreign. Especially the heat.

Her sensible demicorset, as Smith predicted, seemed to be squeezing her breathless. She fanned her reddened face with her hand and stifled the memory of his telling her she should abandon the garment and the senseless propriety it represented.

Arrogant man. She hadn't asked for his advice. Thank heavens he hadn't been on the dock to see her lose her bags before she set foot on Moroccan soil.

"Will we pass the British Consulate en route?" she asked her benefactor.

"The British Consul maintains a house near the *Bab el-Marrakech*, but he spends most of his time in the city of Rabat," he informed her. "If you would contact him, you may have to wait for some time, mademoiselle. It is sometimes weeks between his visits."

"B-but, I was given to understand that there was a *permanent* consulate here." She clamped her hands together in her lap and tried not to perspire.

"London"—LaCroix's dark eyes glinted with amusement—"is very far from Casablanca, *oui*?"

She forced what must have been a weak smile.

She hadn't been in Casablanca more than an hour and she had already had her luggage stolen, learned that her carefully drawn plans were probably based on Foreign Office fictions, and fallen into the debt of a Frenchman who was looking at her as if she were a well-braised brisket.

Her spirits sank further when they drew up in front of the Hotel Marrat and she discovered her proposed lodging was a dusky stuccoed structure with patches of bare bricks showing through a crumbling surface, tile work in dire need of repair, and iron railings that gave a poor illusion of balconies beneath the upper-level windows. The paint was missing from the lower half of a pair of battered front doors that opened at the level of the street itself. She took a deep breath and prayed that the soured milk and moldy leather smells that assaulted her weren't coming from the hotel.

The owner of the Marrat, a gaunt, pasty-faced fellow dressed in a rumpled western suit and fez, hurried out to greet them the instant their carriage stopped. He bowed and smiled excessively, revealing a number of missing teeth and a starched collar that was all but blackened with oily dirt. As Monsieur LaCroix escorted her inside the hotel lobby her nose reported both the good news and the bad. The soured milk smell, thankfully, had remained in the street, but the moldy leather smell was very much a part of the Marrat.

Mister LaCroix—"Ferdi" as he insisted Abigail call him—instructed the manager to treat her as if she were royalty, kissed her hand, and declared he would count the minutes until he saw her at supper. She would be counting the minutes, too, she thought . . . until she could be on her way to Marrakech.

The manager insisted on personally showing her to her room, which was up two sets of worn stone steps and along a narrow loggia. At the center of the hotel was a overgrown courtyard containing a broken fountain. Her room was in a far corner on the third floor, well away from the entrance, and from the quiet of the surrounding rooms, well away from other guests as well.

The decor was a haphazard mixture of Europe and North Africa; walls of stucco set with colorful glazed tiles, but furnished with a mixture of western items. The bed was a tall poster affair with a well-worn mattress and metal springs and there was a dry sink made of parched-looking wood and a Chippendale wing chair with stuffing showing through horsehair upholstery. The chipped tile floor was covered by colorful wool rugs and on the ceiling was a paddle fan with blades of tooled leather, run by a belt driven by something outside the room that made a continual low, thumping sound.

When the door closed behind the manager and porters, she tested the bedding by thumping it and released a haze of dust. Throwing open the shutters, she leaned on the iron railing of her tiny balcony and inhaled deeply several times. It was only for a few nights, she told herself. She had survived deadly storms at sea; she could survive this, too.

Of course, at sea she had had help.

Smith's face rose unbidden in her mind and she felt a

disconcerting pang of disappointment at not seeing him again before she left the ship . . . which she attributed to her failure to express proper gratitude to him and the nagging sense of indebtedness it left in her. If there was anything she couldn't abide it was being in someone's debt.

She thought of her new benefactor. And then tried *not* to think of him.

She had to reassert some control over her life. First thing tomorrow, she would go to the British Consulate herself. If the Consul was indeed gone, surely someone—a trusted secretary or majordomo—would be there in his absence. She would ask for and *get* the assistance she needed.

The dining area of the Marrat, a few steps away from the main lobby, was more like a noisy café than a proper hotel restaurant. The management had gone the proverbial extra mile for Monsieur LaCroix and his guest; their table was the only one with linen and candles instead of a scarred wooden top and a battered Persian lamp. A pall of smoke was collecting over the nearby tables, where men of both European and Moroccan descent indulged in Turkish tobacco, Western liquor, and spirited conversation. There were no other women present, a fact driven home when Abigail realized that she and Monsieur LaCroix were the object of stares.

He had already ordered their meal but, mercifully, the menu contained items she recognized: chicken, squash, garlic, peas, and melons. The things she hadn't encountered before were relatively benign—a thick, clabbered milk they called *yoghurt*, rice-and-meat stuffed grape leaves called *dolmas*, and something like a cross between rice and cracked wheat, called couscous. Most of their conversation revolved around LaCroix's vivid descriptions of local food markets and cuisine and Moroccan life. It was only when the tea came—the same boiling hot infusion of mint and sugar she had experienced aboard the ship—that LaCroix at last came to what seemed to be the point of his invitation.

"What has brought you to Casablanca, mademoiselle? A lovely young woman . . . traveling alone . . ."

Something in the way he caressed the word *alone* as it rolled from his tongue made her glad she hadn't accepted the wine he offered her earlier.

"I am here on a research mission." She countered his increasingly personal tone with professional purpose. "I am a librarian at the British Museum. I study manuscripts and I came to search for some historic texts."

"Texts? *Writings*, you mean? There are libraries of sorts in some of the mosques . . . dusty, silent places tended by withered old men." He gave her a sweeping look. "I cannot see in you that sort of scholar, mademoiselle."

"Then look harder, monsieur." She set her jaw. "For I am just that kind of scholar."

"Truly?" He studied her with amusement, templing his fingers. "Are you sure you did not come to dig for buried tombs filled with precious artifacts?"

Precious? She prayed her twitch wasn't visible. *Priceless.*

"Quite sure. I seek *books* . . . though not books as we know them . . . more like scrolls or *papyri* . . . things the ancient Egyptians would have written on."

"Egyptians?" His smile developed an edge. "You would do well to study maps as well as your 'texts,' mademoiselle. Egypt is a long way from Morocco."

"Nevertheless, I will travel to Marrakech. All I need is a guide, a horse, and a porter or two—"

"What makes you think you will find anything of value in Marrakech?"

He leaned forward slightly in his chair and she sensed expectation coiling beneath his genial expression. She choose her next words carefully.

"I have studied a goodly number of documents collected by a fine classical scholar whose works passed into my hands at the British Museum. Professor T. Thaddeus

Chilton researched these texts extensively, and I am certain he discovered the key to their location. His work points clearly to Marrakech and south."

"So"—he barked a laugh—"you do follow a 'treasure map' after all."

The noise around them lowered the instant LaCroix uttered those fateful words. All around them, grizzled male faces were suddenly turned their way, alight with interest that could only be described as hungry.

"Not *treasure*," she said with increased volume, intending the words to carry to the ears attached to those curious faces. "Unless one considers the words of the ancients to be rich in wisdom."

LaCroix's attention shifted abruptly to the archway leading to the hotel lobby, where two men had just arrived. His gaze darkened as they paused and nodded anxiously, requesting his attention. Both men had sweaty faces and wore dirt-smudged shirts. The smaller of the two was sporting a split and bleeding lip and the larger had a darkened swelling on his jaw and scrapes on his knuckles.

"Pardon, mademoiselle." The monsieur rose with a polite nod of apology and exited, pulling the men just outside the door to the dining room. The pair seemed to be delivering news that upset the dapper Frenchman. His features tightened and his posture grew rigid as he listened. Then he looked up and found her watching his reaction. He forced a smile and gradually turned his shoulder so that she could no longer see his face.

A few moments later, he dismissed the men, who hurried off at a purposeful pace, then returned to the table with a grave expression.

"Is something wrong?" she asked, hoping for an excuse to end the evening early. "Please don't think you must entertain me if you have pressing—"

"No, no. Nothing too serious." He paused and seated himself. "Can you tell me . . . was there anything of great value in the third bag you lost?"

"There were items of great value, but only to me.

Books, papers, and a few personal things. Why do you ask?" she said, coming alert under his scrutiny.

"It seems that my men located your third bag. And as they were bringing it here, they were set upon by another thief who surprised and attacked them." Her gasp brought a mollifying gesture from him. "No, no . . . you saw . . . they were not badly injured. Except for their pride." He gave a rueful smile. "Are you certain, mademoiselle, that there was nothing of greater value?"

"Just simple maps and a professor's journals." She lowered her voice as she spotted curious glances aimed their way. "The journals are all written in classical Greek. The language of Aristotle and Homer and Plato. They would be of no benefit to anyone but me." She winced, reconsidering. "Or some other master of ancient languages."

"You can truly read such things, mademoiselle?" His eyes widened and he sat back in his chair with a chastened look.

"I am quite adept, monsieur. I have studied ancient languages all my life."

"Then you are indeed a scholar, mademoiselle, and I must beg your pardon for not taking your important work more seriously." He pressed a hand over his well-padded heart. "It is simply that brilliance and scholarly achievement seldom come joined in so beautiful a personage."

She lowered her eyes in a counterfeit of modesty and groaned silently.

"You must allow me to make it up to you, Mademoiselle Merchant," he declared, thumping the table with his hand. When she looked up, he gave her a smile so unctuous she wondered that it didn't slide off his face. "You say you need transport to Marrakech. Well, I am the owner of a export company that does much business in Marrakech. I have a caravan leaving for there in two days and would be honored to have you join it." He brightened further as he recalled additional resources: "I can even provide you a guide who knows Marrakech and the roads beyond."

"I am grateful, monsieur." She groaned silently, scrambling for an excuse to decline and finding none beyond her uneasiness at being indebted to a man whose eyes never seemed to register what his lips and words were saying. "But I cannot put you to such trouble. You have already been much too kind."

"Nonsense," he said, breaking into a beaming smile that also failed to reach the dark centers of his eyes. "It is no trouble at all. And you would do me a kindness to allow me to exercise the generosity of my nature." He chuckled and lifted his wineglass in a genial toast. "There are those who might say I could use such practice."

Abigail had to suffer through two additional toasts to her beauty and brilliance before she could call a halt to his effusive adoration and make her way to her room. Even then, the monsieur was so attentive that she was afraid he intended to head straight for her door with her. She forestalled such a happening by stopping by the front desk to inquire after her messages—not that she expected any—and engaged the desk clerk in conversation that allowed her to take leave of the Frenchman and climb the stairs to her room alone.

Her shoulders ached and the nerves of her legs vibrated with unspent tension as she produced her key and turned it in the lock. She slipped inside, locked the door behind her, sagged back against it. Thank heaven that was over. She stepped defensively across the darkened room and felt her way along the bed to the lamp on the bedside table. Reassuring light bloomed around her.

"About bloody time," said a male voice that nearly caused both her knees and her bladder to fail. "I had just about given up on you."

Six

She stumbled back against the bed with a strangled cry.

There, crouched over one of her carpetbags on the floor, was her hard-drinking, hard-gambling, one-eyed nurse-maid from the ship. Smith straightened and as he did so she caught the glint of metal at his side. A knife, she realized as he slipped it into a sheath tucked into the top of his fitted, knee-high boot.

Her gaze climbed khaki trousers and a shirt that had a faintly military look to them, and took in a leather belt rig with a diagonal strap across his chest. There was a fresh bruise on his left cheek.

"What are you doing here?" she demanded, her gaze dropped to that sheathed knife and the bag beside it. "Going through my luggage?"

"Bringing back your property." He nudged the carpet-bag with his foot. It took a moment for her to realize that it was the one that had been missing.

"Where did you—how did you—" She sank to her knees beside it and produced a key from her inner pocket to open the lock. "But, Mister LaCroix said it was stolen from his men."

"Stolen back," he corrected irritably. "By me."

She looked up at him in confusion.

"You stole it from them after they had recovered it from the thieves?"

He tucked his thumbs into his belt, looking pained.

"You don't get it, do you? They were the ones who stole it in the first place."

"Don't be absurd. I saw the wretches who took my things." She yanked open the bag and began to pull items from it to make certain everything was still there. "They were dirty and half-naked—what the sailors called 'wharf rats.'"

"Shills," he declared. "Paid to take the bags so that LaCroix's men could 'recover' them. It's a dodge. A buck." Her bewilderment made him expel a harsh breath. "A *confidence* trick." When she frowned even deeper and shook her head, he glowered. "You really are a babe in the woods. It's a scheme where they fake a crime and then solve it for the victim."

"What could possibly be gained by that?" She located the professor's journals and hauled them out, counting and stacking them in her arms.

"Your *confidence*. And trust. So that later, they can steal something a lot bigger and more important from you."

"That's ridiculous. Mister LaCroix would never permit his men to engage in something so underhanded."

"You don't have a clue who he is, do you?" he demanded, hands on hips.

"He is a merchant. An importer and exporter of some sort."

"He's a crook, a thief, and a double-dealer. Get tangled up with him and you'll disappear before you get to Marrakech and never be heard from again."

"That's absurd," she said, feeling a tightening in her throat at that validation of her doubts about the Frenchman's intentions.

"No more 'absurd' than you sitting in a café at the edge of the Kasbah flapping your tongue about ancient books and treasure maps. Good God, woman—you might just as well have climbed up on a rooftop and shouted 'come, rob me!' "

"You were *listening* to my conversation?"

"The whole damned *Kasbah* was listening. I come to give you back your bag and find you dining with the sultan of Casablanca's seamy side." He leaned closer. "By morning, every criminal and cutthroat in the city will know about Miss Boston America's treasure map. And half of them will have a plan in motion to relieve you of it."

"I don't have a treasure map. If you were *listening*, you must have heard me tell the monsieur that."

"Yeah. And I heard him reading between the lines. I also saw the way half of the café was watching"—he bent and flipped the edge of the journals—"and wondering what is in your bag that makes it so valuable."

The memory of dozens of hungry eyes on her in the restaurant sent an echo of unwelcome agreement up her spine. She finally gave in to the urge to meet his gaze and looked up.

Pirates of the Barbary Coast . . . the 300's . . . History.

"You have to get out of Casablanca—fast." He grabbed her wrist and pulled her up. She was close enough to detect a hint of liquor on his breath and it jolted her back to a rational level of skepticism.

"I intend to do just that. Monsieur LaCroix offered me a place in his trading caravan to Marrakech." He groaned and started to protest, but she talked right over his objections: "But I intend to make my own arrangements. I am going to the British Consulate first thing tomorrow morning to get help securing transportation and a guide. I'll be on my way in a day . . . two at most."

He looked at her as if she'd gone totally daft.

"You don't have a day, Boston, much less *two*."

He reeled her closer by her wrist, studying her with a conflicted expression that was some part exasperation, some part annoyance, and some part genuine concern. That unexpected combination disarmed her momentarily.

She examined his face even as he searched hers. Strong features. Angular. Intriguing. Her gaze settled on that darkening bruise on his cheek . . . acquired from LaCroix's men . . . on her behalf. She inhaled sharply to counter a sinking sensation in her stomach and smelled something else on him, something that seemed to be more like perfume than liquor. She took another slow, quiet breath. Was that honey? Out of nowhere came the disconcerting memory of sweetened oats . . .

He stiffened, looking like he was wrestling with something.

"All right, dammit—I'll take you to Marrakech."

"W-what?" She swayed as he released her, then she backed two steps to steady herself against the footboard of the bed. "I didn't ask you—"

"Keep to this room until I come for you. Don't let anybody in. Not even the manager. *Especially* not the manager; he's LaCroix's tool. I'll be back as soon as I get horses and supplies."

"I'll have you know, I am perfectly capable of—"

"Getting yourself robbed, molested, or sold into a harem somewhere."

"Of conducting my own affairs and deciding who I will and will not hire."

He stepped over her opened carpetbag and headed for the darkened window, where he closed and latched the wooden shutters. She dropped her journals onto the bed behind her and crossed her arms, watching him stalk back and forth, lifting and assessing the furniture.

He was mad, she decided. Or possibly drunk. She hadn't had much experience with drunk men.

"This ought to do," he said, dragging the washstand toward the door, upsetting the earthenware pitcher in the basin and setting both rattling. "Lock the door and push this against it when I've gone. Don't open to anybody but me. I'll be back before daylight. " He paused for a moment, looking her over. "And change your clothes. Wear something to ride in. And no damned cinchers."

Before she could say that she did not intend to let him dictate either her wardrobe or her itinerary, he stopped that thought dead with a simple question.

"Do you have a weapon? Something to defend yourself with?"

Alarm shot like steam through her veins. Hot. Unexpected. The full impact of all that had happened broke through her carefully erected defenses. There were thieves and rascals all around, and two very different men were insisting she place her welfare in their hands. She hadn't a clue who to trust.

"Of course. I-I have a pistol. In one of my bags.' Still. She hoped.

"Load it and keep it handy," he ordered.

It suddenly seemed that her entire expedition was in danger of being waylaid and misdirected by men telling her what she could and couldn't do.

"See here, *Mr. Smith*—if that is indeed your name—" She had to reclaim enough ground to stand on with her own two feet. "I appreciate you returning my bag and your offer of assistance, but I don't intend to travel to Marrakech or anywhere else with you. I've told you . . . first thing tomorrow morning, I will seek assistance from the Consul or his staff in arranging transport and—"

"The British Consulate is about as useful as a sandbox in a shitstorm," he declared irritably. "Believe me—you're on your own here. Except for me. Now load your damned gun and be ready to move when I come for you."

Before she could protest further, he was at the door and producing his own key to unlock it.

"Wait a minute—how did you—" She searched for her key, certain he must have taken it. Her eyes widened as she found it still in her pocket.

"This is the *Marrat*." He held up a straight-shanked key just like hers. "There are a hundred of these for every lock in the place."

Her anger came out as a strangled gurgle. Before she could recover, he was out the door and closing it behind him. She hurried to turn the key he had left in the lock and held her breath, listening, sensing that he was still on the other side of the door. Even so, his voice startled her as it came through the panels.

"The washstand, Boston . . . push it in front of the door."

She had the feeling that he would stand there waiting until he heard the requisite noise. Muttering, she did push the washstand in front of the door. Then she gave it an extra shove to jam it tightly in place and produce a telling *thump* against the door.

"That's better." She could hear the smile in his voice through the parched wood. "Now, go load your gun."

Apparently bullets were made to fit into a gun in only one direction. She stared at the six shiny brass disks visible in the cylinder of the pistol she had purchased for the trip. Clearly, the manufacturer had factored "inexperience" into its specifications.

Mechanics of Firearms . . . the 660's . . . Applied Sciences.

She closed the chamber and wrapped her hand around the pistol grip, looking tentatively down the barrel of the gun as if firing it. The cold steel drew heat from her palm. With a shiver, she laid the pistol on the bed beside her and stared at it.

She'd never fired a gun in her life. Did she really intend to start now? She was a *librarian*, for heaven's sake. A keeper of knowledge. A purveyor of enlightenment. Guns embodied a blind and amoral power that was too often bent to the service of ignorance and destruction. Did she honestly think she could fire a weapon at someone?

Feeling suddenly foolish, she gathered up the bullets scattered on the bed around her and dumped them back into the box. Then she carried both ammunition and pistol to one of her carpetbags and tucked it deep inside.

Smith had intended to scare her with his talk of criminals and cutthroats and the Frenchman's treacherous nature to make her think she needed his help. He was probably just as curious about her "treasure map" as LaCroix and the host of cads and criminals he claimed were plotting to rob her.

Spawn of Satan. Her first instincts about him had been right on target.

He had followed her to the Marrat . . . heard her speak of her search for something ancient and valuable . . . and decided to exploit whatever sense of obligation their previous association might have created in her. He planted himself in her room and began issuing orders right and left, assuming that she—like most well-bred young women—had been conditioned to defer to men.

Well, he had badly underestimated her. She narrowed her eyes and produced a smile of pure defiance. No daughter of Olivia Ridgeway Merchant was going to be frightened into submission by a holdover from the days of Blackbeard the Pirate!

She began to unbutton her blouse and in a few moments had donned a clean nightdress and retrieved her doeskin sheets from one of her bags and spread them over the dusty bedclothes. When she crawled between the sheets, she had a difficult time making her tense limbs relax and her chaotic thoughts quiet.

The swirling blades overhead, just visible in the filtered light, and the low rhythmic thumping of whatever powered the fan slowly worked a spell on her senses. She went over and over what she would say to Smith when he arrived and found her snug and safe in her room in her bed, and in her nightgown.

Wretched fright-monger. Unbidden, impressions of him flashed through her consciousness . . . reckless and intimidating . . . big and male . . . smelling of liquor laced with honey . . . with wind-ruffled hair and a bruise on his cheek. . . .

She came awake with a start, later, to the sound of someone pounding on her door.

"Ouvrez la porte!" came a rough male voice from the loggia outside.

Seconds passed. She sat up and blinked. It couldn't be Smith; he wasn't civilized enough to knock.

"Ouvrez—sur l'autorite de le gouvernement de France. Ouvrez!"

Did he say the government of France?

Other voices rose, all male, all speaking—shouting— French. She froze, watching movement in the fingers of light crawling in under the door, and her heart seemed to climb into her throat. The demand came again in heavily accented English:

"O-pen . . . theeese . . . door!"

The knocking escalated to banging that shook the wash-stand against the door and rattled the basin and pitcher on it. A volley of French invective resulted in concentrated blows against the door that jarred the entire door frame. She bolted from the bed and stood stiff with horror.

"Don't you dare—I'll have you know—*I am an American citizen!*"

The only response was the application of an axe to the brittle center panels of the door. The wood splintered and shouts of fury erupted as her attackers tore away the broken wood and encountered yet another obstacle. Coordinating their efforts with a verbal count, they alternately pushed and pulled to rock the washstand free.

"Keep out—I'm warning you—" She thought frantically of her journals and maps . . . her precious cache of coin . . . her *gun!*

Just as she dove for her carpetbags, the invaders gave a last, mighty heave that sent the washstand toppling across the tile floor and slammed the broken door back against the wall.

Seven

Bodies—*men*—poured into the darkened room from the torchlit loggia. Some paused to locate the room's occupant and others rushed forward with weapons drawn to defend their possession of the room. Her involuntary scream served only to draw them down on her as she knelt by her carpetbags . . . up to her elbows in table linen, metal teapots, tins of sugar, and boxes of quinine. . . .

They hauled her to her feet, shouting: *"Ou est le deserteur?"* When she didn't answer immediately, they gave her a shake and barked: *"Ou est Smeeth!"*

Light bloomed around them from a lantern . . . held by the hotel manager, who was himself being held by two burly men in uniforms.

"How dare you invade my rooms in the dead of—"

"Where is he?" the manager said as they dragged him into the room. The quiver in his voice and the haunted look in his eyes fed her rising fear. "Just tell the sergeant where he is, mademoiselle, and they will leave you alone."

"I have done nothing wrong, and I—" She twisted and shoved against their grip on her arms, mildly astonished by her own behavior. Where did this mad impulse to fight come from? "Tell them where *who* is?"

She stilled long enough to turn to the manager and then the man he seemed to be watching . . . the one he called "sergeant." The man was thickset and muscular, with coarse features and flat, black eyes.

"I have no idea what you're talking about."

"Smeeth," the sergeant spat out, shoving his grizzled face into hers. "*Ou est*—Smeeth? *Dites nous.*"

They thought Smith was here with her? It was only then that she made sense of the fact that they wore khaki uniforms and white cylindrical hats with neck flaps and military badging. They were dressed like those men on the dock earlier . . . the ones who had refused to go after the thieves . . . "Legionnaires."

"Tell them I have no idea what they're talking about," she ordered the manager, to translate. "I've been in my room since I left dinner with Mister LaCroix." The sergeant's response to the translation was a guttural snarl that sounded like an oath and a rough wave to his men that ordered them to search everything.

Suddenly teapots, petticoats, shoes, brushes, linen, and journals were being dragged out, examined, and tossed onto the floor.

"Stop!" She strained against the Legionnaires' grip. "Make them stop! I have no idea where this 'Smith' person is." She looked to the ham-fisted sergeant, whose sullen gaze was roaming her nightgown with alarming interest. "I swear to you, I have no idea where he is!"

The sergeant looked to the men at the window who had opened the shutters to search the tiny balcony and the street below. They shook their heads. Then he looked to the men who were riffling her bags and then to the soldiers who had checked under the bed and behind what little furniture might offer concealment. Nothing there, either. He turned back to Abigail.

"Smeeth is *deserteur.* You know thees word? *Deserteur?*" He began to speak freely in French and snarled an order at the manager, who translated: "He says . . . Smeeth abandoned duty . . . fled under fire. His cowardice cost many lives. They will not rest until he is found and punished."

Her gaze caught on the sergeant's huge hand, which was clenched in a fist so tight that his sun-darkened skin was turning white. She looked up, and the soul-deep malice in his face stopped her breath.

"The sergeant says"—the manager's final translation seemed to stick in his throat and he swallowed hard before continuing—"those who give Smith aid will suffer the same fate as him, when he is caught."

The sergeant swaggered closer to her and ran a callused hand inward along the shoulder of her nightgown, pausing to grip the flesh beneath it with a force that was just short of punishing. When he transferred that grip to her face, she yanked her head back and glared at him with full Ridgeway-Merchant fury . . . no longer caring that her anger might provoke something worse.

"How dare you touch me?" She jerked her arms free and backed away, pouring all of her anger and contempt into her gaze. "Get out of my room." She flung a finger at the ruined door and by some miracle, it didn't shake. "And prepare your excuses. I intend to lodge a complaint with your commander first thing tomorrow morning!"

The sergeant assessed her determination and after a long moment, jerked his head toward the door, ordering his men out.

"Remember, mademoiselle." He paused in the doorway to construct a final warning in English. "We . . . watch . . . you."

R*emember*, the beast had said. How could she *forget*? The brutality in their faces and actions, the fear that made her heart pound like a locomotive piston, the horrifying helplessness of watching men burst through her door in the dead of night . . . all on account of Smith. If she had entertained any thoughts of allowing him to escort her to Marrakech—the disappointment sinking through her middle said she had—such thoughts were banished now.

How had they known he came to see her earlier?

Her hands, her knees . . . her whole body was trembling.

We watch you.

Someone had already been watching. She glanced at her shattered door. She had done nothing wrong, but it was all too clear that innocence was no protection in this part of the world. Like Smith said: She was on her own here.

Taking refuge in action, she inspected the damaged door. The soldiers had dragged the manager off with them and she was not about to go searching through a darkened hotel to demand a change of rooms. She would have to make do . . . stand her own guard until morning, when daylight would provide greater safety. After what had just happened, she wouldn't sleep a wink, anyway.

The washstand hadn't been effective as a barrier when the door was intact; she looked around for an alternative and set about shoving the heavy wooden bed against the door. The physical exertion helped to dissipate some of her tension. Then she was able to face the mess the wretches had made of her possessions.

As she knelt by her bags, refolded and repacked her linen and equipment, her eyes began to sting and unshed tears trickled down the inside of her nose. She blinked repeatedly and sniffed. Stop that. No Ridgeway-Merchant woman would allow herself to be threatened and bullied into tears. She made herself think of the intrepid Mary Kingsley facing leeches and headhunters in West Africa and of Harriet Martineau facing the crocodiles of the Nile.

Then her hand brushed something cold near the bottom of her equipment bag and she recognized the metallic feel and shape. Her gun. The Legionnaires had either missed it or considered such a weapon no threat to them. She hauled it out and sat back on her feet to stare at it. An hour ago, it wouldn't have been a threat to anyone in her hands. But now . . .

Mariana Starke had included a pistol on her list of necessities for a woman traveler, and Abigail had assumed it was meant for protection against wild animals. Hazards to safety, she was learning, came on two legs as well as four.

Desperate to overcome the feeling of vulnerability the Legionnaire invasion had left her with, she set about dressing in clothes that would bolster her sense of control and make her feel less exposed. She chose her gray tweed split skirt, riding boots, and a simple cotton blouse with a band collar and sleeves that could be rolled up. She debated stuffing her pink satin demicorset in the bottom of her bag, then with a surge of defiance, donned it instead.

Before long, she was dressed and her belongings were packed. She intended to leave the hotel, first thing in the morning, and head straight for the consulate. Surely someone there would be able to carry a complaint to the commander of the local regiment of the Foreign Legion. Then she intended to hire horses, find a proper guide . . . or at least a reliable map . . . and set off for Marrakech before the day was out.

When she was ready, she blew out the light and stationed herself in the chair with the revolver on her lap . . . watching both the door and the window and listening to the sounds of the Moroccan night. Every dog bark, every distant voice, every squeak of a wheel that floated up from the streets below caused her pulse to jump. Some time later, in the distance, she heard a single, plaintive voice, crying out in what sounded like a lamentation. A call to prayer, she realized with relief.

Hour after hour dragged by. Her eyes grew so accustomed to the darkness that she could see clearly in the room. She began to be able to tell which were ordinary night sounds and which were unusual. Soon the ordinary were all she heard and the darkness and the slow unwinding of tension overwhelmed her. In spite of her determination to stay awake, her eyelids drooped and her head came to rest against a wing of the chair.

Thus, she didn't hear the scuffing sound just outside the shutters as dawn arrived. She didn't see the glint of the blade inserted beneath the latch of the shutters, hear the creak of the hinge, or notice the soft thud of leather-clad feet onto the tile floor. Her breathing continued slow and shallow . . . until a hand clamped over her mouth and she jolted awake with a cry and a flail of limbs.

"Quiet!" came a harsh whisper. "It's me."

A face and eye patch materialized out of a fog of sleep and anxiety. She stilled and after a moment he removed his hand.

"Legionnaires," he continued to whisper. "They're everywhere."

"Including here," she said in a vehement whisper, drawing his gaze with hers to the shattered door. "They were looking for *you*."

"Dammit." He straightened and made a gesture of exasperation. "I figured LaCroix would . . ." He paused for a moment, shaking off that train of thought. "They left men in the courtyard—we'll have to go out the window."

"Not me," she said furiously, shoving to her feet. The gun on her lap tumbled to her feet with a *thunk* that sounded like a thunderclap in the darkened room. She scooped it up and held it awkwardly by the grip, unsure of where to point it. "I'm not going anywhere with a wanted *deserteur*."

"I'm not a—" He stared at her for a moment, then exhaled steam in a hiss. "Fine. Once we're out of here, you're on your own."

"I'm not going anywhere with you. Every minute you stay here makes it more likely they'll find you here and accuse me of helping you."

"I'm not a criminal. And you've got more to worry about than just—" He grabbed her by the arm and pulled her to the opened shutter. "See that roof?" He pointed to the top of a nearby building.

"Of course I see it. What's it got to do with—"

Something—*someone*—on that rooftop moved.

"And over there." He pointed another direction, to a stepped line of roofs that were silhouetted against the gray of the predawn sky. The horizontal line developed a series of bumps that moved like an undulating snake, paused and blended into the roofscape, then moved again. Something about that sinuousness and stealth caused her toes to curl inside her boots. "And there . . ." He pointed to still another roof.

"Legionnaires are only a part of your problems, Boston."

Human figures were clearly visible in the third direction. She could make out heads . . . turbans . . . moving silently, steadily . . . toward the Marrat. And then she saw the glint of metal . . . a grizzled face . . . a blade clamped between teeth. . . .

"W-who are they?" Her voice sounded as dry as her mouth felt.

"Locals, most likely . . . who've decided to have a look at your blessed 'treasure map' for themselves."

"How do they know—I said I don't *have* a treasure map!" It came out much louder than she intended. She clamped a hand over her mouth and looked to the door.

A heartbeat later, an alert was being shouted from the loggia to the central courtyard below.

"Dammit!" He took the gun from her, turned her around, and shoved it down into the back of her belt. Then he pushed her toward the bed. "Grab one of those sheets!" He seized the dusty cover and by the time he had finished tying one corner to the sheet, the sound of running outside the door was growing louder. "*Damn, Damn, Damn!*"

There was just time for one more knot, before the Legionnaires arrived at her door and started pounding and shoving, yelling to each other, "Take them alive "

Them? Abigail froze for a moment with disbelief.

Smith pulled her to the window and shoved her out onto the tiny balcony, where he tied one end of the sheets around the rickety railing. "Over the side," he ordered through gritted teeth as he finished fastening the end to the ironwork. "There are horses waiting in the alley. You better be able to ride."

When she hesitated, trying to think whether escaping with him was the best thing or the worst thing she could do, he roared, *"Now!"* and her flight instinct took over, propelling her to the edge and making her swing her leg over the rail. Below, she could indeed see horses and someone waiting.

"My journals—my maps!" She tried to swing her leg back over the railing, but he prevented it. "I have to have my bags!"

"Go!"

"I can't go without them!" She tried again to climb back onto the balcony.

"I'll get them!" He ducked back and grabbed the first of her carpetbags and flung it across the room and onto the balcony. She lifted the bulky bag, slung it over her shoulder with both hands, and then looked down. Three storeys below, she could see the waiting figure waving, beckoning, and she freed one hand to grab the railing and slip her other leg over the edge.

Nothing in her orderly college-to-library-to-museum life had prepared her for letting go of a solid iron railing and trusting her body weight to a rope of hastily knotted bedsheets as she was being chased out of a hotel room by force of vengeful soldiers.

The fabric groaned as she grasped it and slid her weight down over the edge of the balcony. She could see the knots tighten, slip, and finally grab again, and abandoned her grip on the carpetbag to use both hands. The bag fell into the darkness below with a sickening thud, and seconds later, her second bag went hurtling past her to join the first on the ground.

"Whaaat—" She looked up to see Smith on the balcony with her third bag. Before she could call to him not to throw it, he already had.

Thudding, splintering sounds now came from the room behind him. He climbed over the railing and lowered himself so that he hung from the edge of the narrow parapet by his hands.

"Slide, dammit!" he roared. She realized he was swinging his legs over to grab the sheets above her and that the knots would never hold them both.

"Oh, God!" Slamming her eyes shut, she relaxed her hold and flew down the bulky rope that ended a good six feet above the ground. Somebody grabbed her as she fell and the next thing she knew she was in a heap on the ground with her hands on fire.

"Ow, ow, ow . . . ow, ow . . ."

Staggering to her feet, trying to right her vision, she spotted four horses and a rotund little figure in a turban dragging her bags toward the horses. A familiar figure.

"Haffe?" It was disorienting seeing him here.

"Merchant M'am." The *Star*'s steward gave her a breathless grin as he deftly threaded a rope through the handles of two of her bags, then heaved them across what appeared to be a packhorse.

Something hit the ground behind her with a thud, but before she could turn to see what, she was pushed wholesale toward the nearest horse.

"Mount up—move!"

She apparently didn't react quickly enough; she was picked up by the waist and practically thrown onto a hard wooden saddle on the nearest horse. When she righted herself, Haffe handed her a set of reins and Smith smacked the rear of her mount to set it in motion. As the horse lurched, she was thrown back and barely grabbed the pommel to hold on for dear life.

"My bags!" she called over her shoulder.

Smith's only response was to shoot past her on his mount and lean down to grab her horses' bridle and pull it into a run.

Behind them, Legionnaires burst out onto the balcony just in time to see their horses disappear into the gloom, and faceless predators on three different housetops sounded the alarm that their quarry was on the run.

Shouts and gunshots spurred Smith and Abigail through the narrow, still, darkened streets. When she managed to lift her gaze, she saw the upper floors of the buildings beginning to glow with the first rays of morning sun; dawn had arrived. From mosques and minarets all over the city, a siren of voices began a haunting and already familiar call to the faithful. Her perception became a gritty kaleidoscope of shape and color as dust boiled up from the horses' hooves. Here and there, they passed through widened intersections setting shopkeepers and peddlers scattering for cover and food sellers with carts and unlit braziers careening out of the way.

The thought kept drumming through her head that the die was cast; she would be his accomplice now in the eyes of the French Foreign Legion, even though all she had done was allow herself to be pushed out a window and dropped down a rope of bedsheets onto a horse.

What choice had she had? They were watching her . . . all of them . . . Legionnaires . . . thieves . . . adventurers . . . cutthroats. . . .

That was when she saw it: the British flag, hanging from the iron grille of a street-side gate just ahead. Reaching for the security it represented as a man in the desert reaches for the shimmer of water on the horizon, she straightened in her saddle and pulled back on the reins. She looked back. That had to be the Consulate! It took some tugging on the reins and flapping her heels against the horse's sides to make it turn, but she was soon back at the flag-draped gate, grabbing and rattling the ironwork.

"Hello in there! Open up—it's an emergency!"

A turbaned fellow in a long, hooded cotton tunic headed for the gate.

"This is the Consulate, yes?" she called as he headed for the gate. "Is this the British Consulate?" When he nodded and repeated "British Consulate," she nearly melted. "I'm from the British Museum! Let me in—quickly—please!"

As the heavy wood and wrought iron gate swung open, she kicked her mount and it shot into the small courtyard of the consul's residence. The man swung the gate closed behind her, then hurried over to help her down.

"I must see the Consul straightaway—it's vital," she said, handing off her horse's reins. He answered her in a mixture of English and a Berber dialect, bowing and gesturing to the front doors.

"Inside, ma'am. Inside."

There was no doorman at the front entrance; no one to admit or greet her. The great wooden doors opened easily, despite their massive weight. She found herself in a tiled loggia that surrounded an inner courtyard. She called, "I've come on urgent business," and "I must see the Consul straightaway," but received no reply.

Stepping into the dawn-shaded court at the center of the house was literally stepping into an oasis for the senses. Lush trees and flowering shrubs were grouped around stone benches and beds of blooming flowers and trellises of vining jasmine surrounded a marble fountain that sat at the juncture of paved paths. The trickling water sounded almost musical. The noise and danger of the streets seemed a million miles away.

An unreal and somewhat disorienting sense of calm continued as she wandered down what seemed to be the main corridor of the loggia, peering through stone archways and past carved latticework, calling for someone, anyone.

The stillness, at first comforting, now began to worry her. She had decided to turn back to the outer courtyard to look for the man who had taken her horse, when a slender Moroccan-looking man in traditional dress of turban and a long-sleeved tunic stepped out onto the loggia and into her path.

"May I help you?" he said, nodding formally over folded hands.

"Thank Heaven." She clasped a hand to her heart. "I

was beginning to think—I need to see the British Consul immediately."

"I fear that will be impossible, ma'am," he said in lilting tones. "Consul Battingale is in Rabat and will not return for several weeks." He gave her a wan smile and somewhat apologetic shrug. "I am Ravad Qatar . . . house steward. Perhaps I can be of service."

Her spirits rose as quickly as they had plunged. "Bless you, Mr. Qatar. I am in dire need of horses and a proper guide to . . ." She thought of Haffe and her bags and her detoured cache of money. "To Marrakech. I've come to search for some books that belonged to an old library . . . I work for the British Museum." His eyes widened at the mention of her employer.

"Truly? I have heard of this place . . . this great house in London . . . where many wonders and treasures are assembled. If I can help—"

Just then shouts and the sound of men and horses and confusion roiled through the half-open door to the outer courtyard. Dread seized her as the steward looked alarmed and nodded to excuse himself to see about the disturbance. Before he reached the main doors, Abigail had already recognized the voice shouting demands.

"Ouvrez! Sur le nom de la Republique de France! Ouvrez les portes!"

That voice—they had found her! The memory of the sergeant's hand digging into her shoulder and the blunted rage in his eyes came flooding back. They couldn't touch her here, could they? This was essentially British—

Qatar's voice rose into the confusion, declaring "No, no!" and "No right to come here!"

Rights or no, they seemed bent on invading and searching the consulate.

She backed down the loggia toward the rear of the courtyard, looking for a rear exit. Spotting a promising doorway, she ducked inside and rushed to a far doorway and down a passage that led through what appeared to be a kitchen pantry. She paused for a moment, listening and collecting her breath, inhaling the scents of spices and flour and strings of dried garlic.

The sound of movement and men's voices came from all directions now; they were searching the consulate. How long would it take for them to reach such an obvious hiding place as a pantry? She peered out through the curtain into the adjoining kitchen. On the far side was yet another door. Its size and the heavy wooden bar across it suggested it led to the street.

Her only thought was to escape the consulate and find a place to hide until the Legionnaires left and it was safe to go back for her horse. Smith's face and voice rose in her mind proclaiming the Consulate useless as she listened to the search drawing closer to her. She would be well on her way to Marrakech by now, if she hadn't stopped to seek sanctuary where there was none.

The sound of something being overturned in the room behind her caused her to bolt from the pantry and race across the kitchen. The bar was heavy and tightly fitted into its metal brackets. She pounded upward on it with the heels of her palms and the dull thuds drew the attention of a nearby Legionnaire. When he appeared in the doorway—rifle forward—she had just begun to move the bar. With one last panicky blow from her hand, the bar was free. He shouted what had to be an order for her to stop and she whirled to face him and shrank back against the door . . . where she felt a lump in the back of her belt.

"Stay back," she called, reaching behind her for her pistol . . . the one Smith had jammed into the back of her belt . . . mildly surprised that she hadn't remembered it until now. "I'm warning you—I'm armed—"

The soldier advanced on her and in desperation she raised the pistol up and out from her with both hands. He halted immediately, assessing both her and her weapon.

It was loaded, but she was trying to recall what she had to do to fire it. The soldier sensed her uncertainty and started forward again.

"Stop, I said! Halt!" She jabbed the gun at him to show she meant business and he stopped again, scowling.

It had something to do with pulling that lever back. As he decided she wasn't a serious threat, she reached up with both thumbs and pulled the hammer back. It clicked once, then a second time, and the soldier froze. She realized from his reaction and the fact that she couldn't pull back any farther that she must be ready to fire.

"Back away! I'm warning you—"

She shifted control of the heavy pistol to her right hand and edged sideways to dislodge the bar from the door with her left. When the bar fell to the floor she glanced down . . . and everything happened at once.

The soldier lunged for her, his comrades burst into the kitchen, and her fingers reached the metal door handle. In the space of a heartbeat, she yanked the street door open, braced, and squeezed the trigger.

The blast from the gun sent the soldier diving to the floor and caused his comrades to lurch for cover. Jarred by the violence of the explosion, she whirled and charged out the rear door at a run.

Outside was a dark and narrow alley—just wide enough for a man on horseback or a small cart to pass. Instinctively, she headed for the light coming from one end, sensing it would be a broader street that might offer a means of escape or a place to hide. It was indeed a wider street, with a number of people on foot, donkey carts, and a number of stalls visible down the way.

Behind her, the soldiers had recovered enough to charge after her and once in the alley, they made the same decision she did. The minute they reached the street, one began shouting orders and they split up to search for her in both directions. She could hear them coming through the pounding of blood in her head and the shouts of the people escaping their path.

Every door was shut, every stall was too open and visible, there was no place to hide. Her lungs were burning . . . her legs wouldn't move fast enough . . .

At the edge of her vision she glimpsed a horse charging her way, and sensed it was determined to intercept her. She tried to dodge and plowed into a stall filled with hanging scarves and kaftans that clutched at and slowed her. By the time she fought her way free, the horse was on top of her and as she tried to dart away the animal blocked her way and a hand reached for one of her arms and dragged her against the side of the horse.

"Come on, dammit!" came a command that penetrated the chaos in the marketplace and in her own reeling wits. She looked up into Smith's furious face. "Climb—put your foot in the stirrup!" She managed to help him drag her across his lap—just as the whine of the first bullets reached them. "Hang on!"

Sprawled across his legs, with the wooden pommel of the saddle pounding into her stomach, she had neither breath nor inclination to question his orders. He spurred the horse and raced through the streets at a breakneck pace. Everything careened past, tilted and disjointed. There were more shots, but the winding streets made sighting impossible and the firing quickly stopped.

As they rounded yet another corner, she spotted what appeared to be an opening, a huge, stone arch in the city walls. A caravan of heavily laden camels was entering the city, and traders, hawkers, and food vendors were greeting it. The accompanying confusion was their salvation. Smith crouched over her, bending to his horse, and headed for that opening. She instinctively tucked her head and held on for all she was worth.

As they reached the arch, the shouts of sentries on the ramparts above blended strangely with the call to prayer being issued around the city. She took a breath, squeezed her eyes shut, and answered that call.

Eight

Ferdineaux LaCroix stepped over the debris that was once a door and entered Abigail Merchant's vacant hotel room . . . careful not to snag the silk of his pristine white suit. The portly Frenchman took his time looking over the toppled washstand and displaced bed, then the flat-faced sergeant who stood by the open window grinding an anxious fist into a meaty palm.

"So, you let them get away," LaCroix observed with an air of deadly calm, using his silver-headed walking stick to rake the edge of the naked mattress.

"They had help," the sergeant said with a sullen glance at the bedclothes still tied to the balcony railing. "They had horses waiting."

"He was prepared." LaCroix stepped out onto the balcony, peered down into the shadowed alley, and then turned back to spear the sergeant with a look. "Enterprising, don't you think? *For a dead man.*"

"We give chase." The sergeant reddened furiously, casting the numerous scars on his face into pale relief. "They go to the British house. And you say to take them *alive.*" When LaCroix was silent for another moment he grew impatient. "We know where they go, *non?*" He put a hand to the pistol he wore at his waist and started for the door. "We overtake them on the road to—"

"No." LaCroix brought up his walking stick across the sergeant's path, halting him. "You will let them complete their journey . . . reach Marrakech. You will let them search for and find whatever it is the American woman seeks. Why deprive them of the pleasure of finding this 'treasure' of hers? Especially when we intend to deprive them of the pleasure of keeping it." He glanced again at the knotted sheets on the railing and began to turn the fat gold ring he wore on his little finger . . . thinking.

"Sooner or later they will have to return to Casablanca to seek transport back to London." He straightened, having decided on a course. "All you have to do, Gaston, is keep track of them and bring me word when they've located the treasure. Then you will see that Apollo Smith dies. Permanently, this time. And I will see that the very independent Miss Merchant learns a woman's proper place in the world."

The shadows of the great walls and the constriction of the enclosed city fell away as they raced through the city gate and into the countryside. Groves of date palms and cultivated green fields produced a disjointed patchwork of landscape in her head. When she managed to raise her head, she spotted tents, stalls, and corrals lining the mostly empty road. It was dawn, and there were few people about; only a few men facing east on prayer rugs.

As soon as they were past the encampments that surrounded the city Smith abandoned the road and struck off across country.

They rode for what seemed like forever . . . until they reached a spot sheltered by a large outcropping of rock and he finally stopped and lowered her to the ground. She staggered, dizzy, and hung on to the horse's blanket to stay upright. Every bone in her body had been shaken loose at the joints, and from shoulders to knees she felt like she'd been tenderized.

"What the hell were you doing back there?" he demanded, swinging down. She sensed that only the exertion of the ride kept him from roaring full force at her. "Where in blazes did you go?"

She looked up at him, seeing spots of dark and light as blood drained from her air-starved brain. "I saw the Consulate and thought they could help. Then the Legionnaires came and bashed their way in—they just *invaded* a foreign mission—a *consulate*! How dare they?"

He reached for her right hand and pulled it up between them. Her wrist hung limply, but there was nothing half-hearted about her grip on the handle of the pistol she had fired at the soldier in the kitchen.

"Good God." Apollo looked from the gun to her flushed face. "Did you shoot this thing?" She winced at the sight of the gun, and he raised it to take a sniff at the barrel. "You *shot* at them? Dammit all—it's a wonder they didn't haul out the mobile artillery on us." He pried her taut, bloodless fingers from the pistol grip and dangled the gun between them. "Legionnaires don't like being shot at, Boston. They take it personally. And they make it a point of pride to return fire at a ratio of *four-to-one*."

"What was I supposed to do? Let them arrest me and send me to prison for the rest of my life so they wouldn't be offended?" She punched a finger at him. "This is all your fault. They broke down my door in the middle of the night and ran me out of my hotel room, my consulate, and finally Casablanca itself because of *you*! You're a *deserter*!"

He jerked his chin back at the charge and glared at her.

"Well, at least I'm not a damned *lunatic*—charging off to Morocco by myself, nearly dying of seasickness, getting robbed before I even set foot on shore, and then taking on the French Foreign Legion singlehanded." He leaned steadily closer to her. "No, you're worse than a lunatic—

you're a *menace*! You're going to get somebody killed. But it's *not* going to be me."

They faced each other, hands on hips, chests heaving, eyes hot . . . fear-fueled tempers roiling . . . pride burning. She had never been so exercised and overwrought, never vibrated physically with fury and leashed emotion before. She was desperate to do something and was terrified of what that something might be. He was so big and hot and angry and . . . and she was a hair's breadth away from grabbing him and . . . and . . .

It was the uncertainty of *and what*? that kept her from freeing that furious and utterly unprecedented impulse. She had no idea what she would do to him. Or with him. Her gaze fastened of its own will on his mouth. Her own lips began to feel hot, sensitive, and alarmingly conspicuous.

"Get on the damned horse," he said with a growl, withdrawing and jamming the gun into his saddlebag and his foot into the stirrup. When he swung up and was settled in the saddle, he assessed both her and the situation. Looking as if it cost him a few years off his life, he stuck out his hand to her.

"You ride with me or you walk to the nearest village. Which will it be?"

It was a minute before she could bring herself to take his hand and use the stirrup he vacated for her. She struggled up behind him, and then found herself confronted with his big, overheated back. The only handhold seemed to be the rear of the saddle, but they hadn't gone a hundred yards before she was losing her grip and struggling just to stay aboard. He halted the horse and spoke through gritted teeth as he reached for her arms and drew them around his middle.

"Hang on to me." He made a low, growling noise. "Just—keep your hands where I put them."

That was how she came to be trekking through the equatorial noonday sun with her arms full of hostile, sun-maddened male and her own overheated body aching and burning strangely in some very alarming places.

Heatstroke induced delusions . . . Medicine . . . the 600's.

His back seemed as broad as the Sahara and she could feel the hard ridges of his ribs beneath her wrists. Every sway and shift of his body created a fresh awareness of the columns of sinew running up his spine and of the broad, smooth fans of muscles that stretched out to his shoulders.

After a while she decided that even monosyllabic conversation was preferable to dwelling on the intimate details of how his muscular male body differed from her own.

Comparative anatomy . . . Zoology . . . Mammalia . . . 599.

"Where the devil are we?" she asked, squinting first at one side of the landscape and then at the other. Rocks. Hardpacked red and brown earth with the snowcapped Atlas Mountains in the background. The occasional stand of scruffy palms and parched grasses, and a sky as blue as polished turquoise.

"Taking an alternate route."

"To where? The back of 'beyond?'"

"Marrakech."

She absorbed that for a moment.

"Well, where is Haffe? He has my bags."

"He'll catch up."

"How will he know where we are?"

He nodded to the open landscape. "We're the only thing out here."

After a while, he headed for one of the larger stands of palm trees, and as they stopped in the meager shade, he peeled her hands from his waist.

"Climb down and stretch your legs."

She swayed first one direction, then another, trying to decide how to dismount. That mixed effort merely sent her sliding down one side.

"Whoa!" Before he could reach out a hand to help, she landed flat on her rear on the hardpacked dirt.

"Oh—ow—ohhh. *Blessit!*" She sat for a minute biting her lip and letting the pain wash through her. Her legs defied all orders. She finally propped them up manually and made two tries before successfully rolling onto her hands and knees. He swung down from the horse and hauled her onto her feet.

"You act like you've never ridden a horse before."

"I have so." She bobbed as she tried to make her legs support her weight.

"When?" he said. "In the park on Sunday?" He apparently took her silence as confirmation. "Just how did you think you were going to get around in Morocco? Hansom cabs? Gondolas, maybe? Or didn't it occur to plan for a little thing like transportation?"

"I planned. I knew I had to hire horses or camels." She wobbled over to one of the palm trees and braced against it, trying not to show how miserable she was. "I'm just not accustomed to riding bareheaded in scorching sun for hours at a time. Any more than I'm accustomed to having soldiers break down my door in the dead of night, threaten me with guns, and ransack my belongings."

"Welcome to Morocco," he said dryly, maneuvering the horse into the shade and tying him up. Then he sank onto a hummock of dried grass with a weary sound and closed his eyes. When he opened them again they wandered her direction and lingered.

"What are you doing here, Boston? What did you really sail thousands of miles and brave seasickness, thieves, and Legionnaires to find?"

She braced with her chin raised, knowing how it would sound to him.

"Books."

He assessed the defiance in her eyes and the determination in her jaw.

"Books." He sat forward and put his elbows on his knees. "You leave London, where there are bookstalls on every other street, and come to Marrakech, where they've never even heard of moveable type, to search for *books*?"

"I explained it to the monsieur," she said irritably.

"Well, apparently I missed that part of the conversation."

"I'm looking for very *old* books . . . in the form of scrolls . . . parchments or papyri . . . things like the ancient Egyptians wrote on."

"Egyptians? A little off in your calculations, aren't you? Egypt is about a thousand miles—"

"*East.* Yes. Monsieur LaCroix was kind enough to point that out as well. And I'll tell you precisely what I told him: I have convincing evidence that a cache of ancient manuscripts and scrolls is to be found"—she halted just short of full disclosure—"south of Marrakech."

As he considered that claim, a memory apparently shot to the surface. "Those books and papers—that map—you're headed to Timbuktu?"

It was no good denying it; he'd seen the map in her cabin aboard the *Star*.

"Near there," she admitted, dreading his reaction.

"There's nothing *near* Timbuktu but desert." He watched her gaze evade his. "What's so special about these scrolls that you'd travel thousands of miles and endure weeks of desert travel—"

"Weeks?" Her eyes widened.

Apollo groaned. "Yes, *weeks*. What's in these scrolls that's so important that you'd risk your neck for them?"

"I . . . don't know."

He ran a hand back through his hair, holding some of it for a minute as if it contained the wits he was suddenly at the end of.

"*Guess*, dammit!"

"It could be anything. Religious writings . . . history . . . natural philosophy . . . treatises on governance or agriculture . . . epic poetry or plays. . . ."

"You've come all this way to search for writings you know nothing about?" He studied her with deepening alarm. "You're certifiable."

He got to his feet and headed for the horse, determined

to mount up and put as much distance between them as a single continent would allow. But just as he lifted his foot into the stirrup, she grabbed his arm.

"I'm looking for a library." When he turned, she looked as if she'd just been trampled by the wild horses dragging it out of her. "A lost library."

Nine

Apollo lowered his foot to the ground and trained an expectant look on her sunburned face.

"A great library from ancient times," she continued.

"From Egypt," he clarified, and she nodded. Then it struck him. "Good God." The blank on his face was a placeholder . . . until either the disbelief or the horror in him won out. "The Great Library of Alexandria? You're looking for that? Here? In Morocco?"

"You've heard of it?"

"Who hasn't?" Then he stepped back, scowling, realizing why she was so surprised. "Oh, I see . . . common cannon fodder like me isn't supposed to know about the glories of the great classical civilizations. We're just supposed to keep to our place and content ourselves with cheap liquor and spilling our blood every time our betters get an empire-expanding fart crosswise."

Five years' worth of resentment rushed up out of his depths.

"Well, hang on to your knickers, Boston." He jacked his shoulders forward, sending her lurching back. "Some of us grunts and gilhooleys have had enough education to spend our time between bloodlettings trying to maintain what little humanity is left to us. We aren't all dumb brutes and criminals."

He advanced again, taking satisfaction in the way she retreated from him. Suddenly he wanted to see them all retreat—all of the comfortable citizens of the world who sat on their fat bottoms by their smug little firesides while the poor, the uneducated, and the just plain unlucky did their bleeding and dying for them.

"And *some* of us have studied enough to know a cock-and-bull story when we hear it. The Great Library was destroyed in two stages; part of it burned in the great fire that swept the harbor and docks of Alexandria and the remainder was destroyed after the Arab conquest. All that remains of it is the legend of what was lost."

It didn't take her long to recover.

"Until now." She took the offensive with a step that brought her nose to nose with him. "Professor T. Thaddeus Chilton spent a lifetime searching for a remnant he believed had been carried away by devotees of the library's mission to preserve knowledge. He tracked it through literary references, hieroglyphic evidence, and field work. He came to Morocco himself and was on the verge of finding it when he became ill and returned home, where he died."

"And where he took you into his confidence as he lay on his deathbed."

"No. I never met him. His books and writings and papers were donated to the British Museum, where they came into my hands."

"What were you doing at the British Museum?"

"I work there."

"As what?" His gaze drifted purposefully down her, and then back up.

"I am a librarian."

"A librarian." It took a moment to register. Then it made entirely too much sense—her unworldly air, her inexperience, her obsession with her books and papers—and yet it made no sense at all. He gave a derisive laugh. "Try again, sweetheart. There's no such thing as a female librarian."

Her face reddened and puffed like a pomegranate.

"In Britain, perhaps—where ignorance, stubbornness, and blind adherence to tradition seem to be perennially in vogue. But in *America*, women are leading the way in developing libraries and in training professional, college-educated librarians. I, myself, graduated from the New York State University School of Library Science after graduating from Wellesley College."

He stood for a moment feeling like the finger she was jabbing into him was beginning to penetrate his chest wall.

"You attended university?" he said, recognizing the tell-tale signs even as he spoke: precision of speech, erudition, stubborn confidence in her own course, and a startling lack of both feminine artifice and deference to the judgment of men. She had bluestocking written all over her!

"College," she informed him. "A fine *women's* college."

"And they hired you at the British Museum?"

"They most certainly did," she snapped back.

For a moment he was speechless. Anger and frustration he couldn't quite explain boiled up in him. Suddenly, all he knew was that he had to move . . . had to put some distance between himself and the reminder she had just planted of the way his home had changed . . . was still changing . . . beyond his recognition. He backed a giant step, then another, then wheeled and headed for his horse.

"There goes the bloody empire."

"*One* horse, two arses. We ride by Legion rules," Smith declared, after several minutes of stomping back and forth, arguing with himself, and pulling a hat out of his saddlebag. "Mounted companies are supplied with only one mule for every two men. Legionnaires alternate walking and riding on a 'march.' " He turned to Abigail. "I'll give you first choice."

She was so furious that she struck off on foot, leaving him to mount up and ride along behind her.

Behind her was a bad place to be, he thought, watching the exaggerated sway of her hips as she lengthened her stride to cope with the rocky surface. She was wearing a starchy white blouse, a neatly fitted split skirt, and well-made riding boots. And that damned cincher. He'd felt it beneath her blouse as she lay across his lap. He took a steadying breath and told himself to ignore her damned undergarments. And the way her auburn hair shone in the sun. And the way his body came to attention whenever she turned his way.

The woman had a way of finding every sensitive nerve in his body and every sore subject on his mind. If some diabolical fate had handcrafted a female just to torment him, the result would most certainly have been Abigail Merchant. Educated, opinionated, respectable, headstrong, and too caught up in her high-minded pursuits to recognize, much less respond to the lust she inspired.

Worse still, he was starting to feel like a first-class heel for dragging her into his problems. When he saw LaCroix send his men off to recover her bags and watched them come back with only two out of the three, he had known what was happening. He headed for LaCroix's office and found the Frenchman's men with the third bag, starting to pick the lock. Knowing full well they would recognize him and report his presence to LaCroix, he still charged in and stopped them before they got it open.

Sooner or later the Frenchman would have learned he was alive and back in Morocco, he told himself. And he had to get that bag away from LaCroix's thugs; Abigail Merchant wasn't the only one who had valuables in it.

He emerged from such thoughts to find himself staring fixedly at her hair. She had pinned it up earlier, but in the mad scramble out of Casablanca some of it had come loose and was bobbing with each step she took. It was soft, he knew. Silky. Red-gold lights spun through it. Probably still held some faint scent of soap. He could almost feel it sliding through his—

Oh, no. Not that. No damned way.

Abigail's eyes were narrowed to aching slits and her head felt like her brain was beginning to sizzle when something plopped down over her head and blocked out the punishing solar rays that caused it. She looked up to find an oversized wide-brimmed hat providing much-needed relief. *His* hat. Innate good manners and a sense that it might be a peacemaking gesture of sorts forced a response from her.

"Thank you."

He, apparently, felt no such compulsion where manners were concerned. There was no answering "You're welcome" or "Think nothing of it."

Her anger cooled to mere annoyance as she concentrated on walking . . . an effort which surprised her with its necessity. The weedy, reddish ground was littered with sharp rocks perfect for turning ankles and lacerating shoe leather.

She was in Morocco and headed for Marrakech . . . so far, so good. But she was also afoot in a difficult country with a wanted man being pursued by a small army . . . not so good. She glanced over her shoulder at the horse and the man on it. He was arrogant and annoying and probably even more dangerous than he looked. But right now she didn't have an alternative to traveling with him; she had to get to Marrakech in order to begin her search.

"So, do you know where we're headed?" She finally broke the silence, thinking that she would trade her virtue for a cool drink of water just then.

Dehydration Madness . . . Tropical Medicine . . . the 610's.

He surveyed the countryside and pointed toward a spot in the distance where the mountains on the left and the plains on the right seemed to meet.

"We have to avoid the main road. A day's ride straight south is a small village. There will be food and water and perhaps another horse."

"A day's *ride*? How long will it take *walking*? I'm dying of thirst."

He reached behind him and then held out a military style canteen to her. She looked up briefly as she accepted it. When she turned away, the image of him, Sahara-hot and Barbary-fierce, was burned into her mind.

"Do you know this country well?" she said, taking a long second drink before replacing the stopper and handing it back to him.

"You could spend a lifetime in Morocco and still not know the place."

"How long have you been in Morocco?"

"You should know. I arrived on the same ship you did."

"But you were here before, in the French Foreign Legion. For how long?"

"A full enlistment. Five bloody long years."

"If you served a full enlistment, why do they call you a deserter?"

"Someone must have decided that I hadn't quite finished putting in time." He looked around before letting his gaze return to her. "For every day you spend in a guardhouse cell, they tack two onto your obligation."

"And I take it, you spent a good bit of time in a military jail."

"My share."

"For what?"

"Drinking and fighting, striking an NCO, striking an officer. The usual."

"That's usual?"

"For a Legionnaire."

"That's . . . depraved."

He sobered.

"No. Feeding men so poorly that they get sores on their bodies and paying them so badly they have to sell their clothes to get a drink of whiskey—*that's* depraved. Forcing underfed men to 'march or die' thirty miles a day under a boiling Sahara sun . . . that's *depraved*. Drinking when liquor's available and battling bare-knuckled for some respect from your comrades . . . that's just surviving as best you can."

She was silent for a moment, studying his defense of his fellow soldiers.

"They said you fled during battle, deserted comrades under fire."

"They lied."

"Why would they do that if you've done nothing wrong?"

"Good question." He turned to scan the sunbaked red terrain around them and when his gaze came back to her, he swung down from the horse and leaned close to her with a probing look that turned into a sardonic half smile as he handed her the reins and took back his hat.

"Maybe they can't do without me."

Wretched man, she thought. He clearly enjoyed being a puzzle. She sat studying him for a moment after she climbed aboard the horse, trying to put the pieces of him together.

An Englishman. Well-educated. Well-spoken, if occasionally profane. Not without a few civilized and possibly even chivalrous impulses. He served five years in the French Foreign Legion . . . fled to England . . . then returned to Morocco, where he had become a wanted man. It didn't make sense that he would voluntarily come back to a place where he was wanted and hunted. The longer she thought about it, the deeper her itch to know the truth became.

"You must have been safe in England," she said, riding after him. "Why did you come back here, knowing it would put you in danger?"

His answer accompanied a slight straightening of his spine, suggesting that the question had stirred a greater reaction than he wanted to reveal.

"I told you. It's a *family* matter."

She watched him stride faster across the stony ground and thought he was proving as difficult to decipher as T. Thaddeus's journals. It was beginning to seem that the only thing more irresistible to her than an undeciphered text was an undeciphered man. One specific man. Why else would she keep making these distracting side-trips into his personal sagas?

As she mounted the horse and headed after him, her gaze settled on his broad shoulders and slid down his back to linger on the mesmerizing strength of his long, muscular legs. He was enigmatic and opinionated and infuriating, and she wanted to grab him and .. shake him until he ... until she ...

She realized her gaze had settled on his buttocks and jerked her head.

Just ride, Abigail, she told herself. *And pray he really does know the way to Marrakech.*

Ten

Well into the afternoon a "haloooo!" followed by a warbling high-pitched cry stopped them both in their tracks. They scanned the horizon from different directions, but their gazes converged on the sight of a squat, turbaned figure on horseback coming out of the northwest toward them.

Haffe waved as he neared them and made his curious cry again.

"Smeeth! Miz! I find—I find you!"

Behind the voluble steward's mount trotted another horse laden with several bundles and three large carpetbags. Abigail swung down out of the saddle and hurried to greet him.

"Haffe! Thank God you're safe!" The little steward shrank from her touch, so she transferred her attention to her things, circling the horse, touching the bags. "The Legionnaires didn't bother you?"

"They want Engleesh." He gave a smile that was a pure burlesque of "canny" and patted the rolled up rug tied behind him. "Not faithful of prophet . . . at prayer."

"What the hell's in these things?" Smith demanded, untying and lowering one bag while the one he freed with it dropped with a crash on the other side.

"Hey—some of those things are breakable!" She hurried around the horse to see what might have broken.

"What's this?" Smith opened the bag at his feet and held up a large cream-colored sheet of doeskin in one hand and a doeskin clad pillow in the other.

"Bed linen—which, in case you have forgotten, is something civilized people sleep on.'

"You won't need it," he declared, tossing both items aside.

"The blazes I won't." She ducked around the horse to pick the things up and cradle them against her. 'I've already used them. Accommodations here are primitive at best.'

"What the hell's this?" He held up a bolt of translucent cotton gauze.

"Haven't you ever seen a mosquito net?" She tried to snatch it back.

"A mosq—" He pushed it behind him, out of her reach. "Look around you, Boston." He gestured to the semiarid landscape. "You're headed for the desert. They don't *have* mosquitos in the desert."

"Who knows where I'll end up before my search is over?" she declared.

He gave it a toss so definitive that it landed some distance away, and while she charged over to retrieve it, he pulled out yet another stack of cloth.

"Towels?" His mouth pursed in disdain. "Plan on taking a lot of baths while you're here, do you? And is this what I think it is?" He held up one of the several napkins she had brought and let it fall open to dangle from his hand. "You brought *table linen*?"

"A woman never knows when she might be required to entertain some important local personage, and proper linen might not be available." Her arms were already stuffed with textiles, but she made room for more. "Let go!"

"You have an interesting notion of desert travel,

Boston. Beds with linen . . . mosquitos . . . tea parties for
Berber tribesmen. . ." Holding up a cracked wooden box
leaking tea leaves and the handle and bottom half of a shattered ceramic teapot, he fixed her with a look somewhere
between incredulity and horror. "Whatever possessed you
to bring such stuff?"

"I consulted a most authoritative source. Mariana
Starke published a list of things a woman would need
while traveling—"

"Published?" He winced. "In a *book*?"

"*Travellers On The Continent*." When he started to
groan, she felt compelled to explain: "There weren't any
experienced women travelers for me to consult firsthand.
So I consulted the next best thing: books written by them."

With his jaw set, he trudged around the horse to the
other bag and worked the buckles free. He drew out a
small set of cutlery; a sugar cannister; thick ceramic mugs,
slightly chipped; a block-tin tea kettle; calico sheets; an
oilcloth tarpaulin; a sewing kit with shears, tape, worsted,
and needles; wooden clogs; a universal dispensary kit;
matches; a collapsible rubber bladder for carrying water;
spools of cotton and hemp cord . . .

Every item he tossed aside she picked up and set in a
growing pile, intending to repack as soon as he quit vent-
ing his urges for male domination on her things. Then he
held up a canvas cot sling, staring at it in dismay, and she
pounced to the ground opposite him and grabbed it. He
tried to pull it away, and she grabbed one of the wooden
legs out of the bag and brandished it at him.

"Let go! This is none of your business!" she shouted.

"It is my business. I'm not risking my neck so you can
drag half of England along through the desert with you."

"It's not half of England, it's three carpetbags. And if I
had a proper packhorse and a porter or two none of this
equipment would be in question."

He studied her and her weapon for a moment, then
headed for the third bag . . . the one with the built-in lock.

"Don't touch that!" She scrambled to her feet and

rushed over to drag the bag away from him. "That contains my personal things."

"Open it," he demanded, slipping a knife from his boot. "Or I will."

There was a tense moment before she produced the key and opened the case lock. There in the midst of her clothing and toiletries lay T. Thaddeus's journals and two ribbon-bound sheaves of maps.

He pulled out one of the journals and then another, thumbing through each as if looking for something. Halfway through the fourth one he came across an envelope that he yanked out and stuffed down into the front of his shirt.

"What are you doing? Put that back!" She stared at the lines of the envelope visible through the fabric of his shirt. "How dare you?" Emboldened by anger, she made for his shirt front, but he grabbed her wrists.

"It's mine," he said straining to contain her. "I slipped it into one of your books before I left the ship." Her struggles eased.

"What is it?" She glared at his midsection, not convinced.

"It's personal. None of your concern."

She suddenly recalled what he'd said on the ship.

"*Family documents*?" she said with a furious edge.

"Exactly."

She fought the impulse to seize his shoulders and shake him until he yielded up—wait—that was why he'd gone after her stolen bag—to retrieve something he'd put in it! A memory materialized in her mind of him with a knife in his hand, bent over her missing bag. She'd caught him starting to open her bag when she surprised him in her hotel room!

That was why he insisted on taking her to Marrakech. He just wanted his envelope back! Nothing chivalrous about it.

Anger and disappointment competed for her control. She stood toe-to-toe with him, feeling his hands hot on her wrists, feeling her knees weakening at his nearness, and feeling utterly, humiliatingly beguiled.

He released her and took a huge step back, then another. "Fine. Take what you want." He raised both hands, palms out, to say he was finished. "But we're a horse short and that means either your precious mosquito nets and tablecloths ride or you do. You decide." And he stalked off.

She turned to look at the chaos he'd created in her things and feeling a similar chaos churning her usually rational and predictable internal workings.

Her or her bags.

Put that way, it made a wretchedly compelling argument. She sank to her knees by the pile of discards and, with stinging eyes, began to sort her things and repack. Haffe knelt beside her to help and she swallowed hard.

"Spawn of . . . why didn't he just say that in the first place?"

That evening they stopped in a small grove of palms to make camp. There was no spring or well, but there was lush green all around, rich grass for the horses and long shadows of sweet shade for them. Abigail took it in with aching eyes. Strictly speaking, they weren't in desert country yet, but the grove of palms was an oasis all the same.

Haffe set about gathering fuel for a fire, while Smith unloaded and unsaddled the horses. She busied herself carrying the supplies and carpetbags to a sheltered spot between the trees. Haffe had taken pity on her and agreed to take some of the items, packed in her second bag, onto his horse with him.

By the time the sun set, Haffe had started a fire in a circle of stones and was feeding it flat brown disks that resembled mashed coconut husks.

"Camel sheet," he said with a beaming smile. She dropped the piece she was inspecting. "Make good fire."

Rubbing her hands thoroughly on her skirt, she watched him feed the dried dung to the flame until there was a glowing fire and then set a battered pot on a metal grate above it. She didn't want to think about the "flavor" his choice of fuel would add to their food.

The sun that had been so unrelenting earlier mellowed into a hazy red ball that painted the surrounding landscape in gold, rose, and deepening purple. As she collapsed against one of the palms to watch the half moon brighten against the darkening sky, she felt something bite her and smacked the side of her neck. Moments later she heard a determined buzzing and looked around to see several large mosquitos hovering around her.

"Aghhh!" She shot to her feet, batting aside a small swarm of the insects and stalked over to Smith to yank aside the collar of her blouse.

"See that?" she demanded.

He gave it a cursory glance before looking pointedly away.

"I've seen better," he said dryly. It took a moment for that to register.

"Not *me*." Battling the urge to smack him, she pointed at the lump forming on her neck. "The bite. A *mosquito* bite. You said there weren't any mosquitos here."

"I said there aren't any in the *desert*," he said frowning and suddenly starting to scratch his own neck . . . and chin . . . and the back of a hand. . . .

"Well, we're not in the desert, and you made me throw my mosquito net away," she said irritably. "Now I won't sleep a wink, and I'm going to look like a victim of some sort of desert plague!"

Haffe, who had been watching between them, pulled her deerskin sheet out of her bag and carried it to her, motioning for her to wrap it around her.

"Berber wrap up. Engleesh ma'am wrap up. No more bites." Haffe nodded and motioned to her to do as he suggested.

Waving the buzzing from around her head, she draped the sheet over her shoulders and clamped it under her chin so that only the most essential parts of her face stuck out.

The swarming insects soon transferred their attentions to Haffe, who merely huddled closer to the smoke of the fire, and Smith, whose flexing jaw muscles betrayed just how miserable he was and whose refusal to scratch revealed just how stubborn he could be.

"I believe I did bring *two* deerskin sheets," she said with a taunting lilt.

As he stalked off toward the horses, the sound of him slapping mosquitos wafted back and she smiled vengefully. Arrogant man. Thought he knew everything. Well, it didn't matter what he knew and didn't know . . . as long as he got her to Marrakech in one piece. He *owed* her that much.

Night had fallen fully by the time Haffe dished up some of his concoction of coucous and peas and dried squash of some kind. He was humming and seemed to be quite at home cooking over a campfire of camel dung.

"Haffe, what are you doing here?" She glanced up at Smith, who was standing, finishing his food, with his shoulder against a nearby palm. "You're a ship's steward."

"No, no. *Star* first sheep." He pointed to himself and then held up an index finger. "Too much water." He made a two-handed dismissing motion toward the harbor he had just abandoned. "Son of desert." He smacked his chest proudly with an open palm. "Berber."

"Then why did you go to sea in the first place?"

He frowned a moment, then caught her meaning.

"To get wife." His toothy grin, huge brown eyes, and his rounded face made him seem strangely cherubic.

"You hoped to find a wife aboard the ship?"

"To make money to take a bride," Smith inserted from above, scratching the side of his jaw. "He needs money to give to a father of daughters to convince him that he will be a worthy husband."

"You mean, he wants to *buy* a bride?" She looked between the two men and frowned. "Barbaric. Selling women like chattel."

"No more barbaric than dowries and marriage settlements in England."

"I wouldn't know," she said with a frosty smile. "I'm from Boston."

"*L'argent est pour les cadeaux,*" Haffe was either embarrassed or overcome enough by the subject to lapse entirely into more familiar French.

"Silver for gifts," Smith translated.

"*Cadeaux pour le papa.*" Haffe rubbed thumb and fingers together in a universally understood gesture for money. "*Et maman.*" More rubbing. "*Les frères.*" Still more rubbing. Apparently a lot of people would have a hand out. "*tout la famille.*" Then his eager face softened. "*Et la belle fiancée.*" For a moment his gaze drifted into vistas of delight that only he could see. Then he returned with a wistful air. "*Et les chameaux. Beaucoup de chameaux.*"

"*Chameaux?*" she echoed, wishing she had stopped to absorb at least one other living language before immersing herself in dead ones.

Smith made an impatient "tsk" and took a seat on the far side of the fire.

"Camels," he said. "Lots of camels. The proper currency, apparently, for the acquisition of a Berber bride. The more desirable the girl, the more camels must be given to her family."

"*Oui. Chameaux*—camels." Haffe looked back and forth between them, nodding eagerly. "Man-ny camels."

"Just how many camels are we talking about?" she asked. Bartering animals for women. Appalling.

Smith asked him and Haffe sighed and rattled off an explanation of the local pricing scheme that included words that sounded like "dozens" and "beauty" and "grand."

"Three or four dozen should do it," Smith said, producing a small cigar from the top of his boot and lit it. "Haffe here has fairly exalted tastes."

"So I gathered." She tried not to scowl at Haffe. "He wants a great beauty."

"A great *big* beauty, actually." He did a pantomime with his hands of expansive feminine curves. "Berber men, like their Arab cousins, appreciate a bit of heft in a woman." He looked to Haffe. "*Grosse.* Fat. *Oui?*"

"*Oui.*" Haffe was nodding hopefully. "Beauti-ful *fat* wife."

A muffled sound halfway between a whine and a groan escaped her. Brides by the pound. And she thought Boston's society balls were degrading.

"Sweet wife. Sleep soft." The little Berber made a cuddling motion. "Make babies. Man-ny babies. Fat little babies." He gave a deep, wistful sigh.

The hiss that came from her was the sound of outrage being deflated.

"Which brings up another matter," Smith interjected. "Our Berber friend here needs money, and, considering the sort of trouble I seem to be in, I certainly could use some extra coin. I think it's time we talked about our fee for getting you to Marrakech."

"*Fee?*" She nearly choked on her own juices. "I'm not paying you a cent. You got me into trouble with the authorities and used me and my luggage to carry your papers. Consider yourself already more than fully compensated."

Then she looked to Haffe's anxious face and felt her anger going a bit spongy. Something about his eagerness for a plump wife and fat little babies made her want to make him an exception to her belief in the superiority of the Western concept of women's rights.

"You on the other hand, I will pay," she said, thinking she must be losing her mind. "One silver coin per day . . . for your help as porter and cook."

"I don't think so," Smith said, calmly, stretching his long legs out before him and leaning back to prop an elbow on his saddle. Haffe looked at him in confusion. "Haffe and I come as a package deal. I'll tell you what . . . we'll make you an offer. We'll guide you and help you find your library, wherever it is, for . . . half of the proceeds."

"Don't be ridiculous," she said, straightening. "There won't be any 'proceeds.' I'm searching for books."

"Old books," he countered. "Very old books. Probably worth a fortune to some museum somewhere."

"Not 'some museum,' the British Museum. Which I represent. I am here to find the library and secure the right to remove whatever books or manuscripts it contains to the British Museum for study and preservation. The 'prize' is a footnote in history . . . which will enrich nothing but a scholar's reputation."

"*Your* reputation." He drew from his cigar and blew a stream of smoke.

"And T. Thaddeus Chilton's, since it was he who first uncovered the references and did most of the research work."

"And that's all you want? Just a bit of respect and scholarly renown."

"Yes."

"Bullshit."

Eleven

"I beg your pardon!" She was suddenly furious. "I am here in a scholarly capacity and I resent—"

"The truth is, Boston"—he shot to his feet, his body taut—"you don't have a clue what's at the end of your search."

"Yes, I do. *Books*."

"And nothing else? For all you know, there could be temples of gold and vaults filled with treasure beyond your wildest dreams."

She got to her feet and stood her ground, her blood boiling with the urge to take a cot leg to him. Unfortunately, she'd left them all behind. Never in her life had she met anyone who incited her to physical violence like he did!

"It's a *library*," she declared. "Long-dead and completely forgotten."

"What about the people who carried it out here? Those forward-thinking devotees of learning? Hard to believe they wouldn't have had the foresight to take a little traveling money with them."

"Fine—they brought money. Whopping great bags of it. And fabulous jewels and altars of gold—whatever makes you dream in color at night. But it's long since spent and they're long since dead."

"And what if it's not all gone?" He sat abruptly forward, staring up at her. "I have a proposal. How about this: You take the scrolls and books and we'll"—he pointed between Haffe and himself—"take the spendable stuff."

"Don't be absurd. *There is no treasure!*"

"Then we will have gambled and lost."

"Absolutely not. In Marrakech, we part company. You go your way and I'll go mine."

"Look, hiring us right now will save you time and headaches. You're going to have to find somebody who knows the desert—"

"You mean . . . someone who knows better than to throw away mosquito nets?" she snapped and he had the grace to redden.

"All right—I forgot that some oases have a little bug problem. I was thinking about the desert, further on. How are you going to be sure some other guide won't just take you into the desert and take the rest of your money and just leave you there?"

"How do I know *you* won't?" she tossed back.

He shoved to his feet in one fluid motion, clearly angered.

"Look, Boston, I've already rescued your hide *twice* now. And I returned your bloody bag to you"—he rubbed his bruised cheekbone—"at some cost to myself. Then there's the little matter of the coin I spent to provide you horses and help."

"All so you could get your own precious papers back," she charged.

"I'll not deny I wanted them back, but I also knew I had put you in jeopardy and wanted to make it right. I'm taking you to Marrakech, aren't I?"

Abigail took several deep breaths, trying to calm herself to think.

The prospect of continuing for weeks in Smith's overbearing company had to be weighed against the time she would save by not searching for another guide and having to go through lengthy explanations and caveats concerning the object of her search. And, of course, there was the little problem of finding someone knowledgeable, capable, reliable, and honest . . . at least honest enough. What were the odds of finding such a desert-wise saint in Marrakech . . . without even a sham of a British consulate to ask for help?

She looked from Smith to Haffe and back. He had helped her aboard the ship . . . and there were those men on the rooftops. . . . Her best bet, she reluctantly admitted, might be the devil she knew. S.O.S. Smith.

"All right, I'll give you a chance." She prayed she wouldn't come to regret this. "You guide me to Marrakech and help me do my research there . . . and I'll consider purchasing your services for the rest of the expedition."

Partners. That was what Smith called them. Each time he used the term she objected and insisted their relationship—if and when they got to Marrakech—would be strictly employer-employee. Partnership, she declared fiercely, implied both shared goals and a high degree of trust . . . neither of which applied to them.

Whatever they were, they were stuck with each other for the foreseeable future . . . through good weather and bad . . . riches and disappointment . . . ease and discomfort . . . in sickness and in—wait—they'd already had the sickness part. No more sickness.

But if the conditions that night and the following day were any indication of what lay ahead, they were going to be hard-pressed to avoid the "disappointment" and "discomfort." He insisted they get an early start and after a night spent in a half-sitting position against a palm tree, every bone and joint in her body ached at the thought of climbing back on a horse. Then he set a grueling pace and refused to stop until they reached the village. She looked forward to a night under a roof—or at least on a roof pallet somewhere, but when the locals said there were no horses or mules to spare in the village, he insisted they move on and camp in the open countryside.

"I don't see why we couldn't have stayed the night," she said feeling every mile they rode etching its way into her saddle-sore bones.

"They didn't want us there," he said shortly. "Berbers love horse trading. If they won't trade horses with you, you're not welcome. And in Morocco, if you're not welcome, you'd better not hang around."

Disappointment didn't quite capture her darkening mood as she dragged together a pallet of palm fronds that evening, donned her safari jacket and deerskin sheet, and sat down to remove her boots.

"I wouldn't do that, if I were you," Smith said. She looked up to find him on the opposite side of the fire, staring at her, wrapped against the mosquitos in a ratty-looking wool blanket.

"I haven't had these boots off for two days," she said irritably. "Mary Kingsley says that too much time in damp footwear in equatorial climates fosters all manner of rashes and foot maladies."

"Oh, well, if *Mary* says so," he muttered.

Ignoring him, she wrestled with her footgear until one boot came sliding off. She extended her stockinged foot into the cooling night air and wiggled her toes with a sigh before removing the other boot.

"Just be sure to shake out your boots before you put them on in the morning," he said, lying back and propping his head and upper shoulders against his saddle. "The spiders and scorpions that collect in these groves love to crawl into empty boots at night."

She stared at her stocking-clad feet and dusty boots, then warily around at the vegetation and rocks. When she looked back at Smith, his eyes were closed but she could have sworn he was smiling. More of his alarmist nonsense; he was determined to make her think she couldn't get along without him. She clutched her boots to her chest, tucked her doeskin sheet tighter, and lay down to rest.

Eventually—despite aching joints and anxiety over every rustle of grass and leaf—she managed to fall asleep. But not even bone-deep exhaustion could keep her from feeling something moving across lower legs some time later. She came upright with a start and was on her feet and kicking frantically to dislodge something large and dark and many-legged from the cover at her feet.

"Aghhhhh!"

She wasn't aware of her scream as the creature fled for nearby underbrush and rocks. She was startled by Smith's arms clamping around her, and she slapped and shoved at his arms

"Whoa! Boston—take it easy!" He lifted her off her feet briefly to get her attention before dragging her back against him.

"Something was *on* me." She suffered an eloquent, whole-body shiver.

"Did you get a look at it?"

"It was big and had a lot of legs!" The edge of hysteria in her voice alarmed her almost as much as the crawling beast had.

"How many legs? Did it have pincers?"

"It was running, for pity's sake—in the dark—I didn't get a good look!"

"All right—it's all right." He tightened his arms fiercely around her for a moment. "You're safe."

"I know that—" But her heart was beating a thousand times a minute and every nerve in her body was screaming for release.

"Any burning? Stinging?" His voice softened, as if he were soothing a panicky horse. "If you were bitten, you'd be feeling it by now."

She twisted around in his arms to face him with wide eyes. He searched her face with an anxiousness that belied the calm in his voice, even as she searched her internal sensations. Jangled nerves, wild heartbeat, and a searing flush of heat—none of which seemed to come from a bite or a sting.

She shivered again and suddenly every volatile, impassioned impulse she had harbored toward him boiled up within her. So many times in the last three weeks she'd wanted to set hands to him, and now she was. Her arms were sliding around his waist, pulling him closer as she lifted her face to him. . . .

His mouth was descending over hers. . . .

"Look! See! Here!" Haffe's voice broke over them like icy water.

They lurched apart. Smith swiped a hand across his mouth and blinked across the fire at Haffe.

"What?" he demanded, his voice strained.

"Scorpion." Haffe held up a sizeable dagger with a large black scorpion impaled on it, still wriggling. He was beaming. "Fat tail. Very bad."

"Is that what was on—" Abigail turned, having reclaimed some composure, but lurched backward at the sight of that formidable arachnid.

"You're sure you weren't stung?" Smith demanded.

"F-fairly sure. Nothing hurts or burns." She looked down at her stocking-clad feet in the dirt and then at the creature that had just given up the ghost on Haffe's blade. She rushed to pick up her boots, shook them frantically, then sat straight down on the ground to pull them on.

Smith grabbed up his blanket and used it to beat the nearby grasses, looking for anything that might be lurking. Hidden within the grasses was a rocky ledge with a number of ominous crevices.

"Scorpions are dangerous, right?" She couldn't take her eyes off the long, dark body and curled tail with its all-too-visible stinger.

"Only if you hope to live to a ripe old age." Smith stalked back into the dim circle of light and used his feet to slide her bed of palm fronds closer to the fire. "The rule on scorpions is . . . a skinny tail and skinny pincers—

you'll survive . . . fat tail and big pincers—say your final prayers."

"This one had a fat tail." She saw Haffe fling the carcass into the brush.

"Most of the ones in Morocco do," Smith added rolling his shoulders. "Might be good if one of us kept watch tonight." He sent Haffe a speaking look that the little steward acknowledged with a nod.

"You think there could be more?" She stared off into the underbrush, feeling vulnerable and unable to keep that feeling out of her voice.

Smith finally looked directly at her.

"Tell you what," he said, much too innocently, "I'll sleep beside you tonight. That way if something gets past Haffe, it'll get me before it gets you."

Twelve

Abigail was caught off guard by his offer, then she recalled what was happening before Haffe interrupted and
she flushed crimson.

"No thank you." She busied herself recovering her
sheet and shaking it out. "I have no desire to be responsible for your death-by-scorpion-bite." She dragged her doeskin around her and sat down on her pallet.

"You don't have to worry about that. I've been bitten
quite a few times." He strolled over and sat down beside
her, causing her to inch closer the fire to avoid him. "Spiders, snakes, scorpions—you name it. Used to give my old
nurse an apoplexy on a regular basis."

"You had a nurse?" She looked at him with surprise.

"Until the governess came. And after that a tutor. Tutors, actually. Quite a number of them." He grinned defi-
antly. "It seems I was a regular beast as a child. Always
bringing home some vermin or reptile that made the female help climb on chairs and scream."

"The child really is 'father to the man,'" she muttered.

"And, of course, there was my fascination with
heights." He waxed a bit nostalgic as he recounted: "I was

always climbing things . . . trees, bell towers, drainpipes, roof gables . . . breaking bones. By the time I reached public school I was fairly well indestructible. Which has come in rather handy in Morocco.

"The little scorpions, up north . . . I was bitten regularly enough to become immune. Then when we were transferred south and the scorpions got bigger, I tangled with a number of them, too. But I always recover. And the next bite generally doesn't seem quite as bad as the last."

She was staring at him in amazement, seeing clearly in his face the exasperating and yet appealing boy he had been. And she was so focused on that vision that she wasn't prepared for what came next.

"That's why I figured I could put up with you for a few weeks."

She was so dazzled by his grin that it took a moment to register. With a gasp, she started to rise, but he grabbed her arm.

"Just a joke, Boston." Then his eyes sought hers and his voice lowered. "I won't let anything happen to you. You have my word."

She looked down at his hand on her arm, realizing that she was in the grip of an appalling desire to curl up in his arms and believe him. Glaring at her own thoughts, she freed her arm and removed herself to the base of a palm tree well away from both him and the scorpion-concealing vegetation.

Wretch. She refused to look at him or to dwell on the fact that one minute she had been ready to throttle him and the next she was setting hands to him. She had been in fear for her life and wasn't thinking clearly. Thank heaven his "charm" had jolted her back to her normal desire to strangle him.

To take her mind off her unthinkable behavior, she went over and over the list of hazardous wildlife Mary Kingsley and Mabel Crawford had painstakingly described. Mosquitos, leeches, snakes, lizards, crocodiles, leopards, blowflies . . . neither had seen fit to mention the boot-loving arachnids of West Africa.

Venomous Nocturnal Arthropods . . . Vertebrates . . . the 595's.

But every time she dozed and her conscious defenses began to slide, the memory of his lips brushing hers returned. It wasn't the first "almost" kiss she'd received, but it was certainly the most haunting. By morning it was all too clear that despite a lengthy recitation of Smith's faults and failings, she was in danger of suffering a similar lapse of sanity if the opportunity presented itself again.

Thus, when she opened her eyes and found him stretched out on the ground beside her, watching her sleep, she was anything but reassured. As if he could read her thoughts in her face, he shoved to his feet and shook out his blanket.

"Don't get your knickers in a twist, Boston." His gaze stroked her visually before he turned away to start packing up the horses. "You're the key to my treasure. I'm just protecting my investment."

Midday, they came to another isolated stand of palms growing in a sheltered depression and stopped for a rest. As they sprawled on the weedy vegetation in the shade, drinking water and eating flatbread, olives, and potent goat cheese, Abigail hauled out T. Thaddeus's final journal and map, and soon had one and a half pairs of eyes peering over her shoulder. She tried to close the book but Smith stuck his hand in it to hold the place, citing first their partnership and, when that didn't work, his curiosity . . . which finally won her over.

Sighing, she opened the book and held it up for them to see.

Smith scowled. "Tell me it's not all Greek to you, too."

"T. Thaddeus kept his journals in Ancient Greek to practice his translation and interpretation, but also to keep the work safe from prying eyes."

"Beta, iota, beta lamda . . . omicron . . . sigma . . ." He pointed to a group of letters. "B . . . I . . . b . . . l . . . is that *Bible*?"

"Close. *Biblos*. It means 'book'—which is where the word 'bible' comes from." Her surprise at how close he'd come was evident. "You know Greek?"

"A few words and phrases." He shrugged. "The basics came from public school . . . the rest from a Greek fellow in our company who taught me a few words in exchange for some French."

"Here"—she ran her finger along a line—"the professor talks about the guardians' trip into the *erimos*, the desert. He says they built a *naos*—temple—and dedicated it to *thea Athena* . . . goddess and keeper of wisdom. A whole settlement. With walls and homes and chambers for the *grafi*—the writings."

When she looked up from the pages, Smith was looking at her strangely.

"And where was this settlement?" he asked, dropping his gaze to the page.

"South and east of Marrakech. At least that is what T. Thaddeus calculated. He compared old navigational star charts against the few accounts of the library's location in existing texts and engravings. And he knew the length of the journey and the location of the nearest city . . . Timbuktu."

"Timbuktu?" Haffe's eyes lighted with recognition. "Born Timbuktu." Then his pleasure evaporated. "Long journey. Very hot. No water."

"Well, I doubt we'll have to go all the way there," she said. "After two fruitless trips to search for the site, the professor revised his calculations . . . concluding that the library and settlement were closer to Marrakech."

"So, the old boy already looked for it twice and found nothing?" Smith's amusement faded. "What makes you think you'll do better?"

"Because the professor found new evidence. A fragment of a letter that was included on a scroll describing the city administration of Alexandria."

"And no one had noticed this fragment before?"

"It was written in code." She warmed to her subject. "There had been damage to the original scroll and other translators apparently thought it was too fragmented to deal with or would turn out to be mere gibberish. But the professor glimpsed linguistic organization in the piece. After some work, he realized it was encoded and deciphered it. It proved to be a message to some of the old keepers of the library, reporting that the guardians had found a suitable place in the desert and had begun construction of a scriptorium."

She paged through the journal to the place where T. Thaddeus had painstakingly copied the manuscript fragment on which he had pinned his hopes and calculations. She pointed out the letters and identified the corresponding letters indicated by the code, growing steadily more animated.

When she finished, she looked up and found Smith staring at her with an odd look. He rose, stood for a moment, then wagged his head.

"You were one of those little girls who always got 'perfects' on her schoolroom papers, weren't you?" When she didn't answer straightaway, he nodded for her. "Yeah. I'll bet you were a nightmare for your parents."

"My parents happen to both be classical scholars," she said defensively. "My father is a distinguished classicist at Oxford and my mother was a renowned curator and translator at a fine museum library in Boston."

"So, you're following in your father's footsteps."

"I haven't seen my father in nearly two decades." That statement and the thoughts and memories it stirred tapped a seldom acknowledged reservoir of resentment in her. "But perhaps I'll meet him, face-to-face, when I take the remnant of the Great Library of Alexandria back to the British Museum."

He stared at her for a long moment, then turned away with an "Ah."

"Ah?" She set the journal aside, watching as he collapsed on a nearby hummock of grass, stretched, and drew his hat down over his face. "Just what does that mean: '*ah*'?"

"It means"—she could hear the smugness in his voice—"I finally found the real reason you came to Morocco."

Her pursuit of the lost library had nothing to do with her father. Abigail was adamant about that as they rode through the dregs of the day's heat toward yet another stop before reaching Marrakech. She was here to make an historic discovery, to make a reputation as a scholar, and to prove the point that women were capable of the same dedication and sacrifices for the advancement of knowledge that men were. Henry Merchant—a man who thought more of the opinion of his peers than he did of the dignity, brilliance, and spirit of his wife—had failed the test as a husband and father long ago. She had no need to prove anything to him.

Her mother, however, was a different story.

Brilliant but impetuous, Olivia Ridgeway-Merchant had fallen in love with and married a serious young scholar while touring England. When she began to work with him on a variety of groundbreaking translations, his department was scandalized and insisted he cease the collaboration and remove her name from their joint work. Devastated, Olivia found the role of faculty wife stifling, degrading, and ultimately intolerable. When Abigail was five, her mother fled Oxford for her home in Boston, intent on raising her daughter in a freer atmosphere.

But Olivia had not reckoned with the caprices of heredity. Abigail, it seemed, was very much her father's daughter; studious, obsessively orderly, and adverse to risk of any kind. When she finished college and announced she intended to become a librarian, Olivia reacted as if she'd announced she had sold her soul to the devil. She entreated Abigail to travel instead, to start a business of her own, or even to become a devotee of free love. In short, to embrace the freedom Olivia had bought for her at such a cost.

It was only at Olivia's bedside, during her last illness, that Abigail truly understood the sacrifices her mother had made on her behalf. She swore to Olivia she would do something vital and adventuresome with her life. And when her mother's modest estate was settled, she wrote a letter to Oxford and booked passage on a liner bound for England and the British Museum. . . .

But something about Smith's taunting conclusion about her motives had struck a nerve that hours later was still tender. She reluctantly examined her motivations and had to admit that . . . though this expedition was for her mother . . . she did harbor the desire to carry back the remnant of the great library to Oxford and set it before her father's eyes.

Her gaze intensified on Smith, riding ahead of her, and she felt a rush of resentment that he had dredged up a forgotten layer of silt from the bottom of her soul. That old bit of family business seemed to add still more pressure to her already burdened quest.

But the most irritating thing was that she felt somehow disarmed by Smith's incisive assessment of her. Exposed, somehow. Vulnerable. How could a man like him see through her—*into* her—so effortlessly?

And with only one eye?

The wadi Smith had promised would make a good campsite turned out to be a broad valley with a rocky, dry riverbed and a sinuous strip of green flowing along its fertile heart. There were groves of date palms all over the lower valley and plantings of olives and citrus on the slopes. After a long day of dry grass and reflective rock and sand, the lush vegetation was like a salve for the eyes.

Their party, however, was not the only one enjoying the comforts of the river's fertile plain. A band of nomadic herdsmen had claimed the grazing areas for their flocks and set up a camp near the wells at the center.

Smith led Abigail and Haffe to the only well not surrounded by sheep or tents . . . identified by the low stone wall that surrounded the hand-dug shaft and a bracketed pole from which hung a long bucket. Haffe went straight to work watering the horses and setting up a camp, and Smith ordered Abigail to avoid looking directly at any of the tribesmen. Before she could demand an explanation, he went striding off toward the largest of several sprawling tents.

While Haffe replenished their canteens and filled a waterskin for cooking, Abigail paced back and forth, stretching her cramped muscles, amazed that her legs still functioned after so much riding. Her back ached, her bottom was sore, and her skin felt gritty. She was desperate for some clean water, pear soap, and cold cream. Perhaps in Marrakech, there would be time for a bath. . . .

By the time she had drunk her fill, the canteen she used was half empty and she decided to refill it for Haffe, who was busy unloading supplies and preparing a fire ring for the evening's cooking. She drew a bucket of water and carried it back to him.

"You've been to Marrakech, Haffe. What is it like?" she asked, perching on the side of the low stone wall. When he looked up, she repeated her request. "Marrakech . . . tell me about Marrakech."

But his gaze, she realized was focused behind her. She turned to see what had caused him to pale. A number of the herdsmen had advanced and stopped a short distance away to watch them and exchange heated comments among themselves. She couldn't help studying them; they were fascinating in their flowing desert robes and black turbans that extended in veils over the lower part of their faces. Curved daggers were displayed prominently in the dark sashes around their waists. Their eyes were more hostile than sociable . . . or perhaps it was simply their veiled faces that made them look like angry bandits.

Behind them collected a number of smaller figures without veils, some wearing circlets of silver coins across their foreheads, most shading their faces with their hands as they stared her direction and commented furiously about what they saw. A number of children raced back and forth, and pushed each other in her direction, apparently daring one another to approach.

She rose and smoothed her fitted split skirt with her hands, confused by such mixed attention but prepared to greet them cordially.

Thirteen

꧁

It all happened at once: the women began to make that strange whirring cry with their tongues, the men let out shouts of what seemed to be outrage and headed for her en masse, and Smith charged out of the main tent with a fierce look on his face. Seeing the men headed for her, he bolted across the oasis to intercept them and took up a position between her and them . . . his hand on the gun at his side.

Behind Smith, at a more deliberate pace, came a short, stout man in a more elaborate version of the nomads' dress. As he surveyed the situation, he scowled and began shouting orders that brought his men up short. The fury in the camp subsided into a static turbulence that threatened to reerupt at any moment.

Knowing the chieftain's men still gripped the handles of their knives, Smith gave the chieftain a respectful bow that the head man acknowledged with a nod. Then Smith whirled on Abigail with eyes blazing.

"What the hell did you do?" he demanded.

"I have no idea," she said, crossing her arms irritably. "I had just stretched my legs and drawn a pail of water . . . Haffe and I were talking. . . ."

"You drew water?" he said, looking pained.

"Of course. I intend to pull my weight on this expe—"

"I should have told you—the nomads are very touchy about their water. They don't like foreigners, especially infidel females, polluting their wells."

"Polluting? All I did was draw one wretched bucket of water!" she cried, causing another murmur of alarm to sweep through the clan.

Smith turned to assess the way the assembled herdsmen—including the chieftain—were watching them. They sensed she was defying him. If he didn't do something, their hostile eyes said, then they would.

Murmurs turned to ugly shouts and a confrontation seemed inevitable, when a woman broke free from a group near the chief's tent and ran forward with something in her hands. She threw it at Smith, but it fell short. It was a minute before he realized it had been thrown to him, not at him, and he retrieved it.

He unfolded and held up a long, indigo dark garment like those worn by the women of the camp. Bowing in the woman's direction, he came straight to Abigail and draped it over her head and shoulders, covering her from head to toe, as if she were a threadbare couch that had to be made presentable for company.

"What in blazes are you doing?" she demanded. He grabbed her hands to keep her from removing it.

"Saving your hide," he ground out in furiously compressed tones. "It's this or make you a ritual sacrifice to the 'spirit of the watering hole.'"

"Don't be ridiculous." Through her irritation, she realized that there was a marked easing in the turmoil and anxiety the nomads displayed. "Berber nomads don't practice human sacrifice. They're a deeply hospitable people who always welcome strangers."

"How would you know what they are and aren't?"

"Eliza Beaverton listed them as such in her book, *A Three Year Sojourn Through The Barbary Coast*."

He didn't move, didn't blink for what seemed like a very long time.

"That's the most *idiotic* thing I ever—" He removed his hat and ran his hand back through his hair. "Look, you may have lived your life between the covers of a book until now, but this is the *real* Morocco! Out here, things are messier and uglier and a damn site more complicated. Here, anybody who doesn't come from the same desert clan is fair game for plunder or punishment." He punched a finger into the tip of her nose. "You may not have caught it, sweets, but you just came within a hair's breadth of being thrown down a well!"

That took a moment to register.

She stood there with her nose throbbing and her face aflame, watching him wheel and head for the horses. At first she thought he was going to mount his horse, but instead he began to unsaddle it. She looked to the nomads' camp and found several of the men still watching, though from a greater distance and with a casual air she knew to be anything but casual. Then she looked to the well. Berber nomads were a superstitious lot. Eliza Beaverton had been careful to mention that as well.

She suddenly had difficulty swallowing.

Gripping the cloak around her, she headed for Smith.

"What are you doing?" she said, watching him unbuckle her cinch and draw her saddle from her horse. "We can't stay here tonight. Not after this."

"We have to."

"I won't sleep a wink," she said, with a slight tremor in her voice.

"None of us will. But if we leave now, we'll have rejected the chieftain's hospitality and be considered fair game for an attack. If we stay, the chief is honor bound to see that we are treated as guests."

It made a convoluted sort of logic; the sort that seemed to be all too common in Morocco. She glanced again toward the nomads' tents, recalling the fury in the men's veiled faces.

"They were really going to throw me down the well?"

He paused in the midst of carrying the saddle closer to the fire and looked down at her. Cords were visible in his neck and his upper arms bulged beneath his sleeves. Her gaze lowered to those reassuringly solid muscles.

"Only if they got past me," he said, looking like he meant every word.

She watched him deposit the saddle and return for the final one. Did he really mean it when he said he wouldn't let anything happen to her? He would have fought them for her? Something in her chest began to quiver.

In the space of a few erratic heartbeats her entire universe ground to a halt and when it resumed spinning it was going in the opposite direction. His overwhelming strength and male stubbornness went from primitive-and-debasing to protective-and-reassuring so quickly she was left dizzy.

She wobbled over to the campfire Haffe had started, picked up several of those smelly brown disks, and began to feed them to the flames.

There was still an air of unreality about her perceptions later that night as they wrapped themselves in blankets and lay down to sleep . . . so much so that she couldn't tell if she was awake or asleep when she felt someone lift her head and tuck a rolled blanket beneath it. When she looked up and saw that it was Smith and that he was lying down beside her, she couldn't resist a sigh of relief.

The nomads had decamped the next morning when the sun woke Abigail. It was a good two hours past sunrise and one side of her face was already hot where the sun had found it. She staggered to her feet and found Smith and Haffe lolling in the shade, waiting for her rise.

"Why didn't you wake me?" she asked, her heart beating frantically to catch up with her movements.

"You needed the sleep. We all did, after they left."

"What happened to them?" She nodded to the vacant spots where tents had been. "Where did they go?"

"East. Probably to another watering hole. One that's not contaminated." Smith flicked a taunting glance at her and she threw off her protective shroud and planted her hands at her waist.

"That's not my fault. I will not be held responsible for every ridiculous superstition the sun burns into these peoples' heads."

"If I didn't know better I'd swear you were British." He gave a short, ironic laugh. "Look, Boston . . . you're in their land, eating their food, breathing their air, and treading on their ancestral soil. You have to play by their rules."

He strode past her to the horses waiting in the shade. They had already been saddled and loaded for travel. But instead of climbing aboard, he began searching his saddlebag for something.

She turned away, annoyed, and visited the tall grasses on the far side of a cluster of palms. She was busy brushing her rumpled clothes and running her fingers through her disheveled hair as she returned, when he stepped into her path with something in his hands. Her gun.

"Not a bad piece of iron," he said, breaking it open. "Haven't seen this particular model before. A Webley top-break .455 . . ."

"Mark Two," she added. "The proprietor said it was the latest model . . . easier to load . . . an improved barrel. . . ."

"A little large for a woman. Bet it packs a whale of a kick."

"It does." She noted the ease with which he handled the gun and hoped he hadn't decided just to dispose of her down the well himself.

"He should have sold you something smaller."

"He tried. I was advised to get something with 'stopping power.' "

"Yeah? By whom?"

"Maude Cummings, if you must know. In *A Female Adventurer Abroad*, she said you never know when you might have to stop a water buffalo or stampeding herd of zebra."

He closed his eyes, looking pained, then opened them

and focused on checking the cylinders. Evaluating the balance and handling, he aimed it to the side and sighted down the barrel. Then he twirled it on his trigger finger, caught it by the grip, and offered it stock-first to her.

"Keep it with you at all times." He shoved into her hands. "And it wouldn't hurt for you to keep some extra bullets on you."

The fact that he was returning her gun to her seemed an ominous sign.

"Why?" The gun was heavier than she recalled; she had to hold it with both hands. "What's going to happen?" It couldn't be good.

He draped her cloak over her shoulder and nudged her toward the horses.

"We'll be covering a lot more ground before we reach Marrakech."

"And?" Dread crept up her spine. She might need to shoot at someone?

"And everyone you meet on the road in Morocco is either your new best friend or your new worst enemy."

"It sounds to me like you're betting on 'enemy.'"

"Experience"—he headed for his horse—"is a hell of a teacher."

So it was. She stood for a moment, considering the lesson this experience had taught her: He knew more about the land and people than it had seemed at first. More importantly, he had proven that he was willing to side with her and even stand between her and danger.

"All right." She took a stand beside her horse as the others mounted. "I've decided. I'll hire you. For *half* of whatever treasure we find. The rest goes to the British Museum. No wheedling or whining or last-minute demands."

Smith thought on it for a moment, then jerked a nod and grinned at Haffe.

"Congratulations, my friend. You'll soon be a married man."

• • •

From a distance, the city of Marrakech looked like a grand, idealized painting intended for the main salon of a London men's club. The massive walls glowed the color of deep roseate ochre in the waning rays of the sun, and the great prayer tower at the center of the city shone like beaten gold. The road that wound through the palm-littered countryside toward the great northern gate was filled with caravans and people in colorful desert robes and turbans. It was the very essence of Morocco . . . the vision embodied in every book, painting, and illustration she had consulted.

Five days of fatigue and anxiousness gave way to excitement as they joined the camels, donkey carts, and pilgrims afoot on the main road. This was the exotic stepping off point to adventure that the professor had described in his journals. She was finally on the threshold of discovery.

But the relief she experienced was only partly for their safe arrival. The rest had to do with her unacknowledged fear that T. Thaddeus might have let his hopes for his lifelong quest affect his interpretations . . . that he might have imagined more than was really here. But now, seeing the city real and alive all around her, she felt a fresh flood of certainty that they would find the library. Anything— everything seemed possible in a place like this.

"Boston!" Smith's voice finally broke through her preoccupation. He reined his horse and waited for her to catch up. "Put on that cloak from the other night. No sense drawing unwanted attention."

She reached for the dark cotton cloak tucked between the bags behind her and dragged it on over her head and shoulders. Ahead of her, Smith was removing his hat and donning a long, hooded tunic that was Morocco's traditional outer garment. Then he slumped somewhat in his saddle, making himself less conspicuous, and she instinctively copied him.

Looking around at the colorful turbans, veils, and exotic robes of the people milling about the gate, she recalled the reaction of the nomads to her simple curiosity and redirected her gaze to the walls and gate itself . . . looking for rifle barrels . . . troops of angry soldiers . . . blades clamped between teeth. . . .

As they passed under the ornate arch of the Bab el-Khemis and into the shade cast by the great walls, she felt the temperature drop and experienced a chill. Beneath her cloak, her hand went to the gun wedged in her belt, against her back. The steel was no longer cold; it had absorbed heat from her body and now felt strangely in place there, at her back.

"How much money do you have?" Smith dropped back to ride beside her.

"Some," she said defensively.

"Enough for a night or two in a decent hotel?" he asked, his gaze moving continuously over their surroundings.

She nodded, imitating the way he scanned the area for any hint of danger . . . though in truth she had no idea what might constitute a threat . . . outside of dockside thieves, Legionnaires, scorpions, and superstitious nomads.

"This way, then." Smith kneed his mount and turned onto a broad street lined with the walls and gates of prosperous houses and neat-looking shops.

Before long, they arrived in a plaza planted with palms and surrounded by the front gates of buildings that looked more imposing than anything she had seen in Casablanca. Smith halted in front of a series of artful concentric arches that formed the entrance to a sizeable residence. It turned out to be the Hotel Raissouli, a place so respectable and expensive—according to Smith—that no one would think of looking for them there.

The price they were quoted for rooms seemed excessive, but when they were shown through the lofty corridors to their rooms, Abigail took one look at the damask draped bed and pale pink ochre walls and thought the coin well spent. A bath, she told the porter as he handed her the key to her room. She wanted hot water as soon as possible.

She fell asleep twice—once in a chair as she waited for

water and once in the tub—before finally crawling into the clean sheets and sleeping the clock around.

She awoke the next afternoon with the feeling that she wasn't alone. When she sat up, there in a chair pulled up to the bed sat Smith with his boots propped on the mattress.

"What are you doing here?" She pulled the covers higher and blinked repeatedly, trying to focus eyes that still felt like parboiled onions.

"Checking our maps," he said lifting the curled bit of parchment dangling from his hand.

"How did you get in?" When he didn't answer, she glanced at the door, expecting to see it in splinters. "What is the matter with hotels in—*our* maps?"

"Now that we're partners—"

"We're not *partners*. We're employer and employee," she declared irritably, climbing out of bed to grab the map from him.

"I thought I'd better see what we're in for." He sat forward, coming so close that she felt compelled to back up a step. "And what we're in for is disaster." He flipped the edge of the parchment now in her hands. "Except for Timbuktu, there isn't a recognizable place name on the entire thing."

"The professor was careful." She glanced at the map she knew by heart and then rolled it up. "He kept his journals in Greek and his maps in code."

"Yeah? Well, where's the key to this 'code' of his?"

"I have it." She omitted the qualifying: *mostly.* "I just need to consult someone here in Marrakech."

"Someone *who*?" His patience was thinning. "Partners don't keep secrets," he said hotly, his gaze roaming over her in a way that made her too aware of the nakedness inside her nightgown.

"Really?" The heat radiating from him made her feel jittery. She couldn't help noticing that he was newly shaven and his sun-streaked hair was damp. The scent of soap reached her. Her gaze dipped impulsively to his mouth and she prayed this wouldn't turn out to be another of those worrisome "opportunities." "Then tell me what kind of trouble you're in, *partner*. Why did you go to England and then come back? What is in those papers you hid in my bags?"

He glowered at her for a moment, then looked away.

"I know where we can get some decent food at a reasonable price." He rose and shoved the chair back across the tiled floor. "Get dressed." He flicked a disapproving look at her exceedingly proper nightdress. "And try not to look any more *American* than you have to."

Fourteen

Two hours later, after a meal over which a list of supplies and equipment had been hammered out, Abigail announced she had to meet with someone and tried to dismiss Smith while keeping Haffe with her.

"You're meeting your *mystery man*. I'm coming along," Smith said flatly.

Her protests did nothing to convince him he wasn't needed or wanted. She was forced to lead both Haffe and him on a search through the heart of the city for the Ben Youssef Medersa.

"A Muslim holy man?" Smith was incredulous. "He'll never see you."

"He'll see me," she said striding on. "He's an enlightened holy man."

The *medersa* was a Koranic school of some renown, dedicated to the study of Islamic law and scriptures, and as such was forbidden to non-Muslims. Haffe was the only one of the three who could rightfully enter. After some discussion and the dispensing of yet another silver dollar, Haffe was persuaded to take the message she had written and make his way down a long, cool entry passage to the center courtyard.

The ban on clerics' contact with infidels had not stopped T. Thaddeus from meeting and getting to know one of the foremost teachers of that revered academy: Moulay Karroum. The Berber-Arab scholar figured notably in all of the professor's writings about Marrakech; it was clear he had taken Karroum into his confidence regarding his search for the library.

After a time, Haffe bustled back down the passage to collect her and Smith and lead them down a side street to a well-kept door. They were admitted by an older man with a frizzled white beard and lively eyes, wearing a white turban and the dignified white tunic and black sleeveless robe of a cleric.

Karroum welcomed them with a bow and addressed Smith exclusively at first. When he learned that it was Abigail who had come on behalf of his old friend, his eyes widened, but, as she hoped, he accepted conversation with her—an infidel and a woman—with surprising ease.

Then she informed him of the professor's death. Loss silenced him for a time, then he turned aside to collect himself and murmur a prayer. Then, recalling the Prophet's mandate for hospitality, he invited them into the house's reception room and offered them refreshment.

Over potent Moroccan tea, Abigail told him an edited version of how she came into possession of T. Thaddeus's work and that she hoped to honor the professor by completing it. To authenticate her story, she produced the professor's final and most complete map, which she had decided now to carry with her at all times. As the old cleric stroked the meticulously drawn letters and features of the map, prisms of tears appeared in his eyes.

"There are legends, of course." Karroum wagged his head. "And my dear friend had searched for so long, he was convinced that his library could be found. 'But even if it is found,' I told him, 'the scrolls will all have turned to dust long ago.'" He raised a gnarled finger. "The mighty desert does not permit the insignificant works of man to endure for long in its domain. He knew this . . . he had seen the desert reclaim whole villages in storms . . . but still he searched."

"The professor wrote in his journal that you helped him with his 'navigation,'" she said, hoping to steer his reminiscing to more productive topics.

"Ah." His leathery face creased with a self-deprecating smile. "There are those who say I am a fair student of the heavens. An astronomer of sorts. It is good for a servant of Allah to study the glory of the stars. It keeps him humble."

"There is cause for humility all around." She smiled. "In the colors of the sunset. In the cry of a newborn child. In the impatient heart of an olive seed."

He folded his hands and settled a searching look on her. She had a strong sense of being weighed, and she prayed she would not be found wanting. After a productive silence, the old scholar seemed to have made his decision about her.

"You are indeed a student of my dear old friend. He too understood the impatience in the heart of the olive seed."

The knot in her chest loosened. "I was hoping you might take a look at something the professor wrote—or copied—in Arabic. It may be a valuable clue."

He nodded and when she produced a page from T. Thaddeus's journal, he carried it to the light of a window and held it at arm's length to study it. She joined him and when he finished, he seemed unsettled.

"It is phrases taken from the Qu'ran. Our most holy scriptures." He scowled, taken aback. "It is from the Prophet's descriptions of Paradise."

"What does it say?"

"It speaks of the maidens of Paradise . . . the virgins granted to those at the right hand of Allah . . . maidens with large, dark eyes and translucent skin . . . the ones who are immortal and do not age." He handed her the page and shook his head curtly. "That is all."

"But on the other side . . ." She turned the page over

and showed him more characters text . . . some of which were juxtaposed to familiar Greek phrases.

He took the page back and studied it, then swayed back to his chair.

"Here are a number of Arabic words and phrases translated into Greek. Protector is *prostatis*, Caretaker is *epistatis*." He frowned in concentration. "Thaddeus speaks of the guardians entrusted with the books using two terms . . . 'protectors' and 'caretakers' . . . as if there were two groups." He scowled. "One group, he equates with the houris of Paradise."

"Perhaps he meant that women tended—cared for—the books," she said.

The old scholar looked dismayed as he handed her the paper.

"Women scholars? Caring for books?" He shook his head in disbelief. Abigail caught Smith's taunting smile and battled an infantile urge to stick out her tongue at him. "I fear my old friend was ill and merely anticipating the pleasures of Paradise. Perhaps he did indeed embrace our faith before he died. I wish I could be of more help, Miss Merchant."

After a lull in which she folded away her documents, he made a decision.

"I do have something," Karroum said. "Thaddeus gave it to me to keep for him on his last visit."

He levered himself out of his chair and swayed deeper into the shady house. He returned with a flat, polished wood box and placed it in her hands.

"I believe he would wish you to have it."

She ran her hands over the beautiful marquetry work on the top. When she opened it, her eyes widened and Smith left his chair to kneel on one knee beside her.

In the box, on a bed of formed red velvet, lay a polished brass disk that she recognized as instrument used by sailors to take navigational bearings.

"An astrolabe?" she said, realizing instantly how it must have applied to the professor's work and just as instantly how useless it would be in her own hands. "Did the professor actually use it?"

"Oh, yes." He smiled at her expression of dismay. "He spent many hours with me, becoming adept. It is a dying art, you know, to use such an instrument for navigation."

Smith reached into the box for the engraved disk, and she was forced to either let him take it or risk rebuking him in the cleric's presence. She had no way of knowing how far the teacher's tolerance of women extended.

"It is quite beautiful," she said, trying to contain her irritation at the authoritative way Smith handled and examined the pieces. "But I'm afraid it won't be of much help. We have limited time and don't know how to use it."

"Speak for yourself," Smith said with a glint in his eyes, assembling and dangling the instrument from the ring and chain that accompanied it. "The astrolabe and I are old friends."

"*You* might have given me some hint, some indication," she said irritably after they exited the cleric's house and reached the main street.

He tucked the box under his arm and struck off for the nearest market at a fast pace. She had to work to keep up.

"That I know how to use an astrolabe? Fine. Notice is hereby served that I may possess a number of arcane but potentially useful abilities."

"Like what?" She strode faster, infuriated by her own curiosity. "And how do you even know a word like 'arcane'?"

"Misspent youth." He quickened his pace and cut her a brief glance from the corner of his eye. "And what was all of that nonsense about 'virgins in Paradise' and 'ignorant olives'?"

"*Impatience* in the heart of an olive seed. It's a metaphor for eagerness to embrace life and growth . . . the professor used it in his journals." She slashed a look back at him. "It's profound. You wouldn't understand."

She regretted the words the instant they left her lips. He stopped dead in the street, his humor evaporating, his mouth tightening into a thin, hard line.

"Oh, yes. For a minute I forgot." He strode back to stand over her, each step jarring free more emotion until his whole body seemed to be humming with it. "I'm a functionary . . . a tool of colonial military expansion . . . a strong back and weak mind . . . a means to a bloody end . . . literally."

Deep in his hazel gaze, powerful currents were moving.

Snatches of comments hinting at betrayal and loss came back to her. She realized with sobering certainty that he had lived at the extremes of human existence: education, class, and privilege . . . ignorance, powerlessness, and servitude. He was a son of the cultural and economic elite who had become an expendable drudge serving the impulses of that same group. And he was raw inside from experiencing life both ways.

What began as another of their bantering exchanges had become something far more revealing.

"I don't know what you are," she said quietly.

In her awareness the people on the street around them disappeared. . . . there were no ochre-red walls or carved cedar screens, no scent of animals and dust and spice. no cries of vendors plying their wares in the nearby square. There was only him . . . the turbulent, fascinating, sometimes troubling essence of him: A man with a murky past and an uncertain future.

She felt drawn in a way she didn't understand toward the disturbance in his depths. She wanted to delve into it and shake it up . . . explore it more fully.

He lurched back a step and she felt like some of the strength in her bones went with him. She fell back a step herself, to regain her bearings as she watched him stalk off down the street with his hands in his pockets.

Struggling to shelve those new insights deep in personal reference, she collected herself and headed after him. They covered several blocks and made two turns before entering a huge open-air market that she guessed must be the central *souk* of Marrakech. Whatever lingering effects he might be feeling from their encounter, he obviously intended to get on with the business at hand.

Rows of stalls and awning-covered carts filled the rocky, ill-paved square. They displayed everything from garments to decorative weaving . . . copper pots to woven baskets . . . and large wooden trays of fresh vegetables to burlap bags of dried fruit and nuts. Between the rows, jugglers, snake charmers, and musicians plied their trades, surrounded by customers of every size and description.

Smith headed straight for a section of garment sellers and selected three heavy, white woolen burnouses from one stall, speaking French and indicating with vengeful clarity that the bill was to be presented to *her*. Then he moved on to a turban seller and selected lengths of both light and dark cloth.

"We don't need these," she said firmly as the merchant piled them into her arms and held out his hand for payment. "We have *hats*."

"Which won't be worth a damn when the desert wind picks up," he declared, abandoning the central stalls for the permanent shops around the great square.

He found a tentmaker and bargained for a piece of oiled canvas.

"You made me leave *my* tarpaulin behind!"

"Too small," he said flatly.

He found a shop that sold harnesses and equipment of metal and leather, and purchased three sets of wire goggles.

"My smoked-glass spectacles are just as effective."

"Only if you actually *want* to go sun-blind," he said tautly.

Next, he located an apothecary's stall and bargained for camel butter, camphor oil, and a number of foul-smelling substances to put in them.

"I kept my universal dispensary." She winced at the

bizarre animal and insect parts displayed as potential cures. "I have all the medicinals we ll need."

"English remedies for England. Desert remedies for the desert." He bit off the finish of every word and pointed to the merchant's outstretched hand.

He piled the items he had ordered in Haffe's already laden arms and headed for an instrument maker indicating he needed to bargain for a compass. She caught up and grabbed him by the sleeve to pull him to a halt.

"That wasn't on our list, either. I already *have* a compass." It seemed he was spending her money as much to punish her as to acquire what they needed.

He wheeled on her, his gaze hot and temper flaring.

"Our lives will depend on it. I need a real compass, not some tin trinket!"

She stood her ground, refusing to let him either dominate or dismiss her, insisting he deal openly with whatever it was that had surfaced between them.

"It's not my compass we have to worry about." she said furiously, "it's your sense of direction. I'm not sure you know which way is up!"

Tension arced between them making the air heavy and charged. Her skin prickled as he reached for her. When his hands closed on her upper arms, she felt a hot, jagged surge of excitement. Then he pulled her closer.

"Smeeth—" Haffe's voice intruded, sounding oddly choked. "Smeeth!"

Smith's head snapped up. A moment later, she jerked her gaze around to see what had caused him to all but abandon his grip on her.

Entering the square, not far away, was a wall of khaki.

Legionnaires.

She looked around for a place to retreat and found none. The late-day market crowd had given the disputing "Europeans" a wide berth and they found themselves standing virtually alone on one side of the great square. Smith took a step backward, then another, sweeping Abigail and Haffe behind him.

The Legionnaires were talking loudly and pointing to various parts of the *souk* . . . apparently off duty. Then one of them looked up and spotted Smith's stare and hasty retreat.

Abigail's heart stopped as she saw the Legionnaire gather and direct the others' attention toward Smith and her.

"Hey, you! You there—" one of them called.

"Run!" Smith growled, giving her and Haffe both a shove. She wheeled and rushed for the corner, but by the time she reached it she sensed Smith wasn't behind her and stopped. When she looked back, she saw him with his hand on his revolver, backing her way under the scrutiny of a dozen Legionnaires.

All she could think was that she couldn't let them take him; she *needed* him. She looked to Haffe, who was laden with purchases and probably not much of a fighter anyway, then frantically around the souk for someone—anyone who looked like an authority. The only "official" presence in the marketplace was the Legionnaire force itself.

That left only her. She felt beneath her jacket for the gun at her back, squared her shoulders, and charged back into the square.

Fifteen

The sight of two Europeans—one an unveiled female in Western dress—was enough to attract the Legionnaires' attention. But it was the pair's look of surprise and immediate retreat that triggered the Legionnaires' impulse to run a quarry to ground. The faster Smith fell back, the faster they approached . . . until they drew close enough to get a better look at him. A man from the rear pushed his way forward, yelling to the others: "Wait—"

"Smiff?" The tall, lanky Legionnaire's eyes fairly bulged from his head. "Good Gawd! Apollo Smiff, is zat *you*?"

Smith froze and returned both the scrutiny and the disbelief.

"Crocker?" he blurted out. "Will Crocker?"

"Good Gawd—I fink it's 'im!" Crocker stalked cautiously forward to give him a poke on the shoulder and report back to the others: "It's 'im all 'oight. Apollo Bloody Smiff. In livin' flesh."

A moment later, Smith and Abigail were surrounded with Legionnaires swearing with surprise and laughing.

Smith's boisterous hand-clasps and shoulder butting caused Abigail to release her grip on the pistol.

He knew these men. More importantly, they knew him and they didn't seem to want to shoot or arrest him!

"Gawd, let's 'ave a look at ye," Crocker declared, seizing Smith by the shoulders and holding him at arm's length. "Not bad fer a corpse, eh, lads? That's wot they told us, Smiffy old boy—you're *dead*."

"Who told you that?" Smith said, grinning and cuffing Crocker's shoulder. "Bet it was an officer. Damned liars, officers."

"No, no. It was a sergeant," said an Indian-looking fellow with a musical accent to his English and a broad, toothy smile. "I am sure of it."

"An NCO, then. A damned *bad* liar." Smith laughed.

Smith realized the men were all staring at something behind him and turned to find *her* standing with her arms folded and her chin tucked.

"An' who might this lovely slip o' muslin be?" Crocker pushed past Smith, his eyes alight. " 'E rose from th' dead *and* found hisself a woman!"

"This"—Smith cleared his throat and with two giant steps arrived at her side—"is my partner. Miss Abigail Merchant. From Boston. That's in America, for all you brutes and numskulls."

"Will Crocker, miss," Smith's friend offered his hand, and when she accepted it, he bowed gallantly. "Any partner o' Smiff's is a partner o' mine."

"Pleased to meet you," she said, still struggling to understand what was happening. "But in fact, Mr. Smith is—"

"One lucky bastard," injected a red-faced fellow with curly auburn hair and the bluest eyes she'd ever seen. "Private Joseph Ryan Flynn, at yer service."

In short order, she was also introduced to Ravi Phant, Giotto Mancini, Fritz Neiburg, Cruz Sanchez, and Elijah Johnson . . . all of whom claimed to have served with Smith when he was assigned to the Legion outpost in Marrakech. They were off duty, they said, and insisted that Smith and Abigail join them for a drink. Haffe, eager to escape the presence of so much French khaki, volunteered to carry their purchases back to the hotel and departed.

Not far away was a café at the corner of the *souk*, with an outdoor loggia and a number of tables. There was already a lively trade in the place, as customers and merchants adjourned from the waning market for food and drink. But the minute a horde of Legionnaires appeared, the native Moroccans evacuated tables and exited the bistro.

"It's like that everwhere we go," Crocker said with a rueful laugh, nodding to the locals' retreat. "They ain't too keen on our comp'ny."

"Nor should they be," Joe Flynn declared loudly. "We're a colonial force, we are." He broke into a wicked Irish grin. "And damned proud of it!"

A howl of agreement and some pounding of the tables ensued . . . until the proprietor hurried out of the café to see what was the matter. They gave them their order and were soon drinking toasts to Smith's return to the living, to the Legion's miserable record keeping, and to the day each and every one of them mustered out *alive*.

No ladylike demurring was allowed; they set a glass of wine before Abigail and insisted she partake as well. And when the first glass of wine was finished, they ordered her another.

"Forgive me," she said, looking at the variation in the faces around the tables they had pushed together. "but, none of you look or sound very French."

They laughed and began to spout butchered French phrases and sing what were probably scurrilous French songs.

"Not a Frenchie amongst us," Flynn declared, "for which we all thank the Good Lord. 'Tis the French *Foreign* Legion, miss. Made up of foreigners Frenchies themselves are 'discouraged from applyin.' It's just us poor grunts an' gilhooleys bleedin' an' dyin' out here. Us with the dim wits and strong backs." He gave a wicked grin. "Us that got sucked in by them sweet-talking recruiters."

The others laughed raucously and called out the promised benefits of Legion service: "Great pay," "Delicious food," "Lots 'o travel," "Betterin' yerself," "Payin' a debt to society," and "Impressin' the ladies!"

"All 'o that," Crocker said laughing at his comrades, "and th' chance to be declared a French citi-zen . . . *if* ye survive th' full contract."

"What more could a man want?" Ravi Phant said, eyes glistening.

"Of course, Smith, here, he's half a Frenchie a'ready," Flynn informed her. "Parlays with the best of 'em."

"Yeah, but 'e's no ponce. He come to th' Legion the right an' proper way, jus' like the rest o' us," Crocker declared.

"Yeah," Flynn said, beaming mischief. "From prison."

"Prison?" Abigail turned to Smith with wine-muffled shock. "What for?"

Smith swung at Flynn's head, missing by a mile.

"Nothin' I can remember."

"The usual," Flynn said drawing back.

"And what's the usual?" she asked.

"Killin' a man."

Abigail sat in shock, listening to the banter resume and the high spirits flow around her, trying to absorb the fact that Smith had been imprisoned for killing someone. His arrogance, his stubbornness, his secretiveness, his drive to profit from helping her . . . those had been enough to make her wary of taking him fully into her confidence. Now she learned—and he didn't deny—that he had taken a life and was in prison when he was inducted into the Foreign Legion! Just as she was beginning to trust him. . . .

She was so absorbed in stealing glimpses at him and going over every step of their association—wondering how she could have missed the taint of such violence in him—that she lost track of the conversation around her.

"Who else got transferred when I did?" Smith was demanding of Crocker.

"No one." Crocker wiped his mouth with the back of his hand. "We figured ye'd found one o' yer fancy kin to buy ye out . . . an' forgot so much as a 'sod off' for yer old pals."

"Just me, then," Smith concluded, scowling. "They came and got me—put me in a detachment headed for Casablanca. I hardly had time to snag my kit and rifle. They were splitting up the company, they said, and sending experienced men to the mounted companies. But it seems they didn't."

"That's where you were sent? A mounted company?" Flynn whistled. "No wonder they thought you were dead. The mounted companies were sent up north— the Algerian border. Scarce one in three came back alive."

"South and east of Tangiers." Smith nodded, tossing back another whiskey and waving for another round for them all. "A lot of killing and a lot of dying."

To a man, the Legionnaires went silent for a moment.

"To the bastards who bought it up north," Flynn said, raising his glass. It was oddly somber. Such talk brought each man present face-to-face with the fact that as long as he was in the Legion, death was never far away. A moment after the toast was drunk, Flynn cleared his throat and the spell was broken.

"Tell us homesick lads, miss," he turned to Abigail, "what an ugly brute like him did to merit the company of such a beautiful young laidy as yerself."

"Rescued her," Smith cut in, his chest swelling to almost the size of his inflated head. "Twice."

She sent him a dagger of a look that failed to puncture it.

"Aboard ship, on the way from England"—he went on—"and again in Casablanca." Clearly, the whiskey was having an effect. "Then, I damn near had to fight a band of bloodthirsty nomads over her on the road to Marrakech."

Modesty had never exactly been his long suit, but this was too much.

"I have taken to calling him S.O.S.," she said with a strained little smile.

"S.O.S.?" He grinned and leaned close to her. "Yeah. It fits."

"Better than *Apollodorus*," Flynn put in with a taunting laugh.

"What's that?" Abigail turned to the garrulous Irishman.

"His Christian name. Didn't he tell you?" Flynn dodged Smith's lunge across the table.

"He apparently omitted a few things," she said, as Smith caught him and wrapped a steely arm around his head.

"His ma thought the sun rose and set in her baby boy—" Flynn groaned.

"So she named 'im after th' Greek god Apollo." Crocker finished for him.

"Apollo-dorus," one of the others said, thumping the tabletop. The others picked it up. "Apollodorus . . . Apollodorus . . ."

The men of Smith's old company were still chanting his name as they staggered through the streets, escorting Smith and Abigail back to their hotel. The doorman of the Raissouli spotted them coming and called the manager, who confronted the crowd of drunken Legionnaires in the lobby and insisted they vacate the premises.

Smith was sober enough to prevent the others from starting a fight that would only get them all thrown in a cell for fifteen days. They swore they didn't mind doing a little time if it was the price of teaching the hotel man a lesson. Smith declined the offer and gave them each a fierce hand clasp and hug, vowing to see them again on his way back through Marrakech.

Abigail fought the wine-warmed steam in her senses to

watch him part from his friends with glowing eyes, scandalous language, and a booming laugh. He charmed them the way he did her, with his curious blend of educated gentleman and hard-scrapping line soldier It was clear he felt deep respect and affection for these men with whom he had shared hardship and adventure. His loyalty, once given, was apparently steadfast. In their company she began to understand that his arrogance indeed came from hard-won experience and his stubbornness could be viewed as survival-honed tenacity.

And yet, he sat in a café drinking whiskey and casually acknowledging that he had been in prison for a killing. . . .

She watched until the Legionnaires left, staggering out into the street and calling a gallant good-bye. Then she requested her key and headed down the corridor that led to her room. Her legs felt rubbery and the walls around her didn't seem to be as straight as they should be. As she leaned against a pillar to get her bearings, Smith came up behind her and lifted her into his arms.

"What do you think you're doing?"

"God, you're heavy," he muttered, breathing hard as he carried her across the courtyard and down the loggia near her room.

"Then put me down." Frantic to avoid being dropped, she slid one arm around his neck and hung on. "I can walk."

"I saw how you walked on the way back to the hotel." He sobered quickly under the exertion of carrying her. "I never met a librarian yet who could hold liquor."

"Oh? And just how many librarians have you met?"

"Counting you?" he said, glancing down at her.

She nodded.

"One."

He had her lean over to unlock the door to her room and he carried her straight to the bed. She didn't release him quickly enough as she fell back onto the mattress and he was pulled down with her. He caught himself on an arm and a knee above her.

The inches between them were suddenly filled with charged potential . . . attractive force . . . a raw magnetism that excited both her senses and her fears. He was big and hot and full of a kind of experience she hadn't considered acquiring until—

She arched her back and scowled, fishing behind her for something. A second later, she dragged her gun from behind her and held it up.

"Give me that thing," he said, taking it with two fingers and dropping on the floor by the bed.

She looked up at him, knowing what would happen, wanting it to happen . . . afraid to let it . . . afraid to prevent it. . . .

"I don't think—"

"That a girl. Don't think." His mouth lowered toward hers. "Damned annoying habit, thinking."

Before she could respond, his lips covered hers and pleasure washed through her, saturating every tense and tingling part of her body. So this was what she missed the other night . . . this lush, possessing warmth swirling in her blood . . . this soft, sensuous kneading of her lips . . . this ache rising in her skin for closer . . . fuller . . . deeper. . . .

Deeper trouble. Something in her mind refused to dissolve heedlessly into that hypnotic flood of sensation. And as he shifted more of his weight on top of her, the shock of such intimacy helped her remember what it was.

"I have to know, Smith," she gasped out, dragging her mouth from his.

"Know what?" He kissed his way across her face and fastened his lips on her neck just below her ear. Ripples of excitement washed the underside of her skin and she shivered eloquently, trying to remember what she meant to say. Her very bones seemed to be melting.

Go on. Ask.

Just shut up and enjoy something for a change.

Do it now or you'll be kicking yourself later.

Don't do it, or you'll regret it for the rest of your life.

You can't turn your back on the truth and pretend it doesn't matter.

It bloody well doesn't matter—not now!

When will it matter? When you re in the desert and there's room for either a chest of gold or you on the only horse?

"Who did you kill?" She swallowed hard, half hoping she hadn't said the words aloud. "When they put you in prison . . . who was it you killed?"

He raised his head. His gaze was dark and only half focused.

"I have no idea." He lowered his mouth toward hers, but she avoided it.

"No—" She pushed on his shoulders to open some space between them. "Flynn said you killed someone."

"Ancient history," he said, dropping kisses down her chest as he released the buttons of her shirt.

"Tell me." She caught his face between her hands and raised it. He stilled and searched her for a moment as if deciding how much to say.

"It was a bar fight. They said I killed somebody."

"Who said?"

"My jailors. And the Legion recruiter." Heat began to drain from his face. "I don't remember anything from that night. I was drunk as David's sow."

"Then what did they say at your trial?"

"A trial? In Morocco?" He gave a sardonic laugh. "No such luxury."

"But what about the Consulate? Surely they allowed you to speak to—"

"Look, I woke up sweating in a metal box in a prison yard. They told me I killed someone and was sentenced to life in prison unless I joined the Legion. After some pretty uncomfortable 'persuasion,' I signed the damned papers."

"You never even had a trial?" she said, trying to comprehend the outrage that represented and how he could now speak of it almost casually.

"Or a visit from my uncle or the blessed British Consul." He stared at her, then shifted onto his elbow and pushed up to a sitting position.

"Your uncle?" That "family matter" he spoke of earlier, she realized. He'd come back to confront—"You have an uncle here, in Morocco?"

"So it seems."

"And he didn't try to help when you were arrested and put in prison?"

"Regrettably, no."

She studied his hardening face, feeling conflicted . . . needing to know more, but already feeling the distance her demands were putting between them. She had to understand, had to risk one final question.

"Why not?" she asked.

"Next time you see him, why don't you ask him?" he said swinging his legs off the side of the bed and standing up.

"When I see him?" She scowled, watching him swipe his hair back from his forehead and adjust the belt of his trousers. "The only other person I've met is"—it hit her and she blanched—"Ferdineaux LaCroix?"

"One and the same," he said with a fierce glance, heading for the door.

She slid from the bed and darted around him, inserting herself between him and the door handle.

"Why didn't you tell me?" she stared up into a face dusky with an altogether different passion than had filled it moments ago.

"Would you have believed me?" He leaned into her with his body, pushing her back against the door. "Do you believe me now?"

For a moment he let the hot press of his body against hers speak for him and watched her response in her eyes. Her doubt, fears, and desire were all there for him to see.

"Proper and precious Miss Merchant. You're not sure if you should let a killer touch you like this." He dragged his knuckles down the side of her cheek. "You're not sure if you should take pleasure in a murderer's kiss. . . ." He dipped his head and caught her lips with his, delivering a kiss so hot that it all but melted her bones. When he lifted his head, she slid down the door and he caught her by the waist and held her, his breath quick and ragged.

"But you want me, Boston. No matter what I may have done."

She knew she should protest that, but a strange tenor to his voice stopped her. It was a pained quality that kept his statement from sounding like intolerable arrogance. It was doubt. His own.

"They said."

"I don't remember . . ."

"Do *you* think you killed someone in a fight?" she asked.

Emotion welled in him as he pulled her against him and kissed her quick and hard. Then he set her aside and walked out the door, slamming it behind him. She staggered to the bed and collapsed on the side of it, staring after him.

He honestly didn't know if he'd killed someone or not. But he'd lived with it and paid for it with five grueling years of Legion service. His reaction just now showed that it weighed on him. Relief released the last of her control and she fell back on the bed with her eyes burning.

He was right. She did want him. With everything in her.

She touched her throbbing lips.

And after what she'd just done, he might never touch her again.

Damned impossible woman.

Apollo stormed blindly along the corridor, intent on waking up the entire hotel if necessary, to find a bottle of good Irish whiskey. He was going to get roaring drunk and . . .

And what? Forget that the instant his lips touched hers, something in his blood ignited? Forget sensations he'd never felt before cascading through him . . . spreading along the muscles of his chest . . . raking his skin into gooseflesh as they flowed down his belly?

He stopped at the edge of the main courtyard, his fists clenched and his chest heaving. He saw again, felt again the way her mouth had reached for him.

Nothing in this world or the next could have prevented him from pouring a kiss over those soft lips and into the wet velvet heat she offered.

It shocked him at first how her tongue darted and explored and tasted him. She was a librarian, for God's sake. How did she know how to do that? Did somebody write books on it? Every flick and stroke of her tongue had sent another swirl of pleasure spiraling through his body. It felt like his whole being had begun to melt—lips first—into hers.

And *her*. For a few stunning moments she had been soft and lush and feminine. No more prickliness, no more intellectual disdain, no more resistance.

Then she opened her mouth and demanded to know the name of the man he'd killed. She wanted to know, maybe needed to know. But he couldn't help feeling she had used her questions to fend him off, to keep him from—no, to keep *herself* from having to surrender some of her precious self-control.

"Dammit, Boston—"

He looked down at the hot bulge in his trousers and groaned. The whiskey would have to wait. He bolted out into the starlit courtyard, where he removed his boots and climbed clothes-and-all into the middle of a mercifully cool fountain.

Abigail woke the next noon facedown in her own bed, fully clothed and wearing her riding boots. She had a pounding headache, grainy, light-sensitive eyes, and a tongue that felt like a caravan of camels had trekked across it. With supreme effort, she pulled off her boots and dragged herself from the bed.

She managed to find her dispensary and headache powders and downed a healthy dose. The wages of sin. Clearly.

It took effort to piece together coming back to her room last night. The shards of memory lying on the bottom of her mind had smudges of Smith all over them. And the evidence both for and against his character seemed to change from minute to minute.

Whether he had killed someone or not, it was a relief to learn the *entire* French Foreign Legion wasn't after him. Apparently only part of it wanted to arrest him for not being genuinely dead. But, if that was the case, why didn't he just go to Legion headquarters somewhere and straighten everything out?

Because there was more to it. How much more, she didn't want to think. Was there anything about the man that was clear and straightforward?

She cleared the haze away from the last few moments before he stormed out of her room when he'd held her against the door.

There was *one* thing that was perfectly clear. He wanted her as a woman. All right, *two* things. He was right when he said she wanted him.

When she had collected herself enough to face him again, she left the hotel for the horse *souk*, which was where the Raissouli's head porter informed her Smith had been bound when he and Haffe left that morning.

Just like him, she muttered to herself: spending her money without a single thought of consulting her. Wretched man. With each step she dug in her heels a bit harder.

Sixteen

❦

Apollo had difficulty concentrating on horses that morning. His head felt like a brass-smith's anvil and every throb in his temples generated a taunting echo in his oversensitive loins. He struggled to keep his mind on number of teeth, hoof and tendon condition, and water consumption, instead of his testy mood and his equally testy partner.

Damned woman. Dredging up all kinds of internal misery he thought he'd made peace with long ago. He didn't have time for taking her on a tour of the worst moments of his life and justifying his existence. He had business to take care of today . . . the kind that didn't allow for distractions.

Midafternoon, as he and Haffe were nearing the hotel, leading an Arabian-Barb and two mules, he caught sight of *her* striding toward them and stopped in his tracks, preparing for an onslaught of temper or temptation. Or both.

"You bought these?" she asked, ignoring him as she circled the animals. She was dressed in a brown split skirt, starched white blouse with a brown velvet ribbon laced through the standing collar, and her customary riding boots. In the afternoon heat, she looked fresh, composed, and maddeningly self-contained.

"Either that or we stole them," he said irritably, holding out the horse's reins to her. "This one is yours."

"A mare, I see." She posted herself by the horse's head, assessing it, and then looked askance at the mules flapping their long ears to ward off flies. "Mules?"

"Better for carrying supplies in the desert. They drink less than horses."

"If that's the criteria, why didn't we just get camels instead?"

He was about to say he'd considered them, but figured her brains were scrambled enough without being rattled to-hell-and-gone on a hump six feet off the ground, when she dusted her hands with a "she'll do" and headed off.

"Where are you going?" He looked at her receding figure, trying not to absorb the swaying lower half of it. Was she wearing that damnable cincher?

"Tools," she called back, over her shoulder "Haffe, you come with me."

The Berber gave him a shrug and the reins to the mules, and followed her.

Apollo stood for a moment, battling searing flashes of pink satin and the urge to—what? Shake her? Tie her up? Sell her into the first caravan he saw?

"Dammit. There's never a white slaver around when you need one."

He headed for the hotel stables, dragging the animals along. He didn't have time for this nonsense. He had a couple of important calls to make. After all, that was the real reason he'd come to Marrakech.

"Shovels, picks, rope, hand spades, brushes, lanterns and oil . . ." Abigail stood in the street at the edge of the great open-air market some time later, recounting the items in Haffe's arms and trying to recall if there was more on her list. Dismissing whatever might have been overlooked, she picked up two bulky parcels. "This will have to do. I can't spend any more money, if I expect to—"

Her gaze snagged on a patch of khaki on the far side of the souk.

Legionnaires. She raised a hand to shade her eyes for a better look and spotted a tall, stringy-looking fellow in the middle of the group.

"Crocker," she murmured, feeling like she could use a dose of the Brit's thick accent and irreverent humor. When he looked her way, she waved and started for them. Behind her, Haffe hesitated, she paused to wave him along with her, assuring him they were not to be feared.

She turned back and glimpsed the tall, rangy fellow's sunken cheeks and strange, bulging eyes . . . the opposite of Crocker's mischievous, boyish face. She searched out another face . . . a short, wiry fellow with a nose broken to a grotesque angle. She didn't recognize either of them.

Then a stocky figure at the front of the group, wearing several stripes on his sleeve, turned toward her and she stopped dead.

His face was broad and flat, covered with dark stubble, and he had a thick mouth that twisted into an unpleasant smirk at the sight of her. Him she recognized. The sergeant from the Marrat—the one looking for Smith!

The tall, bony soldier pointed at her and said something. The rest of the group turned, but she was already in motion.

"Run!" She pushed Haffe into a crowd of his countrymen milling about the market, praying he wouldn't be singled out, and headed for the nearest corner. As she ran, her head and heart raced to catch up with her limbs. Her best hope was to blend in, too—to look like anything but American or British—

Spotting a garment stall, she ducked inside and despite the uproar of the merchant and his assistants, managed to rip a robe from a peg, empty her arms, and shove them into the sleeves. She just had time toss some coins at the proprietor and get the hood up before the soldiers went rushing by the shop. Seconds later, they reappeared and a harsh voice barked orders that sent them charging into all of the nearby stalls.

"I can't let them find me," she said, grabbing up her packages and scrambling over stacks of garments to get as far from the front as possible. "Is there a back way out? A door?"

Seeing the source of her fear and apparently sympathizing, one of the youths moved a screen used to display garments and waved her behind it. There was no time to question where it led; she lunged through the opening.

Shocked faces greeted her—men stitching garments in a workshop littered with fabric and yarns and a hanging forest of half-sewn garments. Spotting an open door at the rear, she headed for it and plunged into a maze of narrow, sun-starved paths that ran between shabby mud-brick walls.

The alley narrowed without warning; she scraped her shoulders and hands as she banged into the walls and kept going. No other doors opened onto the passage and she was bewildered by the frequent twists and turns that left her with no sense of direction. Unpleasant and probably unhealthy smells saturated the stale air she held her breath as much as possible . . . taking every turn on faith and praying the maze would lead someplace recognizable   •

In the darkness, her eyes adjusted. She could see better, but that meant she could also see small furtive shadows darting underfoot and sinuous shapes scurrying up the dank walls. Shortly, a human form materialized in the alley ahead. She choked on a scream as the turbaned figure bashed her against the wall and barreled past. She stayed against the wall where he had shoved her, feeling her heart battering her ribs and trying not to dwell on the thought that the man could have had a knife and she could be lying in a lifeless heap.

As she peeled herself from the wall and continued, her one thought was of Smith. If she could just get back to the hotel . . . back to him . . . she would be . . .

Then she turned a corner and spotted light—literally at the end of the tunnel—she couldn't believe it at first. It was only when she reached the end and stood staring into a broader, sunlit street filled with people, carts, and wagons, that she realized she had made it.

Sagging against the wall, she searched for landmarks. Across the broad thoroughfare was a massive mud-brick wall in ruined condition. The facing stone had been stolen and the stucco had weathered away. Craning her neck, she recognized a French café down the street and realized the ruin across from her was the Badi Palace.

Grounded now, she tried to recall the way they had come on the way to the great market yesterday. Then she stepped out into the street, lowered her face, and headed for the stream of people moving east . . . forcing herself not to run.

It seemed to take forever to reach the quiet, palm-lined square in front of the Hotel Raissouli. That sunny, prosperous quarter presented a stark contrast to the dark bowel of the city she had just traversed. She made herself walk calmly through the front arches and into the lobby and ask after Smith at the desk.

The clerk found his key on the peg, which indicated he was not in his room, and suggested she try the stables. She found Haffe pacing anxiously and talking to the horses and mules. When he recognized her in her oversized robe, he fell briefly to his knees with a prayer of gratitude.

The little Berber conveyed that he had managed to escape the Legionnaires, as she had hoped, and had taken a roundabout way back to the hotel, arriving not long before she did. He had no idea where Smith was, either. She fought down a surge of desperation.

"We can't wait—we have to start packing," she said, sagging against a nearby post. Packages fell from her cramped and burning fingers. "He saw me. Recognized me—"

"Who saw you?" Smith's voice from the stable door startled them. He quickly reached her side, pulled her upright, and looked her over with concern.

The sight of his sun-bronzed face and reassurance of his strong hands on her arms made her knees go weak. A flood of relief washed over her. He was here. He was holding her. . . .

"The sergeant who broke into my room that night is in Marrakech. I saw him in the square with his men and I waved, thinking it was Crocker and the others."

"A sergeant?" He squeezed her arms. "Did you hear his name?"

"I don't know—it was all so—" She closed her eyes, trying to retrieve a memory she had worked adamantly to forget. "The manager of the Marrat knew him . . . called him Garvin—Gaspar—*Gaston*!"

"Gaston? You're sure?"

She nodded. "He's short and thick, with muscular arms . . . a flat sort of face . . . dull, hateful eyes."

"That's that one. You're sure he recognized you?"

"He chased me. He must have followed us here from Casablanca."

"Let's hope he didn't follow you to the hotel." He looked at the horses and then at Haffe, charting a new course. He pushed her toward the stable doors and prevented her from turning back to retrieve her packages. "Leave those for now. Go. Pack. We have to get out of here."

Under cover of darkness, three riders leading two pack mules exited the city to the south and east, through the Bab Hmar. All three wore *jellabas* and turbans and seemed like ordinary residents of Morocco and Marrakech, if one didn't look too closely. Unfortunately, someone was watching very closely.

Most of the evening traffic through the gate was entering the city; the fact that the three were leaving drew the attention of a tall Legionnaire with sallow skin and precious little flesh on his lanky frame. He focused on them, reading in the way they were bent to their horses and keeping their heads down, that they were trying to escape notice. He edged closer to the gate for a better look. The clinching detail was the European style boots on two of the riders.

It was them, all right. The Legionnaire licked his lips as he stepped out of the shadows of the stone pillars beside the gate and hurried off to make his report. This should be worth a drink or two.

Sergeant Gaston sat in a cramped and smoky café on the east side of the city, drinking whiskey and watching the halfhearted undulations of a hard-eyed dancer veiled in sweat-stained silk. When one of his men entered the café, he straightened and waved the man into the chair across the table.

"Bab Hmar," the Legionnaire panted, winded from running. "I saw them."

"When?"

"No more than a quarter hour ago. Headed east."

"They take the high road to Ouarzazate? Then they go toward the desert." Gaston's smile bared brown-edged teeth. "The woman escaped us earlier today, but—as I suspected—the sight of us has caused them to bolt."

His strategy of posting men at the gates to watch for them had paid off. Now all he had to do was take his men across the mountains to Ouarzazate and wait for Smith and the woman to locate that "treasure" of hers.

Satisfied with the way his plan was unfolding, he spied hunger in Legionnaire's gaze on the bottle of whiskey and his mouth curled into a smirk.

"Thirsty, Schuller?" He poured a glass and with vengeful amusement drank it himself before the soldier's covetous gaze. "Go, collect the others from the gates and tell them to get some sleep. We march at first light."

Mountains. Abigail had studied both official and T. Thaddeus's hand-drawn maps for weeks and she had seen the snowcapped Atlas peaks nearly every day she had been

in Morocco. But until now, it hadn't really registered that
they were bound to cross a mountain range on the way to
the desert. It was only in the depths of that seemingly endless night, as they followed the pale slash of the road
across a rising landscape, that she realized they would be
climbing steadily for the next two days.

T. Thaddeus had marked the next stop on their journey
as "QKQ" on his map . . . which she had decoded into
"TNT" using the professor's transposition scheme. When
she asked what it was, Smith told her it was a mountain
pass called the Tizi-n-Tichka. It was the only place of note
on the map between Marrakech and the last outpost before
the desert . . . which the professor had cleverly labeled as
the indecipherable "Lrxowxwxqb" and which Abigail had
just as cleverly deciphered as "Ouarzazate."

"What did you tell LaCroix about where you were
headed?" Smith dropped back to talk to her. "Did he see
any of the maps?"

"No," she said, thinking back to that night in the Marrat's dining room. "I told him my search would take me to
Marrakech and south. That was all."

"South could mean Tiznit or Agadir or even Tata. With
any luck they won't realize we're headed for Ouarzazate.
Tizi-n-Tichka is the highest of two passes through the High
Atlas range, from Marrakech east. It's controlled by
Berber chieftains who are vassals of the Sultan of Marrakech. Haffe's Berber . . . he should save us some grief
dealing with them."

She made herself concentrate on his dissertation on the
geography and convoluted politics of the pass ahead and
on his hope that Gaston and the others would pursue them
toward the less difficult mountain passes to the south.

"So what you're saying is: They'll think we have better
sense than to take this route."

"Exactly." He produced an unrepentant smile.

When they stopped to water and rest the animals, she
shivered and ran her hands over her arms.

"I'm freezing, my rear is numb, and I can't seem to get

enough air," she complained, trying not to let her gaze stick to his moonlit features. She was afraid he would interpret it as relief or even pleasure that he was still with her. Because that was exactly what it was. "Are you sure there isn't a better way to get to Ouarzazate?"

"Don't blame me for the thin air and bad scenery. I'm just the hired help. Here . . ." He pulled out one of the burnouses he had purchased. "Put this on."

The garment was blessedly warm and she found herself joining Haffe in nodding off from time to time as they continued on through a silent patchwork of gray pastureland and cultivated fields that glowed strangely blue and purple in the moonlight.

By midmorning the next day, they had reached a wadi with a small farming village and traded for some bread, cucumbers, and goat cheese. After watering the horses, they left the road and climbed into the hills overlooking the narrow valley, where they made a day camp in the shadow of several large rocks. They ate, curled up in the shade, and slept until dusk. It was a pattern they were to repeat as they traveled further up into the mountains; resting by day and traveling by moonlight.

It was the evening of the second day, just past the modest Tizi-n-Ait-Imger pass that Smith awakened Abigail with a hand over her mouth to keep her from crying out. Night was falling and in the cold, dry air near the pass sound carried long distances. He whispered that he had just spotted light and smoke from what looked suspiciously like a Legionnaire encampment below them. It could be Gaston, or it could be another patrol; they had no way of knowing. They had to move on.

"No." She scrambled to her feet and crossed her arms.

"No, what?" he demanded, throwing her saddle onto her blanketed horse.

"I'm not going another step until you tell me the truth about Gaston and what you're doing back in Morocco."

"The less you know the better," he said, lifting the stirrup and tightening the cinch. "Now, get on the damned horse and let's ride."

"No." She raised her chin. "I'm not moving until you tell me what's going on. You obviously knew this 'sergeant' in your Legion days. He says you're a deserter, and you deny it. Your friends say you're supposed to be *dead*. What am I supposed to believe?" She sensed he was preparing to stonewall her demand and played her trump card. "I think I deserve to know, seeing as how I may get caught in your cross fire. Then at least I'll know why I'm being killed."

Muttering an oath, he stalked away to climb up one of the rocks at the edge of the ledge to look down at the campfire in the distance.

Her reminder of the danger he had put her in was clearly working on him. He slid back down the rock and sat for a moment staring at her, then he headed for his saddlebags and retrieved the envelope he had secreted into her baggage. She watched him sort through three papers, select one, then return the others to the envelope and the envelope to his shirt.

He strode over to her and shoved the open document in her hand.

"Here." He propped his fists on his waist, waiting.

She squinted to make out the official-looking type in the dying sunlight, and the first three words caused her breath to catch.

CERTIFICATE OF DEATH.

Seventeen

"All right, you're dead." She handed the document back to him. "I want details."

He looked exasperated and started to turn away, then turned back.

"Mount up," he said quietly. "I'll talk on the way."

Something in the resignation of his eyes said he would honor that promise.

"Sergeant Gaston came from Casablanca to Marrakech with dispatches for our commandant that included orders transferring me to a mounted company," he said when they had quietly put distance between them and the Legionnaires. "When I asked what was happening, he said they were breaking up our unit—they needed experienced men in the mounted companies. I went with Gaston and the regular dispatch patrol back to Casablanca. Along the way, we ran into some bandits and barely escaped. Something about Gaston's actions in that fight didn't feel right. After that, I kept an eye on him.

"We arrived in Casablanca just in time to head off with our company for the Algerian frontier . . . where we were in constant fighting and never had enough ammunition or food or water. It was a long, slow slaughter. And every time I turned around, Gaston was behind me . . . with his rifle pointed at my back.

"Finally, in one really ugly battle in a border village, he ordered four of us to enter and secure one of the houses. As we went in the front, the rebels went out the back and set the place on fire. When we tried to withdraw—there was a hail of gunfire. We were pinned down; rebels at the rear and somebody else at the front. I made it to a window and saw that it was Gaston firing and directing fire at the house he had just sent us into."

"He tried to kill you." She felt a chill even inside the burnoose.

"He damned near succeeded. I managed to crawl out the back . . . the rebels had fled. I was wounded and choking—half-dead from smoke. When I woke up, I was in a sheepherder's tent; he found me in the desert and took me in." He rolled his shoulders as if uncomfortable with the memory. "Gaston—and the Legion itself—assumed I died in the fire along with three others. I decided to let them continue to think that. I figured my obligation to the Legion was finished, and I made my way to Tangiers, where I worked on the docks until I had enough money for passage to London."

"And that's why you came back? To find Gaston and punish him?"

"To find who *sent* Gaston," he said grimly. "And punish them both."

The Tizi-n-Tichka Pass was a natural cut in the mountain range that divided Morocco's fertile west from its parched and arid east. To the west lay forests of Atlas cedar, pine, and holm-oak, interspersed with stony pastures and thickets of thorny vegetation; to the east, nothing but wind-scoured red rock, dry, craggy hills, and increasing drifts of sand. Moisture from the spare snowfall on the east side was channeled down the mountains into narrow wadis that became patchy ribbons of green extending into the edge of the desert.

Passage through the pass and access to the resources of the eastern wadis were controlled by Berber warlords with blood ties to the Sultan of Marrakech. Gifts to the chieftain were the preferred route to obtaining passage but, lacking more impressive offerings, simple coin worked just as well.

The tents of the settlement matched the brown and gray of the granite surrounding the pass, and were closed and battened against the capricious winds. The only inhabitants visible were a few men in traditional robes and striped turbans who carried military issue carbines, and directed them to the corrals and sheds for animals.

While Smith and Abigail purchased feed and stabling for their animals, Haffe went ahead to the chieftain's tent to make inquiries. By the time Smith and Abigail caught up, he had the guards outside the main entrance smiling and pocketing tobacco he had doled out for the information he received.

He advised Smith and Abigail on the protocol for their "gift" to the chieftain, Barek, and agreed to speak and translate for them. Inside they were met by hard-eyed youths who took their cloaks and insisted they change from their boots into soft yellow leather slippers before ushering them inside.

The interior room of the enormous tent was as colorful and exotic as the exterior was drab. The floors were covered with intricately patterned wool rugs and the walls were hung with silk and velvet curtains and artistic weavings with rich brocade borders. The open center of the floor was ringed by a low, circular banquette strewn with colorful pillows, and the air was heavy with the scents of lamp oil, tobacco smoke, and sandalwood.

A number of men in simple robes and vividly striped turbans were clustered into groups, conversing and smoking water pipes. They looked up, then went back to their conversation—until they spotted Abigail walking behind the two men. A Western woman. Their interest was piqued. A number migrated toward the chieftain's chair to scrutinize the proceedings.

Barek himself was a large, portly man of indeterminate age, sporting a huge multicolored turban, a nattily trimmed black beard, and a great gold earring in one ear. He assessed them as Haffe and Smith bowed. When Haffe introduced Smith, whatever he said caused the chieftain's eyes to widen and the men behind him to whisper.

Abigail's previous experience with Berber clansmen caused her to tense as the men stared at her and commented openly on what they saw. She was so distracted by self-consciousness that she didn't realize she hadn't been introduced until after they were seated near the chieftain. But it was clear the chieftain had taken note of her; when they were served a drink of something and fermented honey, Barek watched her sample the strongly alcoholic drink with surprise and smiled behind a heavily ringed hand.

After a time, Barek turned to a gaunt, granite-faced man on his right and began to ask questions, which were repeated verbatim to Haffe. Haffe, who had remained on his feet, bowed as he answered and seemed surprisingly at ease. Several words Abigail recognized came up in Haffe's report, which he paused periodically to paraphrase for them.

They were noble and important emissaries, Haffe told their host. From a great palace called the British Museum that a dead prince had bequeathed to Abigail . . . but which was missing some precious scrolls . . . without which the Queen of England's lands could not prosper for much longer.

Abigail tried not to let her dismay show as she leaned close to Smith to whisper: "He's telling a pack of—"

"Details the chieftain wants to hear," Smith muttered, for her ears alone. "It's not wise in this land to be too modest. Nor is it wise to assume that people don't understand you simply because you hear them speaking a different tongue."

Two pairs of young women entered, one carrying large trays of food to place in the center of the gathering, and the second carrying an elongated brass pitcher of hot water, a basin, and toweling to the three visitors. Abigail, following Smith's lead, washed and dried her hands. But when the women came to Haffe, he sat motionless, staring fixedly at one of them, who smiled and lowered her eyes at his reaction. When he extended his hands over the basin, she caught his gaze as she poured water over them and her expression changed. Her expressive eyes widened then softened and soon she was oblivious to the water pouring over the pillows beside him.

The chief's advisor barked out a sharp rebuke and an older woman came rushing in to scold the girl and shoo her out a side entrance. Haffe protested that it was his fault and offered to take whatever punishment might be dealt her . . . making Barek and his men, who had seen the exchange, laugh. Haffe reddened sharply and seemed both chastened and relieved by the advisor's response.

"She ees . . . daughter of Barek's sister," he reported to Abigail and Smith. "She will not be beaten."

They were invited by a wave of Barek's hand to partake of the food and as they ate of the fruits, nuts, dolmas, and breads, the chieftain directed a question to them, which Haffe quickly translated.

"He says . . . what is written . . . in scrolls? Ma-gic? Treasure?"

"No treasure. Just writings." Abigail ignored Smith's attempt to glare her into silence. "Probably a history of Greek and Egyptian times and events . . . stories of the past."

Haffe turned back and rattled off some things in Berber that caused the chieftain to look delighted indeed. He gave an emphatic order, waved to the others to give attention, and settled back onto his cushions with an expectant gaze.

When Haffe turned to them, the smile on his face couldn't cover his anxiety.

"He wish . . . hear . . . theese stories. Now."

"Of course," Smith said clamping off her protest with a timely hand tightening on her arm. "Miss Merchant here has lots of stories, don't you, Miss Merchant." He leaned toward her and whispered: "Tell 'em a damned story."

"I—I don't know any stories," she shot back, struggling to keep her voice down and expression neutral. "My worst grades in library school were in children's literature and storytime."

"Tell a Bible story—Noah and the Ark or something. Count yourself lucky. He could have demanded to see you *dance*."

She grabbed Smith's honey drink and finished it in one gulp before rising and giving an elaborate curtsy to Barek, who watched her with a wry expression.

"A story is told of a great man of long ago named Jacob," she began. "He had many sons . . . twelve, to be exact." When Haffe translated her words, sounds of approval swept the tent. "Jacob was also very rich among his people . . . had great herds and flocks. All in his possession and within his reach prospered." Prosperity. Barek looked very pleased and the men seated on cushions around the tent nodded and muttered amongst themselves

"Though the man had many sons, he loved one above all the rest. This son's name was Joseph. He was handsome and quick-witted." She tapped her temple with a canny look. "It was said he even knew how to interpret dreams.

"Now, Jacob favored young Joseph in all things. To show his love, he had a beautiful striped coat of many colors made and gave it to Joseph to wear." Here, frowns and scowls appeared on one side of the circular banquette. "The favored son wore it proudly and even flaunted it before his brothers." She pantomimed donning a coat and opening it and showing it off with a smug expression. The scowls grew to murmurs, which grew to rumbles of disapproval. "Joseph told his brothers that in one of his dreams, all of his brothers bowed down before him to pay him homage. His brothers knew that Joseph claimed to see the future in his dreams and grew even more jealous and resentful. They began to plot against their father's favorite son."

The excitement that shot through the men of the chieftain's council let her know she had struck a nerve and, heartened, she began to put her all into the telling. She had never held an audience so rapt with a story before!

"But Joseph was young and ignorant of the wickedness that can creep into a man's deprived and aching heart. He didn't heed the warning in his brothers' anger. One day while they were in the fields together, tending their flocks, the brothers seized Joseph, bound him, and sold him into a caravan headed for Egypt." There were gasps of outrage and mutters as glares flew back and forth across the tent. "Then the brothers killed a lamb and smeared its blood on the beautiful striped coat they hated so much. They carried that coat to their father and told him that Joseph had been attacked by a wild animal and carried off. Jacob was grieved and cried out to the heavens."

Dark looks gave way to shaking fists and Barek leaned forward, as tense and unsettled as the others. She felt Smith's hand on her arm, but shook it off, absorbed in the dark looks Barek was giving his men . . . assuming he was annoyed that they were interfering with his enjoyment of the story.

When she got to the part where Joseph was bought by an important official in pharaoh's household and then wrongly accused by the wife of his owner, tensions simmering in the tent erupted.

Blades hummed as they cleared sheaths, and Barek's guards bolted for the chieftain's side with weapons drawn. Barek shot to his feet in a ring of armed guards, roaring orders. In the conflict and confusion, Abigail and Smith were seized and dragged bodily from the tent.

Despite valiant resistance, they were bound hand and foot and left on the ground in a dark tent, against a pole, back to back. She could scarcely get her breath and her hands were beginning to throb from the tightness of the ropes binding her wrists. His battered mouth was stinging and he suffered a sharp pain in his right side whenever he drew a deep breath.

"The story of Joseph?" he said on a groan.

"It's a pivotal narrative in the Old Testament and the Torah"—hurting, frightened, and miserable, she was in no mood for a critique of her storytelling—"and is revered by two of the world's great religions."

"Neither of which is likely to be appreciated in a Berber chieftain's tent."

"Well, it was *you* who said I should tell a Bible story," she snapped. "I said I wasn't any good at it!"

"How was I supposed to know you were *right*?" he grumbled.

She clamped her mouth shut, refusing to waste energy on a response, and turned her attention to their surroundings. Around them, she could just make out stacks of crates, barrels, and bags of what smelled like grain. Outside she heard furious cries, the sound of horses, and the sharp retorts of guns. The silence that settled after that brief surge of violence weighted the darkness so that it soon became claustrophobic.

"This has to be some kind of record," he said, breaking the oppressive quiet. "A woman nearly beheaded by two separate Berber tribes in one week."

"What do you think they'll do with us?" she asked, feeling a little sick from both the honey-wine and the situation.

"Gut us and drape us over a spit, most likely. Roasted infidel."

"Can't you be serious for one minute?" she demanded, hoping to hide the tremor in her voice. "We're in real trouble here."

"Just like these hotheaded Berbers to stuff us away without gagging us." He groaned. "Now I have to listen to endless hours of 'This-is-all-your-bloody-fault.' Leave it to old Barek to devise a torture worse than being roasted alive."

After the urge to throttle him passed, she realized there had been a peculiar thickness to his voice as he trivialized their predicament, and her indignation began to dissolve. His insolence was purposeful. He was keeping his spirits up. And hers. Legionnaire style. Spitting in the face of danger. Suddenly the situation didn't seem quite so bleak.

Then she felt his fingers groping for hers and latched on to them as if she were drowning and they were a life preserver.

At his suggestion, she laid her head back against the pole and tried to get what rest she could. It was difficult; her thoughts kept roiling.

"What about Haffe? You think he got away?"

"I didn't see him in the melee, and he's not here with us. Maybe he did." After a few minutes, he looked over his shoulder at her. "I don't think they'll do anything to us before Barek has a chance to question us. Even in these remote reaches, he can't just execute two Westerners on a whim."

"I don't understand. What did I say to make them all so furious?"

"Good God, woman, did you not see the stripes on their turbans? You were telling a story about a rich nomadic lord in the tent of a rich nomadic lord. Barek would naturally assume you were talking about him. Five will get you fifty that he has a lot of sons. And if he has a lot of sons from several competing wives, there's probably a helluva lot of rivalry. And you've seen how possessive and hot-tempered Berbers can be."

She groaned. "We're dead."

"Not yet," he said with a chuckle. "I refuse to die until I get my hands on the book that taught you to kiss like that."

Her heart lurched and quivered before resuming it's usual rhythm.

"What makes you think there's a book involved," she said tartly.

"With you, sweetheart"—she could hear the smile in his voice—"there's *always* a book involved."

Deep into that long night, as they slumped against the pole and dozed fitfully, a heavily cloaked figure slipped under the rear of the tent, paused, and then made his way toward the captives using the stored crates and bags for cover.

Something—a rasp of sand underfoot or a stir of air—caused Abigail to come awake with a start. She held her breath and her heart paused as she scanned the darkness for what had triggered her sense of alarm. The merest whisper of a sound both confirmed her suspicion and started her heart pounding. Someone was in the tent. Someone who hadn't come through the main opening.

In a heartbeat, a chilling host of possibilities visited her . . . warring sons . . . jealous mothers . . . angry tribesmen . . . not to mention the vengeful Gaston and his Legionnaires. . . .

An amorphous dark shape materialized from a stack of nearby barrels, moving steadily toward them. In the dimness she caught a dull glint of reflected light . . . long and smooth . . . a knife!

She sucked a breath to scream and the intruder lunged for her in the same heartbeat.

Eighteen

"No, no, Merchant ma'am—meee!" A frantic whisper came through her panic just as Smith rolled to his knees and launched himself into the little Berber's side, knocking him to the ground.

"No—it's Haffe!" she cried softly.

"Haffe?" Smith groaned as he rolled closer to the invader to see for himself. "Dammit, man—you better have brought a knife."

Moments later Haffe had cut their ropes and, as they rubbed feeling back into their constricted limbs, led them to the rear of the tent. He fell to his knees and peeked under the tent wall to see if the way was clear, then quickly scrambled outside and held the bottom of the tent for them. They followed one at a time and were soon sliding between the skin and canvas walls of closely packed tents. As they neared the cliffs behind the tent settlement, they had to flatten against a sheer rock face and edge sideways. At the end of that passage was a sheltered opening where three horses and two well-laden mules stood waiting.

As they approached, a diminutive cloaked figure stepped out of the darkness and joined Haffe. Abigail was shocked at first to see it was a woman, then not-so-shocked to realize it was the young woman who had traded gazes with Haffe in the chieftain's tent.

"Joleef." Haffe introduced her. "She help."

The girl produced two pairs of English-style boots from beneath her cloak and smiled.

Soon they were in their own boots again and staring at the sheer cliffs that formed the pass itself and at four armed guards crouched around a campfire in the middle of it. They had little chance of making it past the guards. And even if they managed to get through, the road beyond hugged the mountain in clear sight and easy rifle range for two hundred yards.

What they needed, Smith said grimly, was a diversion. Haffe exchanged whispers and a tentative handclasp with Joleef . . . who whirled and began to run quietly toward the road leading into the main pass, her cloak billowing. Seconds later, she started to scream and run up the road toward the pass.

The guards bolted up, searching the darkness, and spotted her. Three pulled their rifles from their shoulders and rushed to investigate, leaving the fourth reaching for the gun he had propped against the rocks nearby. Just before the men reached her, Joleef turned sharply toward the center of the camp, screaming and drawing the soldiers after her.

In the brief interval before the camp sprang to life, Smith, Abigail, and Haffe mounted up and dug in their heels to charge the remaining guard.

Startled by onrushing horses, the man jolted back against the rock and lost his grip on his rifle. By the time he recovered, located the gun, and fired at them, they were well along the narrow track around the mountain and his adrenalin-racked aim missed them by a mile.

The path on the east side of the pass fell steeply along the mountainside, but the knowledge that they would soon be pursued drove them to a reckless pace. At the first curve it felt as if they might go plunging over the edge of a cliff, and at the next straight section the path narrowed and the horses slid and stumbled on loose rock.

Haffe went first on his Arabian-Barb and after the first harried curves, the mules' surefootedness began to steady the horses. By the time they reached the second major switchback, both horses and riders were moving with greater assurance.

But not for long.

The sharp retort of rifles sent them barreling down the road, through crevasses of wind-scoured red rock and along narrow drops that made Abigail close her eyes and Smith curse under his breath. Dawn found them lowering into the foothills with Barek's men still in pursuit.

With richer air and surer footing, they began to run for the ribbon of green that would lead them to the oasis village of Ouarzazate. The horses, which had displayed their fearless Barb heritage on the perilous mountain tracks, now proved their Arabian blood by stretching out to cover ground with an air of release. The mules had difficult keeping up at first, but soon were pounding along doggedly after the horses.

The sun was overhead when they paused on the brow of a craggy hill to look back and spotted their pursuers arrayed above them on the rim of a cliff.

"They've stopped!" Abigail panted. "Why?"

"Who cares why," Smith said, shading his eyes. "They *stopped*."

"Lands of brother," Haffe declared with authority. "Barek not welcome."

Just as the relief of that registered and Abigail closed her eyes with a murmur of gratitude, she heard Smith's "What the devil?" and snapped back to the edge of her nerves.

Far above on the cliff, Barek's men remained poised and still, but someone or something was moving at their backs and heading down the winding track. Another minute passed before Smith and Abigail could make out splashes of white over patches of khaki. Uniforms. White hats—kepis—like those worn by Legionnaires.

"Dammit!" Smith swore. "No Legionnaire patrol would give chase at a chieftain's command—if they're coming after us, it's because they were already after us! It's Gaston and his cutthroats."

Without another word, he reined his horse around and dug in his heels. Abigail followed suit and once again they were racing across the rocky hills, headed for the trickle of green visible on the northeastern horizon.

They rode hard through the heat of the day, pushing their horses, knowing that there was no relief to be had except in the river valley that carried life-giving water down from the mountains. There they could find shade, water, and most importantly, cover.

The grueling pace seemed to have paid off that evening, when they stopped at a grove of palms outside a dusty village in the Draa Valley. They hadn't seen their pursuers in hours and had to gamble that Gaston and his men were as exhausted as they were and would have to stop as well. The sun was fully set and the dry air had began to take on a desert chill before they stopped to make a fireless camp. They drew water for the horses, ate food from their supplies, and wrapped up in their burnooses to settle down for the night.

As she tried to make herself comfortable propped against a date palm, Abigail couldn't help thinking about how narrowly they'd escaped . . . and about the young woman who had helped Haffe and made their freedom possible.

"That young woman . . . Joleef . . ." she said to Haffe, "she took a great risk in helping us."

He nodded with a smile that quickly faded. "Barek take to Imilchil." When asked what he meant, he reverted to French and Smith had to translate.

"Imilchil apparently is a marriage fair. Berber clans from all over come to find brides and make family connections. As Barek's niece, the girl is valuable for making ties. Barek intends to take her to the fair and arrange a marriage for her and an alliance for himself."

"Need camels. Soon." Determination filled Haffe's cherubic face as he pointed emphatically to the ground. "Find treasure. Fast."

She stared at him for a moment, her stomach sinking at the thought that he was depending on the riches of her "treasure" to help him win his much-anticipated bride. She turned to Smith with a muted glare.

"See what you've done."

Halfway through the next day they reached the first village and joined a number of other travelers watering their animals . . . including a small caravan that had stopped to take on water. As Smith and Haffe filled their canteens and water skins, Haffe talked with the camel drivers and learned they were bypassing Ouarzazate to head directly south. Seeing an opportunity, Smith spoke with the leader, a merchant named Abu Denaii, about joining the caravan to travel toward the southern oases and the route to Timbuktu. Denaii was a leathery, hard-eyed trader who quickly named an exorbitant sum for such a service. After spirited negotiation, pointing out that they had their own animals and water and would not slow the others down, Smith and Haffe got him down to a reasonable price.

"We're doing what?" Abigail said, coming wide awake from a doze of exhaustion and batting away gnats that swarmed everything that moved.

"This makes sense, Boston," Smith declared. "If we travel with them, their camels will obliterate our tracks and Gaston will go on to Ouarzazate and search for two days before realizing we never arrived there."

She handed over the money and they left the comforts of the wadi an hour later, setting off to the south in the company of two dozen heavily laden camels.

The terrain changed the instant they crested the edge of

the river valley. Beyond lay sections of dry, stony ground that alternated with drifts of sand rippled by the wind. As they settled into a steady pace, the sway of the camels ahead and behind became lulling. The temptation to close her eyes and sleep was almost overwhelming for Abigail, until Smith said they needed to abandon their hats in favor of turbans because they needed to look more like Berber traders.

She spent the better part of the next hour learning to twist and tie a turban, and as irksome and tedious as that was, the reaction of the camel drivers to her attempts was worse. They snickered and guffawed and occasionally called advice to Haffe, who persisted despite their derision. Lacking a mirror, she had to trust him when he said her final attempt was adequate. But the way Smith chewed his lip when he looked at her gave her no confidence in her newly acquired skill.

It was when she put on her burnoose for protection from the sun that the muttering among the men of the caravan went from teasing to the edge of taunting. Her donning of a predominantly male garment marked her too clearly as a foreigner and infidel. Smith told her to ignore it; women in the desert also wore them for protection from the sun. But she began to feel a familiar dread when the men untucked the ends of their turbans and drew them down over their faces . . . veiling themselves against her eyes.

That night, Smith and Haffe made their camp apart from the others and, knowing desert custom, Smith made a point of inviting Abu Denaii to sample the hospitality of their fireside. However, the merchant arrived with a bottle of whiskey and insisted they join him in a drink. Abigail declined and withdrew to sit by the fire with T. Thaddeus's journals, unsettled by the fact that Denaii—part Arab and part Berber, ostensibly Muslim—carried alcohol with him and drank it freely. When she looked up from reading, she caught Haffe scowling at Denaii across the flames. He, too, was uncomfortable that the chief trader was not a good Muslim. In this part of the world, a man who was faithless to his religion could not be considered trustworthy in anything else.

Despite her uneasiness, she managed to fall asleep and had to be shaken awake the next morning. The camel drivers were mostly packed and ready to travel, but Denaii was shouting and snarling orders at them, holding his head.

The sun grew stronger and hotter as the day progressed. The rocky soil disappeared altogether and beneath their feet, the base of sand deepened. By midday they shed their burnooses for lighter *jellabas*, but kept their turbans, which shaded their eyes and kept their heads surprisingly cool.

When they crested a rise and glimpsed the seemingly endless sea of dunes around them, Abigail caught her breath. Here, at last, was the desert she had come to search. Her heart pounded as she began to go over and over in her head the professor's accounts of visitors to the library.

"South of the last oasis, the land becomes sea," he had written. "Neither bird nor beast calls it home, for there is no sustenance to be taken from its depths. The sun pierces your bones . . . illuminating your darkest secrets, sorting your desires . . . measuring your will . . . even your will to live. And it decrees, based on its own relentless test: This one is strong enough . . . that one will perish. . . ."

She had thought he must have been a little delirious from the heat to resort to such melodrama, but she saw now the overwhelming vastness and desolation that had generated such musings in him. And she also saw why the professor had been forced to abandon his final expedition: He simply hadn't the stamina for such a grueling undertaking.

As midday passed and the sun shone in their eyes, Smith pulled out their wire-mesh goggles. The contraptions screened out—literally—much of the brightness and kept them from going sunblind. Her lips dried, but licking them only seemed to make them dry faster. She thought of the beeswax balm deep in the bowels of a bag somewhere. A lot of good it did her there.

Her gaze was drawn to Smith, who looked exotic in his robes and turban, and strangely at home in the desert. These last few days had been no less than a revelation regarding the man inside him. He'd had plenty of chances to throw up his hands and abandon her to her ignorance and stubbornness. Heaven knew . . . he'd had plenty of provocation, too.

But he hadn't left. He'd given her the benefit of his experience with the brutal extremes of mountain and desert. She reached up to feel the goggles she wore. From the start he had known what sort of hardships she would face and tried to warn and even protect her. In the end, he had decided to take her himself . . . despite the sun and heat and sand and scorpions . . . despite vengeful Legionnaires and plots to make him conform to the official record of him. Somebody wanted him dead, and he was out here in the blistering desert helping her look for a semimythical pile of papyrus.

She shook her head and prayed there would be something of value at the end of this eventful journey for them both.

A shaggy brown dot appeared on the horizon that evening, and as they approached, it grew into an uninhabited oasis that jutted out into the sand from a larger ridge of solid land that ran to the west for a distance before submerging back into the sands. A low stone wall and pole hoist were visible beneath clusters of palms and the animals, sensing water ahead, picked up their heads and their pace. There was daylight left, but Denaii told Haffe and Smith he knew the country well and this was the last good water for a hundred miles. They would camp early and get extra rest before continuing.

Since there was no grass to harbor scorpions, Abigail

made a pallet on the ground by the fire and pulled out her map, her journals, and the astrolabe.

"Hey—there's still some light." Smith scooped up the astrolabe as he returned from unloading and watering their mounts, and he headed for the top of a nearby dune. "May as well get in some practice."

He was back soon with a pensive scowl. "Well I can still read the angles, but it doesn't mean much unless you have a map or chart as reference."

"I do have a regular map the professor used . . . it has grid coordinates in mostly empty space. I've tried to compare it with the one the professor drew. . . ." She spread both out between them, giving him a chance to study them firsthand. "I can see now why neither map includes many features. There's nothing out here to represent." She pointed to the professor's cryptic drawings. "There's Ouarzazate. But, we headed south before reaching it . . . perhaps along this route. Is it just me, or do those little figures look like camels?"

But Smith was focused on the oddly ornate compass rose T. Thaddeus had drawn in the lower right corner of the map. It contained a ring of Greek letters at the center in addition to the customary flowers and star points and was far more intricate that the rest of the map.

"Is it possible that he used this compass rose to mark a destination as much as direction?" he asked, pulling the lamp closer. Then he pointed to what appeared to be a gap in the arc of the compass. "And what happened there?"

She squinted to study the notch he indicated.

"I don't know. It doesn't seem to have been erased." She looked up at Smith. "He must have spent hours drawing that. More time than all the rest of the map put together. Why would he leave one ray of the compass empty?"

"He was an eccentric old cod, that's why. He used an astrolabe, for God's sake. Who uses such a thing these days? Present company excepted."

"Do you think you can use it well enough to help us find the library?"

He picked up the central disk of the astrolabe and studied the engravings . . . arabesque designs and sinuous curves that resembled . . . "Hey . . . does that look like script to you?" He handed it to her.

She rose and held up into the fading sunlight. "A bit. Elongated like waves . . . looks like Arabic. . . ." She straightened, rethinking it. "Or *Greek*." She traced the letters with her finger. Alpha . . . pi . . . that looks like an omicron . . . that one resembles a lambda. . . ." She scowled and pressed fingers to the inner corners of her eyes. "No, no. I'm probably just reading things into it."

"Like what?" He leaned closer to stare at the disk. "What do you see?"

She looked up at him through her lashes. "I think they're the Greek letters A . . . P . . . O . . . L . . . L . . . and O."

He looked straight into her eyes. "That's me."

The shiver that ran through her raised gooseflesh all over her body.

"Don't be ridiculous." Her disclaimer was aimed at her own reaction, as much as his. "It's a old brass disk used to determine position from the angle of the sun. Of course they'd refer to the Greek sun god, Apollo. Half of the round objects unearthed around the Mediterranean have Apollo's name on them."

"Yeah? Well, I happen to be *touching* this one." He pulled the disk from her hands and tossed it onto the map. "And I actually know how to use it." He edged closer and his mouth quirked up on one side. "I'm going to find your library for you, Boston. You're going to owe me . . . *big*."

She refused to retreat. The warmth of his breath on her lips was too much of a challenge. Or a promise.

"You help me find the library, Smith," she said, drinking him in like a potent elixir, "and I'll pay you . . . *big*."

His laugh was low and provocative and climbed inside her skin as he glanced down her front. But his gaze caught on the astrolabe lying on the map, and he drew back so abruptly that she felt the air being pulled from her.

"Wha-at's the matter?" she asked, watching him move the central disk of the astrolabe over the drawing of the compass rose.

"That notch on the compass"—he pointed to an unnoticed similarity—"there's one almost like it on the disk of the astrolabe."

When he placed the brass disk over the compass rose and turned it, sure enough the notches aligned.

"What does it mean?" she asked, frowning at it.

"It means . . . we have an angle, Boston." He traced the angle between the map's North and the compass notch, and grinned. "The old boy gave us a direction after all. Midday tomorrow, I'll take a reading and chart a course for your library."

Reassured, she poured over her map and journals, translating by lantern light. Later, after having a bite to eat, she curled up inside her burnoose and fell immediately asleep . . . so, did not see Smith stretch out on his blanket beside her, nor did she see him bolt upright later and sit listening in the darkness.

He drew his knife and crept to the palm trees where their horses were tied. There he watched and listened, nerves straining to detect what he thought was a voice. Then he spotted a lone figure walking along the top of the nearby rock ledge and climbing down it to head for the caravan camp. When the figure reached Denaii's camel, he delved into the saddlebags and drew out a whiskey bottle. It was the head man himself. He returned to the canvas shelter his men erected for him each night and sank onto his pallet with an audible groan.

Smith watched and listened a bit longer, telling himself that the trader had probably just been answering nature's call. Everything else seemed quiet . . . even the camels. Rolling the anxiety from his shoulders, he returned to his own blanket and fell asleep like he was falling off a cliff.

It seemed he had no sooner closed his eyes than he was

struggling back toward consciousness with inexplicable urgency.

Something was wrong. He lurched up with his heart pounding and found Abigail and Haffe still sleeping and their horses and mules still tied to the line he had strung between palms. Their cache of supplies appeared to be untouched. The only cause for alarm seemed to be the fact that the sun was already well above the horizon and it was unnaturally quiet.

He shoved to his feet and looked toward the caravan camp.

It was empty. Abandoned. Lock, stock, and camel.

He rushed to the cold remains of the fire the drivers had sat around the night before, then went over the area where they had bedded down the camels, finding only churned sand and camel dung. Denaii and his drivers had packed up quietly and stolen away like the proverbial thieves-in-the-night. He climbed the rock ledge and scanned the dunes to the south for sight of them. A tiny fleck on the horizon might or might not have been them before it disappeared.

Uttering a few choice oaths, he stalked back to their camp and dropped to one knee to give Abigail's shoulder a shake.

"Wake up, Boston," he said. "We've got trouble."

Nineteen

"The trader and his camels are gone," the tall, rail-thin Legionnaire known as Schuller reported as he flung himself over the crest of a tall dune and onto his belly beside his sergeant. "It is only Smith, the woman, and the servant."

Gaston grunted a laugh, baring teeth misshapen from decay.

"Take a lesson," he said to the men lying on their bellies along that slope, cradling their rifles across their arms. "These Berbers are fools for the clink of silver. Always eager to strike a deal . . . even if it means reneging on one they've already struck."

Garnering sly nods and looks of appreciation from his men, Gaston considered his next move carefully. LaCroix's orders were to track the pair and to watch and wait until they had whatever it was the Merchant woman sought. But LaCroix was a fool. Anything Smith could do, a squad of Legionnaires could do better . . . including persuading a nubile young female to yield up the location of the valuables she hunted. The thought of "persuading" her repeatedly sent a shaft of heat through his loins.

Then his mind went back to the slippery nature of his prime quarry. Every minute Smith stayed alive was another minute Fate might decide to yank him from Gaston's grip yet again. And he did not intend to allow that to happen.

Apollo Smith was going to die today, whether he had the pleasure of killing him personally, or not.

"Check your lead," he ordered and took satisfaction in how quickly his men obeyed. "You have one target: the Englishman, Smith. I want the woman and the animals untouched. We will have use for them later."

Gaston sent half of his eight men around the rock outcropping in a flanking maneuver. When that contingent reached the ridge and began to climb, he motioned the rest over the peak of the dune with him. They kept silent as they started down toward the oasis, counting on the element of surprise. It was habit more than strategy, for at this range—and with odds of nine-to-one—the outcome was all but assured.

Abigail was draping her burnoose across the back of the saddle, and contemplating retying her turban . . . which seemed to have loosened as she slept on it. Who could have imagined that a turban would double so effectively as a pillow and save her from a serious crick in the—

Her gaze snagged on movement at the top of a large dune, not far away. Her eyes widened and for a fraction of a second she was struck dumb with horror. The movement took form . . . *human* . . . moving stealthily.

"L-Legionnaires!" Her shout set Smith crouching and pivoting—drawing his revolver.

"Take cover!" he thundered while ducking behind the nearest palm. He got off several shots that sent the Legionnaires diving onto their bellies, then glanced back at Abigail. Her head was still clearly visible among the horses. "Forget cover—get out of here!"

"Not without you!" She found her gun in her saddlebag

and searched blindly with her fingers for the extra bullets she had emptied from her skirt pocket because she always managed to roll over on them in her sleep.

From the rock ledge came another volley of shots that whined past or cracked into the palms around her. Cradling her gun with both hands and stiffening her arms, she pulled back the hammer and squeezed the trigger . . . once, twice . . . more. Her bullets gouged out stone chips all over the ledge, but at least they kept that contingent from returning fire for a few critical moments.

"They're on foot! Mount up and ride!" Smith yelled to her.

"Only if you do!" She broke open her gun, dumped the hot, spent cartridges, and loaded new rounds with shaking hands, vowing to actually aim at something this time. Her ears were ringing and the smell of burned gunpowder stung her nose. When Smith's gun was empty, Haffe pulled the rifle from Smith's saddle and threw it to him.

When Smith's firing halted, the contingent on the dune lurched up and charged and a second group dropped over the rock ledge in a flanking maneuver. Abigail jammed her boot into the stirrup and swung herself up onto her horse. Haffe was already mounted and crouching low in his saddle as he grabbed the mules' lead reins and bolted for the desert. She looked back to call to Smith and found him trapped behind that tree. Instinctively, she bent low in the saddle, pointed her gun, and fired at the Legionnaires rushing him. Two of them dropped to the ground and the others crouched to make themselves smaller targets. She could hear Gaston cursing and ordering them on, but that short delay had already allowed Smith to reach his horse.

"Go!" he shouted at Abigail, kicking his frantic mount into motion.

Abigail's horse reared slightly, then exploded under her and shot out across the sands after Haffe.

Gunfire exploded at their backs, but with every wild heartbeat they were yards closer to being out of range. Then she spotted the nose of Smith's horse at the edge of her vision and put all of her energy into catching up with Haffe. The shooting stopped as they raced away, but unless they quickly put miles between themselves and Gaston, all they had done was delay the inevitable.

They rode as fast as their horses hearts and the shifting sands would allow. It wasn't long before she learned to ride the troughs between dunes and when necessary, ride straight down the side of one instead of angling across it. The wind rose steadily. Her heart pounded and her lungs burned; her eyes felt gritty from the swirling dust. After a time they had to slow the pace and bring the loose ends of their turbans down across their faces in order to breathe, but they rode doggedly, heading south into a rising wind and worsening weather.

By midafternoon strong winds had begun to kick up loose sand that pelted them like rain. The horses lowered their heads and pushed on, fighting for every step in the swirling sands that battered their legs Haffe finally turned back to shout above the wind that they needed to take shelter and Abigail followed the alarm in his eyes to Smith, who was slumped in his saddle, looking as if he might be blown off at any minute.

She called to him and got no response. Dismounting, she hurried to help Haffe drag him from his saddle. There was a blackened gouge in his turban and a grisly red flow of blood down the side of his head.

"Smith!" She shook his shoulders and pressed an ear tight to his chest to listen for a heartbeat, reporting to Haffe: "He's alive, but we have to find out how badly he's hurt."

The little Berber nodded and quickly retrieved the large canvas tarp from the mules to fashion a surprisingly effective lean-to against the side of a dune. Together they dragged Smith into it, and she quickly determined the blood had come from a single head wound. Bracing for the worst, she removed his turban and found a slash along the side of his head that ended on his forehead just above his patch-covered eye.

"Water . . . and my medical kit . . . from the bag with the lock on it," she shouted to Haffe above the wind. He nodded and left to retrieve them.

"You'd better not quit on me, Apollo Smith," she whispered, fighting the grip of panic on her throat. "We've got miles to go, you and me. Don't you dare die on me."

Steeling herself, she removed his eye patch and was surprised to find he seemed to still have an eye beneath a scarred eyelid. It didn't look so bad . . . she gently pushed open the lid and found a relatively normal looking sclera and iris inside. There were probably a number of ways to be blind if your eye was . . .

Just then, Haffe arrived with her medical kit and a lantern and she hastily lowered the eye patch and set to work removing Smith's upper garments and laying out the contents of her dispensary. She tore strips from his turban and wetted one of them to swab the blood from his wound . . . while trying to recall what she'd read about stitching lacerations. *Dr. Parker's Home Physician . . . Medicine . . . the 615's.* It was a long furrow of an abrasion, and as she cleaned it thoroughly with the stinging American antiseptic, Listerine, that she had brought from Boston, she thought he registered a bit of discomfort.

"Head wounds bleed a lot. Maybe it looks worse than it is," she said, mostly to herself. "We'll have to keep it clean and bandaged, and hope for the best." She placed gauze over the wound and secured it with strips of his turban.

The wind intensified, sometimes rumbling like a distant locomotive, sometimes howling like a wounded animal. Sand pelted the tarp and invaded every vulnerable pore of the oiled cloth and every unsecured crack and opening. They could literally taste dust. Their only consolation was that Gaston and his men were caught in the same storm and were probably faring no better.

"The horses!" She looked to Haffe, whose eyes were big and bright in the dimness of their battered shelter.

"Horses smart," he said, tapping his temple. She glimpsed a flash of large white teeth. "Close eyes. Arse to wind." His confidence in the animals' survival instincts allowed that worry to fade.

Then the meager daylight began to go. In the closing darkness she listened anxiously to Smith's breathing and wondered if she were somehow marked for disaster. She'd never felt so alone or so vulnerable . . . adrift on an ocean of sand . . . at the mercy of raging forces of nature.

With a lump developing in her throat, she threaded her fingers through Smith's and closed her eyes, praying that her longing and determination would somehow travel through the warmth of that contact to call him back to her.

"I need you, Smith. Wake up. Please," she whispered, trying not to think about what would happen if he didn't. She looked at Haffe, unable to hide her desperation. "I can't do any more for him. When the storm breaks, we'll have to turn back to Ouarzazate and get him some help."

Haffe nodded gravely and extended a hand . . . almost patting her arm before remembering himself.

"Rest, Merchant ma'am." He gave her a wan little smile. "I watch."

Nodding miserably, she curled up beside Smith and listened anxiously for each of Smith's ragged breaths until fatigue claimed her. The darkness softened and the roar of the wind gradually faded in her consciousness.

It seemed like mere minutes later that she awakened with a start to a strange, dusky light coming from the opening at the front of the shelter. Haffe was gone and she crawled over to the canvas opening to look for him. Through the haze of dust she could see him swathed and bent against the wind, leading the horses and mules back toward the shelter. Though caked with dirt, the animals appeared to have weathered the sandstorm with no ill effects. She drew back inside and checked Smith, finding him still unresponsive.

"Come on, Apollo," she whispered, wishing she could will some of her strength and health into him "Wake up." On impulse she bent to brush his lips with hers and stroked his cheek. "Please, wake up."

Moments later Haffe scuttled into the shelter with a bag of food and two canteens. Hunger was the farthest thing from her mind, but at his urging, she made herself eat some of the flatbread and wash it down with water.

"How long do you think it will be before the wind dies enough for us to go on?" she asked, unsure just how much of it he understood.

"Sand cut. Like knife." He shook his head. "Stay here."

"But we have to get him to better shelter and some proper medical treatment. He could be dying—"

Smith groaned and for the first time in hours, moved of his own volition.

"W-who's"—his voice rasped as he turned his head slightly—"dying?"

"Smith?" She lurched over him and grabbed him by the shoulders. "Oh, thank God." His half-focused gaze caused relief to erupt in her, making it hard to breathe for a moment. She stiffened and blinked until a potentially cata-strophic wave of emotion subsided. "We thought you were—how are you feeling? Can you move? Can you see? How many fingers am I holding up?"

"I can see well enough to know you're not holding up any. My head hurts." He explored his bandaged temple, and his hand stopped abruptly on the part of the bandage just above his eye patch. "How bad is it?"

"Now that you're awake and back to being 'SOS Smith,' I'd say it's probably not so bad." She kept him from his bandage. "A bullet grazed your head and you lost some blood. Then we ran into a storm. We're waiting for the wind to die down so we can take you back to Ouarza-zate."

"Why Ouarzazate?" He moved his limbs stiffly, taking inventory.

"We have to get you some medical help," she said, pushing his shoulders back down when he tried to rise.

"What makes you think we'd find any in Ouarzazate?" he said hoarsely.

"But your head—"

"Hurts like a sonuva buck," he said, grimacing as he tried to raise his head. "But it won't hurt any less on the way back to Ouarzazate. Or any more if we go on from here."

"You can't be serious. You're a long way from being on your feet."

"I'll be on my arse in a saddle—feet won't figure into it." He made tasting motions and grimaced. "Did I eat half of the Sahara? I could really use some water. . . ."

There was no doubt about it; he was awake and fully, annoyingly himself. As the day wore on, he wanted whiskey to dull the pain. She gave him headache powders. He demanded whiskey to slake his thirst. She gave him water. He insisted on having a mirror to see his injury; she declared that was one of the things he had made her discard on the way to Marrakech. When the powders took effect and he turned his back to sleep, she offered up a terse prayer.

"Thank God."

It was the middle of the next day before the wind abated enough for her to leave their shelter and have a look around. With the sun directly overhead she had difficulty orienting herself when she climbed to the top of a nearby dune.

Wind-sculpted drifts of sand stretched as far as she could see, unbroken by smoke from fires, lines of camels, vengeful Legionnaires, or tracks of any kind . . . not Abu Denaii's tracks leading south, nor their own leading from the north. The storm had scoured every trace of human movement and activity from the landscape. She stalked back down the dune.

"We're lost."

Haffe crouched in front of the shelter by a hollow in the sand.

"No, no. Follow caravan."

"Look for yourself. There aren't any tracks."

"Camel tracks." He said adamantly holding up two flat, brownish clumps and grinning. "We follow."

"Dear God," she muttered, staring at those sand-crusted chunks of camel dung and feeling herself teetering on the brink of full-blown hysteria. "We're escaping an ambush . . . forging across the Sahara . . . risking life and limb to look for a priceless archaeological find . . . guided by *camel droppings*."

A rusty sounding laugh from behind her caused her to turn.

"The latest in nomad navigation." Smith was crawling out of the shelter. "Little wonder they spend most of their time wandering around the desert."

"Thank heaven you're up." She hurried to his side and insisted he lean on her. "Any chance you could try the astrolabe and find out where we are?"

When he said he could probably manage, she snagged her map and astrolabe and helped him to the top of the closest dune. Then he looked down at the arm she hadn't yet removed from his waist.

"So, I take it you're glad I didn't die."

"Just protecting my investment." She blushed, feeling her lips heating suddenly and her skin coming to life . . . and she started to withdraw.

"Yeah?" He trapped her against him and pulled her closer.

Flustered by an impulse to raise her mouth to him, she shoved the astrolabe and map into his hands and ducked out of his arms.

"Imagine how it would sound to the old boys at the British Museum: 'We reached the Great Library by following a trail of camel dung.' Find us a direction, Smith. And pray that the 'Apollo' in you gets it right."

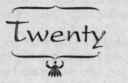

Twenty

An hour later, fortified with bread and goat cheese and Haffe's sweetened tea, they set off in the direction Smith identified. Each time they crested a dune, she rose in her stirrups to look around, and each time the landscape was barren as far as she could see in all directions. The storm had blown away both their tracks and the caravan's. In this contrary land, every bit of fortune seemed to come with a nullifying bit of disaster attached.

The next two days brought only more of the same: searing sun and endless plodding through freshly sculpted drifts of sand. Weighed down by goggles, turban, and burnoose, with the sun burning her cheeks and sand burning her feet through double-soled boots, Abigail felt alien and unwelcome in the desert. But by sunset of the second day, she had given up wasting energy on such musings. She had more pressing things to think about ... like the way Smith managed to stay upright in the saddle, though it clearly cost him a great deal.

Just at sunset on that second day, Haffe spotted a rare outcropping of rock and they decided to make camp beside it. After she and Haffe erected a shelter with the tarp and helped Smith inside, she removed his bandage to check his head. He was too exhausted to put up more than a token protest when she mixed him another headache powder, and insisted he drink water and sleep.

As he dropped like a stone into unconsciousness, she exited the tent and quickly encountered Haffe's anxious expression.

"No more tracks," he said, gesturing to the last nugget of camel dung lying on a burlap bag by his feet. She had lost track of the last time she'd seen him dismount to pick up one of those smelly little way markers.

"We're completely off the caravan trail?" Her heart sank when he nodded. "Then we're on our own out here. Lost."

"Not lost." He smiled and waved at the sand all around them. "In desert."

Haffe, she decided, was the living, breathing incarnation of optimism. And she wondered—not for the first time—what he would say if he truly understood just how little she and Smith knew about what they were doing.

The next morning the sun rose blearily over the horizon at dawn and seemed to grow more hostile as the day wore on. Smith was sagging badly and the horses were even beginning to droop in the heat. They stopped at noon to erect a shade for themselves and the horses, and Haffe doled out a single cup of water for each of them . . . giving the horses and mules twice that amount. It was a harbinger, Abigail realized, of privations to come.

Smith roused a few hours later and insisted on staggering up a tall dune to take another sun reading.

"How certain are you that we're on the professor's course?" she asked, watching him compare the sun's angle with the angle indicated on map.

"Fairly certain," he said. "But the old boy was mad as a March hare. Who knows if he had a clue what he was talking about?"

As midday passed and the sun grew less punishing, they set off again following a course that took them still further out of the way of caravan and commerce, into uncharted desert wilds. They rode until night fell and the desert around them became a dark, moonless void that forced them to stop for the night.

Smith didn't argue when she and Haffe thrust him into the tentlike shelter they erected and insisted he drink part of their cups of water. His lack of resistance stoked Abigail's growing anxiety.

Two hours later as a desert-gold moon rose in the east, Abigail and Haffe sat wrapped up in their burnooses by a long-dead camp fire. Haffe was snoring softly, and Abigail had lit the lantern and was once again pouring over the professor's last journal.

T. Thaddeus' final discourses rambled and were filled with arcane references. But in the middle, she found once again the account of travelers who stumbled across a place they said was called the "Temple of the Keepers." The story came from a three hundred-year-old scroll the professor discovered in a mosque library in Timbuktu. A mixed party of Berber traders and Spanish merchants had gotten lost in a sandstorm and wandered in the desert for several days before encountering a vision . . . a tantalizing mirage of clear, sweet water . . . over which rose a great columned edifice made in the style of a Greek temple. She held the journal closer to the lantern and read aloud to herself.

"Some of the party—maddened by lack of water and the searing heat of the sun—ran toward it and were 'swallowed by the desert.' The missing men were found later by their companions, raving about a great 'reservoir of knowledge,' from which wisdom flowed like water into the desert. The reunited party later stumbled across a caravan route and were picked up by traders. When they recovered, the men spoke of their experience in dreamlike terms and regarded the event as a vision of a long-dead world."

"Lost." Her spirits and shoulders both sagged. "Like us."

Was she making fool of herself . . . having squandered her best chance for a secure life on the scheme of a man who was as mad as a March hare? Anxiety coiled around her stomach and began to squeeze. It wasn't just her money she was risking out here. What if Smith had been gravely injured or Haffe had taken a bullet? What if they ran out of water and supplies?

She looked over at the sleeping Haffe and knew she had to move in order to purge the anxiety building in her. She strode up and over the first dune . . . and then across a second . . . dragging her heels to leave furrows that would mark her path.. . then sat down on the side of a dune to look up at the night sky. Its simple grandeur and immensity seemed to mock her ambitions.

"Well, Mother, I hope you're happy," she whispered irritably. "I'm having my big romantic adventure."

When she started back she had difficulty finding the tracks she had left. The sand had flowed back together like a liquid, filling in her trail, and the moonlight wasn't strong enough to give her a view of the minor disturbance left.

Heaving a sigh, she walked back and forth looking for the dune she had crossed. She could always call out, she supposed; Haffe would probably waken and rescue her. But she would never live it down if Smith awakened, too, and learned she had lost her way so close to camp.

After a few minutes of searching, she admitted she was lost. Worse, she began to worry that her searching might be leading her further away from camp. In desperation, she climbed to the top of a dune and searched the darkened area visually. As she feared, there was no sign of their camp or animals. Turning, scanning the moon-silvered landscape, she froze . . . staring through the moonlight at something that shimmered.

Impossible. She rubbed her eyes and squinted, looking harder. There was a brief, bright shimmer, like that of moonlight on water. Knowing it couldn't be their camp, she still felt compelled to move toward it. Just one dune—she would climb just one dune closer.

From that vantage point, the shimmer seemed even more pronounced. She slid down that dune and clamored up a third, feeling a surge of excitement.

Shafts of pale, silvery light resembling solidified moonbeams began to appear . . . first one, then another parallel to it . . . still another. Columns, she realized. Arrayed in a line. She leaned one way and then another to see if it was some trick of light, but was unable to make them disappear. She continued to approach and glimpsed an entablature above the columns and a sloped roof above the frieze and cornice. It looked uncannily like the entrance to the British Museum!

She stopped dead, staring at a ghostly Greek temple that seemed to be made of moonlight. Such things were called mirages if seen under the burning desert sun. But what were they called if they were seen by moonlight?

Crazy, that was what.

She headed for the columns, bent on exploring them, but her foot caught in something. She looked down to find both feet sinking in a strange, slippery kind of sand. Alarmed, she strained to lift her feet and step out of it, but her movements only caused her to sink faster. She was up to her knees before she realized she was caught fast and sinking even faster. The sand seemed to be flowing downward and—like water seeking its lowest level—was pulling her down with it.

She was submerged to her waist before she admitted she couldn't climb out and began to call for help with everything in her.

"Help! Smith! Haffe—help!—I'm trapped in the sand—sinking! Help!"

She clawed at the ground that continued to sink around her and dug in with her feet, seeking purchase, feeling like she was swimming against a thick and determined current.

"Please—please God, don't let it—*Help! Help!*"

Despite her struggles, she continued sinking . . . chest-deep . . . shoulders under . . . calling out for help . . . gasping to breathe as she tried to stay afloat on that smothering tide until the sand choked off her cries and closed slowly over her head.

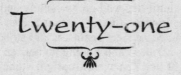

Twenty-one

Buried alive, unable to move more than an inch in any direction, she struggled with urges to both cough and gasp for air. Panicky thoughts flashed through her mind as the air in her lungs was depleted . . . Apollo . . . her mother . . . the museum . . . adventures she would never . . . kisses she would never . . .

Something shifted beneath her; the pressure on her feet and legs decreased. She began to slide again, this time in a flume of free-flowing sand . . . descending.. . then falling. She crashed to an abrupt halt in a sitting position, with sand raining down on her head. She had found a bottom of some sort and flailed in one last, spasm of will. Her hand hit a void—an open space!

Frantic with hope, she dug in that direction until she broke abruptly into nothing. No, not nothing—*air*! She sucked deep, glorious breaths of air that made her cough repeatedly. Dust-laden and probably as stale as Pharoah's beer, the air felt marvelous. She collapsed at that boundary between solid and gas . . . listening to the shushing sound of sand still falling behind her.

It took a few moments for her wits to reassemble. She'd

fallen through a hole of some kind and was underground. But underground in what?

Waving her arms, she investigated the space around her. There was nothing above her or on either side, so she slid down the slope, pausing here and there to feel her unseen surroundings, until the sand grew shallow and ended on a solid surface. It was stone . . . *stones* . . . set together. A floor! She planted her feet against it and stood up slowly, feeling above her head and finding no barrier.

To her right she discovered upright stonework . . . set with mortar. A *wall*. Reassured by the prospect of being in something man-made, she felt her way along with both hands and feet. If it was a wall, it had to lead somewhere.

She had the sense that the floor sloped downward and the sound of her movement began to echo around her, as if the size of the space was increasing. From a distance she heard a sound like a trickle. *Water*. Alarm filled her. Was she in a well? Had fate thrown her down a well after all, as punishment for—

"For God's sake, Abigail, get a grip," she said shakily, and was buoyed momentarily by the sound of her own voice.

Then the passage dropped out from under her and she tumbled and fell, smacking into stony edges and she careened arse-over-elbows into darkness. When she stopped, she groaned and sat up. The sound of water was significantly louder—closer—almost at hand.

She blinked repeatedly, and the darkness lightened and surfaces became visible. A block wall on four sides—a passage! And she was sitting at the bottom of some steps. Pushing to her feet again, she ignored her screaming knees and hips and the burning in her shoulder to explore further.

The passage ended in a large underground chamber filled with water. A pool at least fifty feet across and a hundred feet long was bordered by paved walkways and, at one end, water seemed to be squeezed from pure rock and tumbled down a stone face into the pool. The light came from the openings of several other passages apparently leading into the pool chamber.

A man-made pool, below ground, in the middle of the desert!

She rushed forward and dropped onto her stomach at the edge of the water, plunging her cupped hands into it and drinking greedily. It tasted sweet and she began to laugh and splash the water into a wild, impromptu fountain that expressed her relief at being alive.

Light bloomed around her, blinding her momentarily. She rolled up to a sitting position and brought her hands up to shield her eyes. When she was able to focus past the lanterns illuminating her, she found herself facing four old humans. Very old, very wrinkled humans. With fuzzy white hair, age-yellowed eyes, and sunken mouths. Wearing earrings.

One of them spoke using a word that Abigail understood in theory, but was unused to hearing or speaking except in her own head. It took her a moment to trap and translate the word properly.

"Gyni i." An ancient word for "woman." Moderns used the word *gynaika* instead. Greek. Her heart stopped. *Old* Greek.

"parthena," *"neos,"* and *"oraia"* . . . opinions came thick and fast.

Virgin . . . young . . . lovely . . . Her mind dutifully translated each word, while somehow holding the full sense of its meaning at bay. Women . . . old and withered . . . speaking ancient words. . . .

Smith rushed to the edge of the cone-shaped depression, calling to Haffe as the little Berber's frantic face disappeared into the streaming sand. The sound of Haffe's frantic voice had roused him from sleep with something about Abigail being in trouble. By the time he stumbled from the tent to see what was happening, he found only Haffe's tracks settling and disappearing in the sand. He followed them at a lope over several dunes and arrived just as Haffe's shoulders were sinking into the same depression that Haffe said had "swallowed" Abigail.

There wasn't time to go for a rope. Making a split-second decision, Smith dug his toes into what seemed the stable edge of the depression and launched himself across the sand, his hands outstretched. But he fell short and as the little Berber disappeared, he crawled forward and plunged his hands into the sand, feeling for Haffe's head or hands. Then he began to sink himself, though he scrambled to support himself with his arms. The treacherous sands pulled and the edge under his feet slowly gave way.

Panic seized him as his arms and shoulders were pulled under, and he just had time to suck a breath before his head was engulfed in sand as well. Shoulders, waist, hips—he was encased upside down in a streaming current of earth. Clawing and resisting as much as the sand would allow, he felt his blood rushing into his head and lost all semblance of thought and reason. Instinct took over as his lungs began to burn and he began to flail and dig with his arms and hands while trying to shield his face.

Then he felt a release of pressure beneath him and fell straight down in a shower of sand and dust and landed with a thud on something that groaned and moved. A torrent of sand poured over and around him, and he scrambled to one side and rolled downward until he came to a jarring halt.

He gasped and lay there for a moment, stunned, grateful to be breathing. As he took inventory of his battered body, he realized he was lying on what seemed to be a flat surface in breathable air and that nothing seemed broken.

The darkness around him lightened suddenly, allowing him limited vision. From behind him came the sound of human groaning and from the front came a scraping, scuffling sound.

Bright light burst over him, blinding him momentarily, and he raised his hands to shield them from two merciless beacons that illuminated a stone floor . . . a block wall . . . air hazy with dust . . . a massive pile of sand. . . .

"Smith?" Abigail's voice coming from the light caused his heart to thud and then race wildly.

"Boston?" he managed to choke out between coughs. "Are you all right?"

"I'm fine." A moment later, she had her arms around him and was helping him to his feet. "But you don't look so good. Is that Haffe with you?" As soon as he was stable, she abandoned him with a hasty squeeze and a "Stay here," to respond to Haffe's groans and plea to Allah to be merciful.

Squinting against the light, Smith dragged a steadying breath and pressed both hands to his throbbing head. As he began to sway Abigail arrived with Haffe and they slid under his arms to keep him upright.

"Where the devil are we?" Smith said, blinking to clear his vision.

All three explorers stared dumbstruck at the quartet of old women holding oil lamps aloft and scrutinizing them.

"Who are they?" Smith said on an indrawn breath.

"I have no idea," Abigail said, staring at the women and wondering if they were entirely mortal. The old girls all began to speak at once using the same word in sundry variations: "anir o," an ancient form of "andras."

Man. One of the old women stepped forward and poked Smith with a finger . . . in the stomach . . . hard.

"Owww." He flinched.

Her age-hooded eyes widened at that undeniable evidence of his corporeal nature. *"Anir o! Anir o!"*

"Now wait a minute—" Abigail intervened to push them back. "Is that any way to treat a visitor to your . . . your . . ." Home? Maze? Netherworld?

Just where *were* they? Abigail righted her wits enough to register that they wore white linen tunics and chiton-like overgarments pinned at their shoulders with tarnished gold brooches. Around their waists were frayed golden cords and on their feet were ancient-looking sandals. The entire group looked as if it had stepped right off a Grecian urn. A very *old* urn. And they spoke a form of Greek that was even more ancient than they were.

Abigail's knees went weak as the recognition struck and she stiffened, bracing to keep both herself and Smith up. She had to be sure.

"Who are *you*? And where are we?" she asked, using Greek words she couldn't recall ever speaking aloud.

"Who are you?" One of the lantern-bearers demanded in a recognizable phrasing of the old language. She seemed a bit younger than the others and wore a great golden amulet on a chain around her neck. Her hair wasn't entirely white and her skin wasn't quite as desiccated.

"We're explorers . . . from London, England," Abigail said haltingly, praying her pronunciation was faithful enough to be understood by these living anachronisms. "What is this place?"

"Where is this 'Engle Land?' " the woman asked more slowly.

Abigail glanced up at Smith, who was sagging, and came up with an answer that—if they were whom she hoped they were—they should understand.

"North of Gaul. The land of the Brettons. I am a librarian . . . come in search of the last remnant of the Great Library of Alexandria."

"*Librarian*?" The medallion wearer twitched as if she had been pinched. "The *Librarian*?"

Abigail's words had struck a spark in the women's eyes and after a word from the medallion-clad leader, the old girls withdrew a pace and fell into heated consultation, glancing over their shoulders and huddling together, clasping hands. As they talked their manner changed, their bearing grew more erect and dignified.

"Welcome, *Librarian*," the medallion wearer said, leading the others in a bow. "We have been waiting for you. By what name do the gods know you?"

"I-I am Abigail Merchant," she managed to get out. Expecting her? She glanced at Smith with growing concern.

He was shaking his head as if having trouble staying alert, and she could swear there was fresh blood on his bandage.

"Idera. Chief priestess. Your foremost servant," the leader said with a bow so low that Abigail feared she might hurt herself. But she straightened and gestured to the others. "My sister priestesses are Hathor, Calla, and Mercredes." Each nodded when her name was spoken. "Come with us." Then she turned back and flicked a look at Smith and Haffe. "Your servants may come, as well."

At a flick of Idera's wrist, two of the old women hurried to take Abigail's place under Smith's arm. Reluctantly she relinquished her hold on him and followed their guide.

As the threesome accompanied the old women through a maze of passages, Abigail kept glancing back at Smith, who seemed a bit dazed but was walking on his own. Telling herself he would be all right, she turned to the head of the contingent of "priestesses" with a dozen questions.

"Who are you? Who is responsible for this tunnel? How long have you lived here? Where did you come from? How have you managed to survive in the middle of the desert?" And finally: "Priestesses of what?"

Idera put off all of her questions with the same response.

"Soon. Soon. You will see."

Frustrated but wary of giving insult, Abigail divided her attention between monitoring Smith's condition and examining the maze of worn steps and ancient passages they were negotiating. Smith seemed to be getting both his balance and his wits back, but Haffe was busy fending off the curious hands of the old women who escorted them.

"No, no. Bad woman. Bad! No touch—"

After a few minutes, the passage broadened abruptly into what appeared to be a street lined with doors that looked as if they hadn't been opened in a generation or two. At the end of the street, they arrived at a paved stone plaza dominated by a neglected but still working fountain and the startling façade of a replica of the Greek Parthenon.

Abigail stopped in her tracks, staring openmouthed, and Smith came alert to give a low whistle. Above the temple, which seemed to have been carved from the surrounding stone, rose an arched vault that looked like it was part natural cave and part human-made dome. The man-made parts were plastered with crumbling frescoes depicting stars on one side and the glory of the absent sun on the other.

But it was the temple itself that drew Abigail's attention and held her spellbound. It was the very image of the mirage she had seen earlier.

"Our temple," Idera said with a wave of hand. "To honor Athena, Goddess of Wisdom. It was her that sent us into the desert."

"A-Athena sent you here?" Abigail's heart was hammering.

"To preserve the knowledge and wisdom of the ages," Idera said calmly. "But you must already know that. Since you are the one prophesied to come."

Abigail could hardly breathe.

"This is our New Alexandria." Gooseflesh rose all over Abigail as the old woman smiled and turned halfway to the plaza, holding out arms as if to join Abigail to the city. "Forty generations of protectors and caretakers honor and welcome you."

Abigail's throat tightened as she surveyed the plaza and temple and tried to come to grips with the fact that she had indeed found the remnant of one of the most noble legends of ancient history, the Great Library of Alexandria.

Gradually she began to focus on the details of the subterranean complex, all of which lent credence to the priestess's claims of great age for the community. The stonework in the paving of the plaza was foot-worn and badly buckled in places. There was stucco missing from the fronts of the buildings facing the plaza and there were crumbled or missing bricks and cracks in every structure around the plaza. Even the elegant temple itself seemed the worse for wear . . . chipped stone and worn steps . . . figures missing from the frieze above the columns. . . .

"Well, it was 'new' once," ancient Hathor said flatly.

"It has to look better than the *old* Alexandria," Calla opined wickedly.

"It has been a few hundred years," the one called Mercedes declared. "And with no Protectors left to repair the walls and vault . . ."

Protectors? The old woman had used the term *prosiatis* . . . one of the terms that cleric Moulay Karroum had interpreted from Arabic into Greek for Abigail. These women called their long-departed cohorts "protectors." She looked in broadening dismay at the women. Were these the "caretakers" that had been likened to Muslim "houris," the virgins of Paradise?

Only now did the full impact of it register.

"This is it—this is really it!" She grabbed the priestess and hugged her, laughing wildly. Then she abandoned Idera to throw both arms fiercely around Smith. "We found it—*you* found it! You and the professor's astrolabe! You really are *Apollo* Smith!" As she released him and staggered down the steps to stare raptly up at the temple, the head priestess and the other old women chuckled with approval of her awe and excitement.

Abigail began to walk and then to run toward the half-toppled fountain where she spun around and around trying to take it all in. Then she raced to the steps leading to the temple, hardly able to contain the joy rising in her.

Idera and the others followed at a much slower pace.

Abigail threw her arms around one of the thick stone columns that formed the front of the temple, hugging it, running her hands up and down the grooved stone, absorbing with her entire body the wonder of its existence.

"We're really here!" she cried. "We really found it!"

As Smith, Haffe, and the old priestesses reached the pillars, she rushed into the temple and stopped dead, halfway through the sanctuary, staring in awe at a great statue of the goddess Athena sitting on an altar perusing a scroll. The altar was flanked by ranks of ancient oil lamps . . . only two of which were burning, giving off a sooty, flickering light.

"Athena," Abigail was finally able to exhale on a breath.

"Our patroness," Idera said, clasping her chest and puffing with exertion.

"You came here with the scrolls and books from the Great Library," Abigail declared, her face flushed. Idera nodded and continued.

"Well more than a thousand years ago, our forebears brought what writings they could secret away from the Great Library of Alexandria . . . to protect and preserve them until it was safe to return them to the world."

"And they built this place, this temple." Abigail looked around her with awe, taking in the worn stone carvings and faded frescoes that celebrated the goddess's command and the journey of the forebears from Alexandria.

Idera drew Abigail behind the altar to see the pictorial representation of their history arrayed behind Athena's image.

"This place was chosen because there were natural caves. The first servants of Athena widened the entrances and built passages between the cave chambers . . . which became the scriptoria for the books. Later, they discovered the underground spring and built a plaza and carved out the temple. We lived peacefully among our nomadic neighbors and traded, even married among them.

"But then the Arabs came and converted the Berbers to Islam." She sighed. "They declared our temple to be an abomination and the trading and marrying stopped. Then the era of raids and storms came upon us. Year after year . . . howling winds and oceans of sand invaded our village . . . until we realized it was a sign from the gods that we should let the desert overtake and hide us. The Protectors extended the walls over us as the desert invaded . . . and finally finished the vault you see." She pointed to the dome over the plaza.

"But with each generation that passed, there were fewer

of us to do the work and to keep up the city,' the oldest priestess, Hathor, said tiredly. "Now there are but a few of us left. We have grown old in the service of our goddess."

The priestess named Calla stepped forward.

"We are grateful you have come at last, Librarian.'

Just then, Smith sagged against the altar and the women gasped and hurried to help him.

"He was injured. He needs rest." Abigail would have gone to him, but she was restrained by Idera.

"My sisters will see to him." The priestess gave quick orders to escort him and Haffe to nearby quarters, then as he and Haffe were led away, she turned back to Abigail. "Stay with me. There is something I must show you."

Abigail watched Smith being led away and was torn between going with him and satisfying her curiosity about this remarkable place. But when she turned back to Idera, the priestess had unpinned the brooches at her shoulders and allowed her draped chiton to fall to the floor of the temple.

Underneath the chiton, atop her linen tunic, she wore a halterlike garment made of two rounded metal hemispheres that fitted closely over her breasts and were held together and fastened around her body by rows of chains overlaid with flat metal plates like armored scales. Abigail gasped. The anatomical faithfulness of the thing was a bit shocking, but even more astonishing was the fact that the thing seemed to be made—from breast cups to scales—of pure gold.

While Abigail stared, the old woman unlatched the garment, removed it, and laid it on Athena's lap. And while Abigail's gaze was fixed on it, the old priestess attacked the buttons of her blouse.

Twenty-two

"What do you think you're doing?" Abigail tried to keep the edges of her blouse together, but the old woman was determined and surprisingly quick.

"You must take the mantle of the high priestess of the Temple."

"I am no priestess—much less a 'high' one," Abigail insisted, yanking her blouse free of the old girl's hands. "I'm just here to find the books and carry—"

Idera retrieved the golden garment and held it up to Abigail's breasts, which seemed to fit it perfectly. "You see? You truly are the one."

"Because I fit your bosom holder?"

Idera edged closer and trapped Abigail's gaze in hers. It was a disturbingly potent stare—those dark, penetrating eyes, so deep, so fathomless—privy to both knowledge and mysteries Abigail couldn't begin to guess. And the old woman seemed sincere in her urgency to introduce Abigail into the workings of her world.

Her mother's voice rose in her mind: *"For heaven's sake, Abigail, do something adventuresome, something bold and unexpected for once."*

Being declared a priestess of Athena certainly qualified. Besides, if she hoped to take some of the library back to England with her, sooner or later she would probably have to borrow some of the old priestess's authority.

"All right. But if I have to wear it, I'll wear it *inside* my garments."

She unbuttoned her blouse and set it aside. When she turned back she found the old woman staring at her pink satin corset and scowling.

"You already serve another goddess?" Idera demanded, confused.

"No," she declared, muttering to herself as she worked the laces of her corset: "Not unless you count 'Fashion.'"

As soon as her blouse and corset were off, Idera dragged her around to the front of Athena's great statue and made a grand obeisance, calling on the Goddess of Wisdom to "look with favor on the prophesied one, *Able-gale* . . . who, like her name . . . is both clever and full of wind." She called down the blessings of great wisdom and foresight for the task ahead.

"Task?" Abigail said, frowning as old Idera slipped the straps of the metal bosom-corset up her arms and over her shoulders. "Exactly what sort of task will I need all this wisdom and foresight for?"

"To return the library to the world," Idera answered, tugging and shimmying the metal cups into place over her breasts with alarming intimacy. "What else?"

For that she needed a solid gold bosom-holder? Abigail looked down at the thing being strapped around her. It weighed a ton; her respect for the old woman's stamina soared. Then, with the ceremonial breastplate secure, Idera turned with arms upraised to address Athena again.

"Bless this courageous—" She hesitated and leaned toward Abigail to whisper: "A woman, yes? And not a maid?" Abigail flushed crimson.

"A maid."

Idera looked distressed and it seemed for a moment that she might abort the entire proceeding.

"Not one of those miserly Vestals?" she demanded.

"No! I mean, certainly not," Abigail said, realizing she referred to the famed Vestal Virgins of Rome. The priestess couldn't honestly think . . .

The news that Abigail was not yet mated could not quite eclipse the fact that she was The Librarian and had come from the ends of the known world to retrieve the library. Reconciling herself to the Fates' unfathomable decision, Idera sighed and continued.

". . . this courageous *maiden* . . . and give her the strength, judgment, and passion to accomplish this great task." She glanced darkly at Abigail and turned back to Athena, lowering her voice. "And give her a proper partner to open her mind to the great mysteries and make her worthy."

Abigail's cheeks were still burning with embarrassment and lingering indignation as Idera led her down the steps of the temple minutes later. She was struggling to both understand why the state of her virtue would matter and absorb the fact that the breastplate she was wearing had probably been worn by thirty or forty successive generations of priestesses who served the Goddess of Wisdom.

It was all true, she thought, standing on the steps and staring in renewed wonder at the dilapidated plaza that had anchored the keepers' world for centuries. Part of the Great Library had survived in the hands of *female* caretakers. She narrowed her eyes and pulled her shoulders back, determined to be worthy of bearing the honor and the burden that had just been placed on her. Moulay Karroum was going to have a heart attack when he learned about this.

Before she entered a single scriptorium—Idera announced as she conducted Abigail toward her quarters— she would have to undergo a purifying ritual. Imagining all manner of instruments and elements that could make her life a pain-ridden horror, Abigail asked what the ritual involved.

Water, spiced and scented oils, and a thorough rubbing with sponges.

Abigail solemnly declared she would do her best to endure.

The halls and passages of the library and temple complex had once represented the pinnacle of Alexandrian style. Now the walls were in dire need of both repair and paint, the stone tile floors were missing pieces, and the wooden furnishings were warped and parched-looking. The lamp stands in the chambers and hallways had traded most of their gilding for a coat of cobwebs. A number of the doors they passed hung askew on broken hinges. The one thing in plentiful supply seemed to be dust.

"About bloody time!" Smith roared the minute she stepped into the main chamber of the apartment she was given. He was standing stark naked in the center of a huge marble tub filled with water, holding a bit of toweling across his privates and batting away the eager ministrations of half a dozen old women collected around the basin. "Tell the old tarts to keep their hands to themselves!"

Their attentions had apparently brought him roaring out of his exhaustion. Against her better judgment, the sight of his big, well-made body was bringing her roaring out of hers. Her eyes flowed over him in the golden light of several oil lamps, taking in his tanned upper body and his pale lower—

"They're only helping with your 'purification,'" she said, chewing her lip and trying not to be too obvious in her curiosity. "You have to be *purified* before they will allow you into a scriptorium."

"I'm as pure as I intend to get," he said irritably, climbing out of the bath in spite of the women's attempts to stay him. "What the hell's a 'scriptorium'?"

"I believe we covered this. It's a chamber where writing is done and where books and manuscripts are kept." She folded her arms and her attempt to avoid staring at his bare flanks caused her gaze to rebound to his face. She froze.

His eye patch was gone, leaving only its outline visible in skin lighter than the rest of his face. He was staring at her with two eyes that from all appearances were perfectly healthy.

"It makes sense," she said distractedly, "from a manuscript conservation standpoint. Contaminants from the outside . . . grime, molds, human pests, and parasites, body oils, could ruin fragile documents."

"I didn't come for documents," he declared, wrapping the toweling around his lower half and bracing before her with a glower.

"Well, I did." Embarrassed by her reaction to his nakedness, annoyed by the way the women were ogling their interaction and nudging each other, and dismayed by the realization that he was seeing her with both eyes, she went for something off-putting. "And apparently the good priestesses are concerned you might contaminate *me*."

The light struck in his gaze said her comment had had the opposite effect. Her irritation and her awareness of his maleness rose apace. As he headed for her, she could see his muscles moving smoothly beneath his skin and took in several scars. The old girls made to intercept him with toweling and scented oil, and he lurched back with a "Dammit!" instead, and turned away.

As he escaped into an adjoining chamber, Idera intervened to order the women to attend The Librarian instead. Disappointed, they turned on Abigail with the same intense scrutiny they had trained on Smith. They pulled the few remaining pins from her hair, shaking it out, brushing, and examining it. They patted her curves, stroked her face, examined her eyes and teeth, and gently poked her breasts.

"I had these once. And better," old Hathor cackled.

"My hips were the talk of the city," Elysia giggled, giving Abigail's derriere an assessing pinch. "But hers are young and firm enough. . . ."

It was by far the most immodest and uncomfortable half hour of her life. By the time she had been scrubbed, rinsed, and laid out on a bench to be oiled and kneaded like a loaf of bread, she fully shared Smith's discomfort. As if they read his name in her thoughts, they began to ask questions about him.

"What's he like, the tall one?" the very elderly Hathor asked as they gathered around to rub scented oils into her skin.

"As a lover," Calla with the thinning, wiry hair clarified. "Is he gentle?"

"Or does he ride like a pillaging Hun?" ancient Mercedes asked, her age-faded eyes suddenly bright with speculation.

"Always favored lovers that were tough and vigorous, myself," declared the soft-spoken one, Elysia. "Makes the taming and training all the more fun."

"It's been such a long time—tell us, Librarian." Hathor leaned closer. "Does he growl like a tiger or howl like a wolf when pleasure overtakes him?"

"I—I wouldn't know," Abigail declared, reddening such that even her hair seemed to be blushing. "He is not my lover."

Even as she said it, some vulnerable, sensually starved part of her groaned with disappointment so keen it verged on outrage. Smith was right; she did want him as a man. He was handsome and strong and capable and interesting and sensually beguiling. . . .

But he was also arrogant and secretive . . . possibly violent . . . not especially trustworthy. He had made it clear he was here for treasure to fund his quest for vindication . . . perhaps revenge. He looked out for himself, first and foremost, and when she managed to forget it, he always managed to remind her.

"He is merely my employee," she said, taut with conviction.

"Employee" was not a word that translated easily into ancient Greek. The old priestesses gasped as she explained it to them, and they looked to Idera in dismay. The chief priestess sighed, reiterated Abigail's place in prophecy, and then turned to her to explain their concern.

"Before coming with the Protectors to New Alexandria, we served Athena in a small society devoted to pursuing wisdom through initiation into the mysteries of the union of male and female."

It took a moment for Abigail to understand. The union of . . . *oh*. She had encountered allusions to such things in scholarly tomes, but had avoided indulging in unseemly interest in them. Now she was not only confronted with the fact of their existence, she found herself being judged by their sensibility . . . which held her upright, abstemious ways to be suspect.

"We—*ahem*—expected the goddess to send us a Librarian initiated fully in the path to wisdom," Idera said, looking somewhat apologetic.

Abigail looked around at the old girls' long faces and her shoulders sagged.

It wasn't enough that she had her mother's expectations to fulfill, she thought as they dressed her in garments resembling theirs while her things were freshened, now she had a goddess's expectations and the disappointment of a half dozen octogenarian priestesses to deal with! Just when she was feeling good about finding the library. . . .

By the time she had taken some food and wine with the priestesses and they escorted her back to her chambers, she was a little fogged in the head and looking forward to a much-deserved sleep. When the door closed behind her, she stood for a moment looking at the door where Smith had disappeared, then turned emphatically to a second door several yards away. There had to be a bed here somewhere.

She quickly found herself in a dimly lighted chamber, facing a dais topped by a huge, linen-draped bed . . . occupied by Smith, wearing nothing but a smile and a pale shadow where his eye patch had been. She glared in surprise at the doors that both led into the same chamber.

Then he said her name, low and soft.

"Hello, Boston."

Her entire body erupted in gooseflesh.

"The old girls are unusually progressive in their sleeping arrangements." His deep, resonating tones caused her fingertips to tingle.

"They're daft as dodos," she said, folding her arms over her chest and raising her gaze to him, "the lot of them."

"The bed is really soft." He patted the bedclothes. "Climb in."

"Do me a favor," she said, seizing the one thread of her reason that wasn't unraveling. "Put your hand over your right eye and tell me what you see."

He scowled, then raised his right hand and cupped it over his eye.

"A beautiful young woman. Wearing way too many clothes."

She tucked her arms tighter.

"So, the eye patch is just a ruse."

"Is that what you're all prickly about?" He gave an indulgent laugh and swung his legs out of the bed. She was relieved to see a linen wrap around his lower half as he rose. "All right. I can see out of my left eye. My vision has gradually improved. But I still have trouble with bright sunlight producing glaring halos around things, and it's less of a strain if I wear the patch in bright sunlight. Taking it off and putting it back on is a bother . . . so in Morocco, I wear it all the time."

"And?"

"And . . . it . . . makes for something of a disguise." He halted, assessing her stubborn pose and skeptical expression, looking a bit less sure of himself. "There are people who want me dead, remember."

"So, you never thought to tell me—your *partner*—that you actually have two good eyes," she said irritably. "Just like you never bothered to tell me that you were in prison for killing someone . . . or that you knew about Ferdineaux LaCroix because he was your uncle . . . or that the Legion had declared you officially dead. How many more secrets do you have, Smith? A harem tucked away in some steamy little corner of the local kasbah? A lucrative little side business in stolen antiquities, perhaps?"

The last bit of humor drained from his face.

"Of all the damned hysterical—" He strode toward her, but she braced and put up her hands, palms out, to stop him. "You've got quite a little tally going there, haven't you? My sins of omission." He flushed hot and bronze. "Repeat them to yourself like a rosary, do you? Thinking it will keep me at bay? How about a little garlic around your neck while you're at it?"

"I'm sure there are other beds nearby," she said looking to the door.

"I suggest you find one," he growled, stalking back up the dais and climbing back into the bed. "Because I'm not going anywhere."

"It's *my* bed. The old priestesses—"

"Figured we'd been sleeping side by side, more or less, for some time and assumed a few more nights wouldn't kill either of us."

"Get out of my bed!" she shouted, flinging a finger at the door.

"Just what is your beef with me, Boston?" he demanded, sitting ramrod straight. "What have I done to earn this anger of yours?"

Very well.

"Every time I think I can depend on you, I stumble across another of your secrets and realize . . . I don't know you at all."

His eyes glimmered darkly.

"You don't want to know me," he said tautly. "It's easier that way. You get to go on living in your precious books and don't have to cope with the real world. The real world is filled with real men. And real men are messy. Conflicted. Inconvenient. Complicated. You have to take the good with the bad, the bitter with the sweet. But you're no picnic yourself, Boston. One minute you're sizzling hot, the next cold as ice. One minute you're a wilting lily, the next you're bloody Annie Oakley. . . ."

Before she could respond, he was down the steps and closing the distance between them. "Wait—you can't—"

"Oh, but I can." He grabbed her by the shoulders and pulled her against him. "Because you're going to let me."

A wave of heat from his kiss, liquid and rising, engulfed her objections and made it impossible to put an end to this demonstration of pure unadulterated lust. *Hers.* If she raised her hands to push him away, they would probably just curl around the smooth, hard skin of his sides instead. So she stood not resisting and not responding, hoping to conceal the turmoil his kiss was stirring in her.

When he raised his head, his eyes were dark and he was breathing heavily.

"Are you sure it's me you're fighting?"

She fell back a step when he released her and stood feeling utterly dismantled . . . fault by fault, fear by fear.

She watched him stomp back up the steps, blow out the lamp, and throw himself onto the bed. He was challenging her to prove she wasn't afraid. Of herself.

"What are you waiting for Abigail?" Her mother's voice rose in her head. *"Take a lover. Make a child. Do something wild and wonderful! What are you afraid of?"*

In the dim light coming from the other room she stomped up the steps to the other side of the bed and flopped down on it with a spiteful flourish. As her heart rate slowly returned to normal, she could feel him waiting . . . listening . . . so she gave him back the bit of insight he'd just handed her.

"You know what I really hate about you?" She hoped the answer would be as annoying to him as he was to her. "You're just like my mother."

Twenty-three

The first scriptorium, Idera said the next morning as she unlocked the heavy cedar door and led them inside, was also the largest of the three main library chambers. The torches around the walls were quickly lighted and revealed several long tables in the center of the chamber and rows of shelves stacked with scrolls of parchment and papyrus along the walls. On the table were pots of ink and quills of various kinds . . . under a significant layer of dust. Cobwebs drooped from the ceiling and shelves, and the oil lamps and candle stands on the tables were covered with soot and dust.

Abigail glanced at Smith, who frowned at her, then forced her thoughts from their argument last night to the discoveries at hand. Clearly no one had been in this chamber for a very long time.

"You don't tend the manuscripts?" Abigail couldn't hide her concern.

Idera sighed and looked to Hathor and Calla, who sagged visibly.

"For centuries we recopied scrolls that were damaged or deteriorated," Hathor declared. "Some were copied several times . . . always faithfully, always with great love and care. Women, our forebears discovered, were better at the fine copy work, and so the men applied themselves to keeping the community safe and healthy. They oversaw our protection and the trading and the growing of crops." She smiled at their disbelief. "In those days, we were not yet taken over by the desert. We were able to cultivate crops in the two large oases connected to our settlement."

"How did you manage that?" Smith asked.

"Passages like the one you fell into form a maze in the rock beneath the sands," Calla continued. "At the oases, some of our community farmed and traded from a permanent settlement, blending in with the nomads. But then the desert sands began to advance, and we were forced to abandon our fields and buy more of the food and supplies we needed."

"Now our eyes dim and our hands are no longer steady enough for the copy work. Our days here are numbered," Idera concluded. "We are proud to have executed our duty. But we are relieved to place it now in your hands."

Abigail looked around at the scrolls and realized the magnitude of the task being handed to her. It would take a lifetime of work to examine, evaluate, authenticate, and conserve these priceless relics. She gently removed a scroll from one of the shelves and carried it to a table. Calla and Idera wiped away the dust with their robes and pulled out a stool for her to use.

Unrolling the parchment, she found the ink still dark enough to read and the script quite legible. But, the skin was brittle and cracked as she opened it.

"What is it?" Smith said, reading over her shoulder. "Greek?"

"Hebrew." She looked up with tears in her eyes. "The writings of a great rabbi and thinker of ancient times, Gamaleal . . . once the teacher of Saint Paul."

She went on to find copies of Plato's dialogues, Callimachus's writings on the Great Library, Pliny's natural philosophy, the *History* of Herodotus, the Babylonian

Tiglath-pileser's codex of laws. Each discovery seemed more wonderful than the last. It would be difficult to choose just a few to carry back with her to the museum.

An hour later, her eyes burned from the dust and her back ached from the weight of the hidden breastplate combined with sitting bent over manuscripts. When Idera suggested she see the next scriptorium before continuing, she reluctantly pulled herself away and accompanied the chief priestess to another great cedar door guarded by a stout iron lock.

Inside, the air was moist and fetid, and when the torches had been lit they saw why. Moisture had seeped through the walls and collected on the chiseled stone to migrate into some of the scrolls. Most susceptible was the ancient papyrus, rolled in mats of reed and kept in wooden boxes that had absorbed moisture. Idera called for the other priestesses and they began to carry many of the works to a common hall, just off the plaza, where they could be assessed and repaired. Smith and Haffe, who had followed with surprising interest, were also pressed into service and soon the chamber was cleared of everything salvageable.

As they carried the last load from the scriptorium, Smith spotted another massive door and asked if there were more scrolls in that chamber. His eyes lighted when Idera said casually, "No, no, Engle-lander. Not scrolls. Gold."

Suddenly there was a low rumbling sound from afar, and the earth itself vibrated for a moment. They dove toward the walls as dirt sifted down through the cracks in the passage roof. But the ceiling held and the trembling stopped.

"What was that?" Smith demanded, straightening and brushing sand and dust from his newly cleaned shirt.

"Probably another tunnel collapsing." Idera shrugged, looking grieved. She looked to Abigail and brushed some dust from her cheek. "We have lost a number of tunnels in the last few years . . . including the one you fell through."

"About this gold . . ." Smith said, eyeing the door.

"Oh. Yes." Idera merely leaned a bony shoulder against the heavy, iron-bound door and it creaked open.

They hurried into the chamber, holding a lantern aloft, and found . . . nothing. The stone floor and benches were empty except for a couple of bent and discarded cups whose veneer of gilt had mostly worn away.

"This is it?" Smith picked up the cups and studied them.

"There are a few other pieces in the temple, but the rest is gone," Idera said, turning to Abigail. "As I said, you came just in time."

But not in time, they soon learned, to save the holdings in the third scriptorium. When they opened the door, there was water a foot deep over the entire chamber. Chunks of stone and masonry had fallen from the weeping rock that formed the chamber, allowing water to trickle in rivulets down the walls. Some of the shelves had floated and toppled and they could feel rotting manuscripts underfoot as they waded through the water to check other scrolls.

Mold and rot were everywhere. The entire collection was a loss. They led Idera and old Hathor from the chamber in tears.

When they sat the old women down in the common hall and got them wine to steady their nerves, Hathor told them: "Idera and I . . . we have known for some time the walls were weakening. Our dome, our passages, our temple . . . the desert is reclaiming what we once took from it. We have held the news from the other sisters, hoping we could continue on a while longer."

"We must act quickly to get the manuscripts out of the city," Idera said, gripping Abigail's hands.

Abigail nodded and looked up at Smith, who scowled.

The camp was deserted, that much was clear. Gaston sat on his horse, watching his men tear through Smith's supplies and ransack the woman's belongings . . . dragging out a silk petticoat and holding it up to themselves, doing a dirty little parody of "feminine" and laughing. His mouth curled into a half smirk. Four days of searching had finally paid off.

"Spread out!" he roared as he swung down from his horse. "They can't have gone far. Their animals are still here!"

As his men reluctantly abandoned their spree to begin searching the nearby dunes, he walked through the camp, ripping back part of the tent and kicking several of the leather bound books his men had dislodged from a carpet-bag. "Books," he snarled. That was what he hated most about Apollo Smith. "Always flaunting his highborn kin and fancy education. Acting like he knows everything. Getting all the breaks." One of his men located a bottle of Irish whiskey and he confiscated it, taking a deep pull of the liquor as he waited for reports. Damned fine whiskey. He almost spit it out. "Nothing but the best, eh, English? Enjoy your whore and your treasure while you can. When I get my hands on you, you'll wish you'd never been born."

"Here!" One of his men came racing back over a nearby dune, waving his arms, beckoning wildly. "We found something!"

Gaston dropped the bottle, ripped his gun from its holster, and went running to see what they'd found. His disappointment turned venomous when he stood looking down at a large, conical depression in the sand.

"This?" He lashed out with his gun barrel to strike the soldier on the side of the head. "You called me out here for *this*?"

"It's a hole, Sergeant," the tall, gaunt Schuller declared, stepping in front of his comrade. "And there is a faint trail . . . movement . . . running this way."

"A hole, eh?" Gaston considered the unusual nature of such a thing in the desert. "Get a rope," he ordered the lanky Legionnaire. "Climb down there and see what it is."

A short time later, Schuller disappeared down the rope in a shower of sand, but moments later reappeared, his dusty head popping through the sand at the bottom of the depression.

"A tunnel!" he called out. "There's a tunnel down here, partly caved in."

With a grim new sense of urgency, Abigail, Smith, Haffe, and Idera hurried back to the main plaza where the volume of manuscripts had outgrown the nearby chamber and the old priestesses were now unrolling manuscripts on the steps of the plaza itself. Abigail and Idera brought up the need for transport, and Haffe volunteered to take a ladder back up the passage they had fallen through . . . to climb out and retrieve their equipment and horses.

Sensing their time was shortening, Abigail began to survey and select the manuscripts from known thinkers. Her throat tightened as she went from scroll to scroll, knowing that in choosing some to take with her, she might be rejecting others that were more important . . . ones that might not be here when she returned with a full expedition.

Smith watched her with the books the way she chewed her lower lip, the anguish in her gaze each time she laid a manuscript back and moved on, the way she paused periodically to square her shoulders—as if adjusting the burden the old priestesses had thrust upon them.

Making such choices grieved her. As he watched her fingers lingering on the rejected scrolls, wanting them, regretting leaving them, he recognized in her actions the poignancy of first love. She had fallen in love with books early on, and had devoted her life to them. In that brief moment he glimpsed the workings of her heart and began to plumb unexplored depths of his own.

His chest felt tight and his stomach seemed to be sinking lower. It struck him that not only did he understand the longing and desperation she was feeling, he was feeling it, too. Her feelings had somehow migrated into his chest and his stomach and his . . . What was happening to him? He was soaking her up feelings like a damned sponge!

It was those kisses. And the touches. And talking. Arguing. Battling. Every encounter had infected him a little more. She was under his skin in a big way and giving him a helluva fever. In his head. In his heart.

Good God.

Dizzy suddenly, he staggered backward and plopped down on the plaza steps. He was in love with Abigail Merchant. The knowledge spread through him like a good whiskey's fire, starting in his core and spreading outward, warming and claiming as it went. He was in love with a woman who made him randy, furious, and crazy . . . all at the same time!

He shoved to his feet, determined to walk it off or at the very least to put some distance between himself and this appalling revelation. Then she looked up with a scroll in her hands and caught him in her sights. He froze like a rabbit before a hunter, feeling his gaze drawn into hers.

Dove-gray eyes, shimmering with fulfillment and sadness. Suddenly he was feeling the same thing. That peculiar pleasure tinged with pain. And he couldn't walk away. He couldn't just leave her there; he might never be able to leave her. He strode over to her and pulled the scroll she was holding from her hands.

"Come on, Boston, you need a break." He dragged her to her feet and led her along the loggia to the common hall, where he made her sit down and thrust a cup of wine into her hands.

"It's all so much," she said looking up at him with turbulence in her eyes. "I never imagined I'd have to make such decisions—not by myself."

"There's no one better equipped to do this than you." He sank onto the dining bench beside her and realized that his hands were trembling.

"But if I choose wrongly—if I don't realize the significance of a scroll—"

"Look, the world has gotten along without these books for nearly two thousand years. If you miss a few . . . we'll survive." He reached for her hand and the feel of her skin against his sent a ripple of intense pleasure up his arm.

She glanced down at his hand covering hers and raised a soft smile.

A sharp *crack* of a sound lashed through the open door. Something about it sent a frisson of alarm through him. He straightened, listening, and soon there was another, then another. He looked at Abigail and explained his fear and his bolt for the door with one word: "Gunfire!"

In the plaza, the old priestesses were standing like gophers caught out of their holes, staring in dismay at various tunnel entrances. The sounds weren't anything like the rumblings and shifting of earth they had grown accustomed to hearing. They were sharp, sporadic, and sounded alarmingly man-made. The acrid, biting smell that wafted out into the plaza was quickly followed by several men in dirt-covered uniforms, bearing rifles and forcing a battered Haffe ahead of them at gunpoint.

The old women were startled at first, but they had some experience with invaders of one kind or another. One look at the men's scarred and pitiless faces and they knew they were in for trouble. Hathor put down the scroll she was rewinding and backed away along the nearest loggia, escaping the ranting of a thick, flat-faced man demanding their submission. She darted into the commons as quickly as her arthritic limbs would allow.

Gaston. Abigail glimpsed him from the doorway of the common hall and shrank back inside the door as Hathor burst inside and scurried past her toward the corridor beyond. She caught sight of Smith standing at the base of the plaza steps and was barely able to stop herself from calling out to warn him. He headed for the fountain and crouched behind it, stealing glimpses of Gaston. She watched helplessly as the sergeant and his cutthroats rounded up the old priestesses and demanded to know who was in charge . . . demanded their valuables and the whereabouts of *"l'homme Smeeth."*

None of the old women spoke French. For several harrowing minutes, Gaston went from woman to woman, shouting Smith's name into each face and driving home his demand with an occasional raised fist or bullying shove.

Idera rushed into the plaza and planted herself before Gaston with a fearless mien and an erect bearing. She insisted they leave, but Gaston didn't understand until she pointed toward the tunnel they had arrived through and uttered commands so regal that they transcended mere language. With a snarl, he swung a meaty fist and sent her sprawling back onto the pavement.

"Bastard!" Smith launched himself from behind the fountain and into Gaston's side, knocking him off his feet and crashing to the ground with him.

Twenty-four

Smith managed to get in a few savage punches before Gaston's men pulled him off and dealt him the same. Abigail groaned and flinched with every blow he received. She felt for the gun at the back of her waist before realizing it was in one of her bags, at their camp . . . somewhere in the desert. There was no time to look for another weapon; she would just have to count on the element of surprise to give Smith some advantage —

"Wait." Someone grabbed her arm and she looked back to find it was old Hathor. "That matters not, out there. You must come with me to prepare."

"Prepare what?" Abigail tried to shake her off and turn back to the scene unfolding in the courtyard. Smith was moving, crawling to Idera's side, pulling her into his arms and cradling her under the barrel of Gaston's pistol. The other old priestesses had each targeted one of the invaders and now advanced on him. In a heartbeat, the old girls were stroking and rubbing up against Gaston's men in a startling parody of seduction. The men, horrified by the old women's advances, lost track of Gaston's orders in their own desire to get away. They brushed and shook the women from them, growing increasingly frantic when the priestesses tried to renew their attentions.

Beside Abigail, Hathor shook her head in dismay at her sisters' failure.

"It always used to work," she muttered. "Come. *Now.* We must hurry."

"Seize the old whores," Gaston roared, "and lock them up!"

The men grabbed the old priestesses and dragged them screeching and clawing toward a nearby doorway. Gaston turned on Smith, giving him a savage kick that would have caught him square in the gut if he hadn't released Idera in time and curled away.

"Where is the treasure you came for?" he shouted.

Smith rolled back, holding his side.

"Look around you." He was gritting his teeth. "These scrolls are the only treasure here. That's what we came for. These books."

"Liar," Gaston snarled, then strode over to stare down at some of the open scrolls. "You didn't come here for paper!" He gave several of the scrolls savage kicks. The sound of papyrus and parchment ripping seared Abigail's heart. "Where is the treasure?" He kicked Smith savagely again. And again.

"No! Stop!" Idera threw herself over Smith with her hands stretched out to ward off further punishment. "Tell him I'll show him the treasure!"

"But, there is none," he protested in her language.

"Not true, Engle-lander." She caught his gaze and in that brief glance convinced him to trust her. "There is something I have not yet shown you."

Gaston watched the tension between Smith and Idera, and when Smith translated, he snarled at one of his men to bind "Smeeth" and bring him along.

Soon the old priestesses were locked into a chamber just off the plaza, and Idera and Smith were being dragged by Gaston's men through the corridors toward the scriptoria. Idera stopped before the door to the flooded chamber.

She made a show of selecting the right key to open the door and the soldiers raised their torches and knocked her aside in their rush to enter. The water shocked them and they turned back, shouting the place was flooded. Gaston turned on the old priestess, brandishing his fist and spitting oaths.

"Tell him there is another door,' she told Smith, without quailing. "But to get to it, his men must remove a beam that has fallen in front of it."

She lifted her garments and waded into the water . . . leading them to a niche at the far end of the chamber. In front of the alcove were several beams that seemed to have fallen from some of the wooden bracing that had been used to shore up the ceiling over time. One of the beams was still blocking the way to a small metal-bound door set into the stone wall. Gaston studied the situation and the old woman, clearly suspicious, then leveled his cocked gun on Idera.

"You—Schuller—" he ordered, "go find some axes."

Shortly, as Gaston inspected the door his men had to open, Idera caught Smith's gaze in hers and covertly directed it to the main door behind them.

"This way." Hathor led Abigail through a series of narrow passages carved out of rock. The more she talked, the slower she had to walk; she had only so much breath available. "We have planned for this day."

"What day?" Abigail glanced over her shoulder. "I have to go back and—"

"You should be about your task, Librarian," the old girl admonished. "Your man will survive."

Abigail reddened. *Her man.*

"Gaston wants to kill him."

"That brute?" She gave a snort. "He wants gold more."

They arrived at the temple and Hathor led her to the back of the altar, and despite her obvious desire to hurry, the old woman took her time locating a small iron circle with a star-shaped hole in the center. She then produced a straight-shanked, star-shaped key and inserted it. Something in the lock gave with a *clunk* and Hathor slid back a panel of the marble base. As she turned a geared handle, the image of Athena began to pivot to the side, separating from her seat. Abigail had to help the old priestess lift the hinged lid of the altar and together they stood panting softly, staring at a chamber containing fired clay jars bearing seals . . . amphora.

"Here, Librarian, are the most valuable of our texts . . . dedicated to Athena—our legacy to the world. If no others survive, you must see that these are kept safe."

The tenor of resignation—or forboding—in Hathor's words put Abigail even more on edge. She helped the old woman remove the amphora from the chest. The long, thin jars with handles on either side of the necks were heavier than they looked. When all seven lay on the floor beside the altar, Hathor produced three lengths of stout rope from inside her garments and tried to get down on her knees to thread them through the handles. Abigail watched a moment, then took the ropes herself and sank to her knees to link the jars in pairs as Hathor directed.

When she looked up, Hathor was holding a jewel-crusted collar she had just pulled from the chest. It was a wide flexible circle made of the same golden "scales" that formed the ceremonial breastplate Abigail wore under her clothes.

"This was worn by the chief priest, the foremost *Protector*," Hathor said, softening visibly, clearly revisiting a memory. Then she stood on her toes and pulled out a short golden staff with a bale at the end and a matching crook— symbols of Egyptian royalty used in Ptolemy's Alexandria.

"These things are priceless." Abigail fell back on her rear and stared in awe at the things the old woman was handing her.

"So they are," Hathor said with a sad smile, producing more. There were golden lamps and altar furnishings, bale ends for scrolls, golden plates and chalices, golden wrist cuffs, and great chains with jeweled medallions. "These are symbols of our culture and our mission to safeguard knowledge." Last, came a small bag of gemstones and a pair of large leather bags that were still supple enough to hold the treasures securely.

The old woman gripped the side of the altar and endured the pain of sinking to her knees beside Abigail. She placed her hands over Abigail's, holding her tightly, willing her to hear and understand.

"You must take these with you, too. They will help you tell our story."

Abigail couldn't swallow. These were final words. Hathor did not expect her life or the life of her community to continue much longer. She thought of the scrolls stacked in the common hall and spread on the plaza steps—then made herself quit thinking of them. Nodding, she began to place the treasures into the leather bags, moving faster, feeling a growing urgency.

There was an ominous boom and crash that exploded into a roar. Everything around them shook like it had when the tunnel collapsed . . . except that this vibration was many times stronger.

Abigail thought of the cracks in the stucco and stonework of the dome over the plaza. There was hardly a place in the city that was structurally immune if the dome roof decided to. . . .

Smith!

She ran through the temple to the front columns and peered out at the plaza. Dust and sand were drifting down from the stonework overhead, filling the air with an ominous haze. A single Legionnaire stood watch in the plaza, fingering his rifle and staring uneasily at the stonework overhead. But Abigail's attention snagged on the scrolls piled and unrolled on the steps nearby and then flew to the door of the building where the old priestesses were being held.

She had just decided to go for the door and free Calla,

Elysia, and the others, when Hathor swayed past her, headed down the steps in open sight.

"Hathor, wait—let me—" Abigail shouted softly, trying to call her back.

By the time the preoccupied Legionnaire spotted her, she was more than halfway to the door leading to her sisters' prison. The guard challenged her, but she gave a dismissive wave and kept going. Clearly, without Gaston's direction the Legionnaire didn't know whether to shoot her or not. Conflicted, he finally raised his gun—just as another, larger crash rocked the entire complex, causing everything to shake violently. He staggered and flailed, trying to keep his feet, forgetting the old woman as the first stone fell from the dome.

Halfway up the man-made part of the expanse, a narrow trickle of sand funneled through the opening left by the fallen stone. The moving sand forced a second block free, then a third. Suddenly sand was pouring in a steady stream into the far side of the plaza. The Legionnaire panicked and ran for the tunnel that had brought them into the complex. Hathor reached the door and opened the latch, but instead of calling her sisters out, she entered, leaving the door standing open.

The stone pillars of the temple portico around Abigail swayed violently enough to dislodge pieces from the capitals above. Massive stones came crashing down around her and she bolted down the steps to the main plaza . . . just as Idera, Smith, and Haffe emerged from one of the streets leading to the scriptoria. The three were battered and scraped, and holding on to each other for support, but the minute they spotted her Smith waved her back.

"Go back!" His voice was barely audible above the continuing roar and rumble of stone falling and structures failing. She defied his order to run to them and insert herself under Idera's arm, taking much of her weight from him.

"Into the temple!" Idera cried weakly.

Moments later, they limped through the debris on the front colonnade and into the safer space inside the temple.

The ground gave one last powerful shudder and then abruptly ceased trembling. There was an unnatural feeling to the sudden stillness. In the distance rocks could still be heard falling and rolling.

"What happened to Gaston?" Abigail asked, looking to Smith.

He shook his head grimly and said only: "Later."

Idera grabbed Abigail's arm as they hurried through the sanctuary.

"Hathor—did she show you the books? Did you prepare them?"

"She did." Abigail helped the priestess to the rear of the altar. When Idera saw the amphora laid out on the floor, linked by ropes, she sagged against Abigail to gather her strength. "Thank the goddess. You must take them and go—now—before the dome fails completely."

"Not before I get some of the other books." Abigail started to move toward the plaza. "I know exactly where several important—"

"There is no time to argue." Idera pulled her back and draped a pair of the amphora over her shoulder so that one hung in front, the other in back. "Carry them thus. I'll show you the tunnel that is strongest. You will have to move quickly."

"No—I can't leave the books—"

"Go now," Idera said with pain in her voice, "or you may not leave at all."

"What are those?" Smith had shouldered a pair of the amphora, then spotted the leather bags. Lifting one, he found it remarkably heavy. "What's in here?" Before anyone could respond, he stuck fingers into the top of the sack and encountered cool, sleek metal. "What the—" He yanked open the cords and gave a low whistle. He looked up at Haffe, who burst into a joyful laugh and reached for one of the sacks, lifting it onto his free shoulder.

"Come—there is no time to lose." Idera thrust one of the two lighted, sacred lamps into Abigail's hands and then pushed open a hidden door at the side of the altar. The way was narrow, crudely chiseled from the rock that formed the main part of the temple. Smith had to bend and crouch to make it through and Haffe sometimes had to put down his bag of gold and drag it behind him in order to pass. But after a few minutes of harrowing and increasingly claustrophobic descent, they reached a tunnel that was broader and of more reasonable height. The air was thick with dust, and there were sand and small rocks underfoot that made crunching sounds.

"If you bear to the right twice and then to the left once, this tunnel will take you to an oasis that is directly east," she said looking to Smith. "The tunnel you came in by runs directly west." He nodded. "You may still be able to retrieve your horses. If not, nomads come by the oasis from time to time . . ." She looked pained as she gave them each one last touch and muttered a blessing. As she turned to retrace her steps to the temple, Abigail grabbed her hand.

"Come with us, Idera. Your knowledge is priceless. You could help us tell the world your story."

A rumble moved through the walls and passages and vibrations made the sand at their feet shift. The old priestess stiffened, looking sad but resigned.

"A hundred and fifty years is long enough to live," she said. "I would stay with my sisters and share their fate."

Another, more powerful rumble sent a shower of sand and small stones down over them, and Smith muttered something unintelligible and pulled Abigail's hand from Idera's. With a nod to the old woman, he dragged Abigail down the tunnel. She protested and made him halt, but when she looked over her shoulder, there was only darkness. Idera and her lamp were gone. Her eyes filled with blinding tears.

"Hold up the lamp, Boston," Smith ordered, pulling her along.

When she held it up and blinked to clear her eyes, she was alarmed to see dust and rocks spraying down through the roof of the passage. The large stones had once been held in place by force of placement and mortar, but seemed to be slipping both restraints.

"This thing could go at any time," Smith uttered. "Move!"

Abigail went in front since she held the light, but she soon was being pushed by Smith's determined pace. At each juncture he reminded them "two rights and a left," and Abigail was grateful he had the presence of mind to keep track. She kept thinking of Idera and Hathor and Calla, and of all of the archaeological treasures that were being destroyed behind them.

The rumbling seemed closer and the creak and groan of rock around them grew deafening and seemed almost continuous. It was like being in a fog; the light of her lamp reflected off the falling dust, making it difficult to see the way. She extended her arm and veered to the side of the passage to let the wall help guide them. They began to cough and Smith told her to pull her shirt up over her nose to filter the air. She could hear the strain in his and Haffe's labored breathing. The heavy bags of artifacts were becoming a dangerous burden, but Smith was determined to soldier on.

Then there was a huge, ear-splitting crack and thunderous roar. The earth shook and large stones from the tunnel roof began to fall. Abigail yelped as a stone glanced off her shoulder and Smith shouted above the roar: "Run!"

Twenty-five

Dodging rocks and splintered timbers, they charged through the passage . . . gasping for breath . . . battling both a lowering ceiling and a sharpening incline. All that mattered was putting one foot in front of the other and evading the rocks falling around them.

Abigail sensed that Smith wasn't behind her and when she looked back, he was bent at the waist in order to move through the tightening passage. A frisson of panic shot through her as it occurred to her for the first time that they might not make it out. Then she saw that part of his struggle had to do with the bag he carried—the artifacts—the gold.

"Drop the bag!" she called, sliding back down the sand-slippery slope to extend him a hand.

"No!" was all he could spare breath to say. But moments later the lowering ceiling forced him to lower the bag and pull it behind him. This time when she offered a hand, he accepted it. When she called to Haffe. who was behind Smith, the little Berber's only response was a gasping prayer of gratitude that he was not as tall as Smith.

The sand under their feet made traction difficult. Each

of them slipped and fell, banging the amphora against the passage floor. Everything seemed to be closing in on them, as if the earth itself was trying to strip them of the evidence they carried—determined to keep the story of the library its own private secret.

Without warning, the tunnel began to collapse, raining rock and sand down on them, knocking the lamp from her hands and plunging everything into total darkness. Sand started to engulf her feet. With the memory of being buried alive fresh in her memory, she began to churn her legs, running almost in place, her panic rising. Smith's hand released hers and she cried out and turned back, groping for him in the darkness. He latched on to her wrist but when she tried to pull he didn't move.

"I'm stuck—"

"Leave it!" she cried.

"No—I think I can—"

Another rumble caused more rock to fall around them and she screamed, "Smith! Haffe!"

"Here!" Haffe called, sounding far away.

Suddenly the sand and rock filled a third of the tunnel—Abigail was practically crawling as she struggled to haul Smith upward with her. It felt like her arm was being pulled from its socket.

"Leave the bag!" she cried.

"If I could just—there's a damned rock—it's wedged. . . ."

Rocks crashed behind them and the roar of sand and debris filling the tunnel told them they had just missed a massive cave-in. Galvanized, Abigail set her feet against one side of the tunnel and her shoulder against the other, latching on to Smith's arm with both hands and pulling with all her might.

Smith felt his grip on the bag failing and desperation filled him.

"The tunnel is filling up!" she called to him. "Smith—for God's sake—"

He felt inevitability in the way the bag was slipping

and, with a surge of self-preservation, released it and began to climb over the mounds of rock and sand building between them and the exit. Moments later, they reached a spot where the sand sloped downward and sensed they were past the worst of the cave-in.

"Haffe!" he called, panting, bracing against one of the walls, listening past the *shush* of falling sand and his own echo.

The little Berber's voice sounded far away; he was caught in the cave-in. Smith felt around in the dark to locate the slope and crawled back to the top of it.

"Crawl along the top—there's still an opening. Feel for my hands." He called to Abigail: "Grab my feet—when I give the word, pull!" Then he crawled up the slope and stretched out through the narrow opening between the unstable roof and the debris filling the tunnel.

He had to fight for every breath and suppress every survival instinct he possessed to again wedge himself into that narrow space. It seemed like forever before he felt something brush his hand and called out, "It's me—here's my hand—can you feel it?"

Haffe's fingers coiled around Smith's, then their other hands met.

"Pull! Now!" Smith yelled.

After an agonizing minute, Haffe burst from the hole— free—and all three of them tumbled back in the darkness, struggling to breathe. Then the earth rumbled again and they were forced to push on in the darkness, praying there would be no more obstacles.

The tunnel abruptly shortened, making walking impossible. They dropped to hands and knees to crawl along in the darkness. The rocks cut their hands and gouged their knees. Just as it seemed too much to bear, a faint point of light appeared far ahead.

"Light!" she called. "I can see light ahead."

The prospect of breathable air and being able to stand up helped her ignore the pain in her hands and knees. The tunnel brightened continually as they approached the end, and it seemed to her that something like branches or roots had overgrown the opening. It turned out to be vines that had once fed from the spaces between rocks in what appeared to be a man-made wall. She pounded with her fists to break the desiccated vines and was finally able to push the three amphora she carried out the opening and then to drag herself out after them.

She tumbled into a cylindrical structure made of stacked stones—a hand-dug well. Its bottom, where she landed, was at least ten feet below ground level and was bone dry. She staggered to her feet and checked the amphora. Finding them intact, she bent and braced with her hands on her knees, breathing deeply, grateful to be alive. She was more grateful still when Smith pulled himself out of the opening and collapsed nearby . . . still wearing both of his amphora.

She helped him up and together they staggered to the opening of the tunnel to help Haffe. When he scrambled out, covered with sand, he threw his arms around Abigail and then Smith, weeping with joy and relief.

"Praise be to Allah—we escaped! I swear upon my mother's heart I shall never again—"

"Where is the other jar?" Abigail said, staring at the amphora that had fallen by Haffe's feet. She grabbed the rope and pulled it from the vines at the tunnel opening . . . and out came the broken top of second amphora he had carried. The rope was still tied to the handle.

"Sorry, Merchant ma'am," Haffe's big eyes were filled with glistening prisms. "Jar broke."

Abigail's heart stopped as she stared at the jagged shards left around the still-sealed mouth of the clay jar.

All she had learned . . . all she had discovered . . .

"But . . . kept book," Haffe said, pulling a long, narrow roll covered in sheepskin from behind him.

Her eyes widened.

"You saved it?" She grabbed it and pressed it to her heart, rocking, weak with relief. "Oh, thank God."

No one spoke for a few moments as they caught their

breaths, brushed sand from their hair and clothes, and took stock of their injuries.

"What is this place?" Smith looked around as she inspected the scrapes and cuts on his hands.

"Well," Haffe said, confirming Abigail's thought. "Old."

None of them had serious injuries, but all of them felt like they had mud in their lungs from the dust they had been forced to breathe. They began to look for a way out of the well, and Haffe discovered stones projecting from the sides of the well at graduated intervals, meant to serve as steps.

They climbed out into the dying light of the setting sun, piled the amphora together, and collapsed on the ground beneath some palm trees. A sultry evening breeze felt like the kiss of Life itself as they lay looking up through the palms at the deepening blue of the oncoming night.

The next thing Abigail knew, she was awakening to a similar sky, but with the sun visible behind instead of before them. On one side of her Haffe snored softly and on the other, Smith sat watching the sun come up. When she moved, he looked down at her.

"Are you all right?" he asked.

"I'll survive," she said, pushing herself up and feeling every nerve and muscle in her body screaming protests.

"Good." He pushed to his feet. "We have a long walk ahead of us."

Minutes later, the threesome were trudging through the desert, headed due west and praying that the old priestess had known her directions.

As they walked Abigail asked how they had escaped and Smith explained Idera's trap in the flooded scriptorium . . . how she had tricked Gaston's men into chopping through the last remaining support beam to get to a door that supposedly concealed treasure. Instead, they demolished the shoring of the chamber and the scriptorium started to collapse into the pool of water in the cavern beneath it. Apparently the old sisters had known of the dam-

age to the structure for some time, and the water had wors-
ened it to the critical stage. Several of Gaston's men were
trapped in the collapse and as Idera and Smith escaped
from the chamber, they saw Gaston and others scrambling
for their lives.

"So, he's dead now?" Abigail asked.

Smith raised his eyebrows. "I believe so."

"Too bad," she said tightly. "He deserved worse."

Three hours later, standing on a high dune, they spotted
a haltered horse wandering and began to run.

What they found on arriving in their old camp made for
good and bad news. Their horses and mules were still there
and seemed little worse for their time in the hot sun. With
some water and a bag of feed, they soon revived. The camp
itself, however, was a disaster. They stood looking at the
wanton destruction, and Smith ground out one word that
sounded like a curse: "Gaston."

It took a while to clean and repack their gear, and treat
their minor injuries. Haffe rounded up the Legionnaires'
mules and Gaston's horse and declared that he intended to
sell them at the first horse souk he encountered. They
would fetch enough for two or three of the camels he
needed. At that oblique reference to the fortune they'd had
possessed briefly and lost, Abigail looked to Smith, who
set his mouth grimly and looked away.

The threesome donned turbans and *jellabas* against the
sun, and by early evening, were headed directly north, intending to take the same route back to Marrakech and
Casablanca.

The next evening they were still trudging northward,
veering slightly to the west, fighting exhaustion and dreading the notion of having to spend another night on the
ground, when they crested a small rise and spotted in the
distance a small, fortified village—a *ksar*.

As Smith and Abigail paused on the heights to discuss
whether to try to find hospitality there, Haffe straggled up
to joined them and recognized the place.

"Foum Zguid!" Haffe declared with a surge of energy.

He pointed at the village's red mud walls and distinctive red and white gate towers. "Haffe's cousin here!"

With a few inquiries, Haffe was able to locate his cousin's gated house . . . a place apparently known for offering hospitality and lodging to foreigners. His cousin Topsel was delighted to see Haffe and insisted on offering them food and shelter. After introductions, Haffe's rotund cousin showed Smith and Abigail to sleeping rooms and provided basins and plenty of water for bathing.

It seemed like heaven to Abigail as she scrubbed the dirt from her hair and broken fingernails and cooled her sunburned skin. Never again would she take simple bathwater for granted.

After a meal—at which Haffe dazzled Cousin Topsel and the family with tales of his adventures—Abigail excused herself to her room and Smith soon followed. He found her sitting on her bed, staring at the amphora lined up on the floor nearby.

"You did it," he said, watching her pensive mood. "Right there you have proof that a remnant of the Great Library existed and that you found it."

"I know." She arched her back and rubbed her neck, unable to enjoy the success for the weight of loss and disappointment. "But there was so much more. Thinkers and authors that shaped our world with their words, and might have reshaped it with a few more words." Her usually square shoulders rounded. "And that beautiful temple . . . and Idera and Hathor and old Mercredes . . . I can't bear the thought of them lying beneath a mountain of sand and rubble."

"It was what they chose, Boston."

"I know. I just can't help feeling . . . we lost so much."

He sat down on the bed beside her but refrained from touching her.

"But we also gained a great deal." He nodded to the amphora. "Aren't you curious?"

"Yes. Of course." She looked at him and then at the seven scrolls. "But we can't open them. They have to be treated for preservation the moment they're opened and conserved and studied under the most pristine conditions." She shook her head. "Not to mention the fact that the seals need to be intact to authenticate them. I guess we won't really know their contents or their value until we get them back to London."

"Yeah?" A faintly wicked smile crept over his face. "Well, like it or not—one of them has already been opened. Don't you want to see what it is?"

She stared at the scroll lying on top of the other amphora. He was right. The seal was gone; the manuscript was already exposed to the hazards of air and heat and whatever moisture and pests might lurk nearby. Her heart beat faster.

At her fingertips lay one of the seven texts the keepers of wisdom had chosen to preserve specially and return to the world. Something for the ages.

"I could unroll it for just a few minutes." She chewed her lip. "It would probably give us a glimpse of what to expect in the others." She retrieved the scroll and carried it gingerly back to the bed. "Light another lamp."

She knelt by the bed and he quickly joined her, holding the second lamp aloft. Her hands trembled as she drew out the scroll and unwrapped the soft leather covering. The document was written on parchment of excellent quality, still surprisingly supple. She could scarcely breathe as she untied the binding and watched the wisdom of the ages unroll.

"Greek," she breathed out, "thank heaven."

"What does it say?" he asked, barely able to contain his excitement.

"It says . . ." She pointed with her finger along the large letters inscribed at the top of the first column. "The Book of . . . the . . . Seven . . . Delights." She frowned and retraced the words. "The Book of . . . the Seven Delights."

"What is that? A bit of philosophy? A play? A treatise or an epic?" When she didn't answer, he tried something simpler. "Who wrote it?"

"It says: 'From the priestesses of the Temple of Athena . . . to the lovers of Greece and of the entire world.'"

"What? The old tarts wrote their own book?" he said with a grin. "What would they have to write about?"

Alarmed by what came to her mind, she bent over the manuscript with her finger flying along the beautiful script, fitting letters into words and words into sentences that sent a slow current of shock through her. Her face drained.

"What? What is it?" Smith watched her reaction as she sampled various parts of the manuscript, then he tried to parse out a few of the words himself. "I can speak it, but I never really learned the written—it all looks like Greek to—"

She, on the other hand, was having no difficulty reading. It was the content that stunned her: *pleasures of the flesh and spirit . . . eyes that beckon . . . soft breasts . . . adoring tongue . . . a stallion rearing . . . in a most pleasant position . . . with limbs flung wide and body yielded . . . rake the nails of the fingers along the inner thigh . . .*

She couldn't breathe. She gasped and her mouth opened but no air entered. She lurched up and backed away from the manuscript in horror.

"The 613s!"

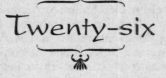

Twenty-six

"What's wrong?" Smith looked between the scroll on the bed and Abigail's shrinking posture. "What do you mean? Six hundred thirteen what?"

"It's . . . it's . . . about men and women and . . ."

"And?" he prompted.

"Being together . . . like in . . . marriage." She could see he wasn't taking her meaning and uttered just above a choked whisper: "It's about *sex.*"

"What?" He blinked and looked back to the scroll opened on the bed.

"Sex." She managed to say it louder and with a less sibilant "s."

"You're joking."

"I would never joke about such a thing," she bit out, feeling betrayed and more than a little foolish. "It's a book of instructions for . . . the act of . . . *procreation.*"

He looked stunned for a moment, then brightened.

"The old girls wrote a pillow book?"

"A what?"

"In the Orient, books meant to educate the reader on sexual practices are called 'pillow books.'" He bent closer to the suddenly tantalizing script. "Why on earth would the old priestesses have written such a thing?"

"Because that was the purpose of their cult of Athena." She stared at the scroll, seeing in a disturbing new light Idera's disappointment that she had never taken a lover. She couldn't believe their bizarre preoccupation with sexual proficiency—both hers and the rest of the world's—was becoming the focus of her discovery. "Idera and Hathor said their sect believed that the portal to true wisdom was the joining of male and female in the procreative act. Some notion of rejoining the separate halves of mankind and making things whole again."

"Ah! Like the Tantric beliefs." He smiled. "Hard to imagine the old girls—"

"Like what?"

"Tantrism. A Hindu philosophy and practice aimed at attaining enlightenment through the joining of male and female in sexual pleasure. Ravi told us about it." He produced a lopsided grin. "Being in a *foreign* legion is a very broadening experience." He leaned over the scroll, staring at the letters, frowning. "Damn. My old language master *said* I'd be sorry if I didn't study my declensions."

"You don't understand," she said angrily, grabbing him by the sleeve to pull him away from the book. She didn't know which was more infuriating: the old priestess's prurient notions, the fact that they weren't alone in such beliefs, or the fact that *he* seemed to know all about them! "I can't take that scroll back to the British Museum. I'd be made a laughingstock."

"You can't help it that the old girls wrote a book about 'the procreative act.'" His grin faded as he glimpsed the genuine turmoil in her. "Look, it's only one of seven. And they thought it was important enough to preserve it for posterity. It may seem a bizarre notion—sex as a path to wisdom—but you have to remember that a lot of the great thinkers seemed pretty outrageous. Like Plato with his philosopher kings . . . Rousseau with his noble savage . . ."

Struck suddenly by a second punch of horror, Abigail

turned to the other amphora that were lying with such deceptive innocence along the wall. Instead of priceless treasures, she suddenly saw them as bombs waiting to explode and rain humiliations down on her.

"Of all the priceless works . . . of all the great thinkers they had to choose from, why on earth would the-ey . . ." Her voice and self-control both broke. The tensions, fears, and anxieties of the last few weeks collided with extremes of fatigue and disappointment and an overwhelming sense of responsibility.

"We came all this way and found a whole library of irreplaceable ancient works." Her anguish rose with each word. "We discovered a beautiful ancient temple and the descendants of a whole community of knowledge keepers. And then lost them all. They're all gone." Angry tears burned her eyes and she balled her hands into fists. "We risked life and limb—I almost got you and Haffe killed—and for what? To gain the approval of a bunch of hateful old men who will never really accept me or allow me to do the work I want to do! What kind of madness is that? Worse—I spent almost every penny of my mother's legacy . . . so now I'll never have a house of my own or any real security. . . . All I have to show for months of planning and expense and misery and hazard is a book I can't show anyone and six pig-in-a-poke jars that will probably turn out to be the world's biggest archaeological joke!"

"Come on, Boston." He headed for her. "You're not responsible for their contents."

"You don't get it, do you?" She swiped at her tears as she backed away, refusing to let him touch her. "I'm a *woman*."

"Ohhh, but I do get that, sweetheart. Believe me. I get it all the way."

"They *hate* women scholars. They hated my mother—made my father take her name off the work they did together. And they hate me—just because I was hired by the museum. They'll use any excuse to discredit these books, whatever is in them, because they weren't found by a man."

She focused on the open scroll through the tears burning her eyes, seeing its dismal future and feeling despair closing around her. "Especially when they see that one. They'll say it's immoral or indecent or an out-and-out fraud. 'The classical masters would never have produced such a thing,' they'll say, or 'It doesn't belong in a muse—'"

She broke into sobs she couldn't stop, and the frantic shushing of her inner librarian only seemed to make her cry harder. Covering her face with her hands, all she could think of was getting out of the room, out of the house . . . away from all the evidence of her colossal failure and her humiliating reaction to it.

But after only two steps toward the door she bumped into Smith, who corralled her in his arms.

"No—no—"

She tried to pull free but he only held her that much tighter. Realizing he didn't intend to let her go, she stopped resisting and gradually melted against him, burying her face in his shirt.

Her turbulent emotions slowly calmed and her sobs faded. Surrounded by his presence, she was finally able to wipe her burning eyes and drag a deep, shuddering breath. She found herself seated on his lap, on the bed, wrapped snugly in his arms. He was holding her, resting his cheek against her temple, letting her purge the accumulated tension of weeks of danger and uncertainty.

She pushed back to look at him. His eyes were islands of tranquility . . . earthy green and gold and brown . . . with dark, luminous centers that seemed oddly warm and comforting. His arms around her felt strong and unexpectedly gentle. It occurred to her that the worst had happened—her lofty ambitions were now probably forfeit—and she felt strangely better than she would have expected. In fact, sitting there with him, she was feeling almost relieved. And when she looked into his eyes, she knew what it was that made the difference. In finding the library and losing it, she had found something that made her feel more vital and glad to be alive than a bunch of scratchings on parchment ever could.

"You make me crazy, you know," she said quietly.

Apollo smiled.

"I know."

"Mostly because"—she drew a fortifying breath—"I'm crazy about you."

His smile broadened.

"I know that, too."

His lips closed over hers, warm and soft and welcoming. When he turned slightly and slid her back onto the bed with him, she reached up to cradle his face between her hands and closed her eyes to focus on the changing sensations of his mouth on hers. Desire flared into the space created and then vacated by more volatile emotions. She sensed what was coming . . . wanted it . . . needed it. . . .

"What the devil is that?" He ran his hand up her side and over her breast. He pulled back, blinked, then went for her blouse buttons. "What on earth?"

She swallowed hard against the grip of desire on her throat. "Idera gave it to me in the temple, after you left that first evening."

His gaze fixed on the bumps at the tips of the golden orbs.

"It looks like a woman's . . ."

"Breasts," she finished for him.

"Made of . . ."

"Gold." She gave a certifying nod.

"Good Lord."

As the impact of the sight registered, his voice lowered a full octave.

"Take it off."

Moments after the metallic garment hit the floor, he sank back onto the bed and pulled her beneath him. Murmuring half-coherent endearments into her skin, he covered her body with kisses and caresses from trembling hands. Gradually, she released her own curiosity and began to explore beyond kisses and nibbles, tracing his body with eager hands. And as tension and pleasure rose apace, she molded her half-bared body against his, seeking that mysterious combination of position and pressure that could assuage the burning in her breasts and the hot ache between her legs.

The rest of the world melted into a darkening blur of shade and color as her awareness shrank to the boundaries of the bed. Sensation bathed the underside of her skin and trickled through her body to pool in her loins. She was suddenly possessed by the urge to hold him closer, to feel him with every part of her hungry skin, to feel him around and even inside her.

As the last barriers of propriety and custom were removed, night-cooled air flooded over her heated skin and she shivered. He gave a soft laugh as he braced above her, staring at her tousled hair and glowing body nestled in a whorl of abandoned clothes. His eyes glinted as he lowered his mouth to hers and whispered against her lips:

"I'm crazy about you, too, Boston."

With a laugh, she pulled him over her like a blanket and gave a ragged sigh of pleasure as he satisfied her desire to be closer to him . . . and in so doing, created another desire, even more compelling.

Then another.

And another.

Later, she lay in a steamy tangle of bedclothes and limbs, watching the painted ceiling of the room come back into focus and thinking she'd never be the same again. The thought was not nearly as frightening as it would have been only a few hours ago. The innocence lost seemed more like ignorance shed. And wisdom gained. The thought astonished her.

She had never imagined that sex could seem so pleasurable and so honorable at the same time . . . so reciprocal . . . so tender . . . so *loving*. She looked at his face lying so close to hers on the pillow and felt an overwhelming desire to share him—no, to share the pleasure and joy she found with him—with the whole, entire world. If she could somehow pull everyone into their embrace, bring everyone into the sense of connection she now felt with him. . . .

Apollo Smith was nothing that she in her buttoned-up, dead-language-loving, book-obsessed core would have expected to want. But he was everything that mattered to her now, everything that brought her joy and pleasure and made her want to grow and experience and give. This, she realized with a growing sense of awe and humility, must be what her mother had felt for her father.

This must be *love.*

When she opened her eyes the next morning, he was lying beside her, propped up on an arm and watching her.

"How do you feel?" he asked, running a hand up her naked side.

"Good," she said, self-conscious and edging toward embarrassment.

"Just good?"

"All right, *very* good."

"Must be losing my touch." He shook his head. "Maybe the old girls can give me a few pointers." Reaching down to the floor beside the bed, he picked up the loosely rolled book and placed it on her stomach. "Read to me."

"Now?" She pushed up to lean against a pillow and yanked the sheet up around her, dislodging the scroll from her lap. "This is hardly the time for—"

"*Au contraire.*" He set the scroll squarely on her lap a second time. "It's the perfect time. After last night, you'll have some basis on which to judge it."

Her jaw dropped.

"You think last night was merely an exercise in validating a manuscript? How could you even think I would—"

He stopped her words with a hand.

"Last night was between you and me, and about you

and me," he declared. "And it was better than good, it was *great*. But then, isn't that what the old girls claimed to write about? Men and women loving each other and somehow learning from it?"

She looked at him in confusion. He had to be the most infernal—

"Read," he demanded. "How else are you going to know if it's immoral and degraded and needs to be destroyed?"

"It's not my place to say what is or isn't immoral. And a true librarian would never, ever advocate destroying published works on such a basis."

"Really? I was beginning to wonder." He stretched out across the bed and propped his head on his hand. "Lucky for you, I happen to have a little experience with immorality. I'm pretty sure I'll know it if I hear it. Read."

Curse him—he was challenging her to live up to her precious ideals. She glared at him, then at the manuscript. She did want to know—*needed* to know—what was in it. She would have to read it sooner or later. Shifting to take better advantage of the morning light, she began to parse out the words.

" 'From the priestesses of the Goddess Athena, lovers of wisdom but also lovers of humankind . . . to all of those children of humanity who would seek wholeness and enlightenment. Since the dawn of time . . . when humankind's spirit was split in two . . . there has been a yearning of the soul, a desire in the heart to join with another . . . to become one . . . to be whole again. And the great Goddess Athena in her perfect wisdom, has shown us the way.' "

"Sounds perfectly high-minded to me," he interjected.

She gave him a silencing look.

" 'The capacity for physical pleasure is a gift from the divine and must be treasured and cultivated. In discovering and mastering the Way of the Seven Delights, a man and a woman will find not only pleasure, but unity. And the great paradox of such communion is . . . when two become one, each discovers a clarity of being, a new awareness of self in that union.' "

"Something of a twist on the old 'the-whole-is-greater-than-the-sum-of the-parts' notion," he murmured. "And?"

" 'The first delight is *Seeing*. Seeing the beloved in all the ways and shapes and moods that can delight the eye and entice the heart . . . studying the form of the body . . . which is so marvelously created and wonderfully made. Let the lover remove his beloved's garments, one by one . . . adoring each part of the body unveiled . . . the lobe of her ear . . . the hollow of her throat . . . the slope of her shoulder . . . the curve of her breast. . . .' "

Her cheeks were hot enough to glow in the dark. She raised her head and found he had shifted closer and was staring at her with darkened eyes.

"Go on," he said, his voice lower than before.

"This is . . . indecent." It wasn't so much a professional opinion as it was a personal feeling. She was going all hot and itchy, deep inside. Reading matter that made her feel like she had to rip off her clothes and drag him naked onto the bed just had to be wicked.

"Looking at someone and adoring them is indecent?" He gave a *tsk* of disapproval. "Shakespeare wrote worse. Read on."

" 'Do not touch, except to remove barriers to vision. And be not hurried in this adoration,' " she said, tracing the line of script with a finger that was beginning to tremble. " 'The world has nothing more important for you to do than to discover the fullness of your pleasure in one another.' "

"Nothing is more important." He pushed himself up until he sat staring intently at her earlobe and the nape of her neck. "Sounds like wisdom to me."

She stiffened, unable to retreat as he leaned closer to nudge her hair away from the back of her neck.

"It is beautiful, you know," he murmured, lowering his face so that she could feel his breath moving her hair. "Your skin. Sleek. Soft."

A cobra watching a snake charmer would have had more control at that moment than she had. Her breath was growing shallow, her mouth was going dry, and her skin prickled with expectation. He was practicing the old girls' suggestions for seduction . . . absorbing her with his gaze, bathing her skin in admiration. And she couldn't summon the slightest desire to object.

He dragged a finger up the side of her neck and out along her naked shoulder. Knowing now where those delicious sensations could lead made them both alarming and irresistible.

"Read on." The vibrations of his voice ignited a slow fire under her skin.

"It's probably just a list of body parts." She shivered.

"Then *really* read on."

" 'The eyes are the windows of the soul,' " she read, glancing up at his eyes . . . the color of forest and earth . . . glowing with possibility.

" 'To know the beloved, the lover must peer through these windows to learn the depth and beauty of the beloved's heart. Let the lovers face one other and look long and patiently through the windows of each other's souls . . . naming what they see . . . adoring all that the beloved is . . . pain and pleasure, sorrow and mirth . . . righteousness and compassion . . . yielding and steadfastness. . . .' "

Again her gaze sought his before she forced it back to the scroll.

" 'But let nothing be hidden . . . by garments, or shyness, or shame.' "

"The old girls must have written this in their *younger* days," he quipped.

She couldn't help the laugh that bubbled up through her or the gasp of surprise she uttered as he wrenched the scroll from her hands.

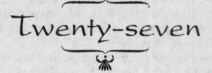

Twenty-seven

"Hey!" She tried to cover herself as he pulled the sheet from her body and dragged her up onto her knees with him in the middle of the bed. "What do you think you're doing?"

"Trying out the old girls' 'first delight.'" He grabbed her hands and refused to let them go. When she reluctantly met his gaze, he smiled. "How else will you know if it's a fraud or true and worth all of this effort?"

She sat on her knees with her arms over her breasts, feeling exposed and uncertain of what he intended and of how she should react. Even after what passed between them in the night, there was still a part of her that held back, wary of yet another surprise.

Determined, he faced her on his knees and held his arms out at his sides.

"Here I am, Boston. Look at me. See me as I really am."

It took a moment or two for curiosity to begin to overcome modesty. Her gaze wandered awkwardly, almost reluctantly over his naked frame, trying not to linger on any one feature. Then he dipped his head to capture her gaze in his and she was unable to free it. Soon she was falling heart-first into those dark-centered gold-and-green eyes, entering the uncharted depths of him.

The longer she looked, the more fully she absorbed the impact of what she saw . . . the sum of the pain and pleasure he had experienced . . . his sorrows and losses . . . his irreverence, pride, stubbornness, and irrepressible spirit. He was a very complicated man, and yet had a way of making things oh, so simple.

And he seemed appealingly simple just now. All there. Open to her. Offered to her. Nothing held back.

Her heart stopped for a moment. She couldn't breathe. It was a revelation. And an invitation. To accept, she would have to take the same risk and open herself in the same way and allow him access to the longing, the desire, and the love in the deepest core of her.

Her mother's example had taught her that love could be difficult and demanding. But, as annoying and challenging as Apollo Smith could be at times, loving him was turning out to be liberating in ways she could never have imagined. It opened her to new ideas, new attitudes, and new delights . . . along with all the new complications it brought into her life. Loving him had changed her, was still changing her . . . opening and freeing parts of her she hadn't realized existed. And in the end, it was those changes that made the difference.

She leaned forward, widening her eyes, lowering her last defenses, inviting him into her heart.

"Here I am, Apollo. See me."

"Earnest," he said as he gazed intently into her soft gray eyes. "And honest. Sometimes too honest for your own good. Rigid at times. But careful and diligent and dependable. Hellishly stubborn. But too softhearted to ever be fully arrogant." He smiled as incidents from their time together surfaced in his mind as a response to each conclusion. Each memory brought yet another realization. "Dutiful. Gentle. Tough. Hungry. Proud. Tender. Compassionate. Proper . . ." He paused for a moment, absorbing her, searching her shimmering eyes, looking for the one thing that would change his life forever.

And there it was.

"And *loving*." Relief and joy both collected in his throat, making his next words sound strangely hoarse. *"Loving me."*

The smile that brought to her lips put the Mona Lisa's to shame.

"Good God, Abigail Merchant—it took you long enough."

He wrapped both arms around her, bore her laughing back onto the bed, and loved her until she not only saw stars, but felt them exploding in the very core of her. There wasn't a particle of her body that wasn't moved and somehow transformed by the experience.

As they lay together later, exhausted but far from sleep, it occurred to her that the old priestesses' first delight had offered a perfect way to lower barriers and defenses between her and Apollo. Surprise filled her as she glanced at the rolled parchment now tucked safely away at their feet. It was almost as if the book had been written all those centuries ago just for—

She stilled and held her breath as the realization struck. It *had* been written for them . . . and for all the other couples striving to love fully and discover the depths of their hearts. And if it worked for them, then it just might work for others, too.

"I think the old priestesses knew what they were writing about," she said with an edge of reverence.

"Holds out hope for the other six jars." He chuckled and stroked her bare breast as she lay snuggled against him. "And makes you wonder what they consider to be their *second* 'delight.'"

Recognizing the light struck in his eyes, she shoved up onto her elbow and teased him with a lingering kiss.

"If I translate it for you . . . I don't want to hear you ever complain again about my desire to do things 'by the book.'"

• • •

Touching, it turned out, was the next "delight" prescribed by the priestesses in their guide to attaining wisdom. By day's end, Abigail and Apollo had explored a few of the wide range of tantalizing contacts that employed the sense of touch. Time seemed to stand still while they embraced and caressed . . . tickled, scratched, raked, tweaked, brushed, and kneaded. They made it through only a small part of an exhausting list before passion flared wildly and irrevocably between them, and they were forced to rest for a while afterward.

Cousin Topsel, their compassionate host, delivered a tray of food to their door that evening and suggested they might like to dine on the roof, under the stars. With tray in hand, they ascended the stairs and found a rooftop haven spread with Persian rugs and fat silk pillows, and furnished with brass lanterns.

They ate hungrily of coucous with almonds and currants, stuffed squash and roasted lamb, then he doused two of the three lamps, lay back on the cushions and made a place for her beside him.

"Look there," he said, pointing to a constellation in the night sky as she nestled beside him. "That's Orion the Hunter . . . the Pleiades, which figure in a lot of local stories . . . and over there is Canis Major, the brightest of which is Sirius, the Dog Star. And that's Mars. See how red it looks compared to the others? Back that way, near the horizon"—he pointed over his head, past the intervening walls—"is the North Star that the sailors used to steer ships. And the Big Dipper that points the way."

"How did you learn about stars?" she asked studying his profile even as he studied the sky above. He chuckled.

"I got tired of lying on the hard ground, night after night, staring up at the stars and knowing nothing about them. So—" He glanced at her from the corner of his eye. "When I finally got paid, I bought a book about them. I carried it with me on patrol and made friends with the night sky. Crocker and some of the others in the company

gave me a bad time about spending money on books instead of whiskey. But soon they were out there with me,
staring up at the sky, learning the stars' stories and how to
navigate by them. It was the first of several books I bought
and shared." He paused. "Ironic, really. When I arrived in
Morocco I was trying to escape books. And tutors. And ex-
aminations—"

"You were at a university for a while," she prompted.

"Oxford. Three interminable years. I was ready to start
my final year when some friends asked me to go with them
on a 'grand tour.' My father was furious and demanded I
stay at home with my shoulder to the wheel of the family
business." He expelled a deep breath. "I told him to take
the Calvinist pole from up his arse and quit hounding me
about 'preparing myself.' And I ran off to join my friends
in cutting a degenerate swath through Paris and Marseille
and Mallorca. Then Tangiers."

"Is that where you . . ."

His arm tightened around her, betraying the potency of
those memories. "I had no idea that my father's health and
the family firm were both in decline. That was why he
drove me so hard to do well at university and prepare myself. He needed me to take the reins." He paused for a moment. "But he also wanted me to *want* the reins."

"When you went back to England, did you see him?"

"He died two and a half years into my contract with the
Legion." His voice flattened. "I didn't find it out until almost a year later . . . when I spotted my uncle LaCroix in
Marrakech. He seemed surprised to see me still alive and
was more than pleased to give me the news of my father's
death."

"He told you . . . just like that?" She reached up to
stroke his face. "Apollo. I'm so sorry." She paused before
asking: "What about your mother?"

"My mother was from the south of France and never did
well in the English climate. A year or so after my father's
death she took to her bed, ill."

"You didn't get leave to go home to see her?" she asked.

The harshness of his laugh was blunted by the warmth between them.

"There's a saying in the Legion that Legionnaires have no family except their brothers-in-arms." He paused seeing events again in memory. "I wrote my mother after I learned of my father's death, but I received no reply. I learned from the family solicitor, when I was in England, that she was heartened by my letter and longed to see me. He said she wrote me back, but by that time I was in a mounted company and constantly on the move. I never got her letter. She died before I made it back to England."

"Oh, Apollo." She gazed into his luminous eyes and glimpsed the pain that he carried on account of his lost family. There were more questions to ask, but guided by a surge of feeling, she kissed him instead.

He took a deep breath and set aside those painful memories.

"It's just ironic that it took five years in the Legion . . . starving, scorching, working myself into a stupor, and spilling my blood all over North Africa to make me finally appreciate the privileges of an upbringing and education that had once been handed to me."

She was deep in thought as they descended the stairs later with their arms around each other. As they strolled along the loggia toward their room, he ran his hand up to the side of her breast and gave a chuckle.

"I've been thinking about this golden breastplate of yours."

"I can tell," she said as she trapped his fingers against it.

"Strictly speaking, it's spendable treasure. Which means Haffe and I are entitled to half of it."

"Hmmm." She canted her head. "This may require some delicate negotiations."

"And speaking of gold," he said more slowly and deliberately, clearly bracing for a reaction, "I'm thinking about going back to the oasis with Haffe and some diggers to retrieve the artifacts from the tunnel."

"What?" She entered the room and turned to look back at him. "You can't be ser—"

A hand clamped over her mouth. Apollo saw a human shape materializing out of the darkness and seizing her. He reacted out of pure instinct, bolting across the room after her.

"Abigail!" Before he could reach her, a second force came roaring from the shadows by the door and blindsided him. It felt like his skull exploded and by the time his knees hit the floor, he was fighting paralyzing flashes of pain to stay conscious.

He managed to deflect part of a second blow, and heard scuffling and a string of oaths, and the hammer of a gun being drawn back.

"Not here, idiot!" a graveled voice snarled in French, just before a third blow—to the back of his head—caused everything to go black.

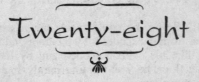

Twenty-eight

"Wake up!"

Water splashing over him caused Apollo to struggle back toward consciousness. He lifted his pounding head and found himself lying facedown on a dirt floor with his hands bound behind him. The place looked like an abandoned house; it had numerous layers of old paint on the walls and crumbling stucco everywhere. From the dingy light of a battered lantern hanging overhead, he could see a dust-covered bench nearby, but otherwise, the room was empty. He dropped his head back to the muddy floor.

"Wake up, damn you!" A pair of worn boots appeared and delivered a fierce kick to his ribs. "Wake up so you can see how you are going to die."

He rolled as far as he could to lessen the force of a second kick and clenched his jaws as pain exploded like fireworks through his belly.

There was a pause, then the battered, bloodied face of Sergeant Gaston appeared above him grinning. Another kick produced a spear of pain through his ribs and kidneys. Gaston grabbed him by the collar and jerked him up.

"Surprised to see me?" He gave an ugly laugh. "You

hoped I died back there in that hellhole with the rest of them."

"Not at all, Gaston," Apollo gritted out. "I was hoping you *lived* . . . for several days . . . trapped under tons of rock. . . ."

Gaston's fist plowed into his mouth and felt like it was stripping flesh from bone. His head snapped back, and he saw starbursts of light after Gaston cropped him back on the floor.

"Stop—leave him alone!" Abigail's voice galvanized him. He fought to focus his gaze and locate her. She was being held at the far end of the room by two men dressed in torn and bloodied clothes what had once been Legionnaire uniforms. One of the men he recognized, a tall, emaciated fellow called Schuller.

"Boston—are you all right?"

"Better than she will be," Gaston said, stepping into Apollo's line of sight. "After I get through with her, she'll be fit for nothing but dog meat."

"You hurt her and I swear I'll—"

"You'll do what, Engleesh? Bury me alive? Steal my horse and leave me afoot in the desert? You tried that." He leaned closer. "But then, you were never good at murder. No killer instinct. You always had to have a little help." He leaned closer and his lips pulled back over his foul teeth in a parody of a grin. "Like the night you killed a man in a bar fight." He gave a vicious laugh. "How does it feel to know you spent five years in hell for *nothing*?"

"What do you mean—nothing?" Apollo said, struggling past the pain to think. Gaston knew what happened that night . . . knew he wasn't a killer. . . .

"You don't remember." Gaston seemed pleased as he squatted before him to better view his face. "It was my men and I who 'arrested' you and took you to the constables. They took my word that you had killed a local—one of their own—and were more than willing to throw you in 'the box.'"

"Why?" Apollo demanded, fighting the temptation to

succumb to the wretch's taunts with paralyzing fury or despair. "I'd done nothing to you."

"Money. What else? I was paid to see you found your way into the Legion."

"Paid by whom?" He needed to keep Gaston talking.

"You cannot guess?" Gaston laughed, clearly relishing his power. "Think harder."

The ropes binding him felt stiff, new. Schuller and the other man had been in a hurry and hadn't bothered to pull them tight enough on Apollo's wrists. He began to work his hands back and forth.

"You think you are so smart." Gaston delivered him another nasty kick. "Who in Tangiers would care about a drunken English schoolboy?"

Apollo spit the blood from his mouth and answered.

"LaCroix."

"It took you long enough." Gaston straightened and inserted his thumbs in his belt. "Despite your books and fancy airs, you are a fool." Another kick took Apollo's breath and caused a stabbing pain in his lower chest. Cracked ribs, he realized, feeling as if his lungs were being squeezed with each breath he took.

"Algeria," he managed to pant out. "Up north. He paid you then, too?"

"Good money," Gaston boasted. "Though, by then I hated you enough to kill you for nothing." His face twisted as he leaned closer. "Son of an aristo whore . . . you think the world owes you . . . others should listen and follow you . . . because your blood is blue and you read your fancy books." He ripped his knife from his boot. "Let us see the real color of your blood. . . ."

Abigail watched in horror as Gaston slashed Apollo's shoulder, wringing a grunt of pain from him and sending a stain of crimson spreading across his shirt.

"Red. Like the rest of us," Gaston said on a growl that caused the back of her neck to prickle.

"Stop!" She was able to shout by thrashing her head enough to escape the hand across her mouth and digging into her cheeks. "I'll tell you about the treasure. Leave him alone and I'll tell you how you can find the treasure!"

Apollo gritted out her name in warning as Gaston shoved to his feet and wheeled on her. "*Tresor*? You think Gaston ees stupid, eh?"

"Abigail—don't," Apollo said, though his words were less than distinct.

"There is a treasure," she blurted out. "Gold beyond your wildest dreams. And precious stones . . . artifacts just waiting to be claimed . . ."

"Lying whore," Gaston sneered, glancing back at Apollo. "You think to buy his life with simple lies?" He turned back to Apollo, his eyes narrowing. "Now you both die."

"I can prove there is gold," she said, straining against the hands that held her. "Listen to me Gaston—I can prove it. Think of it—*gold*. You'll be able to buy your way out of the Legion—"

Gaston raked her with a glare.

"I am gone from the Legion already. Took 'English leave.' Months ago." He drew his pistol. "Like your lover. *Le deserteur*." He lowered the gun toward Apollo's head, which sent her into a panic. He had nothing to lose by killing Apollo and her.

"Are you going to let him kill your chance at riches?" she demanded of the lanky guard gripping her left arm and the grizzled old veteran who held her right. "If he kills Apollo, I'll take the gold's location to my grave—I swear it!"

Gaston must have realized her tactic might succeed with his henchmen. He turned enough to glare at them over his shoulder.

"She lies—she knows nothing!"

"I have proof—here." She struggled to raise her captive hands. "Just look at me!" The men's hold on her arms slackened with curiosity and indecision as she fought to reach her blouse. One button gave, then another. Gaston was cursing in French, berating the pair, demanding they stop her while he cocked the gun he held on Apollo. She flipped a third button, then ceased worrying about fastenings and just grabbed the sides of her blouse and ripped them apart.

"Look!" she shouted, arching her back to thrust her breasts and their covering forward. "Look at this!"

The gasps and mutters of his men caused Gaston to slash a look over his shoulder. A moment later, he pivoted fully to stare at her, his mouth slack with astonishment.

She glanced down at herself . . . at the golden breast cups with their prominent nipples, the intricate metalwork and precious stones around the edges, and the scales of gold glinting in the dim light with every frantic breath she took. She had never felt so exposed or so desperate. She looked up at Apollo's bloodied face and pain-racked form on the floor. Or so determined.

As Gaston and his thugs stared at the breastplate and at her breasts visible at the edges of the cups, she felt a subtle shift in the balance of power.

"This is only a small part of what the old priestesses gave me," she said breathlessly. "There are golden plates and lamps and chains and chalices . . . collars laden with precious stones . . . enough to make you rich men for life." She looked at the men holding her. They were salivating. She could see them swallowing, pushing aside their desire for vengeance in favor of more primal urges, and prayed that riches came before lust in the hierarchy of their desires.

Gaston lowered the gun to stalk over and squeeze the nipple at the tip of one of the golden cups—his eyes glittering—his tongue flicking over his lips.

"So, I see there is something in this gold, after all."

Suddenly Gaston slammed forward into Abigail, knocking her back against the wall. Her scream was trapped in her throat by the impact, but as she fought for breath, she also fought to free her arms from the surprised henchmen. Bashing them with her fists, she felt Gaston's bulk peel away and saw Apollo on his feet behind the sergeant . . .

with the ropes that had bound his hands now stretched taut around Gaston's bullish neck.

One of Gaston's men made a lunge to help, but Gaston's cocked gun went off and sent the man scrambling back to help his comrade with Abigail instead. They began pawing at the breastplate she wore, trying to pull it from her. She beat at them and kicked. Out of pure instinct, she sank her fingernails into one of their faces. He howled and withdrew, only to return with a backhanded blow to her face. . . .

Across the room, Gaston had managed to double up and pull Apollo over him, breaking the choke hold. He jammed an elbow into Apollo's ribs, pounding the breath from him and sending him crashing back against the nearest wall. Gaston staggered around and remembered the gun in his hand. As he raised it, Apollo lowered a shoulder and charged him full out, slamming him back against the far wall. They grappled for the gun, wrestling and straining . . . the gun hit the floor.

Abigail fought furiously as the men combined efforts to overpower her and push her down onto the floor. With her hands pinned on each side of her head and the men kneeling on her legs to keep them down, she could only buck and thrash as they pulled at the breastplate and laughed cruelly as they tried to fondle her in the process.

She spotted a knife in the top of one of their boots and knew it was her only chance. Going still, she began to make sobbing sounds and begged them to stop and not hurt her any more.

"Take it—you can have it!" she cried, turning her face from them and measuring the distance to the man's boot before slamming her eyes shut. "It has a special latch—let me get it off—"

They hung over her, panting, eyes fixed on the gold of the breastplate. They glanced at Gaston, fighting for his life, and turned back to her with heated faces. Gaston's hatred for the Englishman was no longer their concern. Here, it was every man for himself. They eased their weight from her legs and pulled her up to a sitting position.

She reached for her head and swayed as if she might be going faint, then lashed out and grabbed the knife. Before they could react, she slashed one's arm and sent the blade deep into the other's thigh.

Apollo heard the howl of pain and the roar of anger that followed, but couldn't see what was happening. The sergeant's meaty hands were clamping tighter and tighter around his throat. Darkness was closing on the edges of his awareness; he could barely draw breath. Desperate, he tried one last move—bracing with his legs and heaving up, unsettling Gaston for a fraction of a second. That was long enough for him to get his chin against Gaston's wrist and bite down on it with everything in him.

Gaston howled and recoiled. In the heartbeat that followed, Apollo rocked to the side and threw Gaston off. He was dimly aware of Abigail struggling to crawl away from Gaston's men. He glimpsed them grabbing furiously at her, then jerking back when she turned and lashed out at them. An alarming blur of red was all he saw before he reached his feet and Gaston charged him like a wounded bull. . . .

Abigail spotted Gaston's gun on the floor. Crawling frantically—stretching her fingers and gritting her teeth—she managed to reach the grip of the pistol and drag it toward her . . . just as the two men grabbed her feet and hauled her back to face their vengeance. She curled to one side, bringing her hands together on the handle and pulling back the hammer with both thumbs.

One saw the gun, the other didn't. When she squeezed the trigger, the older man jerked and headed over onto the floor . . .

The gunfire sent a bolt of electricity through Apollo. He was vaguely aware of a scuffling near the door, and then it seemed like everything else in the room went still. He and Gaston rolled on the floor, punching, gouging, and kicking . . . each determined to finish the other . . . until a form loomed above them and another shot rang out.

Gaston screamed and rolled back, grabbing his thigh. Above his groans and curses, Apollo managed to hear the double click of a cocking pistol.

"Don't move, you miserable bastard!"

It was Abigail's voice. And when he recovered enough to focus his eyes, he saw her standing over Gaston with her blouse ripped open, her hair a wild tangle, and her hands filled with a gun.

"You?" he managed to croak out. "You shot him?"

"Them," she said tautly. Her eyes were white hot with fury and her grip on the gun was rock steady. He looked over to find one of Gaston's men lying crumpled on the floor and the other gone.

It took a moment for the impact of it to sink in. She'd just shot two men. And probably saved his life. It was all he could do to get to his feet and stumble over to her.

"Are you all right?" she asked, glancing at him for only a second.

"I'll live." He sagged on her shoulder for support.

"That's good enough for me." She gave a strange little smile and after glancing up to reassure herself it was true, she focused again on Gaston. "What do we do with him?"

"If you kill me," Gaston snarled, his lips flecked with spittle and eyes glassy with pain, "it changes nothing. LaCroix will still have what he wants."

"And just what is that?" Apollo wrapped his free arm around his damaged ribs and tried not to breathe too deeply. "Why has he hounded and pursued me?"

"You don't know?" Gaston's laugh was chilling.

Angered beyond reason, Apollo sprang forward and dropped a knee onto Gaston's damaged thigh. The sergeant screamed.

"Tell me! What does he want?"

"Your birthright."

It was gritted out under such duress that it had to be the truth.

"That's almost funny," he said, beginning to feel a little

delirious. "I don't have an inheritance. My father's business was sold to pay off credit—"

He halted and for a moment held his breath to keep the pain of breathing from clouding his thoughts. LaCroix wouldn't know or care about his father's business. He would only care about things that would come to Apollo's mother . . . his estranged sister. "But the LaCroix family has nothing of value. My mother was eager to wed my father because her family was penniless.

"Tell me! What does he think he'll gain by my death?" he demanded, grabbing Gaston by the hair of the head and shaking him.

"I don't know," Gaston finally admitted, his voice hoarse with pain. "But something worth more than *your* damnable life."

Apollo dragged himself from the injured sergeant and stumbled back to Abigail, who pulled his arm up over her shoulders to support him.

"I have to find out what LaCroix is after," he said, looking into her determined gaze. "I have to get back to Casablanca."

"He'll be gone before you get there," Gaston muttered, struggling to stay conscious. "He's selling everything. Fleeing Morocco. You'll never find him."

"I'll find him," Apollo said, "if I have to track him to hell and gone."

"When he learns you're alive, there won't be a safe corner for you in all of Morocco." Gaston ejected one last bit of venom: "When we meet in hell, Smith . . . we'll continue this."

His head dropped to the side and Apollo knelt to feel for a pulse.

"Is he . . ." She looked at the gun in her hands with dawning horror and dropped it. "Did I kill him?"

"No. He's still alive. But he's losing blood fast." He looked at the pool of blood beneath Gaston's leg. As much as he loathed the wretch, his conscience wouldn't allow him to do nothing. He unhooked Gaston's belt and pulled it from him to strap around his leg like a tourniquet. Then he rose and put his arms around Abigail.

"Let's get out of here," he said, turning her toward the door.

"What do we do with Gaston?" she asked.

Apollo halted to look back at him. "He's not going anywhere. We'll turn him over to the local police. If he's lucky, when he wakes up he'll be in a local prison. If not, the locals will save themselves trouble by saving just his severed head for the native *goumiers* who hunt deserters for the Legion."

As she nodded, her gaze caught on something.

Twenty-nine

"Wait—" She ducked from under his arm and hurried back to retrieve something from the floor. As she took her place under his arm again, he saw that it was the gun and stared at her in surprise.

"What?" She looked up at him with widened eyes. "I think the wretches used *my* gun. See? It's a Webley top-break .455."

"Mark Two," he added, his battered mouth quirking up on one side.

"Maude Cummings was right about something after all," she said. "It does pay to have a gun with good 'stopping power.'"

He laughed even though it hurt, and in moments they were stepping out into the gentle light of the breaking dawn.

Their arrival at Cousin Topsel's, looking battered and bloody, sent the whole household into a frenzy. Haffe was frantic that Smith and Abigail had nearly been killed, and Topsel was outraged that the sanctity of his household had been invaded and his guests had been harmed. His personal pride and the family honor both had been assailed.

Haffe and his usually affable cousin charged out into the street to collect men from neighboring households to search for the man who got away—Schuller—and to see that Gaston was seized and punished according to their own uncompromising brand of justice.

Abigail and Apollo were taken immediately to a room on the main floor, beside the courtyard, where Topsel's wife and daughters bound Apollo's ribs, bathed their cuts, and treated their bruises with smelly herbs mixed in camel butter. The pair were made to drink a potent tea and shown to feather-filled beds augmented with soft pillows. Their pain subsided and they were soon asleep.

It was night before Abigail stirred again. Apollo was already awake, testing his ribs and trying to stand.

"Are you all right?" she said staggering to her feet to help him.

"As well as can be expected," he said, smiling with his half-swollen mouth as she wrapped her arms gingerly around him to hold him up. They stood for a minute, luxuriating in that closeness before she looked up at him with tear-rimmed eyes.

"I thought I'd lost you," she said, "and that I'd never have a chance to tell you how much I love you."

"Yeah? Well, watching you rip open your shirt in front of Gaston and his thugs took a few years off my life." He touched her bruised cheek. "I love you, too, Boston. And I'm sorry I've gotten you into all of this. I never meant—"

She stopped his apology with her fingers. "I'm not sorry. I'll never be sorry."

He held her for some time before taking a deep breath that signaled hard words ahead.

"You know, don't you, that I have to go. I have to get to LaCroix before he disappears."

His eyes, that she had so recently learned to read, let her know the decision came from a turbulence deep in his soul. This was no show of bravado or thick-headed attempt to redress a blow to his pride. This was something he had to do. The peace of his heart, perhaps his very life itself was at stake.

"If you go, I go. I intend to be with you through every bit of it," she said drawing herself up at tall as possible. "Give me two days, Apollo. Rest and heal for two days, and then we'll find him if we have to go to the ends of the earth."

The party that set out from the village of Foum Zguid was larger by far than the one that had arrived five days before. Abigail, Apollo, and Haffe were joined by Topsel and two of his nearly grown sons, as well as several male servants, a dozen camels, and the eight Legionnaire mules and lone horse that had belonged to Gaston and his men.

Apparently Haffe had confided his desire for a brave mountain girl to Cousin Topsel, who—being something of a romantic—took Haffe's plight to a family council of other cousins in the town. The family agreed that an alliance with the wealthy chieftains of the Tizi-n-Tichka Pass would be an advantageous thing. After some initial reluctance and a promise that he would return a part of the bride price to them when he was paid for his service to the rich Westerners, they put together a number of camels and sundry other gifts that included silver coin, to help him win over the girl's family. Cousin Topsel agreed to accompany him to see to the negotiations.

Travel, while a bit slower, was certainly more comfortable than before. The extra hands made the tasks of raising tents for the night and cooking less burdensome, and the canvas-sling cots Topsel had provided made their sleep more restful. Apollo's injuries caused him to tire more quickly but in general he seemed to bear the pace well.

Despite the evidence of his improving health, Abigail worried about him. At least once a day, she caught him staring off toward the mountain peaks and what lay beyond them. Marrakech. Casablanca. LaCroix.

But when she approached him as he stood in the moonlight staring up at the mountains on their final night in the desert, he surprised her with his concern.

"LaCroix?" He gave a grim chuckle. "He's probably at least one or two deadly encounters away. I'm worried about the pass. Topsel will approach Barek first and smooth things over for Haffe with wedding talks. But as for you and me . . ." He wrapped an arm around her. "I'm wondering how you and I get through the pass without being spotted and seized. We didn't exactly leave the place on the best of terms." He hiked an eyebrow. "If only you didn't look so . . . American."

She punched him in the ribs.

But the next day as they rode along, she brought it up with Topsel and Haffe and after much discussion, they developed a plan that included Apollo and Abigail posing as servants in the party until, under cover of darkness, they could take their horses and the amphora containing the books and steal off down the road leading to Marrakech. Abigail would have to hide her face behind a veil and Apollo would have to crouch a bit to hide his height, but they agreed it was the only way to proceed until Barek and his people were preoccupied with preparations for a wedding.

The last morning on the trail before the steep trek up the mountainsides to the pass, Topsel and Haffe exited their tent wearing handsomely embroidered *jellabas*, burnooses trimmed with gold braid, and richly colored fringed sashes into which they inserted ivory-and-gold handled daggers. They could have passed for wealthy merchants . . . emirs . . . sultans.

Abigail and Apollo, on the other hand, were quickly divested of their English boots, had their faces rubbed with a smelly brown paste meant for treating horse injuries, and were covered with simple-looking cloaks infested with sand fleas. Worse still, Abigail's hood contained a veil made of thin cotton gauze that made it difficult to see where she was going. Then she learned she would have to ride one of the mules up the mountain track, since servants didn't rate horses.

"This plan had better work," she muttered, hanging on to the animal's neck and gripping the reins of the amphora-laden mule behind her as they reached the last switchback.

There was no turning back now; the track was too narrow to permit it. The camels began to balk and make a bleating sound to show their objections to the difficult conditions. Topsel's sons and servants scrambled from one to another, stroking and reassuring them and starting to sing a strange, lilting chant. The camels apparently had an ear for such songs; they calmed visibly and continued plodding.

"I wonder if they know any numbers that might work on anxious librarians," Apollo called out and Abigail didn't bother to look back, vowing to postpone bashing him until they were on level ground once more.

The pass came into view around the last perilous bend and flashes of memory brought back their previous flight through the pass . . . bullets flying, rocks grinding underfoot and careening off the edge of the sheer drop beside them. Her mouth dried and her palms dampened as they approached the gray granite walls of the pass itself.

There were half a dozen rifle-carrying guards on duty. She rounded her shoulders and crouched lower in her saddle, trying not to stare at them, but feared they could see right through the veil over her face and would know she was a foreigner. She held her breath, but they looked past her to Apollo, who was riding the lead camel. To her surprise, they looked past him as well to focus on the camels themselves.

Topsel and Haffe dismounted and distributed tobacco, asking directions from the guards to the center of the settlement. The guards laughed when they revealed their mission, and pointed them to the right path. But Abigail wasn't able to breathe comfortably until the entire party was through the main street and they were stabling their animals at the corrals.

Two mules laden with gifts and one camel went with Haffe and Topsel to Barek's tent. Topsel did the talking and was soon granted entrance for an audience with the head chieftain. Apollo and Abigail watched from a distance as they unpacked the mules and had Topsel's sons carry the gifts inside the chieftain's tent. All was quiet for a time as they helped the servants erect their own sleeping tents at the edge of the compound and eyed the path to the Marrakech road. They had to hope that Cousin Topsel was as persuasive as he was romantic and that Haffe's heart would be satisfied in the outcome.

When she looked at Apollo, he smiled, shrugged, and went back to brushing the horses they had unloaded. She went back to drawing water for the animals stashed behind the tents . . . still loaded with the amphora and supplies, awaiting their escape. She caught several unveiled women watching her as she went back for more water and prayed they couldn't tell she was a foreigner . . . and wouldn't throw her down the well if they found out she was an infidel.

The sun was sinking fast and the cold, clear sky was reddening when a commotion arose from the front of Barek's tent. Abigail and Apollo froze, watching Haffe and Topsel burst outside with Barek and several of his men. The pair seemed to be in good spirits, trading banter and good-natured jibes with Barek's men as they inspected the mule and camel that had been brought to the tent for that purpose. There were several exchanges that bore the stamp of a universal bit of horse trading, then Barek himself ran a hand over the camel and pronounced it acceptable.

Abigail sagged with relief and then glanced at Apollo, who was so absorbed in what was happening that he was forgetting to slouch. She called his name quietly and made a hiss that got his attention. He quickly mended his posture and faded back toward the tents . . .

. . . just as Topsel, Haffe, Barek, and a throng of men headed in their direction. Their faces were red and their manner expansive, the effect, no doubt of Barek's rule-bending fermented honey drink. They seemed to be coming to inspect the rest of the mules and camels being offered. But it was clear from their curious stares at the tents and Topsel's retinue that they wanted a closer look at all of Haffe's and Topsel's assets.

Haffe tried to intercept their interest, drawing their attention back to the two horses he had brought . . . mentioning the name Joleef . . . indicating that one would make a fine gift for his future bride. But they spotted Abigail and asked point-blank what the men were doing traveling with a woman.

She was a kinswoman, Topsel said, brought to welcome the bride and be her companion on the journey to her new home. Barek studied her for a time, making Abigail nervous and bringing Haffe's patter of persuasion to a fever pitch.

Out of nowhere, a number of women appeared, approaching at a determined pace. They were unveiled and wore colorful striped tunics and skirts, and headpieces ringed with chains that bore rows of silver coins as decoration. They studied Abigail, who lowered her head. The woman at the front of the contingent approached Barek and spoke to him directly, pointing at Abigail.

Alarmed, Abigail bowed and began to back toward the nearest tent.

"Stay where you are!" Haffe declared in French that Apollo translated. "It is Barek's sister. Joleef's mother." He bowed to the woman and forced a broad smile. "She is upset that a woman in our company wears a veil. These mountain tribes do not veil their women. She does not wish Joleef to go to a man who will make her hide her face."

Of all the potential hitches in their plan, this was one they could never have anticipated. Abigail stared at Joleef's mother, torn between applauding her courage in standing up for her daughter and wishing she would just shut up and go away. Reassuring Barek's kinswoman that veiling was not required in Haffe's clan would require stripping her disguise and revealing her identity.

Tension mounted as both objections to the match and attempts at placation flew. Barek's men seemed amused by Haffe's position and began to call out suggestions to him . . . some of which made his face redden.

When Haffe turned to Topsel for help, the cousin tried to explain away her veil as a practice sometimes adopted on journeys . . . to afford a woman protection from strange eyes. It was her choice, he said. And she wanted to wear it.

Barek finally spoke, pointing to the spot on the ground before him. From the panic in Haffe's eyes as he turned to Abigail and beckoned, it was clear that Barek intended to speak to her and decide the matter for himself.

There was nothing to do, but comply. She took modest steps, approaching with her head bowed, trying to behave like a proper Berber woman . . . whatever that was. When she arrived at the spot and Barek asked her a question, she spotted Haffe nodding surreptitiously and followed his lead. A second question caused Haffe to wag his head and she did that, too. The final question made Haffe's eyes widen with alarm . . . not something she could answer with a simple yes or no. She squeaked out a word that sounded like "ariaha," praying that wasn't a Berber word for "stuff it in an orifice of some sort."

All was silent for a moment and she thought she might have gotten by. Then a young woman came rushing up and threw something on the ground at Barek's feet. Abigail gasped. It was an English riding boot. *Hers.*

An instant later, the women were snatching off her veil and cloak and baring her Western clothes.

Barek's eyes widened.

All at once, Apollo ripped off his burnoose, Haffe tried to grab Abigail back out of the way, and Barek's men rushed to surround them with drawn knives and lowered guns. In seconds they seized Apollo and dragged him struggling before Barek, whose looked at him with disbelief.

"You!"

Thirty

Not a muscle moved, not an eye blinked as Barek's re-action echoed through the camp. Abigail was frozen like a desert mouse before a hawk. Apollo braced for what could only be an explosion of epic proportions, followed by a dose of fierce Berber retribution. Haffe prepared to see his friends punished, his suit for Joleef's hand denied, and he and his cousin humiliated and stripped of all of the gifts they had brought . . . perhaps even the clothes on their backs.

Then Barek let out a roar and lunged at Apollo, wrap-ping arms around him and lifting him off the ground. Apollo struggled . . . then heard and felt what sounded like a laugh. A few panicky heartbeats later, Barek dropped him on his feet and pushed him back to arm's length, looking at him as if he were a long-lost relation! Then he grabbed Abigail and did the same, swinging her around and laugh-ing, saying the same things over and over again.

"My friends . . . my very good friends!" Haffe trans-lated, clasping his heart, which had finally started to beat again. "How wonderful it is to see you!"

When he put Abigail down she staggered, disoriented

by that unexpected barrage of goodwill. Locating Apollo, then Haffe, she mouthed the questions: "We're his friends now? How can that be?"

Barek sensed their confusion and laughed in a way that made mirth a command for his followers. They, too, began to laugh . . . even the women. Then the head chieftain wrapped one arm around Haffe's neck and the other around Apollo's and turned toward his tent, calling in perfect English: "You come, too, Englishwoman!"

"You did me a great service, at your last visit," Barek declared after they had been hugged again, kissed on both cheeks, and commanded to sit at his right hand. As they were brought fresh slippers and settled onto the silken cushions, the chieftain explained.

"Your story, Englishwoman . . . it was inspired by Allah Himself . . . to burn the ears of a pair of jealous kinsmen . . . traitors. Hearing your story, they believed I had learned of their plot to unseat me as head of the clans and brashly implemented their coup on the spot. But it was their own guilt that made them believe it was more than just a story and betray their own treachery. My men were able to capture and dispatch them and their accomplices. By the time I learned the truth, you had already escaped through the pass and been chased by my men. Some French Legionnaires arrived shortly after . . . offered to catch up with you and send you back to me. But of course, I did not see them again." He looked with satisfaction around his elegant tent. "In the days since, loyalty and harmony have been restored."

"Drink!" He commanded, waving the serving girls over to fill their cups with honey brew. "And eat your fill. This is a time for celebration. Allah has returned you to me and even brought me a husband for my niece . . . which will save me the expense of a journey to Imilchil."

Haffe's face fairly split with a grin and he let out a whoop of joy that brought laughter from every quarter of the tent. Topsel hugged him roundly, then reached for his own sons and ruffled their hair, admonishing them to take a lesson from their cousin on how to choose a bride.

Abigail and Apollo stared at each other in disbelief and then joined in the laughter . . . and the food . . . and the drink. . . .

When Joleef entered the main tent to help serve, portly Barek rocked to his feet and called Haffe forward to join their hands and declare that the wedding preparations would begin immediately. A roar of approval went up and Abigail spotted Joleef's formidable mother at the side of the tent watching with a critical but not disapproving eye.

Later as the dancing and the music and the feasting settled into a pleasant haze of indulgence, Barek leaned toward Apollo and Abigail.

"You are quite a storyteller, Miss Merchant. I hope the chieftain of this 'British Museum' appreciates the work of so fine a woman."

"Thank you, Lord Barek," she said, tossing a meaningful look at Apollo. "I hope to convince him to do so. I must say, your worship, your command of English is a most wonderful surprise."

"It pays for a ruler or chieftain to keep a few tricks up his *jellaba*, eh?"

"Indeed." Apollo laughed, slipping an arm around Abigail, lest there be any doubt about her availability.

"I am wondering," the head chieftain said. "Whatever happened to those Legionnaires? Did they find you?"

"They found us," Apollo said, glancing at Abigail.

"Bad men," Haffe said, wagging his head. "Deserters. Traitors. One got away, but was no doubt swallowed by the desert itself. The *goumiers* carry the head of their leader back to the French officers even now."

"May Allah send the same fate to all traitors," Barek declared, holding his cup aloft and waiting expectantly for the cheer that quickly filled the tent.

That night they slept in the comparative luxury of Barek's tents and the following day Apollo and Abigail left with fresh provisions, well-rested horses, and a pang of loss in their hearts from saying good-bye to Haffe.

The little Berber's huge, dark eyes filled with a prism of tears as he dug the toe of his boot into the dirt and tried to unstick the words in his throat.

"Much thanks, Miz Abi-gail, ma am," he managed to get out.

"It is I who should thank you, Haffe. Without your help, Apollo might not have survived and I never would have found the Library. I'll see that your name is remembered in all of the reports and publications. And I promise to send you a third share of whatever we might be paid for our work." He nodded and then suddenly threw his arms around her and hugged her for a long, tearful moment.

"Smeeth . . . I wish you well with this bad man. Be careful, eh? I tell you . . . go to the Sultan of Casablanca and ask in the name of Allah for his help. Not even a sultan can deny you if you ask in such a way." He reached out his hand to Apollo, and when Apollo took it, pulled him close to whisper: "I would wish you a gloriously fat wife, but"—he looked a bit woefully at Abigail—"I do not think the milk of six camels would be able to fatten her."

Apollo threw back his head and laughed, pulling Haffe into a full embrace as the little Berber rattled off more blessings and good-byes.

It was difficult to climb aboard the horses and head back out into the forbidding mountain terrain, knowing that they would miss the celebration of Haffe's longed-for wedding. Tears streamed down Abigail's cheeks when she turned in her saddle and saw Haffe and Joleef standing together and waving until they were out of sight.

Apollo looked a bit misted himself as he held out a hand to Abigail. When she placed hers in it, he squeezed her fingers and said, "I know. I'll miss the little wretch, too. But, just think: You can read the third 'delight' to me by the campfire. It will be just you and me." He waggled his eyebrows, then seemed to sober. "There will be vegetation and dried wood around. . . . I hope you won't miss the *parfum de camel dung*."

The third delight was called *Dancing*. And there was no better place to do it, the scroll said, than under the stars.

"Perfect," Apollo said as he pulled her back against him and nuzzled the nape of her neck. "Read on."

They were in a clearing in the middle of thickets of small trees and brambles, just off the road. There was grass and wood for a fire and clear air that made the stars above twinkle.

"'Begin by disrobing,'" she read, then lowered the scroll. "It's too darned cold to take our clothes off. And what's that got to do with dancing, anyway?"

"I suspect they'll find a way to heat things up." He kissed and bathed her neck with hot breath. "Read on and find out."

"In loving there will always be rhythms. The swaying of bodies walking side by side . . . the pounding of hearts . . . the lapping of body against body . . . the rise and fall of breasts in breathing . . . the undulations of hips in a dance of seduction . . . the utterances of lovers as they ride the crest of fulfillment. . . ."

"See?" His fingers slid under her golden breastplate. "You're getting warmer already."

She inhaled sharply, taking command of her senses and forcing her attention back to the book.

"'Lovers must explore the rhythms of their togetherness and find those which are most pleasing . . . for, the combinations of movement and frequency will be as unique to each pair of lovers as their individual faces and bodies are unique from all other faces and bodies. To begin . . . kneel and join hands . . . rocking slightly back and forth until you feel yourselves moving as one. Then stand and hold each other in an embrace, rocking slowly together, side to side. When harmony is reached, vary it and rock so that your bodies brush lightly against each other and separate at the end of each passing. Slowly increase the pressure as you brush against one another, until you can no longer part. Then you are ready for the next step. . . .

Apollo's voice was low and provocative in her ear.

"I think I could skip right to step two."

The delight of *dancing* sounded almost too simple, but in practice was surprisingly enthralling, even with a few garments left in place. When they finally did progress to step two, where they were directed to rock and rub and thrust in a variety of rhythmic encounters, they were hard-pressed not to sink into wild, spontaneous lovemaking. Not surprisingly, the book seemed to foresee that impulse and warned against abandoning control and the spoiling the learning. " 'To persevere and learn control is to learn the essence of wisdom in loving.' "

So they lay together, mostly naked and not yet joined, exploring the rhythms of each other's bodies and the resonance their rhythms could find in each other. The sensations were delicious. But it was more than pleasurable, it was enlightening. And it brought them both to a wild and shattering climax.

As they lay together later, wrapped in her doeskin sheet and several blankets, it seemed they had enough heat to warm the entire countryside. Apollo watched the sky and pointed out a shooting star. A good omen, he said.

"I hope so," she said, snuggling her head against his chest and enjoying in a whole new way the sound of his heartbeat. "You know, I've been thinking . . . about LaCroix."

"I can see I'm going to have to step it up a notch. Can't have your mind wandering while we're doing this." He gave her breast a teasing stroke.

"I'm serious." She turned his face to her. "I know it's never far from your mind either." He couldn't argue that. "I was thinking . . . LaCroix said he does a lot of trading and such in Marrakech . . . he had a caravan headed there shortly after I had dinner with him. Somebody has to know something about his plans. Does he have offices there? Property? Documents? It wouldn't hurt to take some time in Marrakech to find out."

"All of that while I was making love to you?" He sighed and pulled her closer. "I can't wait to see what you'll be like when I have your full attention."

"Ooooh," she said, brightening, already miles ahead on the road. "We could stay at the Raissouli again. They have those lovely marble bathing tubs. . . ."

On the fourth morning, when they donned *jellabas* and descended the main road toward the glowing red walls of Marrakech, their thoughts turned from their romantic explorations to the difficulties they could confront in the city. Both felt a rise of tension stemming from memories of their last stay in the city. From the minute they rode through the Bab Hmar—midday—they seemed to feel eyes lingering on them, judgments being made, and whispers being passed. Whether truly sinister or not, those impressions made them eager to be off the streets and to find a safe place for the amphora.

After they secured a room at the Raissouli, Abigail went immediately to the French Consulate to inquire about LaCroix's local business contacts. She presented herself as a new friend of LaCroix, visiting the city and hoping to contact him. When she exited the consulate, she made straight for The Europa Café, which was known to be frequented by European merchants and businessmen. Apollo was there asking discreet questions of staff and patrons.

"Any luck?" he asked. "This place is a dry well."

"The consulate staff were less than helpful at first," she told him as they took an out-of-the-way table. "But, then I implied I had a more-than-platonic interest in *le monsieur* and they practically tripped over their feet to give me this address." She held up slip of paper with a triumphant expression. "What Frenchmen won't do for a woman who bats her eyelashes."

They headed for the address and discovered that it matched a ramshackle warehouse near the great clearing called the Jemaa El Fna. They tried knocking, then pounding doors, and finally found some steps that led to an upstairs office. The rooms had been recently vacated; there were sun-faded spots on the wooden floors where furnishings had once stood.

"He's gone, all right." Apollo ran a finger over one of the bare spots. "Recently, too. Taking everything that wasn't nailed down."

"We'll just have to go back to the Europa," she said, heading for the outside door. "Or perhaps we should inquire at hotels where Westerners stay . . . see if anyone has done business with him late—*ohhh*—"

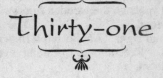

Thirty-one

"Ufff—" A Moroccan-looking man in Western dress smacked into her in the doorway. After a scramble for apologies on both parts, he straightened the crumpled brim of his hat and tugged down his vest as he took stock of them.

"May I inquire what you are doing on these premises?" he said in English that matched the language of their hasty apologies.

"I'm sorry—" Abigail began, but it was clear the man expected the explanation to come from Apollo, who took the cue and stepped up.

"We were looking for Ferdineaux LaCroix. We were given to believe these were the offices of his Marrakech trading company."

"They are his no longer. I, Abdallah bin Narjan, purchased this trading company from him just—where are the furnishings?" The man looked around the empty space, then at them in dismay. "What have you done with them?"

"We've done nothing with them, Monsieur Narjan," Apollo said adamantly. "I assure you. We arrived moments ago . . . were directed here by the French Consulate. You're free to check—"

"Then where are my desks and cabinets? My records? My bills of lading?" Alarm infused his face as he dashed past them to look in the other rooms. Finding them empty as well, he rushed back out the door and down the stairs to throw open the doors to one of the warehouse bays. It was as he seemed to fear: *empty.* He rushed to a second and then a third bay, finding in each the same unoccupied space.

He wilted with disbelief. Abigail and Apollo upended the empty barrel that was the sole occupant of the final space and helped the fellow to a seat on it.

"How could this have happened?" he mumbled. "I purchased the warehouse, the office furnishings, the contents of the warehouses, the trolleys . . . I have bills of lading. I have manifests." He looked up. "I have been robbed!"

"I fear, monsieur, that you may have been robbed by the very man who supposedly sold you the property," Abigail said. "How long ago did you make this agreement with Monsieur LaCroix?"

He thought for a moment. "A fortnight ago. Exactly. I came to these very offices and signed the documents and received the papers of ownership."

Abigail looked to Apollo, who shook his head. There was no way of telling whether that was good news or bad. Two weeks ago he was still arranging deals and engineering swindles. But, a lot could change in two weeks.

"One more thing, Monsieur Narjan," she asked, bending slightly to peer into the man's devastated face. He lifted his head and struggled to collect himself. "In the transaction, did Monsieur LaCroix happen to mention what had prompted him to sell his holdings, or what he intended to do afterward?"

Her heart nearly stopped when the dispirited Moroccan nodded.

"He said he was going home. To France."

After accompanying Narjan to the French Consulate and then to the Sultan's palace to lodge a complaint and ask that a police inquiry be launched, Abigail and Apollo headed back to the Hotel Raissouli.

"Can it really be that simple?" Apollo said, standing in the lobby looking sheepish and feeling like a fool. "An inheritance. Why else would he want me dead?"

She pulled him into the hotel bar where she ordered him some of the Irish whiskey he had declared was the mother's milk of Legionnaires.

"He was your mother's brother, right?"

"The black sheep of the LaCroix family. That was how he ended up in Morocco . . . the family banished him from France." His face grayed as he pulled out old memories for examination under new light. "I felt worldly and wicked . . . looking up the prodigal son of the family . . . discovering what a rich man he'd become . . . sampling his jaded hospitality. Food, liquor, gambling, women . . . he provided it all . . . until that night in the kasbah. . . ."

"Which he himself arranged. Small wonder he didn't respond to your pleas from prison. He wanted you out of the way," she said. "He must have already had thoughts of returning to France."

"He expected I would either be killed in combat or die of some dread disease. Only I didn't die. No wonder he was so shocked when I approached him in Marrakech." He finally sipped the drink. "If everyone else has kicked off, I suppose there might be a ramshackle old house or some land somewhere in France . . . probably deep in arrears for taxes. He's made barrels of money here. Maybe he's going back to salvage the old estate."

"There must be something of value in France that would have come to your mother and now is yours. But more important, once he learns you're still alive . . . he's a thief and a murderer who will stop at nothing to get rid of you. You won't be safe until he's dead or in prison. You have to do something."

"With what? My army of white knights?"

He downed the rest of the drink in one gulp. She had

never seen him so dispirited. He was letting his guilt over his former conduct stop him from—

"You know,"—he stared with bitter amusement at the bottom of his empty glass—"if I was still in the Legion, I'd just order up a couple of bottles of whiskey right about now, and my comrades and I would all get pig-eyed and start a—"

He sobered as he stared at the glass in his hand for a long moment, then he straightened abruptly Purpose flooded back into his face and frame.

"The Legion," he said, smacking the glass on the tabletop, tossing down a few coins to pay for the drink, and heading for the door.

"Where are we going?" she demanded, breathless as he grabbed her hand and pulled her along.

"I have a few friends in Marrakech, remember? They may not be knights, but they *do* wear white hats."

The Marrakech headquarters of the French Foreign Legion were a stone and stucco hodgepodge of Moroccan construction adorned with fussy French embellishments that looked unmilitary and entirely out of place. Exactly as he remembered it, Apollo said, pausing to take a deep breath before ushering Abigail through the gates and into the quadrangle formed by offices and barracks. It was early evening and the men of the garrison were gathered at tables under dusty canvas shades, eating their suppers.

It took a moment for anyone to notice Apollo, but Abigail the men spotted right away. Murmurs of "a woman" and "a proper lady" reached her and she tried not to react to the stares. When Apollo pulled her arm through his and clamped a hand on it, someone with a lilting Indian accent recognized him and called out his name. "Smeeth! Apollo!" Instantly, they were thronged by Legionnaires eager to greet an old comrade and angle for an introduction to the woman on his arm.

In short order, Abigail and Apollo were seated, supplied

cups of "barracks beer," and were recounting their adventures since they left Marrakech. After pausing for breath, Apollo told the true story of his induction and revealed his need for help in chasing down his grasping and murderous uncle. In Casablanca.

"Lor'—I'm in!" Will Crocker was the first to declare. "I'll go wi' ye. Things 'as been a mite dull hereabouts. We could use a right old rumble, eh lads?" He boxed the air with bony fists. "Keep the ol' fightin' blood up."

"I'll go, too," Joseph Ryan Flynn declared. "I've just been sayin' it's high time we trounced some wicked old bugger wi' a ton of loose cash."

That sparked a wave of laughter and prompted a response from Apollo.

"I can't promise you payment . . . except in camaraderie and chow."

"Anything digestible," Ravi Phant declared with a hand to his lean stomach, "would be an improvement over our sad excuse for a mess."

"But surely they can't just leave, Apollo," Abigail said, seeing in his friends' eagerness to help, a fresh disaster in the making. "Won't that be considered desertion? You know what the Legion does to deserters."

"Roight noice of ye to be concerned fer the likes o' us," Crocker said. "But ye needn' fret. The Legion's like yer ol' granny—tough at times, but alwus willing to take ye back wi' open arms."

"As long as you come back within six days," Ravi added.

"Aye, even old grannies have their limits," Flynn said with a grin.

There was agreement all around and the decision was made. Half a dozen men charged off to grab their marching kits and rifles and arrange to "borrow" several of the Legion's finest mules.

Apollo and Abigail were exiting through a passage leading to the main gate when a knotty little fellow wear-

ing clerks' armbands on his sleeves, stepped out of a
nearby office straight into their path.

"Smith!"

"Gilly," Apollo said, offering his hand to the little man.

"I thought that was you." Gilly had an Irish lilt to his
voice. "The captain told me to keep something for you, in
case you came back. Wait here."

He returned moments later with an envelope for Apollo,
who looked at it for a moment before smiling and tucking
it inside his shirt.

"And who might this be?" Gilly asked, staring eagerly
at Abigail.

"Abigail, this is Gilly Farquar, the company's clerk.
Gilly, may I present my fiancée, Miss Abigail Merchant."

Abigail was startled by his invention, but covered it
smoothly and extended her hand to the clerk, uttering
something inane but polite. Gilly blushed and quickly
drew his hand back to cradle it in his other.

"Tell the captain . . . I thank him," Apollo said and Gilly
nodded.

Apollo's friends collected outside Raissouli's and
Apollo and Abigail took them inside and, to the dismay of
the management, insisted they be given a room for the
night. They protested they'd be just as comfortable in the
stable with their mules, but Apollo persisted and they were
finally given a large room at the back of the hotel. It was
palatial compared to their usual accommodations, and after
removing their boots, they strolled reverently around the
room peering at the pictures and furnishings with their
hands clamped behind their backs.

Apollo arranged for food to be delivered and then
joined them with a couple of bottles of good whiskey, and
shared a drink with them. It was almost like old times.

But it wasn't old times. And now he had a far more appealing bunkmate waiting down the hall. Finishing his

drink, he advised them to get some sleep since they would have to travel hard and fast the next day.

"The same advice might go for you, old son." Flynn flicked a wink at the others, who laughed knowingly.

There was something about their winking and subtle humor that annoyed him. It was clear to them that Abigail was his . . . what? Partner? Woman? Lover? And what would she be to him once they reached Casablanca and she bought passage on the first steamer back to Portsmouth or London? The thought stopped him in his tracks.

After a moment, he squared his shoulders and continued on to their room. There would be time to think about all that after he had taken care of LaCroix.

When he stepped into their room he found her ensconced in a marble tub of perfumed water, looking warm and relaxed. He went to the side of the tub and knelt down.

"Are they tucked in?" she asked, opening her eyes.

He chuckled. "You should have seen them . . . meek as church mice."

She gave a throaty laugh. "That's hard to believe." Then she sat up and reached for the top button on his shirt. "Take those clothes off and join me."

He didn't have to be asked twice. Soon he was sinking into the tub and settling back, cradled between her legs, to soak away the dirt of the road.

"This might be our last night alone for a while," she said running her hands over his shoulders and arms. "And since we have a tub for bathing and plenty of water, I thought this might be our best chance to try the fourth delight."

"You read ahead?" He looked at her over his shoulder. "Without me?"

"The fourth delight is *Tasting*."

He sat up and looked at her, then at the tray full of condiments on the table by the bed.

"Ahhh. Then that explains the cinnamon oil and honey and fruit. . . ."

"'First you must learn the taste of the beloved's kisses,'" she quoted, sliding forward to pull his head down and give him a long, lingering kiss. "Ummm. Faintly sweet, like warm whiskey. 'Then progress to the taste of your beloved's skin, in all its variety and texture.'" She slid her arms gently around his healing ribs and nibbled her way up his shoulder, licking and tasting as she went. "Salty, slightly vinegary . . . very . . male," she pronounced. "'Continue until you learn the taste of your beloved's tears and sweat and . . .'"

This delight was intimate in a way Abigail had never imagined a man and a woman could be, and yet, it seemed unabashedly playful in its suggested use of sweet oils and perfumes, honey and cream, wine and peaches . . . including 'a garment of sweetmeats to be nibbled from the beloved's body.'"

Later, after Abigail took her second bath of the night and while Apollo took his, Abigail picked up the envelope that had fallen from his shirt when he undressed earlier. Without hesitating, she opened it and pulled out two letters, both written in French. She carried them to him in the tub and ordered: "Read. And translate."

"It's addressed to the Legion commander in Tangiers. 'Due to an error in casualty reporting, trooper Apollo Smith of the 4th Mounted Company posted to Casablanca has erroneously been listed as deceased. It is my duty and pleasure to report that he is in fact not dead, but presented himself to me this afternoon in my office, along with his own death certificate, which was sent to his family solicitor in England.

"'The circumstances of this error and its reporting after the skirmish at Ati Tinehir, on the Algerian frontier, are highly suspicious. The referenced letter of condolence to his family actually predated the battle in which he was supposed to have died. The incorrect report of his death appears to have been an intentional act by his immediate superior, Sergeant Emile Gaston. This same sergeant, during said skirmish, is reported to have directed fire upon a house into which he had sent Smith and three other men from his own squad. Of the four troopers, only Smith survived.'"

'Also at issue is the matter of the transfer of Trooper Smith from the Ninth Infantry Company in Marrakech to the 4th Mounted Company in Casablanca. I took it upon myself to contact the commandant of the garrison at Casablanca. He neither received nor issued orders resulting in said transfer, nor have there been any other such transfers in recent months.

'I hereby request that headquarters initiate an inquiry into these 'false orders' and into the battle reports made by the officers at Ati Tinehir, to determine if disciplinary action may be required.' "

The second letter stated simply to the chain of command in Marseille: " 'There has been an error in the reported death of Legionnaire Apollo Smith of 4th Mounted Company posted in Casablanca. Trooper Smith is not dead, and in fact completed his contract just prior to the date listed for his demise. It is therefore requested that he be issued an honorable discharge from Legion service.' "

"So you showed the captain the death certificate you showed me," she said, making the connections.

"When we were in Marrakech before. The captain was always a fair and decent man. I asked him to look into it and apparently he did."

"Fine." She gave an irritable sigh. "What's this 'letter' he talks about?"

Apollo rose from the tub, wrapped some toweling around him, and retrieved a worn but familiar envelope from his saddlebag.

There were two letters in it, along with his death certificate. One was addressed to Jeanne Marie Smith, Apollo's mother . . . a letter of condolence, signed by Ferdineaux LaCroix. The other was a letter from a solicitor in London, verifying Apollodorus Smith's identity and stating that the accompanying death certificate and letter from F. LaCroix arrived at his client's home within days of each other.

"Your uncle wrote your mother to express regret at your death, when he was responsible for it? The man's a monster!"

"That's not all," he said, coming to point over her shoulder. "Look at the date of my supposed death and the date on LaCroix's letter."

"Good Lord—he wrote your mother before you officially died."

"A fact not lost on our keen-eyed family solicitor, who saved the letters and gave them to me when I arrived in England."

"So you knew LaCroix was involved." Mixed emotions swirled in her as she turned to look at him.

"I guessed he was involved. But I didn't know why or who else in the Legion had helped him."

"Besides Gaston," she said.

He nodded. "He seems to have been the only one. The rest was just ordinary Legion bureaucracy. He and LaCroix forged orders that sent me to a mounted company and appointed Gaston my sergeant. Once those orders were slipped into the cue, the rest just followed naturally."

She slid her gaze over him, visually caressing his work-hardened and desert-tempered frame . . . lingering over his old scars and fresh bruises . . . thinking of all he had endured and all he had become. It had been a hard path for a hard-headed, arrogant young man with too much time on his hands and too many wrong ideas of the world. But Fate had been more instructive than vengeful. He had been offered an education in the true value of life and loyalty and love, and he had applied himself. He had truly learned what was of value in life, and she was fortunate to have met him after he did.

"I can't believe you didn't tell me that your Legion troubles were being resolved . . . that you're no longer dead and you're being honorably discharged. I should be flaming furious with you."

But instead she was standing half-naked, beside their rumpled bed, with tears of joy in her eyes.

She was learning, too.

She opened her arms and he walked into them.

Thirty-two

Three days of hard dawn-to-dusk riding along the main roads had brought Abigail's and Apollo's party to the eastern gate of Casablanca in the late afternoon. Apollo and Abigail cloaked themselves in their burnooses, lowered their heads, and joined the stream of visitors and traders entering the city through the Bab Marrakech. Crocker, Flynn, and the other Legionnaires rode as a group, some distance back, giving the appearance of a squad of soldiers on dispatch duty . . . a routine sight at that time of day on that road.

As arranged, both groups made their way to the heart of the city and the Hotel Exeter, the place Abigail had planned to stay when LaCroix diverted her to the Marrat. There, Apollo and Abigail took a room and with the help of the hotel's porters, stowed the blanket-wrapped amphora safely in it.

"So this is what I missed," she said, gazing at the comfortable brass bed, thick carpets, and beautiful screened loggia running the length of the room. As the last of their baggage was stowed and the porters withdrew, Abigail headed straight for her small satchel and took out her gun.

"What do you think you're doing?" Apollo watched her nimble insertion of bullets into the chambers and got a very bad feeling.

"Reloading," she said calmly. "You have a gun. Crocker and Flynn and Ravi and Sanchez all have guns. I'm not going out on the street without one."

"I'd prefer you didn't go out on the street at all," Apollo declared, grabbing for the weapon and missing. She narrowed her eyes as she tucked it in the back of her waistband. He knew that expression. "Look, LaCroix has eyes and ears everywhere, and God knows how many hired thugs on the payroll."

"All the more reason for me to be armed and with you at all times."

"Come on, Abigail—" He towered over her, scowling.

"Don't you dare start 'Abigailing' me," she said irritably. "You came along on *my* expedition and I saved your hide more than once. So, don't even think of telling me to mind my place and act like a proper lady. I'm a full partner in this venture and I'm a darned good shot."

There was no arguing that.

"Dammit," he found himself saying. "Swear to me you won't do anything stupid."

"Like what? This?" She pulled his head down for a blistering kiss.

"I was thinking more along the lines of you pulling your gun on LaCroix and shooting him before I get the chance."

She softened with a smile.

"If I see him first, I promise I'll hold him at gunpoint until you get there."

From his place at the parapet of a roof overlooking the intersection of two shadow-cloaked streets, the Legionnaire known simply as Banane could easily keep watch on the comings and goings around the walled house owned by Ferdineaux LaCroix. There was generally not much traffic in this quarter, where houses were large and gates were thick, but he had seen two parties come, pound the gates of a house they didn't know was empty, and depart disappointed . . . one stewing hotter in his suspicions, the other shouting that he would have the money LaCroix owed him or else.

LaCroix? Pay? Banane smirked at the thought. He had made sure he got a partial payment in advance for this bit of surveillance.

And a dull bit of work it had proven, thus far. There had been no sign of an uprising of angry investors, customers, or erstwhile partners . . . much less the local constables or the Sultan's personal guards. So much the better, for the arrival of the Sultan's men would spell major trouble for LaCroix, who was now vacating the city and taking everything with him that wasn't nailed down. He hadn't scrupled to spare even the ruler of the city in his latest bit of plundering.

Banane yawned and pulled back from the parapet wall to pace a bit and restore circulation in his legs. The exercise took him around the edges of the rooftop sleeping rooms and garden and where he paused to peer over the edge into the shadows. A movement in the alley below caught his eye.

He pulled back out of sight, waited a moment, then peered over the edge to count four men. Two were in what looked like Legion uniforms, but the other two wore *jellabas* over Western trousers and boots. The taller of the two wore what looked like an eye patch that was flipped up. He squinted for a closer look as the group tried the doors to the kitchens and the shuttered windows accessible from the street. Finding no entry, they raised their attention up the house and spotted a stone finial at the corner of the parapet. Shortly a rope was lashing through the air.

They knew their way around. Rooftop doors were the least secure.

Banane retreated from the parapet, gathered up his gear, and melted back into concealing shadows of the sleeping rooms with their numerous carved screens. When he saw the first man scramble over the side of the parapet, a bolt of recognition went through him. He grinned to himself as he darted silently down the stairs and worked his way through the empty upstairs rooms to a window he had left unlocked. This information should be worth a bonus.

"No one from the palace, eh?" Ferdineaux LaCroix said as he stood at the center of a maelstrom of activity in one of his lesser-known warehouses.

All around him, men were loading barrels and crates and furnishings onto wooden lorries, preparing them for transfer to the ship waiting nearby. He himself was sorting documents from a stack of pasteboard cartons and feeding some of the records to a fire in a large metal drum.

"Only the Dutchman and an Arab," Banane said, savoring the news that came next. "But this evening, someone else came . . . someone whose name might be worth a few more dirhams." The Frenchman regarded him with impatience that turned to threat and made Banane reconsider his request.

"*Apollo Smith.*"

The papers in LaCroix's other hand fell back into the carton he had pulled them from, and he looked for a minute as if he'd been impaled.

"Smith? Apollo Smith is still *alive*?" His face reddened furiously and he bolted around the barrel to grab the little informer by the shirt. "You're sure it was him? *Certain?*"

Banane swallowed hard. "I bunked near him for months. I know him."

LaCroix released him with a shove.

"Damn Gaston to hell! He was supposed to follow him and the Englishwoman and get the treasure she was after. Then he was supposed to kill Smith . . . for the *second* time." He stalked away and paced for a time before setting aside his anger to concentrate on thinking. "I should have known . . . if you want something done right, you have to do it yourself."

"Smith was at my house." He wheeled on Banane. "Did he get in?"

"They were on the roof when I left. The door there was unlocked."

"Then he knows I've abandoned it. If he's searching for me, he'll probably try my offices next—then perhaps the main warehouse and the docks." He ground a fist into his palm as he fleshed out the plan forming in his mind.

"You—leave that!" He called over a pair of burly dock-workers loading crates onto wagons. "Find my body-guards, Belanger and Patel, down at the ship. Tell them I need them." Then he turned to Banane with a cold smile.

"It has been a long time since our last family reunion," he said. "I think perhaps . . . it is time for another."

Abigail and Apollo met Crocker and Flynn and the others at a side door of the hotel, where they split into two groups: one headed for LaCroix's house and the other for the docks to see if there was word of him taking passage on a ship. Apollo insisted Abigail accompany him to LaCroix's house . . . mostly to keep an eye on her. She didn't object to going with him . . . mostly to keep an eye on him.

Though it was dusk when they arrived, there were no lights in the windows and no signs of cooking fires or servants coming and going. They tried the lower doors and windows and found no easy entry. Crocker pulled a rope out of his pack and threw it up around a finial on the parapet around the roof. Apollo insisted on going first and Ravi went second, promising to open the doors for them if all was well.

Five minutes after they reached the roof, Abigail and Crocker heard a bar being drawn back on the alley door and as both trained guns on the opening, the door swung back and Apollo appeared in the opening.

"He's gone." He led them inside and up to the main floor, where they went from room to darkening room, finding only litter and the occasional broken or discarded furniture. "He's cleared everything out. We have to hurry."

The LaCroix Trading Company offices were near the Bab el-Marsa, the sea gate, in a somewhat dilapidated commercial quarter containing shipping offices and various craftsmen and shops catering to the sea trade. They arrived at the trading company offices to find several men shouting and brandishing fists at the closed and shuttered front of the business. Ravi was able to translate their ranting as: "You son of a whoring donkey!" and "My money or my goods, you thief!" and "The Sultan will have your hands for this!"

"What has happened?" Ravi asked them in the Berber Tamazight dialect. Startled at first by hearing their language from a French uniform, they soon began to rail about their losses, calling LaCroix a thief, a liar, and a filthy dog.

"Do you know where he might be?" Ravi asked.

If they knew, they said reaching for the long, curved daggers prominent in their sashes, the wretch would not live to see the sunrise.

At one man's declaration that he was going to the palace to report this to the Sultan, the others jumped at the chance to go with him, vowing to see justice brought down on the vile Frenchman's head.

"Probably 'is best friends when they 'ad their noses in 'is trough," Crocker said with a snort. "Now they're out a quid or two, an' 'e's the devil in-car-nate." He looked up at the simple roof. "No holds fer a rope. 'Ow do we get in there?"

"I'm not sure we have to," Apollo said, studying the shuttered windows and barred door. "He's sure-as-hell not coming back here to face the likes of them. Which means he has probably taken everything of value here with him."

"Then he could already be headed out of the city." Abigail looked above the houses and buildings toward the sea gate. "How would he travel, a ship?"

"If he's truly headed for France, that's the only way."

He grabbed her hand and struck off for the docks. "We need to find Flynn and the others."

Just outside the Bab el-Marsa, they entered an unregulated district of hastily constructed warehouses and marine suppliers squatting side by side with cafés, brothels, and seedy hotels that ran all the way to the water. The streets were lighted by the open doorways of enterprises beckoning to newly paid and idle sailors.

They hurried along the streets, scanning the fronts of the buildings, being jostled by inebriated sailors, pickpockets, beggars—and the occasional—

"Hey!" Apollo froze, then wheeled to look at someone who had bumped into him. A Legionnaire's uniform . . . a small, wiry fellow whose nose was flatted against his face in a grotesquely familiar crescent. *Banane*. Part of the retrieval squad he had seen on the dock the day they landed. If there was anyone who might have access to information about a rich crook in hiding, it was probably the little squealer himself. Information was his stock and trade.

"Banane!" he called. "Stop—I want to talk to you!"

The little Legionnaire halted at the sound of his name and glanced back over his shoulder. When he spotted Apollo, his face lit with recognition and fear. In a heartbeat he turned and was running off down the street. He knew something—Apollo thought—or the sight of an old comrade wouldn't have made him bolt.

"I'll get him!" Apollo took off after him and was soon regretting his rash impulse to give chase. His still tender ribs were jarred with each stride and he was quickly beginning to feel like his lungs were being hammered. The little informer darted and dodged—as slippery as an eel. Clenching his teeth, Apollo picked up the pace briefly, and then saw Banane scramble to turn down an alley. When he reached it and made the same turn, he caught sight of Banane bursting out of it into the next street at full speed. Panting heavily now, he followed and was relieved to spot Banane again and see him glancing over his shoulder . . . veering . . . heading straight for a group of seamen exiting a tavern.

Banane slammed into them and bounced off one and then another of the men before sprawling headlong on the dusty street. In an instant, he scrambled up and was running again, but the delay had given Apollo time to catch up and as they entered an area of dilapidated brick and wooden warehouses, the gap between them was closing. Another glance over his shoulder told Banane he would soon be caught, and he put on a last, panicky burst of speed.

In desperation, Apollo launched himself at the Legionnaire and slammed him down on the hard-packed dirt. For a moment they both lay on the ground struggling to breathe. Then, fighting through the pain in his chest, Apollo pushed himself up and rolled the informer over onto his back to see his face.

"I'm looking for a man," Apollo rasped out. "A Frenchman named LaCroix. You know him?" Banane was panting so, he could only nod. "Do you know where he is?"

Banane shook his head, but there was more defiance than defeat in his denial. Apollo drew back a fist.

"Tell me!" he roared. "Do you know where he is?"

"He'll . . . kill me . . . if I tell," Banane blurted out.

"I'll kill you if you don't."

After a moment, he felt Banane's body slacken.

"I can't say how to get there. But I'll know it when I see it."

Apollo shoved to his feet and pulled Banane up by his shirt.

"Take me there," he said, pulling his gun from its holster and shoving Banane ahead of him, holding him by the collar.

He could feel the little worm trembling, could see the paleness of his face in the moonlight. They made two hesitant turns through darkened alleys before they stepped out onto an empty, moonlit street and Banane finally announced they were in the right place. He searched the mud brick and planking faces of the buildings until he came to one with just a number painted on its doors.

"Is this it?" Apollo demanded.

"I—I think so," Banane said, quaking now.

Apollo tried the door and found it locked. "Is there another way in?"

Banane turned with a frantic expression but came nose-to-nose with the barrel of a pistol. He swallowed hard, nodded, and led Apollo around the side of the building to where a pair of loose boards could be swung out of the way.

"You first," Apollo said shoving him toward the opening. As soon as Banane's feet disappeared into the opening, Apollo got down on his knees to crawl through himself. It was dark inside and smelled like a warehouse of some kind . . . marine stores . . . rope and canvas, pitch and turpentine. . . .

"The door—I found the handle," Banane whispered. "Now can I go?"

"Open it," Apollo demanded.

The door creaked softly as it opened and a slice of dim light entered the storeroom. Outside, there were stacks of crates and barrels all around the door and a dim light coming from overhead.

"Go on." Apollo nudged him forward along the stacks of cargo and at the end of the stack Banane darted around it. Apollo considered leaving, but he had to know if LaCroix was here. With a silent snarl he headed after the little wretch.

Around that corner he caught a glimpse of Banane disappearing around yet another stack of barrels and pallets. There was something in the way the little squealer moved that seemed odd, almost . . . eager.

Crouching, he stepped around a last stack of cargo and suddenly heard hammers being drawn back on at least six guns. Freezing, he looked up. All around him were beefy dockworkers, holding guns. He looked down.

There before him, on a platform at the end of the empty

warehouse floor, sat Ferdineaux LaCroix with a pistol aimed straight at his heart. Strolling toward LaCroix with an insolent bounce in his step and a taunting smile was Banane. LaCroix tossed him a small bag that jingled when he caught it.

"Well, well. My beloved nephew." LaCroix turned to him with a sardonic smile. "Back for another dose of my 'hospitality' are you?"

Thirty-three

As Abigail, Crocker, and Ravi watched Apollo run after the little Legionnaire, they assumed that he would haul the fellow back to them in short order. One minute dragged by, then two. They looked at each other uneasily. After three minutes, they went after him, searching the raucous nearby streets and then spreading out into the farther, quieter ones.

They didn't find Apollo, but they did find Joseph Flynn and Cruz Sanchez, who had news. There was a ship sailing for Marseille in a day or so. Franks and Johnson were still there, watching the loading. They had followed the empty lorries back to a warehouse on the edge of the docks and had been looking for Apollo, Abigail, Crocker, and Ravi before proceeding.

"That may be where he is," Abigail said, looking frantically to Crocker and Ravi, who nodded.

"Where who is?" Flynn asked. Then his eyes flew wide. "Smith?"

It took a quarter of an hour for them to reach the warehouse and find a way to see inside. They had to climb up to the louvered vents at the top of one wall, where they could hear voices, but couldn't make out what was being said. Nothing was visible but stacks of cargo.

Then one of the main doors opened and out came a diminutive figure in Legionnaire khaki, striding confidently. Abigail, who was perched on a stack of old pallets against the warehouse, recognized him as the man Apollo ran after and waved frantically to get Joe Flynn's attention. The Irishman saw the Legionnaire and a second later, dove off the stack of old cargo crates and landed on Banane.

Quickly, they dragged the little weasel around behind the piles of old wood and demanded to know if Apollo was inside with LaCroix.

Banane nodded, seeming terrified. Then they asked if there was another way inside, one that wasn't so obvious. He nodded again.

"And that lovely Miss Merchant," LaCroix said, watching his men drape the ropes securing Apollo's hands over the hook of a cargo hoist. As they pulled the chains to raise the hoist, Apollo's arms stretched above his head, sending pain through his still-healing ribs. "Snatched her right from under my nose. Did you take her out into the desert and have your way with her?"

"Go to hell," Apollo rasped out.

"*Tsk.* Not very sociable of you." LaCroix set down the wine he had been sipping. "Did she find her treasure?" He laughed. "Did she find yours?"

"What about *your* treasure, LaCroix?" Apollo demanded. "What did you find in France that was worth murdering members of your own family?"

"You forget, I don't have a family." LaCroix came up out of his chair, crimson, his eyes like hot coals. "They disowned me when I was nineteen—younger than you when you came to my house. They bought me a ticket from Marseille to Tangiers and told me I had a whole continent to get lost in. They never wanted to set eyes on me again."

"What did you do to deserve it?" Apollo said, feeling his hands going numb. "Did you steal them blind, too?"

LaCroix halted and abruptly drew a veil over the hatred simmering in him.

"That would have been difficult indeed, since someone had already beaten me to it. It seems their honorable neighbors had stolen their lands from them in life-leases they didn't realize they could reclaim. Half of the family lands—rich olive groves and vineyards—had been swindled from them. Along with interest in a shipping company and valuable property on the island of Mallorca. Sometimes it takes a thief to catch a thief" He gave a light, chilling laugh. "Of course, sometimes it takes lawyers."

"So you found enough to make you a rich man," Apollo concluded.

"I am *already* a rich man. What I found was incentive to go home and do what needed to be done. A bit of poison here, a tumble down the stairs there. My father and his brother were old and feeble . . . no one was the wiser."

"And your sister."

"Ah, yes, Jeanne Marie. Her death, I cannot take credit for."

"You killed her as surely as you killed the others," Apollo spat, welcoming the surge of energy that anger poured into his blood. "Writing her that I had died, only months after my father's death . . . the shock stopped her heart."

"Always such a delicate thing." LaCroix oozed congenial malice. "Everyone's favorite. But the little bitch couldn't keep her mouth shut—couldn't wait to tell on me—they'd never have known about that stupid girl if she hadn't—" He halted, teetering on the brink of losing control yet again. "My sister betrayed me. She deserved to die thinking her son was dead." He licked at the spittle collected on his lips, then again became the cool, genial taunter. "However, it's only a matter of a few months difference. You'll be dead all the same."

"Not necessarily." Abigail's voice floated out over the

warehouse, causing LaCroix to jerk back and look frantically around.

"Boston?" Apollo followed LaCroix's narrowing gaze and found her stepping from behind a stack of cargo, holding a gun. "What are you doing here?"

"I'm here to offer you a deal," she said to LaCroix.

"Don't be absurd," he glanced around the rest of the warehouse, looking for others and finding none. "You're too late. He has to die and stay dead in order for me to inherit. Now, unfortunately, so do you." He motioned to his men, who relieved her of her gun and tossed it on the floor.

"Are you all right?" she asked Apollo.

"I'll live," he said.

LaCroix barked a laugh.

"I said I came to make you an offer," she said to LaCroix. "I found a treasure."

"Did you indeed? How pleasant for you."

"It's priceless—one that museums will pay a fortune to display."

"Don't Abigail—" Apollo said furiously.

"Not to mention, a cache of priceless gold artifacts," she continued. "It can all be yours. . . ."

LaCroix studied her intensity, but then seemed to sweep it aside.

"I suppose you feel compelled to try to save him, Miss Merchant. But really." He winced. "Such an obvious lie."

"I'm not lying. I have six amphora filled with treasure in my hotel room at the Exeter. All you have to do is send your men to fetch them. They're yours." She held up a key on a ring attached to an engraved brass disk and let it dangle.

"You would say anything to save him, wouldn't you? How touching." LaCroix strolled to his chair and finished the wine in his glass. "How futile."

"He doesn't believe me," she said to Apollo. "I can't believe I'm going to have to do it again." Then she turned to LaCroix with a fierce expression. "You want proof?"

"No, Abigail—" Apollo nearly strangled on his own juices.

"I'll give you proof."

She ripped off her jacket and tossed it onto the floor beside her gun. Then she began to undo the buttons of her blouse. LaCroix glimpsed what she was doing and turned to watch with astonishment.

"I went into the desert for books." One button.

"But instead, I found a whole city and an ancient temple." Two buttons.

"Artifacts of pure gold. Altar pieces, chalices, jewelry." Three buttons.

"You don't believe me, LaCroix?" She ripped her blouse apart and shouted, *"Look."*

Stunned silence reigned for a minute as LaCroix and his men stared at a pair of ornate golden breasts set in a web of golden scales . . . women's breasts . . . elegantly rendered . . . in pure, dazzling gold . . .

She stood with her blouse open and her chin high, challenging LaCroix to inspect this unique bit of treasure. But her eyes focused on Apollo with such intensity that he felt himself coiling inside, sensing, anticipating . . .

LaCroix reached to touch her golden breasts, the light in his eyes approaching a whole new level of greed. Apollo was able to nudge himself back a few critical inches, without being noticed. Every eye in the warehouse was on her chest as Apollo took a deep breath, then jackknifed his legs up and slammed his feet into LaCroix's spongy bulk, sending him sprawling.

Abigail dove for her gun, LaCroix's men raised their weapons, and LaCroix tried to drag himself—gasping—over to one of his thugs.

"Stop where you are, LaCroix! The rest of you—drop your guns!" Joe Flynn shouted as the Legionnaires sprang up from the stacks of cargo with rifles trained on LaCroix's men.

Everyone froze except for Abigail, who at Apollo's urging scrambled over to turn the crank lowering the cargo hoist and his arms. Just as she was wrapping her arms around him and helping him over to a seat on a crate, LaCroix grabbed for the nearest gun.

The Legionnaires caught the movement and aimed a shot at the weapon, knocking it out of LaCroix's hands, but igniting a hail of gunfire. The Legionnaires dropped onto their bellies and LaCroix's men dove behind nearby crates, trading fire at will.

Abigail and Apollo scrambled behind a stack of barrels as bullets whined past. "Are you all right? You're not hit?" she demanded.

"I'm all right," he said, grimacing with the pain of just breathing. "Where's LaCroix?"

She stuck her head up to see over the edge of the barrels and spotted him crawling toward the steps that let to the upper floor. "He's over there"—she pointed—"heading for the stairs."

"Stay here." Apollo popped his head up long enough to spot LaCroix, then ducked back down to move in a crouch through the stacks and around pallets of cargo.

"What do you mean, wait? He has a gun, Apollo!" she cried, peering up over the crates to fire a shot at one of LaCroix's men who spotted Apollo's movement and took aim at him. The man dove back behind the crates again, and she headed after Apollo, trying to keep her head down and run at the same time.

The shooting slowed to occasional shots and Flynn called again: "Lay down your guns and come out with your hands on your head."

The answer was the bark of several more rounds, followed by a pause. Flynn signaled his comrades to use the lull to reload, counting that LaCroix's men wouldn't carry additional ammunition and would soon have to either surrender or flee. If they ran, it would be like shooting fish in a barrel.

But their employer was already in full flight . . . crawling up the several steps to the main level of the warehouse. When LaCroix reached the midpoint of the stairs, two shots rang out and he curled into a ball. Realizing he wasn't hit, he lunged up the rest of the steps . . . but then tripped on the splintered wood of the top tread.

By the time he was on his feet again, Apollo was close enough to snatch at his ankle. LaCroix kicked him off and headed for the doors, before frantically remembering something in the railed-off office and wheeling to grab it from one of the desks. It took one heartbeat too long. When he turned back, Apollo loomed between him and the door.

"You're not going anywhere," Apollo said moving slowly forward.

"I should have killed you that first night"—LaCroix spotted a knife used to open packages, picked it up, and brandished it at him—"instead of having you dragged off to prison."

Apollo felt his grip on reality must be sliding; he gave a strangled laugh.

"Prison. Before you die—I should probably thank you for that."

His reaction disarmed LaCroix for a second . . . but a second was long enough to allow Apollo to lunge at him. For a long time they stood braced, opposing, grappling for control of the knife. LaCroix, for all his appearance of softness, was surprisingly strong and he had weight enough to more than resist Apollo's force. But Apollo had the advantage of height and slowly bent LaCroix back over the railing until he could slam that knife-wielding arm sharply against the edge of a desk. The knife went flying to the floor.

LaCroix sensed his only hope was to get Apollo below him and press with his bulk. He rolled from the desk, taking Apollo with him. They landed on the floor straining and thrashing, grasping for advantage—until Apollo abruptly yanked his arm back and surprised LaCroix with a blow to the side of the head.

The Frenchman was a second slower responding to the next blow, and suddenly the tide had turned. An instant later he was atop LaCroix with his hands sinking into that red, corpulent neck.

The fury of prison sweatbox days and endless desert nights broke free in him. His vision narrowed and washed crimson. The pain of years of cascading losses bore down on him. His father . . . his mother . . . his family . . . his youth . . . innocence . . . prospects . . . dreams . . . friends . . . the years he could never replace . . . the time and opportunities that had been stolen from him . . .

He was beyond reason, beyond knowing that he was shouting those losses into a purpling face as he choked the life from the man responsible for them.

"You took everything!" He half-growled, half-sobbed. "You took my whole life! You took my life—you took my life—"

"Apollo! Stop! You're killing him!" Abigail's words barely registered through the blood roaring in his head. But the cool reason those sounds poured into the heat of his fury started to slowly pull him back toward reality. "Stop—please God"—she grasped his wrists but couldn't dislodge his hands—"you can't do this, Apollo! Stop—"

His fingers slowly loosened around that thick porcine neck. But it still took Abigail and Flynn and Crocker all to pull him off of the Frenchman's inert body. Lost in a morass of emotion, he sat on the floor feeling disoriented and repeating over and over, "he took my life" . . . until a cooling, reassuring presence reached him.

Suddenly *she* was there, all around him. Real. Consoling. Stroking his hair and murmuring wordless reassurances. He looked up into her dove gray eyes that were filled with love, shared anguish, and comfort.

"He took my life," he said, seeing the truth of it more clearly than ever before, "and you gave it back to me."

He pulled her fiercely against him and murmured a wordless prayer of gratitude. For in that moment, he understood the depth of a bond between two souls that was indeed the beginning of wisdom and the start of a whole new life.

• • •

Abigail saw Crocker kneel to check on LaCroix and asked, "Is he . . . ?"

"Not dead," he responded, sounding disappointed.

"Too bad." Flynn gave the unconscious LaCroix a prod with his foot.

Crocker spotted LaCroix's ledger on the floor and picked it up . . . then turned to look at the piles of records stacked all around.

"Every piece o' paper is another poor sap who lost 'is shirt."

"What'll we do with 'im?" Flynn asked. "And them?" He gestured over his shoulder to the men being tied hand and foot on the floor of the warehouse.

"A pity," Ravi said, "that we could not just hand him over to those men at the trading company. They would see he received his just reward."

As Apollo got up slowly, leaning on Abigail for support, the thought struck him.

"Good idea. We'll turn him over to the Sultan." Apollo clapped Ravi on the shoulder. "You speak the dialect . . . head for the palace and explain our situation here to the head of the Sultan's guards. I suspect they've been hearing quite a bit about Ferdineaux LaCroix of late."

The office was full of papers detailing LaCroix's larcenous dealings. It became clear as they looked through the record books for references to property in France, that LaCroix had positioned himself as a broker between European concerns and the Moroccan leaders, including the sultans themselves. And he managed to misrepresent both sides . . . insisting on the requirements of "gifts" and inflating prices and fees in order to skim funds from the transactions.

By the time the Sultan's men arrived, LaCroix was making small movements that indicated he was waking. The captain tossed water on him and had the guardsmen drag him to his feet. He was groggy at first; it took him a few minutes to appreciate what was happening to him. Then he looked at the men holding his arms, and at the unmistakable uniform of the captain of the Sultan's guards, and finally understood that his worst nightmare was coming true.

"You cannot do this to me!" he cried. "I am an important businessman—a citizen of France! You have no authority over me. You have no right—"

"I believe you gave them that right, sarr," Flynn said with a smile, "when ye went an' tweaked the Sultan's own nose."

"Look at the bright side," Crocker said as they wrenched LaCroix's arms behind his back and bound them. "This'll likely the last time they'll be binding yer *hands*."

"Oh, yes," Ravi said with an exaggerated lilt. "And the captain was saying on the way here that the Sultan is particularly fond of the press . . . that he sets aside one day a week to witness executions done in that manner."

LaCroix alternately threatened and wheedled, demanding release and then begging for mercy as they dragged him out into the Moroccan night.

Thirty-four

The Sultan of Casablanca was so pleased by the way the French Foreign Legion assisted his valiant guardsmen in the capture of the thief and criminal Ferdineaux LaCroix, that he presented each of the Legionnaires involved with a beautiful gold-handled sword. The men of Apollo's old company went straight from that royal audience to the nearest sword-seller to trade their reward for cash to spend on their extended leave in Casablanca . . . courtesy of a proud and grateful Legion.

Apollo and Abigail were given the finest accommodations the Exeter had, compliments of the Sultan and several prominent and grateful merchants. They slept well and ate even better. Apollo's ribs continued to heal, and at night he was able—even eager—to help Abigail continue with her validation of the Seven Delights.

The only one to suffer at LaCroix's demise, besides LaCroix himself, was the captain of the French cargo ship *Maintenon*, who was forced to delay the vessel's departure for Marseille by several days. Its only scheduled passenger and the owner of a majority of its cargo was gone, and the Sultan insisted on a full inventory and accounting of the items being shipped, lest stolen goods or materials escape Moroccan soil.

Apollo came hurrying back into their room a few days later with news that they'd freed the ship to sail to Marseille.

"It leaves tomorrow morning," he said, looking around the rooms that they had shared for the better part of a week, locating his satchel and laying it open on the bed. When he looked up moments later, she was staring at him as if he'd just announced he was headed for the North Pole.

"Any word on when the next ship bound for London will leave?" she asked, looking at the amphora stacked against the wall and then at her scuffed carpetbags beside them with a sudden, intense feeling of loss. After all she and Apollo had been through together . . .

He turned from the bed and stood looking at her.

"Come with me to Marseille," he said. "It will only be a couple of weeks. I have to set things right and see what is left of my family. And my inheritance." She rubbed her hands together, gazing at the amphora, and he continued: "Then we'll catch a ship to London and stare down your crusty 'old boys' together."

She looked up with tears collecting in her eyes.

"You really want to come with me? You're not just saying that?"

He went to her, feeling every bit of her uncertainty and desperately needed hope in his own heart as he took her into his arms.

"I wouldn't miss it for the world," he said, willing her stiff form to melt against him and let him know that what they had found together was as important to her as her other dreams. "We're partners, remember." After a moment he added: "Besides, we've still got two delights to go and from the sound of them, they could be pretty interesting. *Control.* And *Surrender.*"

And there it was, that melting, that joining he had come to crave on a daily basis. Above her head, he grinned and felt his own body relax. She was his.

As her body molded to his, she heard his chest rumble and then go quiet except for a soft, dependable thudding. She had been listening to his heart like this for nearly three weeks now. And whatever happened between them, that reassuring primal rhythm would be a part of her forever.

"There is one condition," he said, with a tenor to his voice that made her know he was grinning and whatever came next was probably wicked indeed.

"Yes?" She bit her lip, waiting, knowing she would probably agree no matter how outrageous the requirement sounded.

"The next time we check into a hotel as Mr. and Mrs. Smith . . . I want it to be for real."

Thirty-five

※

Assistant Jonas Pratt trotted up the sweeping main staircase of London's Savoy Hotel at the heels of the director and principle librarian of the British Museum, Maunde Thompson. He scarcely had time to catch his breath and nudge the knot of his tie higher before he found himself joining a remarkable congregation of men of letters in the famous Pinafore Room. He stood for a moment, staring like a country bumpkin at the understated luxury of the furnishings and the celebrated illumination of some of the finest minds in all of Britain.

Some he actually recognized from when they visited the British Museum to call on Director Thompson. Lord Edmund Drinkwater of the Royal Society; Sir Amos Greenley of Cambridge Insititute of Antiquities; Sir Chester Edgerton, Balough Scholar at Oxford; B.P. Grenfell, one of the directors of the Oxyrhynchus dig in Egypt; Simon Cresswell, one of the world's leading classicists; Professor Bertrand Hall of Queen's College and Sir Henry Merchant of Christ College, Oxford. Then he spotted Walter deGray Birch, Keeper of Seals at the British Museum . . . one of the few "keepers" who ever seemed to have time for him . . . though in fact—he thought to himself—the man was one of the lesser lights of the museum and hardly anyone to claim as an important acquaintance. *Seals*, after all. A completely dead specialty.

When he realized Director Thompson had moved on and begun to greet still other dignitaries, he hurried to his superior's side in hopes of an introduction to . . . dearest heaven . . . Pierre Monteneau of the Louvre's Department of Antiquities. The dapper fellow looked right through him when Director Thompson introduced him. Cursed French. He glanced down at the man's spats and then up to his silly, pencil-thin moustache. They always thought they were so much better—

The doors opened and a contingent of three men entered, moving with an aggressive stride to take up a commanding position in the middle of the room. They surveyed the gathering with cool analysis, then immediately spotted Pierre Monteneau and Director Thompson.

"Ye gods. Americans," Lord Amos Greenly muttered, heading for the fresh tray of pastries being laid out nearby.

"Harrison Evans," Director Thompson extended a hand as the bluff looking fellow approached. Evans? The Metropolitan Museum Evans? Pratt preened surreptitiously. This was a rare meeting indeed.

"This A. M. Smith has plenty of cheek," Pratt heard the American Evans say. "Inviting the three most prestigious museums in the Western world to view his discovery." The American's teeth were even and astonishingly white. "Have you gentlemen got your wallets open?"

Before Thompson or Monteneau could respond, the main door opened and a young woman in an exquisite gray velvet suit that matched her arresting eyes entered on the arm of a tall, dashing fellow wearing an eye patch. They paused and when she had collected every eye in the room, she smiled.

"Good afternoon, gentlemen. Thank you for coming."

Behind them uniformed hotel porters were pushing linen-draped carts into the room on which lay six urn-shaped amphora. At a command from the one-eyed man, the porters deposited the carts in a line at one end of the room and withdrew. The curators and scholars sorted themselves into an eager circle around the pair and the amphora, murmuring observations about the vessels.

"I am A.M. Smith," the woman declared, causing a murmur in the room. She smiled coolly. "This is my husband, Apollo Smith." The tall, dark fellow bowed slightly. "A few months ago, we undertook an expedition into the deserts of Morocco, guided by the lifelong work of Professor T. Thaddeus Chilton, late of Queen's College, Oxford. We are here to present to you the fruit of that expedition." She waved to the carts.

"In the desert, we located these six amphora containing manuscripts that we believe will be reliably dated from the first through the sixth century A.D."

There was a brief clamor among the scholars at that and in the silence that descended afterward a voice from the back could be heard saying, "Thaddeus Chilton? Good Lord—haven't heard that name in years."

"Professor Chilton is of course, deceased," Abigail said, scanning the faces, looking for one similar to the old wedding photo she had carried with her to Morocco and back. "After studying his work, I realized his theory seemed sound and his research was meticulous. I decided to finish his quest."

And there he was.

Sir Henry Merchant. Classical Scholar. Tall, aesthetic-looking gentleman. Graying but still vigorous at fifty. There was a keenness to his regard and a gravity to his presence that both owed something to the weariness she glimpsed about his eyes. She had difficulty looking away from him.

"Our expedition began in Casablanca and traveled to Marrakech, Ouarzazate, and then southward into the Sahara, which is where these amphora and the books they contain were recovered."

There was some throat clearing and Director Maunde Thompson, of the British Museum, spoke up.

"Excuse me, Mrs. Smith, but how do you know these amphora contain manuscripts of some sort?"

"I was told so. By their keepers. The books they contain were specially selected by a committee of ancient scholars to be included in a temple of learning that was hidden away in the desert for centuries. A temple to the goddess of wisdom, Athena."

The muttering rose to rumbling, equally divided between surprise and outrage. She could see their academic hackles coming up. She knew how they thought and how this must sound to them. They would need time to absorb it.

"And where did these books come from?" Pierre Monteneau asked. "You said they were selected, *non*? Selected from where?"

Abigail felt Apollo's hand seeking hers behind the cover of her skirts and squeezed it gratefully. This was the part she dreaded.

"From the Great Library of Alexandria."

A wave of open disbelief swept the room at that claim and she lifted her head and raised her voice to maintain control of the proceedings.

"Professor Chilton spent his academic career developing and researching a theory that before the final destruction of the Great Library, a portion of it was secreted out of the city and carried into the desert for safekeeping. I stand before you today to say that his theory was entirely correct. I know, because I found that desert repository . . . as well as the temple that formed the heart of the sect chosen to preserve the knowledge it contained."

"You found the Great Library of Alexandria?" a portly, mutton-chop-clad fellow sputtered. "Preposterous! Gentlemen we've been brought here to become victims of a hideous hoax! Good day to you, young woman!" He started for the door, drawing two others with him before she delivered what she knew would be an irresistible challenge.

"I have asked you here not only to announce this find, but to put your brilliant minds to the test . . . to ask you to inspect the amphora, along with the professor's journals and maps . . . to help me begin the process of authenticating this find."

"Authenticate?" The old boy in the door was torn between washing his hands of it and charging back inside to debunk her obvious chicanery. "By thunder, you've got brass—dragging these gentlemen from their most important work to—"

"While you are making your decisions, gentlemen, I hope you will enjoy a bit of champagne and some refreshments," she said with a stiff little smile.

"What is it about champagne?" Apollo muttered into her ear as the men turned to find servers passing among them with glasses of golden bubbly and reluctantly accepted glasses that they sipped eagerly. "Soothes the savage beast."

But Abigail barely heard him. She was absorbed in watching the reaction of her father, who hadn't moved from the spot where he had first seen her . . . nor blinked, from the looks of him. Was anything about her familiar to him? Did he remember her mother and her? Did he have any clue that this day was as much about meeting him as it was about her precious expedition and ancient books?

He seemed so rigid, so untouched standing there. Was that what twenty years of intense and loveless scholarship did to a man? Turned him and his heart to the very kind of stone he studied?

"I, for one, do not intend to participate in this charade!" The old boy with the muttonchops charged out the door, drawing two others in his wake.

Interestingly the major scholars and museum directors all remained, speaking amongst themselves, eyeing the amphora and the pair who claimed to have found them. Abigail began to remove T. Thaddeus's journals from their

bag and placed them at intervals on a draped table provided for that purpose. When Apollo reached for a box of
magnifying glasses and began to lay them out on the table,
Abigail could almost feel the mood of the room shifting.

"Mr. Birch, perhaps you would care to satisfy your curiosity," she said, offering the Keeper of Seals a magnifying glass and access to the amphora.

"Yes, very much so, Mrs. Smith." Walter deGray
Birch jumped at the chance to give the seals on the amphora a thorough examination . . . asking if he might take
one of the carts over nearer the window, where the light
was better.

It was the first hole in the dike . . . followed quickly by
a growing stream of scholars heading for the journals and
maps and availing themselves of the lenses and each
other's professional opinions. The noise and excitement
level rose apace as the old boys rose to the challenge of
shaking the rust from their critical faculties and plunging
into a small mystery with potentially large implications.

The language classicists collected around T. Thaddeus's
journals, excited to find them in Greek and shocked at how
clever the old boy had been in his translations . . . while
others headed for the amphora: feeling, "thunking," measuring, and comparing style and composition to known artifacts in their various collections.

As she watched, Abigail felt a certain gratification that
they had at least taken her seriously enough to begin in-
vestigating her claims. She circulated through the scholars,
listening to their comments and answering their questions
when she could. But her eyes were never far from the tall,
distinguished form of her father, bent over some of the
journals, parsing out phrases and lines.

When she could stand it no longer, she approached the
table where he had drawn up a chair to read some of
Chilton's work . . . and found him perusing a page of her
translation—something she hadn't realized she had stuck
in the book. He looked up, then rose and set the journal
down.

"Sir Henry Merchant, is it not?" she asked, hoping her voice wasn't trembling.

"It is," he said, thickly, clearing his throat afterward. "And may I ask what the 'A' and 'M' in your name stand for, Mrs. Smith?"

"Abigail and Merchant, sir," she said, feeling like she'd just dropped an anvil from the roof into the middle of the gathering.

"Abigail? Merchant?" a thin, disagreeable voice from nearby repeated. "I know that name." Jonas Pratt's sallow face flushed as he peered closer at her. "I know you! You're employed by the British Museum!" he said pointing at her, oblivious to his deplorable lack of manners. "Or you were. You worked in—" He turned to find Director Maunde Thompson examining the amphora and called: "Director Thompson—I remembered where I'd seen her before. She's the female who used to work in our basement!"

Everything came to a halt as every eye in the room turned on Abigail.

She couldn't help the way her face reddened at his snidely worded identification of her, but she could behave in a way that lessened the impact of both.

"Yes, of course," she said, coolly and calmly, reserving the icicles in her gaze for the vicious little Pratt. "I was employed briefly at the British Museum. In acquisitions. I found it a most enlightening—though not altogether pleasant—experience."

Maunde Thompson straightened and came over to see her for himself.

"Acquisitions, eh?" He seemed a bit uncomfortable under Sir Henry's gaze. "Odd choice for a young woman."

"Don't you recall, Director Thompson"—Pratt seized his moment, intending to make an impression by putting the upstart female in her place—"everyone talking about whether there really was a woman in the basement and making wagers? Old Richter, one of the watchman, made a tidy bit of coin taking folks around to prove that she was really down there." His laugh came out more of a giggle than he would have liked, but it did seem to draw a few muffled sounds of derision from the gathering.

For a moment all was silent. Then Director Thompson pulled out his pocket watch and gave it an uncomfortable glance.

"I really do have . . . a pressing engagment. . . ."

"I really should be going as well," Lord Amos Greenley said putting down with an air of regret the magnifying glass he was holding.

Abigail felt Apollo at her side, felt the tension in his frame and when she glanced down saw the fists he had balled and ready. She quickly covered one with her cold fingers, entreating him to hold his temper.

"I say. Sir Henry." Thompson glanced at her father in dismay, having just recalled how she came to be hired in the first place. "This must be your daughter . . . I mean . . . what do *you* think of . . ." Words failed the garrulous director, so he swept the amphora and the journals with an encompassing wave.

Abigail couldn't breathe. Couldn't blink.

She stood before the father she no longer knew . . . recalling the years and choices that had put such distance between them. Choices so heartbreakingly similar that it was almost as if Fate had brought them around a second time . . . revisiting them on him . . . and on her for their own cruel entertainment.

Long ago, when presented with his wife's brilliance and achievement and told to deny it, he had chosen—however reluctantly—the safe and expected route of male superiority, cloaked as academic "rigor" and "purity." He had chosen his career and ambition over his love, his wife, and in the end, his daughter.

Would he do the same again?

Would desire for the esteem of his peers cause him to shun the daughter he didn't know and whatever she had achieved?

"She is my daughter," Sir Henry said, looking as if

every word cost him a piece of a vital organ. Abigail's heart began to sink.

No. Please God. Not again . . .

"But were she a total stranger," he continued in a more emphatic voice, "I would *still* be eager to examine her work and to see the insides of those amphora. Good Lord, if what she says is true—and I have no reason yet to doubt it—then think of it! The Great Library!"

A wave of relief went through the room as Sir Henry turned to Pratt with a raptorlike gaze "I don't believe I took your name sir. And be sure, I want to remember it."

"Pratt." The little worm had difficulty swallowing. "Assistant to the director, Jonas Pratt."

"Pratt," Sir Henry said in a way that made it sound like he was spitting. Then he turned to Thompson, who was edging toward the door and fixed a razorlike gaze on him. "So you put her in the basement, did you?" One of his eyebrows hiked a notch and the entire room inhaled. "Well, everyone has to start somewhere, eh Maunde? Even in the bloody basement. I expected my daughter to be given a chance"—he looked straight at her and met her suddenly moist gaze with a trembling smile—"but I also expected her to earn her way. And by God, I think she has!"

She wasn't even aware of making her way to him . . . her hands outstretched . . . her eyes rimmed with tears. He grabbed her hands tightly and held them for a long silent moment before releasing them.

"And now let's have a look at these amphora!"

$\mathcal{I}$t was dark outside and the electrical lights had been turned on in the salon before the last of the guests exited and Abigail was able to turn to her father in private. Her heart was full enough to overflow through her eyes.

"Do you have any idea how much you look like your mother?" he said to her, his eyes brimming, too.

She couldn't speak, only nod.

But words weren't necessary as he opened his arms and

she walked into them. He had stood up for her . . . demanded respect for her and her achievement by showing her that respect. And it was the pain of his heart, later, to learn that he would never have a chance to redress the injustice he had done to his young wife years ago. He wept at the news of her death, and Apollo and Abigail helped him upstairs to their suite and comforted both him and themselves with talk and stories and news . . . and the whole, true story of their "expedition" and their partnership-become-marriage.

They talked until the wee hours, and Abigail insisted he stay the night with them. The next morning, over breakfast, they both broached the topic uppermost in their thoughts.

"You have to be careful not to take the first bid," Sir Henry advised. "Museums are notoriously stingy . . . that Maunde Thompson's still wearing the first pair of socks his mother ever knitted him. Make them all wait a bit. And make them show you something of their plans to build an exhibit around your books . . . make that part of the deal."

"Sounds like good advice," Apollo said, winking at Abigail, who was glowing after a wildly celebratory bit of *Control* and *Surrender* with some champagne and *Tasting* thrown in.

"We're planning another expedition . . . to retrieve the artifacts buried in the tunnel." Abigail spoke what was on her mind with her eyes shining. She reached for her husband's hand across the tabletop. "Apollo and I discussed it . . . and we want you to come with us."

"Me? On an expedition?" He seemed more dismayed than intrigued by the prospect. "Not me. I'm strictly a library and letters sort of academic. None of that pith and dash the field men have."

"Don't be silly. You've got plenty of *dash*," she said adamantly.

"And pith," Apollo added dryly.

"Come on . . . what have you got to lose? You have to live life to the fullest." Abigail heard herself saying and thought the words sounded astonishingly familiar. "You're way too young to closet yourself away with books and papers year after year. You need to do something wild and wonderful. Something bold and memorable. Something . . . adventuresome!"

"Good God," Sir Henry said to Apollo, looking strangely both alarmed and entranced. "She sounds just like her mother, too."

Epilogue

"*So* that's their story," Leigh Merchant Smith said, closing the book she'd been reading aloud to her fiancé. "My great, great grandmother and grandfather's adventure. What do you think?"

"Quite a yarn," the young man said, clearly striving for diplomacy.

"It's a true story, Michael. Okay—maybe embellished a bit for print, here and there, but basically that's what happened. That's the start of the Merchant-Smith family legacy."

They sat together on the leather sofa in her father's book-lined study, wearing jeans and sweaters. It had been a relaxed weekend . . . as relaxed, anyway, as it could be when meeting prospective in-laws for the first time.

She set the book aside and snuggled against him, pulling his arm from the back of the sofa around her.

"It's why the women of our family always become librarians and always seem to fall for . . . adventurers."

"Venture capitalists," he corrected her. "I work for a venture capitalization firm, remember. I do the back-room stuff . . . research . . . financial projections . . . the boring details."

"Oh. Yes. Sorry. The blazing off to Singapore and Berlin and Paris at a moment's notice sometimes makes me forget what a dull job you have."

"Well, if the story is true," he said, staring at the ornately bound book on the coffee table, "then where are these wonderful manuscripts from the Great Library now? Why hasn't their discovery changed the world. I mean, if it was all that groundbreaking, wouldn't we have learned about it in Western Civ 101 or something?"

"Well, after the auction—which was won by the Metropolitan Museum, by the way—the amphora containing the manuscripts were shipped to New York and were opened with great ceremony by a gathering of eminent scholars."

"And?" He slid to the edge of his seat.

"The scrolls were taken out and conserved and read . . . and found to contain books by some of the most famous classical masters. Aristotle, Epicurus, Ptolemy . . ."

"And?"

"And"—she sighed—"it turned out most of the books were already in existence. They had come down to us through other sources. The few new parts were mostly reformulations of earlier texts. Epicurus's *De Natura* . . . Aristotle's *The Constitution of Athens* . . . Galen's *Book of Medicine* . . ."

"That was it?" he said.

"I'm afraid so. It was a bit of a disappointment to Great, Great Grandma Abigail. But Great, Great Grandpa Apollo, being a devout pragmatist, drew the only sensible conclusion from it, wrote a book detailing their adventure, and plunged into a new round of explorations."

"What was his conclusion?"

She slid up onto his lap, her eyes twinkling.

"That as time had marched on, so had knowledge. Despite the efforts of some to hoard or limit or even destroy learning, it had not only survived, it had thrived. Wisdom, it seems, will always find a way. It has a life of its own and refuses to be imprisoned or restricted or even 'preserved' into irrelevance. Knowledge, pulled out of the stream of ideas, even for safekeeping, slowly withers and becomes obsolete." She laughed, watching his expression changing as those ideas—so familiar to her—took root.

"It's a shame that Gram and Gramps aren't here to see the Internet," she continued. "They would have loved to see how it's breaking down barriers and disseminating knowledge . . . changing the world."

"So this is the family legacy you talked about. This love of wisdom and learning. This passion for knowledge. And libraries."

"Part of it."

She studied his face and the telltale crinkle between his eyebrows that always appeared when he was dubious about something. Michael Phillips made one terrible poker player.

"You still don't believe all this, do you?" she said.

"I'll take your word for it," he said, the crinkle smoothing, replaced by an irresistibly boyish smile.

"You'll do better than that," she said, sliding off his lap and heading for the credenza behind her father's big mahogany desk. Behind the heavy wooden doors was the front of a substantial safe. She opened it and withdrew a rectangular wooden box that she placed on the desk.

"What's this?" He shoved up out of his chair and joined her.

"The seventh scroll."

He glanced at the book now on the coffee table. "I thought you said the scrolls went to the Metropolitan Museum."

"They did. All but this one. This one Grandma and Grandpa kept. It's the most revolutionary of all of them. They were determined this one wouldn't be buried in some vault somewhere and never read."

She carried it to the desk, cleared things aside, then donned a curator's cotton gloves, opened the airtight box, and removed a sheepskin covered scroll of parchment. Then with great care, she unrolled the tattered end and began to read . . . first in Greek, then in English. . . .

"The Book of the Seven Delights."

He stared at her and then at the obviously ancient document.

"They kept a scroll? They really did find the Great Library of Alexandria?"

"Exactly like they said they did. They didn't mention in their book that they kept this scroll themselves . . . shared it quietly with others . . . and passed it down from mother to daughter for five generations."

She could see he was rethinking all of his conclusions and assumptions.

"So, that's your family secret and legacy. An ancient scroll from the Great Library of Alexandria. This *Book of Seven* . . ."

"Delights," she supplied, watching him closely. "It's a path to wisdom through the joining of the sexes in pleasure."

"A sex book?" His jaw dropped. "You mean, like the *Kama Sutra*?"

"It's a wisdom book, it just happens to use sex as it's method of enlightenment." She grinned. "And trust me, it's *better* than the *Kama Sutra*. When we're married, you'll get your own personal translation. But, that's not quite all."

While he was staring at the scroll, she began to unbutton her blouse. When he looked up she pulled it open to reveal a bra made of metal . . . ornate, provocative cups held on with chains covered by scale-like plates of what appeared to be real gold. His jaw dropped. When he could pull his gaze from it to look at her, she was grinning.

"If you're very, very good, Mister Phillips, I'll show you how the latch works."

New York Times bestselling author

Betina Krahn

The Wife Test

Hoping to discover her true parentage, Chloe of Guibray poses as a nun and steals into a convoy headed for England. But one man threatens to make the journey intolerable: Sir Hugh of Sennet, an infuriating sergeant whose masculine presence stirs her most primal marital urges.

"BETINA KRAHN PACKS THE ROMANACE PUNCH THAT FANS HAVE COME TO EXPECT."
—*MILWAUKEE JOURNAL-SENTINEL*

"A RISING STAR THAT JUST KEEPS GETTING BRIGHTER."
—*LITERARY TIMES*

0-425-19092-7

B222